My Life in Dog Years

Erin Pickett

Published by Between The Cornfields Publishing, 2024.

---

1.   http://www.mannisondesign.wordpress.com

And God said,

I will send them without wings
so no one suspects they are angels.

Chapter 1

Oakley's teeth tap against the window over the kitchen sink. I swear the twelve-year-old donkey smiles at me, unlike my wife. She glares in my direction as I pull a carrot from the refrigerator. I open the window and deliver the treat.

"I wish you hadn't started that," Sabrina grumbles.

"It's how he says good morning."

She flips a batch of pancakes on the griddle. "We leave in twenty minutes."

With a carrot in my left hand and a coffee mug in my right, I retreat to the back deck to avoid the Saturday morning we-have-a-dance-recital chaos. Snow crunches beneath my feet as I shuffle my way through the fresh coat of powder. Using the carrot as a brush, I clear enough snow from the railing to place my cup. Inside, dishes clink into the sink and my wife calls to our nine-year-old daughter. I watch Jaycee prance into the kitchen for breakfast through the glass pane of the double door. She's not dressed in her skimpy ensemble yet; probably because she'll spill syrup down the front of herself eating pancakes. I told Sabrina that was too messy, but she insisted it was a recital morning ritual—something I would know if I didn't spend all my time at work. Today is the last one and I'd finally forced myself to take time off from the restaurant to attend. I plan on dropping by Jaybird's after the recital to check that I'm not needed for the lunch rush. But that fight can wait a few hours. Sabrina and I no longer see eye-to-eye on the pressure I feel to run the place myself. She insists my managers can handle the bulk of it, leaving me to the family I'd worked so hard to have. But fear of past failures nags me to work sixty-hour weeks most of the time.

I shove the carrot in my pocket and reach for the snow shovel leaning against the house. The weather drives home the reminder that it's my new manager's first solo shift, and probably not a good day for it. It snowed another three inches overnight. I work on clearing a path to the shed, wondering how Lauren will manage the slick roads. The snowplows haven't

1

made it to rural areas yet and she's inexperienced on snow. Having moved to Wisconsin from Alabama to take care of her nieces after her sister lost her battle to leukemia, she's not used to these conditions. With two slide-offs already this season, I worry about another. She should be there about the time Sabrina and I arrive at the recital. I'll have to trust Lauren will be competent enough to travel safely.

A tug on my Carhartt stops me midway to the shed. With chilled fingers, I clasp the fabric of my coat around the carrot.

A snort and a nudge to my thigh makes me turn to the would-be thief. Large brown eyes stare back at me.

"Yes, I brought your treat, Oakley." The twelve-year-old donkey's ears twitch at the mention of his name. Smiling, I tease the carrot out, his anxious gaze following every movement. He crunches it happily before taking off in a sprint to the far edge of the fence, his long legs leaping over the snow that nearly reaches his belly. I save the shoveling for later and trudge the rest of the way to the shed so I can at least feed him before we leave. After putting down fresh straw, I pretend to be committed to shoveling again, but it's really more about avoiding what's going on in the house than clearing the path.

Jaycee flings the back door open. "Mom says the truck leaves in three minutes. And we'll both stop speaking to you if you miss my dance." She wraps her bare arms around herself and twirls. Her black skirt looks like Sabrina disassembled a hundred of her shower loofah things and sewed them together. Tiny stars cover the weird material and I'm told there's a special thing that's going to happen with them, but it's top secret.

I slowly take the steps and make a mental note to check our supply of salt. "Get inside before you freeze."

Jaycee scoops a handful of snow, flinging a zillion tiny flakes in my direction, and races to shut the door between us.

Leaning the shovel against the porch railing, I retrieve my coffee. I take a quick sip and hurry toward the coffee pot to make a travel mug instead. The cold liquid in my hand sloshes over the side of my mug as I trip over Sabrina's stupid cat, Bobbi, who decided to dart across the room. My wife yells out last-minute orders as I hurry for a mop. The darn cat sits proudly in front of the door that hides the cleaning supplies. If I didn't know any better, I'd swear she does it on purpose. I glare at her flicking tail, daring me to move her. I nudge her with my foot, my jeans and boot taking the claw meant for the flesh at my ankle. The front door slams closed. I've got about a minute to get to the truck. Swinging the mop over to the sink, I spray water on it and turn to tackle my spill. The cat rolls onto her back between me and the mess. I carefully step over her and clean the liquid from the floor. The truck horn blares from the drive. Rolling my eyes, I fling the mop back into the sink to take care of later. Bobbi catches my pant leg as I step over her again, leaving behind the to-go coffee I didn't have time to make.

"You could've shoveled the front walk," Sabrina mumbles as I slip into the passenger seat.

"I had to feed Oakley." I want to mention that I'd gotten up early and shoveled the drive but I'm saving my arguments for the battle over the restaurant.

"One more minute and you would've been walking."

"We have another vehicle. Besides, it was your stupid cat that held me up."

"Blame it on the cat," she says, backing out of the drive. "I thought you were finding another home for that dang donkey anyway."

I nearly laugh. I hate her cat and she hates my donkey. Although, in all fairness, I *did* say we'd only keep Oakley until we found a permanent home for him. But we both know the donkey is staying.

"I'm so excited you get to watch my performance, Daddy," Jaycee chirps from the back, rescuing me from the brewing argument.

"Me too, Jaybird." I smile, leaning back to high-five her.

"Afterward I thought we'd go ice skating," Sabrina suggests. "It's been so long since we've had a day together."

I curl my lip. "Jaycee is hardly dressed for that," I argue, holding back my true intentions of swinging by the restaurant to see for myself that I'd hired a capable employee.

"They wear less than this when they skate at the Olympics," Jaycee argues.

"They aren't outside where it's two degrees," I remind her.

Sabrina points to the backseat. "I brought her a change of clothes."

Jaycee taps her feet against the plastic floor mats. "Can we go? Can we?"

"I don't know," I say, refusing to turn and face her eagerness.

Sabrina scowls, turning onto the highway. "If you think you're going to work after, you've got another thing coming."

I run my fingers through hair that is nearly a month past needing a trim, biding enough time to find words to avoid a spat. "I'm sure Lauren will do a great job."

"I would hope so. You've been her shadow for weeks. If you don't give her a chance, people are going to start talking about...well, you know, how you're following her around like a puppy."

I roll my eyes. "Don't be dramatic. Business suffers without competent management."

"It's either that or your marriage, huh?"

I slap my hand on my knee. "How about we go bowling instead and I promise to take you skating when it warms up ten degrees." I stare out the window at fields of snow.

Sabrina's scowl hits me hard, even if it only lasts a split second. There's no denying a bed on the couch if I demand a few moments at work. "How convenient that the bowling alley is two blocks from the restaurant."

"I'll take you out for dinner afterward."

"It better not be at Jaybird's Country Café."

I reach out to shake her hand. "Deal."

Twenty minutes later, Jaycee runs to meet the rest of her troop, and Sabrina and I find seats in the third row of our crowded high school auditorium. As I remove my coat, I can't help but wish this recital were a youth baseball game and we were in lawn chairs with the sun beating down on us. Of course, it's January, and there's at least a foot of snow outside, but dance is something Sabrina got Jaycee interested in while I'd lost out to *any* physical contact sport I'd suggested.

I glance at my watch. The grills should be fired up, the fryers running, and Lauren should be checking the cash drawers for the registers. We'd had to stop serving breakfast when we lost the last manager or I could've popped in for the early breakfast shift and still made the recital. I mentally check off the list of opening chores, hoping they're being done on schedule. Today probably wasn't the best day to cut her loose from training, I think, reaching for my phone to check for a last-minute question from the manager.

Sabrina nudges me with her elbow as the dance team instructor takes the stage and gives an introduction. "Pay attention."

The girls—and four boys—take the stage and I do pay attention...to their outfits. Entirely too inappropriate for their age. Jaycee's group will be up after this group is done, or so Sabrina whispers in my ear when I cock my eyebrow.

"You've spent the last seven weeks properly training Lauren. She'll be okay."

"It's her first solo shift. You know how the crowd can get on the weekends," I whisper against the music.

"Don't make me take your phone," she threatens, reaching for my fingers that clutch it.

My phone rings and I receive a dozen glares from people annoyed that I'd forgotten to put it on silent. Sabrina tenses beside me.

"I'll ignore it," I offer, stealing a glance at the screen. It's my head cook. I shake my head and slip from the aisle, knowing I'll pay for my actions later. "Hello," I say into the device.

"Hey, man, I hate to alarm you, but Lauren is half an hour late. Nobody can get into the restaurant," Dennis informs me.

"Shit!" Dirty looks come at me from all sides as I hurry to the exit. "Why didn't you call me sooner?"

"Do you think something happened or she just flaked out?"

"I'm about to find out." I end the call and dial a newly programmed number.

Five rings then voicemail. "Lauren's personal answering service—Lauren's working her butt off so she can afford my replacement. Can I take a message?"

I had laughed the first time I heard that recording, but today I cringe, mumbling a profanity under my breath. The phone rings again in my hand and Lauren's number pops up.

"Lauren, where the—" I stop short as a horn beeps on the other end of the receiver.

"No, I've got one called. Thanks," my new manager says, her tone muffled. I catch a brief conversation before she turns her attention back to me. "Jason,

I'm sorry. I took the corner too fast and now I'm stuck in the ditch. The tow truck can't be here for another hour. I've been trying to call around to get a ride in, but it seems everyone is busy...except for the few cars that stopped to see if I needed help. I would catch a ride with one of them, but I'm still pretty new here and I don't know who these people are. I guess I should have put a few of the staffs' numbers in my phone."

I glance toward the auditorium. I could easily call Dennis back and send him after her. I consider it for a minute, but I wouldn't leave Dennis alone with Oakley. Not that my donkey would take any crap off my head cook, but Lauren hardly has the same no-bullshit attitude as my four-legged companion. I zip my coat and head for the door. "Where are you?"

I listen to her directions half-heartedly as I know where her sister's house is and what route she would've been driving. I shoot Sabrina a text, complete with a list of reasons why I have to retrieve my employee myself instead of sending someone after her. By the time I finish, Lauren finally has directed me to a somewhat precise location—between the house where the Halloween goblin hangs in the tree and the barn that's falling down. She apologizes for not remembering the road name, but I assure her I know right where she's at and I'll be there in fifteen minutes. Sabrina's text tone dings as I start the engine, but I ignore it. With any luck, I'll be back before Jaycee's group takes the stage.

Lauren's newly inherited minivan couldn't be in a worse spot. She hadn't made it entirely around the corner but careened off the road as if she hadn't tried to turn at all. Behind us is a blind spot for the drivers coming in our direction. Her back bumper sticks into the road, posing a danger of getting hit if two vehicles happen to come across her at the same time. I cross into the opposite lane and back up toward her van.

She rolls down her window and waves. "Can't really open the door," she says, pointing to the snow piled up around her vehicle.

"It's fine. I think I can get you out," I say, bending to inspect the scene.

I know I should start by getting my pop-up traffic cone and taking it down the curve to alert oncoming traffic, but Sabrina's voice echoes in my head that I'd better be in my seat on time. I reach for my small shovel and work quickly to remove enough snow to hook a chain to our vehicles.

It takes nearly ten minutes for me to clear a path and attach the tow chain to the axle. I'm on my back underneath my own truck when Lauren's voice beckons me.

"I can't hear you! Give me a second," I yell.

The scraping of a snowplow's blade screeches, growing louder as it approaches. My fingers numbly work to secure the connection before it comes around the corner. Lauren shrieks. I turn my head, but the tire blocks my view. Lauren's shrill cry somehow overpowers colliding metal. A blackness like nothing I'd ever seen encases me.

Chapter 2

Tears sting my eyes as a thousand fluorescent lights cast brightness into the vastness suddenly surrounding me. I must've hit my head. *It's warm here. Did I get buried with snow?* The sound of the approaching plow echoes in my ears. *Was there an accident? Am I in the hospital? They must have given me drugs.* I feel like I'm floating. *Did Lauren call Sabrina? I programmed her number, didn't I? The sun feels nice. Did a dog get into the hospital?* There's barking...and...the doctors...they sound like children.

I blink several times, though assume my eyes remain shut. I'm probably in surgery or some sort of medically induced coma. Everything is blank. I blink again. No. Someone is walking toward me. *Man, these must be some good drugs.* Straight out of a fierce light, the silhouette multiplies, seven shapes separating into individual forms. Birds emerge from tiny black spots, soaring overhead across the sky like a flyover at the Daytona 500. Voices chatter happily as the figures pick up speed to reach me. An eighty-pound German Shephard races past them and leaps into my arms.

"Falcon! Is that you, boy?" The dog wags his tail, slathering his tongue over my face. "It *is* you! How've you been?" He knocks me over, his happy barks filling the air.

"We've waited a long time for you to get here," the shortest boy, around ten years old, proclaims.

I tilt my head. He looks just like the pictures I've seen of my grandpa at that age.

"I thought this day would never come," a girl just inches taller than the boy breathes dramatically. She holds her mouth the same way Sabrina does when she's impatient about something.

I stroke Falcon, staring at them a moment. No way I'm seeing what I think I'm seeing. This is the wildest hallucination I've ever had. I was never one to experiment with drugs, but this is still the craziest thing I've ever experienced.

I hug her five-foot frame when she offers it. "Where am I?"

The oldest boy, a lively teenager with the hint of a moustache, steps forward. "Home." The word slips off his tongue like I should recognize my new surroundings.

A timid pre-teen girl reaches for my hand. "Would you like us to show you around?"

I take her hand and a lake appears before us. "I've been here before," I whisper.

I'd fished the lake with my grandpa a hundred times. How it got here, I have no clue. I watch as the older children quickly pluck rocks and toss them into the water. The way the oldest one hides a large stone and waits for the perfect opportunity to splash his friends strikes a memory buried deep inside me. I used to do the exact same thing to my grandpa. Looking back, I know he knew what I was up to, but he was a good sport—he's the one who taught me the trick. My hand is released, and the girl joins in on the fun. I smile watching their simple pleasure.

Taking a seat on the bank, I toss a few pebbles. "What are your names?"

The oldest girl laughs, turning to show me a shiny rock that she plops into the pocket of her dress. "You know our names."

My breath comes out in a huge puff, as if I'd been hit in the stomach. I point to each in turn, rattling off names Sabrina and I had chosen each pregnancy like I've known these children for years. Falcon buries his nose in my side until I drape my arm over him and squeeze gently.

Kelsey hands me a rock.

I toss it in. It sends ripples into the ripples from the large rock Travis just threw. "How is this possible?"

I rest on my elbows, perplexed by it all.

Travis takes a seat beside me. "Don't try to make sense of it all at once," he offers.

I scratch my head. "I wouldn't even know where to start. There was snow on the ground when I got up this morning."

"The weather is always perfect here."

I consider this. The air temperature is comfortable, the sun not beating down heavily, and a warm breeze floats by periodically. But Lauren is still stuck in that ditch, and I still have a recital to get to. Well, probably not,

I think, remembering I'm in the hospital under a heavy dose of strong medication. "I guess there's no need to hurry back then."

Josh brings me a fishing pole. Where he got it, I have no clue. "I've been waiting on you to teach me how to cast," he says.

I leap to my feet. "I've waited my whole life for this day," I say, taking him several feet from his siblings.

I savor every second, splitting time between my lost children. Their energy never seems to run out and, oddly enough, neither does mine. I wonder how Sabrina and I would've held up if this were our daily routine.

We swim in our clothes, throw countless sticks for Falcon, and fish until I'm certain we should be running out of daylight.

"Jaycee would've loved this," I mutter, plucking a blade of grass to show them how to make it whistle.

"Oh, it's not her time yet," Whitney says matter-of-factly.

I smile down at her. "I can't wait to tell your mom all about you." I ruffle her hair and hand her a new blade.

She slobbers over it, creating nothing but a muffled sound of her lips flapping against each other.

"She won't understand," Kelsey remarks.

I pull a new blade of grass and instruct Whitney on the proper technique. She fails again and again.

"Guys, over here," Travis calls, the smell of campfire smoke filling the air.

I turn to see bales of hay circling a small fire. The girls race me to the crackling wood. Travis passes out sticks and Marnie pokes a marshmallow on the end of each.

"Tell me what you've been up to," I suggest as our sugary snacks burn.

Kelsey laughs, her long hair blowing in the breeze. I can't get over how much she looks like her mother.

"Same ole' stuff, different day," Josh replies with a shrug.

I roll my eyes. "You're gonna use that line, huh?" I slide my marshmallow onto a graham cracker and wait for Whitney to place the chocolate on top.

"Wait 'til you try this," she says. "There's nothing like it."

I chuckle, wondering if she knows I've had S'mores before. But I take a bite and she's right. This is the best treat I've ever had. Everything about it is perfect. The marshmallow is black on the outside, creamy in the middle, and the chocolate melts evenly in the middle. It tastes better than I remember.

Josh reloads our sticks and I try another approach. "Tell me about yourselves then. What do you like to do?"

Whitney wipes a string of marshmallow goo from her chin. "You already know us. We're a little bit you and a little bit Mom."

"A little of Grandpa, too," Travis smirks.

"A little of Grandpa is plenty," I tease.

The group exchanges a look I can't decipher.

"What's up?" I put together another S'more and hold it to my lips.

Travis stands. "We have to leave now."

"What? Why?" I leap to my feet, dropping the S'more. "You can't leave now."

My surgery must be over. I'm about to wake up.

They take turns hugging me and I grasp to keep them close. "I'm not ready."

"We'll see you again soon," Whitney promises, but they're already walking away from me. Falcon sits faithfully at my side.

I step toward them but it's as if I'm walking on ground moving in the opposite direction.

"Jason, my child," a soothing voice calls from beside me. "You've been through quite a lot. Why don't you have a seat," he offers, motioning to a wooden bench that replaces the hay bales.

Geese honk overhead. I jerk my gaze to the side when water splashes at their landing.

"I hope you enjoyed your day," the man says.

My eyes bug wildly. "Very much so," I reply.

His hand slides to my knee. "I'm glad." Falcon climbs onto my lap. He'd always thought he was a lap dog. "I wish everyone knew how to love like a dog."

I nod, drinking in the crisp blue sky, the clear water with fish lurking beneath the surface, and inhale the fresh air. "Am I dead?" The man beside me slowly nods. "Should I be bowing at your feet?" Falcon scrambles to his feet as I quickly slip from the bench and fall to my knees because, of course, I should.

With a hand upon my back, He says, "Sit. Please."

I clamber back to my place. "Sabrina needs sidewalk salt." I swear sweat beads across my brow, but a quick swipe with the back of my hand reveals no dampness. "Why am I here?"

"I thought we could talk."

I wring my hands nervously and stroke Falcon's ears when he lies his head on my lap. "Is this where I have to answer for all the things I did wrong?"

He shakes his head. "No. I have a private room all set up for that sort of thing. You know, intimidating white walls with a long table. You'll sit on one end and I'll sit at the other, a clipboard in my hands so I can take notes. Not that I need notes, but you get the idea."

I blink rapidly. How will I ever convince Him to let me in? I'm undeserving of Heaven, that much I *do* know. "I hope you have a lot of time. I've made more mistakes than I can count."

The corners of his lips turn upward. "Relax, won't you? You need to stop worrying about things out of your control. I know you've been told more than once to turn your troubles over to me. I paid the price for your entry inside—" He sweeps his hand from one side to another. "—Is it too much to ask for a little conversation?"

"You let geese in? You know they're terribly mean?"

He smiles. "I made geese too."

"Is Elvis in the . . . building?"

He laughs. "Why does everyone ask that?"

I shrug. "Seems like a good question." I smile nervously, my eyes refusing to meet his. "I don't know why you'd want to talk to *me*."

He points to a weed bank where I'd caught more than a hundred fish. "Remember the first time you got a Muskie on the end of your line?"

I nod, smiling at the fight we'd had. "He 'bout pulled me over the boat. I lost him and my favorite Jitterbug."

He produces a rod and hands it to me. At the end is the same rounded lure I'd hooked that Muskie with. "Now that you've both doubled in size, how about a rematch?"

I cast the line a dozen times, each producing nothing but the lure. "You're sure he's in there?"

Jesus smiles, his hand falling onto my shoulder. "Don't ruin a perfect day of fishing with grumbling. The water is calm as glass, rain is moving in—" He points to a large dark cloud in the west. "—and water temps are in the upper sixties."

He has a good point. I cast my line out, this time not caring whether that dang fish bites the bait or not. A slight breeze carries the smell of impending rain. I inhale deeply. The only thing that could make this better would be if Sabrina and Jaycee could be with me. I immediately regret the thought, knowing what that would mean for them.

More questions plague me but I'm too scared of the answers to ask. "My grandpa loved fishing this lake." My eyelids flutter with excitement. Maybe just *one* question. "Do I get to see him soon?"

"He's been watching over you, you know."

I stand straighter, throwing the line again. The sun beats down on my face. There are so many things I can't wait to see. The streets of gold. The mansion. *Does everyone get their own or is it something we have to share?* "What's the rest of Heaven like?"

Jesus shakes his head. "You know, you're impatient, even after all those lessons."

I think back to the multitude of prayers I'd floated His way, asking for enough money to pay the electric bill, pleading for a better job, begging for children. After four miscarriages, Sabrina and I thought we'd never receive the miracle of a family. Then came Jaycee. And even that wasn't enough for me. I wanted her to have a sibling. Three more miscarriages—one in the second trimester—then came the devasting news Sabrina needed a hysterectomy. I had been so impatient during those years of heartache. I nearly demanded we be blessed. It wasn't until I turned the situation over to a higher power that we realized our family was complete the way it was.

He points to a tiny cove. "Do you remember the day you and your friend, Ryan, pushed each other until you both fell off the bank?"

I hang my head. "We wanted to go swimming, but my mom told us not to get wet because it was too cold for that in September."

He nods. "Yes. And it turned out to be dreadfully hot that day. The weatherman misjudged the path of the cold front."

I turn, glancing slightly upward, pulling my gaze back before reaching his eyes. "We didn't think it would hurt anything."

"Ah, beside the point."

I reel the line in. "Surely, I'll get a pass on that one? I was just a kid."

He unfolds his hands, splaying them open like a book. "If it will make you feel better."

I shrug. Is this some sort of free pass? Maybe I should ask for forgiveness for the time I blamed my cousin for the broken window or the time I walked out of the store knowing they only charged me for six bundles of shingles and not sixteen. Why am I not sweating like a—ooh, better not think that language in present company.

A deer emerges from the woods at the far edge of the lake. As if oblivious to us, she struts to the water's edge and takes a carefree drink. I watch in amazement as a buck follows behind her. A heron dips down from the sky, landing on the lake nearly in front of us. A smile plasters to my face as creatures surround us like a scene in *Snow White*. Never before have I seen so much wildlife in one place. A bunny hops by our feet as I feel myself relaxing.

I point to a fox three yards from where we sit. "My grandpa taught me to skin fish right where that fox is sitting," I say, earning a knowing nod in response. "I'll bet I filleted a million fish right there on that bank."

Jesus lifts a shoulder. "Sixty-two."

I raise an eyebrow. "That's it?"

He laughs. "He only let you use the knife that last summer."

My smile slips to a frown as I remember my grandpa's death that following winter. I want to ask why he had to take him *then*. We were just getting around to all the fun things he'd been telling me we'd do after he retired, and we barely got to do any of them. Nine-year-old me still harbors resentment over that, but is it really something to argue with Jesus about? I'd already done enough of that, and He knows it. "Sixty-two, huh?" Jesus nods. "How many people do you think you could've fed with that?" I ask, thinking it must be more than five thousand.

"Depends on how many are hungry."

I smile at the answer. It's so *Jesus*. I cast the line again and again. I have no idea what to say. Is he waiting for me to say the right thing, the thing that will gain my access inside the Pearly Gates? Where are those anyway? "I'm sorry about the time I stuck the fish in my pocket and took it home," I say awkwardly.

His eyes light up as he turns to me. "You were five and you didn't fully understand fish couldn't breathe without water."

I rub my jaw. "I really thought he would be okay until we got home. I wanted to put it in my fish tank."

"I know."

Of course He does.

My line tugs. I jerk my attention to the fight before me. The fish cranks my line out, tugging against my rod. Stepping forward, I dare a glance at the man beside me. His smile matches my own. It's a beautiful battle of one step forward, two steps back. I wonder if the fish is having as much fun as I am. *He's got a hook in his mouth; of course he's not.* Ten glorious minutes I spend fighting the creature before pulling him to shore.

Holding him up, I bask in the beauty of the twenty-pound fish. "Do you have a camera?" Jesus laughs. I release the large fish into the water and watch him dart away. "May we meet again."

A nagging thought creeps into my head. I never got to take Jaycee fishing. By the time she was old enough, the restaurant was starting to be successful and it left little opportunity for family outings. I always thought there'd be time. Maybe He'll let me go back. I have to ask. "Is there any chance I can go home?"

Jesus cocks his head. "I've made a place for you."

"I know. But I'm not ready." I stare at the ground; afraid I'll see disappointment written on his face. "It's just—Jaycee has a recital. I promised I'd be there."

"You were in a terrible accident. You can't just walk away from it."

I nod. "I think you're capable."

"I have other plans for you."

My heart catches in my throat. "Sabrina...we weren't having the best time getting along today. I need to tell her how much she means to me. How much I appreciate her."

Jesus walks to the water's edge and skips a stone clear across the wide lake. "You are never guaranteed your next breath."

My eyes gape as another stone skids across the flat water. "I know I should've done better. If you give me another chance, I swear I'll prove it."

Jesus rubs a flat stone between his fingers. "I already gave you multiple chances to show your family they came before Jaybird's."

I hang my head, my tongue heavy with excuses. "I know I failed."

Jesus tosses the pebble so high into the air I lose sight of it. "Ah, but you have done so much right."

"It doesn't feel that way now."

His arm slips around my shoulder. "You took your family to church every Sunday. You taught Jaycee's Sunday School class. *That* is so much more important than sacrificing her childhood to pay for college."

"I just wanted to make sure she didn't have to worry about paying for a higher education."

He nods, taking my hand and placing it palm up. "Don't you like it here?"

"I have a kid to raise." His knowing nod presses me forward, my palm still open. "After all we went through waiting for her to arrive...I hate to think I don't get to stick around to see her graduate. Who's going to teach Jaycee to change a tire so she never has to rely on a man?"

"It does seem a tad unfair." The rock He'd thrown lands softly into my outstretched hand. I flinch in amazement, curling my fingers around it. "Tell you what, you skip that rock across the lake, and I'll let you decide where you end your day." The pebble transforms into a perfect skipping stone before my eyes.

I crouch nervously, my entire existence riding on one toss. I'd never been good at skipping rocks. The smooth stone slides from my fingers, skipping five times before sinking to the bottom.

Jesus embraces me in a side hug. "Jason, you were never meant to do the things I can do." Another stone appears in his hand and, with a gentle flick of his wrist, it cascades gracefully across the water.

I watch the ripples, knowing I failed my family. Again.

A smooth, hard form weighs inside my curled fingertips. I brush my thumb over the rock, in awe of its presence in my hand.

"How about I give you a do-over?"

I open my hand. "The only way I'd ever get it across this lake is with your help."

Jesus smiles as if I'm a toddler who'd learned to ask for help pouring milk into a cup. "All you have to do is ask."

I take my weird rock-skipping stance, study the path, and turn my head to the man beside me. "I know I don't deserve another chance—I'll probably blow it. I'm just asking that you don't do this to Sabrina. She's got this vision of us sitting on the front porch when we're old and I'd really hate to let her down. Will you help me?"

Jesus steps behind me, fitting his arm to mine. We move in unison as He guides the rock across the lake. I watch it fade from sight before turning to Him.

He motions for us to return to the bench. "I'm afraid you've missed Jaycee's recital."

I hang my head in shame. I promised to be there. "Maybe it's better if I stay. That girl is *not* going to be happy."

"She'll forgive you. You were helping someone out, after all."

I gasp. "Lauren!"

"She's fine," He says, placing his hand on my knee. "A little shook up, but she'll be okay."

A long minute passes before He stands up, reaching for my hand. "Are you ready to see your grandpa?"

I nod and force a smile. There are far worse places to be than Heaven and I know Sabrina will make sure we're all together again one day.

Jesus wraps his arms around me, encasing me in a peace I've never experienced.

"I trust you to watch over my family," I whisper.

"Make sure Jaycee uses that soccer ball." I wrinkle my nose in confusion. His eyes twinkle a moment, and He nearly laughs. "And enjoy your days at the track."

I fight the tears building in my eyes. So Jaycee is going to switch gears? Soccer and running? It's not baseball, but it sure beats recitals.

He places his hands on my shoulders. "Say hello to your grandpa for me."

My body careens as if I'd jumped out of an airplane with no parachute. The pristine lake vanishes as my surroundings are replaced by a deep white nothingness. Am I going to Hell?! I flail my arms in an attempt to grab *something* but, of course, there is nothing to keep me from falling to my fate. The farther I fall, the darker it turns until I'm encased by blackness.

Chapter 3

Nothing hurts as I expect it to. Maybe He gave me that miracle after all. I open my eyes to a blanket of snow. I don't remember my coat being quite as perfect as what I wear now. Only my ears and the tip of my nose are cold. I turn, expecting to find a mangled truck, but the only thing I see is a brick wall. Snow mounds around me, blocking most of my view in the other direction. I slowly manage to pull myself to my feet, thankful I landed softly from my fall.

"Lauren?" I inch my way through a heaping drift, sinking way farther than I imagine possible. "Where am I?"

I take an awkward step toward the footsteps crunching on crusty snow. Everyone's attire suggests church, but it looks as if some of them got dressed in the dark. One lady is wearing a blue top with yellow pants, but mostly it looks like the dress code is gray. I see my best friend, Kelley, wearing a suit. He only gets that dressed up for two reasons—a wedding or a funeral. I venture out from my corner of the building and head toward him.

"I wonder where that puppy came from," a scratchy voice whispers, stopping me.

Rosie, the minister's wife, steps around the shrub and crouches, planting her large bosoms in my face.

"Rosie, we don't have time to fool with a puppy now. We told Sabrina we'd help get all these flowers to her house." The voice belongs to her husband, Gary.

Instinctively, I turn, searching for the puppy. I spot footprints but no dog in sight. "Have you seen Sabrina?"

Rosie turns to Gary. "I'm not leaving a poor creature out in this weather. He's probably lost."

She looks down at me. Wait, *down* at me? Have I shrunk? Then I notice her smile as she reaches for me.

"What are you doing?" It feels nice, but— "Why is my butt twitching?" I turn my head to inspect. "Oh, hell, no!" There's a tail sprouting from my butt, and it's covered in chocolate colored fur. *I'm the puppy?!*

Before I get the chance to examine the rest of myself, she scoops me up, wrapping me in her coat. Icy Hot so thick it could choke a horse, floods my sensitive nose.

Jaycee's voice crashes the turmoil of emotions brewing inside me. "A puppy!"

Rosie places me on a thinly carpeted floor inside the foyer of our church. I lurch into Jaycee's outstretched arms.

"I'm so sorry I missed your recital! I can't believe I'm actually here!" I slather my tongue all over her face. "I'm so glad to see you! Where's your mom?"

Jaycee giggles, her hands struggling to keep my wiggling body on her lap.

"Sabrina!" I clamber up Jaycee's chest, hanging my arms over her shoulder. I don't see my wife, but the soft scent of her coconut shampoo tells me she's close.

"I think someone dumped him off," Rosie whispers to Gary. "What are we going to do with him?"

Fabric rustles as Gary crosses his arms. "He'll have to go to the pound." Displeasure covers Rosie's face, but I'm not sure how I know that with my back to her. "Rosie, dear, the last thing we need is a puppy to trip over. Do you want to break a hip?"

Jaycee's arms tighten around me. "You can't take her to the pound!"

I struggle out of her grasp. "Her?! No way I'm a girl. Let me go; I need to check something!"

"I'm afraid we have no choice," Gary says.

I casually sit and scratch my head with my foot as if I'd been doing it all my life, discretely 'checking under my skirt' as my grandpa would call it. "I still have one!"

Sabrina's heels clack against the hardwood floor of the sanctuary and softly patter the carpet as she approaches the foyer. I sprint straight for her legs.

"Mom! They want to take this sweet puppy to the pound," my daughter whines, trying to catch me.

I jump against my wife's shins. "Sabrina! I'll never leave your side again! I have no idea what's going on with my four legs and tail situation, but I promise I'll fix this. No more long hours at the restaurant." I laugh to myself as I say the words, as if I have control over anything, including my bladder. Sabrina scoops me up in the nick of time, sending me outside where the cold bites my nose.

"I have to pee in the snow and I can't even write my name," I grumble as a puddle forms beneath me.

The church door opens as the last remaining stragglers exit. Rosie and Gary fill Sabrina in on how I was found while I wait for the door to open again. Ian McPheron shoves the door open half an eternity later. I back away from him, not wanting to get stuck in the same vicinity as his breath. I dart through the crack in the door after Ian passes. Thankfully, he's busy answering his phone and doesn't notice me.

I rub against Sabrina's leg until she bends to scratch my ears. "I wonder why people don't scratch each other's ears. It feels surprisingly nice. Keep doing it," I plead. Even the pleasantness from her touch can't override the smells coming off her hands. It's as if the fragrance of the entire church was bottled and Sabrina washed her hands in it. "Ugh, I see you had to talk to Cathy Wilson. And I see she's still blowing her nose with that snot rag she's been carrying since 2005. Your hand smells like boogers and butterscotch. Maybe a hint of old man Hudson's tobaccy pipe."

"We'll drop him at the pound after we take the flowers to your house," Gary says casually.

Sabrina tickles under my jaw. "I don't think they'll all fit in my house. There are *so many*."

Rosie places her hand on Sabrina's shoulder. "You just point and shout the orders; we'll do the rest."

I play with Jaycee while dozens of arrangements pass through the doors.

"I'm having the weirdest dream," I say. "You're going to laugh so hard when I tell you about it."

These must be some good drugs, I tell myself. Surely this is just a medically induced dream.

Jaycee scoops me up and digs in her mother's purse until she produces a phone. "Stop wiggling. I want to take a selfie with you." I wriggle out of her grasp at the sight of myself. What if this isn't a dream? Am I at my own funeral? I stumble backward, Jaycee crawling after me in her Sunday best. I dart for the sanctuary where my fears are confirmed. I don't have to see inside the coffin to know whose body it holds. My picture is plastered on either side on giant easels. I slump into a ball and whimper.

Jaycee takes a seat and cuddles me on her lap. "That's my daddy. He's in Heaven now."

I'm afraid to look in her eyes. A single tear plops onto the shiny toe of her shoe. I nestle into her side. "I'm so sorry. I should've chosen you."

With the last plant out of the church, Sabrina and the pastor stand, gawking at the two of us.

"Looks like a rottweiler," Sabrina comments.

Gary clears his throat. "Coat's a little light and head isn't boxy enough to be a rott. Might be a mix. My guess is one of his parents could be a black lab."

I scramble to Sabrina's feet. "It's me—Jason! I can't explain this, but you have to help me."

She bends to stroke my head. I cover her hand in slobber. It feels weird to be acting in such a way, but I can't help myself. I thought I'd never see her again.

I turn and pounce on Jaycee, deciding I don't care if I'm destined to four legs, I'm just happy to be back with my family. "Jaybird, it's me," I yap, covering her with slobbery kisses.

She giggles, peering up at her mother, asking a silent question.

"We can't keep him," Sabrina whispers. "I don't know how I'm going to manage things without your dad, let alone adding a dog to the mix."

Gary slides his hand over my back. "I can drop him at the pound."

"I'm sure that isn't the only option," Rosie pleads.

Jaycee's lip quivers.

"Don't cry, Jaybird," I whimper.

Sabrina sighs heavily. "I have an idea." She bends to our level, staring me so hard in the eyes that I'm convinced she knows it's me. "How would you like to come home with us? *Just* until we can find you a permanent home?"

Jaycee shrieks.

"We can make up some flyers and post them around town," Rosie suggests. "Maybe the poor thing's just lost."

Sabrina waves us toward the door. "That would be great. If it's not too much trouble."

"We'll help any way we can," Gary offers.

Sabrina holds the door open. "Would you mind stopping by the store and getting some food and stuff for him?"

"Consider it done," Rosie says.

I sleep on the way home, exhausted mentally and physically from my day. I can't wrap my mind around the accident and my trip to Heaven, let alone the return trip and the addition of two extra legs and a tail. Then, to top it off, I'd found myself at my funeral. Accepting my new existence—and the end of my previous one—is going to take some time. Unless this is still part of the dream...which is what I hope.

Sabrina, Jaycee, and I sit on the floor in our living room. They stare at me as if I'm supposed to entertain them, but a tantalizing smell comes from the kitchen—baked spaghetti and fresh garlic bread. It smells different than I remember. I sniff heavily, trying to figure out my new nose. Apparently, I have to get used to it. There's a hint of flour—which I didn't even know *had* a smell—and eggs, and the tomato sauce is seasoned with just the right amount of basil and garlic. The whole thing is covered in mozzarella cheese. My only complaint is the meat is ground turkey and not beef. But the yeast from homemade breadsticks more than make up for that. The meal smells even more delicious than I remember, and spaghetti is something I only eat because Jaycee loves it.

I leap onto Sabrina's lap. "Let's eat!" I lap a long stroke across her neck. She smells a thousand times better than my memories allow. The jacket I leave hanging on my chair at the table, however, needs washed. I wiggle my nose, a new scent coming in. It smells like...Bobbi...the cat. The striped devil sits in the corner of the room. I wiggle until Sabrina puts me down. Forgetting the food in the other room, I sprint toward the tiny beast, hoping to get a little payback. Bobbi darts over the coffee table and down the hall. I slide across the slick tile in pursuit, Jaycee not far behind us. Hiding underneath the bed in Jaycee's room, the cat hisses as I stare at the mess my child has shoved out of sight. I army crawl three lengths until my back legs slide off the floor and Jaycee clutches me in her arms.

"You have to be nice to the kitty and maybe Mom will let you stay. Be on your best behavior."

I stare at her, a new terrifying thought plaguing me—what if God only let me come back to see them one last time? What if that's what this is? Jaycee squishes me as she holds me football style while she digs a truckload of junk from under her bed. Finding a ribbon on a stick, she pulls it out and drags it behind her as she runs through the house. I chase after it, trying to remember what in the heck she called the thing. She uses it in some sort of dance—if I recall correctly.

I trip over it as we enter the main stage known as the living room. Taking a tumble, I find the yellow and gray satin tangled around my midsection.

"Who puts ribbon on a stick anyway?" I yap, pulling at the odd contraption. "And what's the point of flinging it around? Is it supposed to look like some sort of bumblebee?" My sharp teeth work to free my torso.

Sabrina giggles but Jaycee's lips hold a tight line. "Mom! He's tearing up my ribbon wand!"

Sabrina leaps into action to help untangle me. Even though I know the dangers of the thing, I can't help but chase it again as Jaycee leaps around the room, showing off her skills with the wand. Sabrina whips out her phone to take a video.

"I've got you," I tell her, twisting myself into its trap again.

This time they both laugh and hurry to unwrap me.

After performing the trick, Jaycee scoops me up and takes me to watch the footage.

Jaycee and I continue our game for the longest time and I finally yawn, having forgotten the tantalizing smells coming from the kitchen. I don't know why I'm suddenly so tired. Or why the spot beneath the coffee table looks like a great place for a nap. I crawl under it and curl into a ball.

"He's going to make a good pet for someone," Sabrina says.

"I already love him," Jaycee whispers.

"You just met him." Sabrina pats Jaycee's arm. "Let's go eat."

Is it dinner time? I yawn. It feels more like bedtime. "Save me some."

I want to convince Sabrina to let me stay, but I don't know how, and my brain is heavy with sleep and the hard pill I need to swallow. I slip off, dozing until movement wakes me.

Rosie's thick soles hit heavily on our hardwood floor. "This should cover everything."

My eyes flutter open and I crawl out of hiding to inspect a pile of supplies on the floor. Again, my nose overwhelms me.

"They should not put the dog toys so close to the ferret cages," I mumble, turning my nose up, but when Jaycee tosses the ball, I run after it. "Maybe my slobber will fix that," I mutter.

"Oh wow," Sabrina comments. "You really went above and beyond."

Rosie winks. "We weren't sure how long he'd be staying."

"Hopefully not more than a few days. We've closed the restaurant until the end of next week."

I leap onto Sabrina's calves. "That's too long! Three days would've been fine. We can't afford no income for two weeks!"

"I'm sure he'll have a home soon," Gary offers.

"Maybe he's already found one," Rosie whispers low enough that Jaycee can't hear.

Jaycee wiggles a knotted length of rope in my face. I grab hold, directing her attention away from the adults, but I keep my ears perked in their direction.

Sabrina blocks her mouth with her hand to shield Jaycee from her words. "A puppy is the last thing I need right now."

"It might help her deal with her father's death in ways you can't," Rosie says softly.

"Maybe you're right," Sabrina agrees.

"I don't think it was a coincidence he was found at the church...today," Rosie says with a smirky confidence.

"Now, Rosie," Gary admonishes.

"I'm convinced it was a sign," Rosie argues.

"I doubt that." Sabrina shakes her head. "Besides, if I kept him, I'd feel like I replaced Jason with a puppy."

I place my paws on Sabrina's leg. "But it *is* me," I bark.

Rosie tilts her head sweetly. "God knows what we need when we need it. And I think He sent you a puppy." Rosie's voice holds excitement as if she'd unlocked a secret code.

Gary motions to the front room. "I picked up some sidewalk salt. Wasn't sure if you needed it, but it's by the door."

I dart to the safety beneath the coffee table. God *does* have a sense of humor. It's not what I wanted but I'll take it.

Chapter 4

I yawn, snuggling into a warm blanket. I don't remember my bed being this hard. Blinking into the darkness, I take in the bottom shelf of our bookcase and a dozen photo albums nestled along a thin layer of dust.

"Why am I on the floor?" Stretching, I pull myself up. "Oh yeah, I'm a dog," I whisper, as recent events flood back to me, though I still sort of hope this is all a dream. I whimper a sorrowful cry before pulling myself together when a new noise emerges from the hallway.

The once faint ticking of Sabrina's antique grandfather clock sounds like a gong as it ticks the minutes away. Two glowing eyes float toward me until I make out the shape of the cat attached to them.

Bobbi purrs, her claws extended just enough to tap the wood as she saunters my direction. I wonder if she's always done that or if I'm just now hearing it.

With a tail flicking across my nose, she says, "You and I need to get one thing straight."

I clamber backward into the bookshelf. "You can talk?!"

She sits, displaying a paw with outstretched claws. "Don't be dense."

I inch my nose forward, smelling her scent. A hint of vanilla...and cinnamon? I shake my head. Cats don't smell like vanilla or cinnamon. Did Sabrina get a new room scenty thing? I inhale again. No. The wall plugin produces a Christmassy pine fragrance. I ease closer to the fat ball of fur before me. The vanilla comes from the cat. She reaches out and slaps me with the pad of her paw.

I bare my teeth. "Stop that!"

"Oh, calm down, I retracted my claws...this time," she says, circling me. "I know why you're here and it's best we get the rules out of the way now."

I cock my head in her direction. "Rules? What rules?" I skip over the admission that she knows why we're here, hoping the rules include some sort of code on how to communicate with people. Maybe I can find a way to tell Sabrina who I am after all.

She lands with a lazy thud in front of me, her tongue stroking her belly. When she's properly groomed, she sits in the middle of the blanket I'd chosen to sleep on over the dog bed that *doesn't* smell like Sabrina. "First of all, Sabrina is *my* person. She's doesn't like dogs."

I stare at the bedroom door where my wife sleeps. She never told me she didn't like dogs. In fact, we'd talked about getting one when I got things running smoothly at the restaurant. I hang my head, the weight of another failure landing on me.

"Only slightly less important are quiet hours." I roll my eyes. "They run from 8 PM to 6 AM, naturally. And also, from 8 AM until 10 AM when second breakfast is served. Then again from 11 to 12. I take an afternoon nap from 1 to 3."

"You're about to run out of hours in the day to sleep," I interrupt.

"I need all the rest I can get right now. Sabrina will need me in the evenings. She just lost her husband, you know." I lie down with my head on my paws. "Maybe if he would've stayed where he belonged, Sabrina wouldn't be in so much pain right now."

I lunge at Bobbi before I realize I'm growling. She darts onto the coffee table.

"I am the boss here," she hisses. "If you get out of line, I'll make sure Sabrina sends you away."

I jump at her, but she leaps off the table, taking a coffee mug down with her. Liquid sprays onto my back legs as the cup clatters to the floor.

"You're in trouble now, Jason," the cat screeches and slinks behind the couch. *Jason?* I'm too stunned to move as the bedroom door creaks open. *How does she know?* Before I can move away from the mess to get answers, Sabrina scoops me up.

"You're lucky I wasn't sleeping," she whispers. "And that there isn't carpet in here."

Her feet quietly pad to the back door. The scent of her perfume and fresh tears tickle my nose. I sniff her cheek and gently lick her face. She scratches my head, clutching me in one arm as she lets the cold night air into the warm house. I shiver as she places me in the snow and steps outside with me.

"It was the cat!"

"If you wake Jaycee with all that noise, you're sleeping outside," Sabrina threatens softly.

Ignoring her words, I race into the yard looking for Oakley. I stop beside a sapling to take a leak and resume my search. The donkey snorts from inside the shed I'd built him. I step inside, hoping he's awake.

"Oakley," I whisper. "I hope I'm not waking you. It's just...the cat can talk and I thought maybe you could too."

His frozen breath cloud seeps over the short wall I'd created, giving him extra warmth in winter.

"Oakley?"

His hind flank flinches. I step forward, inhaling the fresh straw, wood, and...starting fluid, oil, and Old Spice, mixed with a tinge of sweat? The enhanced sense of smell may take some time to get used to. Especially when the combinations don't make sense. The pine and straw are smells I'd grown accustomed to since we brought the donkey home, but the rest only sparks a memory of my grandpa. His garage smelled exactly the same as this shed. Funny I never noticed it before.

Snow crunches behind me and I turn at the sound. Sabrina steps inside the shed a moment later with an apple in one hand and a pear in the other. The donkey's eyes open but he remains motionless.

"I'll bet you've missed your treats the last few days." Sabrina's voice cuts through the night air as she strokes Oakley's back and delivers the treats.

I move closer to watch. She leans against the railing. "You probably miss him almost as much as I do." She huffs a thick cloudy breath over her head. "I'll try to take care of you as well as Jason did."

I snuggle against her leg, placing my paws on her furry slippers.

"It was never that I didn't like you; it was more that Jason spent so many hours at work, and I thought when he was home, he should be spending time with us."

Oakley lifts his head over the wall and sticks his muzzle in Sabrina's face. She reaches for the blanket covering the wall and slips it over his back. "Your home will always be here."

Oakley's eyes focus on me. I wag my tail, suddenly afraid any words I might say will come out much like Sabrina's.

"Come on, pupperoni," she calls, slapping her thigh.

I oblige, stopping one last time at the entrance to the shed.

"We'll talk tomorrow, kid," Oakley snorts. I turn and leap toward him.

"Puppers," Sabrina yells, already halfway to the door.

"Go on," Oakley orders. "It's cold out here and I'm not sharing my blanket."

Disappointed—and excited—I do as I'm told.

Sabrina clicks the lock behind us. I head to the front door and check that it's secure. Content the house is safe, I sneak quietly into my bedroom. Immediately I'm hit with the faint scent of vanilla and cinnamon and, sure enough, the cat is on the bed next to Sabrina's head. I stretch as far as I can reach and stare at my wife curled up on my side of the mattress. Bobbi's purring nearly drowns out the soft sobbing made by my grieving wife.

"I'm so sorry I let this happen," I whine. "If I had just stayed where I belonged, I'd be there next to you now."

"Like always, you didn't put your family first," the cat yawns, spewing the words as if she'd said them a million times.

"Lauren needed my help," I explain more to Sabrina than the demon cat. "I couldn't just leave her. What if it had been *you* out there...that's what I was thinking. She had nobody to call."

Sabrina leans up and scoops me onto the bed. For a second, I think she understood my words, but she stays silent.

I lick the tears on her cheek and curl into her. I don't know how to help her, but I know I can't leave her now. She *needs* me. Her hand strokes my belly, the metal band of her ring a painful reminder of the grief I'd caused.

Chapter 5

Jaycee scoops me up and plucks straw from my fur late the next evening. We're outside with Oakley and they hope it's the last trip out for the night.

"Don't tell Mom, but I'm going to give you a name." With a finger to her lips, she whispers. "It has to be a secret, though. She says you aren't staying; therefore, you don't *need* a name. But everyone needs a name."

I lick her face.

"Max?" She takes a few steps away and calls to me. "Chase?"

"No and no."

She steps into the snow, a finger to her chin. "Maybe you'd like something historic. Stonewall? Like Andrew Jackson?"

I tilt my head. "Is that the best you've got?"

Jaycee falls to her back and fans her arms over her head. Sitting, she proclaims, "A girl in my class once named a kitten after her grandma and her parents had to let her keep it after that!"

I pounce onto her belly. "Don't you dare!"

"Waffles? Mom likes waffles." I race around the shed and circle back to her. "Kevin?"

"I'll run away if you give me a stupid human name."

Jaycee sticks out her tongue. "No people names. Unless it's a really good one."

She lists a dozen more names, which I adamantly refuse. I slip off to see what Oakley is up to. I find him behind the shed, yanking a branch up and down. The pine needles slide back and forth over his back. I sit to watch, wishing I had a camera.

He stops upon spotting me. "My back itches," he explains, bending down. "Would you mind climbing up there and getting that for me?"

I chuckle as I scamper up his side. "Jaycee is trying to decide my name. That's good, right?"

"I hope she picks a good one."

"Brutus, Rufus, and Bob the Tomato are not good ones." I slip off his back, disgusted at my prospects but hopeful this is a step in the right direction.

"No, they are not."

Jaycee barrels around the side of the shed. "Moose, come here." I ignore her. "Yogi?"

Oakley dips his head. "At least it isn't Spot."

I feel like my options are the equivalent of having my fingernails ripped off or plucking my eyeballs out.

Sabrina calls us in. I promise to update Oakley in the morning.

Half an hour later, I curl up on the foot of Jaycee's bed, listening to Sabrina read *The Adventures of Huckleberry Finn*.

Sabrina stands at the end of the chapter, closing the book as Jaycee yawns.

"One more chapter," the girl pleads. "Please?"

When Jaycee's eyelids finally drop, Sabrina slips into the hall, a gentle tapping of her hand on her thigh inviting me to come along.

This is my chance. *Make her fall in love with you.*

I watch as she brushes her teeth and applies the wrinkle cream she thinks she needs—but doesn't—and patiently wait for her to change into fresh pajamas even though she's already wearing some.

She pulls the covers on our bed aside, except for the corner the cat has claimed, and points to the dog bed she'd dropped on the floor next to my nightstand. I roll my eyes, though I'm not sure that is obvious. When that doesn't get me invited onto the mattress, I try my hand at the famous puppy-dog pout. Bobbi smirks at me and prances three steps to curl up next to Sabrina's head. I up my game with a whine. It takes a solid five minutes of whimpering before Sabrina reaches over the side and scoops me up.

"I'd sleep with one eye open if I were you," the cat murmurs, retreating to the foot of the bed.

"Funny how easily you got pushed out," I chuckle.

"Just for tonight," Sabrina says softly.

I spin a circle on the sheets. "This is *your* side of the bed." I nuzzle into her pillow, soaking in the smell of her shampoo still embedded in the cotton.

Sabrina seems to follow my lead because she clutches my pillow to her face. "It still smells like you," she whispers and it takes me a moment to realize she's talking to the 'me' who isn't here.

I stretch my neck and wriggle my nose under the pillow until we're face to face. She smiles, though I smell tears forming.

She pulls the covers up to her chin. "Look, pup, I like you; I don't want you to think I don't, but...we have to find you a new home."

I run a circle on the bed, sending the cat scampering for the safety of the dark underneath us. "What?! No! You have to let me stay!"

She reaches out to stop me. "Quiet or I'll put you outside with the donkey." She walks her fingers along the sheets until I can't help but nip at them. "We can't keep you. I wish we could." She shakes her finger as I clamp too hard, her words cutting my soul. "I already have so many responsibilities now—Jaycee, the house, restaurant, not to mention the outdoor maintenance at both places, plus the cat and the donkey that I'll never be able to part with. You see, I really have no time to potty train a dog. I'm really sorry."

I flop onto my stomach, the weight of her words crushing me. If it makes it easier for her, that's what I need to do. I'll leave. I've already caused her so much pain. I can't bear to be a burden. Maybe I can find another family in the neighborhood so I can still check in often.

I stare at her, memorizing the features I took for granted weeks ago. I'd never noticed the wrinkles starting to form around her eyes or the dark circles beneath them. Are they new? Is it because of my death? I crawl onto her stomach as she rolls to her back. Her middle isn't as tight as it was when I met her, but in this moment, I truly appreciate the sacrifice she made with her body to finally bring life into this world, and I find she is more beautiful now than she was more than a decade ago when we married.

"I promise we'll find you a good home," she yawns. "One with a nice yard and maybe some kids. You seem to like kids. Would that make you happy?"

I wag my tail. "If you're happy, I'm happy."

"So, it's a deal?"

I place my paw in her outstretched hand. "I spent the last fifteen years being selfish. Now it's about you," I whisper. "I'm sorry I didn't do it sooner."

I lie on her chest as her eyelids close, feeling her heart beat until the rhythm slows and I know she's sleeping.

Hopping off the bed, I poke my nose underneath the bed where Bobbi had moved when I got too rowdy. Two beady eyes stare back at me. "Looks like you win," I say. "Keep an eye on her. I'm going to spend some time with Jaycee before she sends me away."

I tiptoe out of the room and make my way to the side of Jaycee's bed. The twin mattress is lower than our king-size and I jump onto it easily, landing on a mountain of stuffed animals. Where did all these come from? I step over a tiny gorilla and land on the sheep my mom bought her. Crossing it, I lie down with my butt on a dolphin and my head resting on a stuffed owl with giant eyes. I know they all have names, but I never bothered to learn any of them, not even the ratty old dog she carried around in her younger years. The eyes of another creature seem to stare back at me. I grab its nose and fling it to the carpet. Jaycee lies on her side clutching an armful of fake fur, her mouth gaping open. I softly blow hair off her face, suddenly worried she may inhale it and choke. There are so many things I want to tell her, so many things I'll never get the chance to say. I want her to know I'm proud of her for working hard and graduating high school, the boy she's dating is no good for her, she and her mom will make up after whatever fight they have. Most importantly, I want to see the day she marries the love of her life. But it doesn't look like I'll be around to see these things. I want to explain how this time I'm leaving because it's what Sabrina thinks is best and she will one day understand. Instead of saying all the words that are now in a language she can't interpret, I watch her sleep. I study the scar above her right eyebrow from the time she stood on the edge of the bathtub and had to get six stitches after she fell. I was at work when that happened. There were so many things I'd already missed, and now it looks as if I'll miss the rest of them. With my head next to hers, I let her breathing lull me to sleep.

"Daddy," she mumbles, her single word pulling me from a sound slumber. My eyes pop wide open. Three stuffed animals fall to the floor as she curls her arms around me.

I nuzzle into her and lick salty droplets from her cheek. "I'm right here."

Her hand quivers as she reaches over to me. I shake my head after a finger accidentally pokes me in the eye. The defeated look on her face says more than she ever could. I paw at her arm until she begins stroking my back. Maybe that will get her to calm back down and go to sleep.

"I hope you can somehow understand what I'm about to say," I whimper. "I know you're going to grow up and do wonderful things. I know it's going to be hard. Your mom is going to do her best, but some days she's going to feel like she's messing it all up. Be gentle on her. You're going to make mistakes. Learn from them. Forgive yourself. And always remember nothing can replace family."

As if she understands, she squeezes me tightly.

"I shouldn't have let my work consume me so much. Especially after we tried so hard to get you here. Anyway, it looks like I'm going to miss a lot of things...like teaching you to throw a ball like one of the guys, and driving, though I'm not sure I'm going to actually mind that one. But I really hate that I won't be around to watch you leave on your first date or that I won't be there for your mom when you go off to college. Promise to come home often, okay?"

Tears stain Jaycee's pillow as she clutches me. I lift my eyes to the ceiling. I'm no good at this.

"You're doing fine." I feel the words more than hear them.

"Then why does she want to send me away?"

"Your faith is bigger than a mustard seed. I've seen it."

I bury my nose under Jaycee's chin, remembering the days of lending my faith to Sabrina when she was dangerously close to giving up as we faced multiple miscarriages. Those were hard times, but we got through them together. As I lie there listening to my daughter's soft whimpers, I close my eyes to pray.

Chapter 6

Sabrina brings a large coffee mug into the living room and takes a seat beside Jaycee.

"I know you want to keep him," she whispers. "But this isn't the right time for a dog. Maybe in a year or two."

Jaycee nearly squeezes my insides out. "I promise to take care of him," she argues.

Sabrina sighs heavily. "There's more to having a dog than feeding and house training."

I leap onto Sabrina's lap and shove my snout into her dark hair until her coconut shampoo wafts around me and my wet nose dampens her neck. I wag my tail, hoping she'll see how much I love her.

"I can't expect you to understand the responsibility of a dog."

Jaycee crosses her arms. "We already have a cat and a donkey. I think we have an idea."

Sabrina's hand tenses on my back. "Yes, but your dad is the one who fed Oakley and cleaned his stall."

"I can do that," Jaycee argues.

"Good because I won't have time now that I have to run the restaurant by myself and juggle your activities."

"I'll quit dance," Jaycee offers.

I pounce to her lap. "No!"

Jaycee drops her head, her tangled hair falling over my face. "I don't think I can go back after what happened anyway."

Sabrina drapes her arm over the girl's shoulder. "Your dad wouldn't want that. He didn't mean for this to happen, and you know he'd be here right now if he could."

"I'm here," I bark with as much force as I can muster from my tiny body.

"It's really okay," Jaycee admits. "I'd rather be here with this puppy than with a bunch of girls who fight for attention on the dance floor."

Sabrina smiles, reaching for her coffee. "You know puppies grow up and turn into dogs. What happens when he's not so cute and you're sick of taking care of him?"

I paw Jaycee's shoulder, nipping at her hair. "When will I not be cute?"

Jaycee pouts. "Dad wanted a dog."

"He didn't have time for a dog," Sabrina counters, tears pooling in her eyes.

Bobbi saunters across the living room floor. "Time to pack your bags," she cackles.

I turn on the couch, preparing to leap. "Sabrina has already fallen in love with me; she just doesn't know it yet."

"She's not likely to make the same mistake twice." She flicks her tail as she parades past.

I jump to the floor and get in her face, the scent of vanilla thick in my nostrils. "Clearly you know our history, but I'm not going to let the fact that I'm stuck inside this body stop me from being with my family."

"I may have failed at getting her to dump you in your previous life, but it looks like I get another chance to keep you from hurting her more."

I jump backward, her words hitting me like a truck. "You sound just like my mother-in-law." Could it be? It makes sense. The years flash before my eyes. During our battle with miscarriages and infertilities, Sabrina's mom died after a bout of breast cancer. Sabrina and I were grieving over the loss of a twenty-week pregnancy when her doctor suggested we get an emotional support animal. And that's how we ended up with Bobbi. It would explain why Sabrina took to the cat like she did. And why I always hated the animal.

She laughs. "Surely you didn't think God only sent *you* back to help watch over my daughter and the daughter you claimed to have wanted but never made time for."

I take an aggressive stance toward her. "You know how much work the restaurant took. When we opened it, I had no idea we'd be successful in carrying a child to term."

"And yet it didn't seem to make a difference in the hours you worked."

"I had a family to support. It's not like I could quit working."

"Don't be ridiculous. Your wife and daughter should have been a higher priority than your employees." She scratches her jaw with her hind leg.

"My family has always come first, Audra. Why do you think I worked so much? I worked for them, so they would have the future they deserved!" I bark.

"Is that how you ended up with four legs and a tail?"

My upper lip curls. "I can't believe I passed up Heaven to stay down here with a fleabag like you."

She stops licking her back and stares at me. "I'm confused. You said your family was the most important thing and now you're acting like you'd rather be away from them."

"I'd rather be away from *you.*"

"I'm working on that."

"Don't count on it," I growl.

"That's it, act like you're going to eat me; it will make this sooo much easier," she taunts with a yawn.

Dammit. She's right. If I want Sabrina to let me stay, I have to use what I know. I quickly switch my behavior and pretend to want to play with the loathsome cat. "We won't be the same size for long."

"What are you doing? Get away from me!" She hisses when I try to curl up next to her.

My actions churn disgust in my stomach and I'm thankful she gets up and finds a new place to lay in the corner of the living room.

I follow, nudging her with my nose as I try to cuddle again. "As usual, you're not going to win this battle."

She strikes me with her claws and I let out a yelp as they dig into the sensitive skin along my nose.

Jaycee leaps from the couch and scoops me into her arms. I smile at Bobbi as I'm led back to the couch to soak in the affections from being injured.

"They'll get used to each other," Jaycee bargains. "Your cat is just mean." She peppers my nose with kisses and I slurp the side of her face until she's tied in a fit of giggles.

Sabrina lowers her chin. "That's all fine and dandy, but it still doesn't solve the problem of what we would do with him while you're at school and I'm at work."

"Can't he stay outside with Oakley?"

Sabrina shakes her head. "It's too cold right now."

"Well, we can't leave him alone with your bratty cat." She smooches my face. "She hurt his poor little nose."

"We can't keep him. I'm sorry."

I bark, leaping from the couch. "I have to go *again*. And it's entirely too cold to be going outside every two hours to pee." I circle the living room, searching for a place to squat since I still haven't gotten my back leg to cooperate with hiking. Puppies are expected to make puddles on the floor for a few weeks, anyway, I reason as I glance toward the couch.

Sabrina points about the time I drop my hind quarters. "No!"

Jaycee flies into the air, sliding to me in socked feet. "The bathroom is outside, puppy."

She hoists me up at arm's length and races me to the back door. But it's too late. I stare at her from the other side of the glass, begging to be let back in so I can comfort her. She wipes tears with the back of her hand as she motions for me to go off the deck.

"It's going to be okay," I tell her in my chirpy bark.

She places her hands on her hips and wrinkles her brow like she's trying to figure out the look her mother perfected.

"I need to cheer her up," I mutter to myself. "How the heck can I do that?" Pacing back and forth along the length of glass, I think of all the ways I used to be able to make her laugh. They usually included a witty joke, but that's not going to help me now. I could pretend to fall or try a silly gimmick, but everything I know how to do requires thumbs. Suddenly I remember *America's Funniest Videos*, a show where regular people send in goofy moments they were lucky enough to capture on video.

"Think. There were plenty of animal clips." I turn to see what props are available. The swing set is by Oakley's shed. I could work with that. I leap toward the steps, stopping short when I realize she may not be able to watch from that far away. And I want to see her reaction. The snow drifts are nearly two feet high in some places. With an awkward twist, I bury myself in one and spring out of it. I repeat the action several times, stopping to judge Jaycee's face. Her brow softens and a smile tugs at the corners of her mouth. The image of her doing snow angels pops into my head. I try that. I'm sure I look ridiculous on my back with my feet in the air as I roll from side to side. I stop, lying there with my paws outstretched, wondering how to get up without destroying my creation. Rolling to my side, I try to jump to my feet in a graceful spin that ends with a second dog-sized blob beside the matted 'angel.' I catch a glimpse of Oakley peeking out of his shed, but I don't have time to worry about him now. I rush to the door and cock my head, somehow asking Jaycee if she'd seen what I'd done. Her smile is genuine, but sadness hides behind her eyes. I have to take it up a notch. I shake the flakes from my fur and lick the window a few times.

"Shit! Sabrina won't like that," I grumble.

Without thinking I turn and dart off the deck, landing halfway down the steps. Oakley, fully emerged from his shed, shoves his muzzle in the snow and pulls up a blue ball by its handle. He shakes it vigorously from side to side.

"Sure, *now* you want to play with it," I growl, frustrated with how he's ignored it for two years and now all the sudden he wants to play with it. How he even found it in all this snow, I have no clue.

He throws it three feet and stares at me like I'm supposed to understand his actions. "Well? Go get it," he haws.

I sit, soaking in the fact that a donkey is talking to me and that he's been so stubborn the whole time I'd tried to do this exact thing with him. "I'm trying to help you out. Follow my lead."

I bound to a ball bigger than my body and sink my teeth into the side, thankful the snow has cleaned some of the donkey slobber off. It moves a few inches before I give up, panting.

Oakley comes to my rescue, clinching the handle in his big mouth. "Chase it," he breathes.

I run after it when he throws it again. We continue our game around the yard as the sun creeps into the horizon. When he takes the ball and parades it along the perimeter of the fence, I chase after him, circling his feet.

"Look in the window," he calls, slipping beneath our large pine.

I stop under the branches to soak in the view of my girls standing together watching us. I'm not sure when Sabrina joined the audience but I'm happy to have her.

"I have questions," I pant.

I swear he smiles at me and I feel something oddly familiar about this creature. It's impossible, I think as I stand beside him watching my family watch me.

"Soon enough," he says.

My jaw drops at the line my grandpa had used to tell me I was being impatient on more than one occasion. "Are you—"

Oakley lifts his head, grabs a branch, and jerks his head. Heavy powder showers over me. He'd darted out of the way just in time. "Go to them," he orders.

"That was a jerk move," I yammer, getting out of the line of fire should he decide to do it again.

I smile as I walk toward the door, knowing what he did is exactly the sort of thing I'd pull on Jaycee. Sabrina opens the door and the smiles and giggles coming from them makes it all worth it. Jaycee greets me with a towel. I let her wrap me in it and take me to the couch to cuddle. I yawn, wondering if I have time for a short nap.

Chapter 7

That night I choose to sleep in Jaycee's room. I am afraid she'll have another bad dream and I'll want to be there when she wakes. But it's Sabrina who needs comforting tonight. Her soft sobs get my attention when Jaycee's arm flails and nearly sends me off the bed. The moment I hear my wife's distress, I leap into action.

Bobbi purrs loudly, turning to me when I bound into the room. "I'm trying everything, but she won't stop crying." She steps aside. "As much as I hate to admit it, I think she needs you."

I slowly press my feet onto the edge of the mattress inside the dark room, afraid I'll find my wife in a helpless state. Sabrina sits in the middle of the bed in a pile of what appears to be most of my clothing. She clutches a black t-shirt, holding it to her face.

I stand beside the bed watching her, my heart retching at the pain I've caused. "Baby, I'm right here. Tell me what you need."

"I need you," she murmurs.

"I'm not going anywhere."

"You died in the middle of our 'happily ever after.'"

"But I'm back. God sent me back as a dog. That's why you have to let me stay," I yap. With my front legs clawing to stay on top of the mattress, my back legs equally work to keep from sliding off the thin ledge made from the crack at the box springs. "I never would've left you. In fact, I'm not entirely sure what happened. One minute I was hooking the chain to the truck and the next I was fishing with our kids. Oh, Sabrina, how I wish you could see them!"

Sabrina leans over and scoops me onto the bed with the finesse of picking up a toy left in the middle of the floor. "I hope I didn't wake you," she whispers.

I bounce to her and lick her salty cheeks. "I may be a dog now, but I'll still sit up with you all night," I say, hoping she'll remember how we'd spent the sleepless nights after miscarriages holding each other and talking about what our children would be like until one of us managed to drift off. It was usually me, I remorse. I won't let that happen again.

I plop onto a pile of my shirts, again lifting my eyes toward the ceiling. "They always said You had a sense of humor. I guess the joke's on me. I wasn't the best husband. I put work above the family I nearly didn't have, even after I begged and pleaded with you to make Sabrina's dreams of being a mother come true. It almost didn't happen, and I still couldn't see what was in front of my face. Dogs understand all this without questioning it. They're loyal and nothing comes before family. Get her to let me stay and I'll prove I've learned my lesson. I'll never make her question where she stands again. And, if I can ask one more thing, please help me help her."

Sabrina's hand slides onto my head, her fingers scratching the back of my neck. "What's the matter boy? Are you missing someone too?"

I lurch onto her lap. "Everyone I need is under this roof. I'm sorry if I ever made you question that."

"I just lost my best friend." She raises a shirt to her face, stifling a sob.

I lower my gaze, my eyelids drooping slightly. "None of this is fair." Bobbi comes out of nowhere, jumping onto the bed. I face her as she spins a circle and plops onto a corner at the foot of the bed. "How am I supposed to do this? I can't comfort her if we're speaking separate languages."

Bobbi runs her tongue down her back and peers at me with her glowing yellow eyes. "Just love her. You already claim to."

I smack my tail onto the bed. "What if she doesn't love me back?"

"People are hard to love. Animals are not."

I hate when she's right. Turning back to Sabrina, I position myself into a crouch and leap off her lap, landing in the mound of clothing she'd shoved to her side. Somehow, I envision the laundry as a pile of leaves and scatter them about. My efforts will either do exactly what I desire—make her laugh—or they will backfire and I'll be kicked out of the room. There is no room for error when she's in this state. Tears tend to make Sabrina angry and she's been known to snap when someone tries to make her feel better but, on rare occasions, a laugh isn't too hard to work up and she may soon forget why she was crying. I root through the shirts and pick a fight with the one Audra bought me the last Christmas she was alive. It goes flying, landing perfectly over my mother-in-law. Sabrina laughs and I don't know if it's because she's remembering my disdain at the item or if she finds my current actions amusing.

Bobbi saunters off the bed. "Just as annoying as always," she says, slipping from the room.

I chase Sabrina's hand as she playfully uses it as a toy. She finds a shirt splattered with paint from the restaurant, rolls it like a rope, and hands me an end. Getting on her knees, she entices a game of tug-o-war. The clock on the nightstand ticks off minutes as I distract her from her sorrows.

I yawn. "I know I said I'd stay up all night with you, but this new body isn't the same as my old one."

Sabrina pats her pillow, carefully guarding mine. "You're right, we should get some sleep."

She curls up beside me, throwing her hair over me like an itchy blanket.

"I can't count the times I've rolled over and found a face full of hair," I whisper.

"Get some sleep, boy. We'll figure this out one day at a time."

"Yes! I want to stay. I'll do whatever it takes," I plead, exhaling into the quiet of the night.

"I'll make it happen." The voice floats in the air and I instantly relax.

Chapter 8

It's been a week since I found myself in a new body. It feels like it's been a year. I still can't fully grasp my new situation and part of me still worries Sabrina will send me away. I try to keep my faith, knowing God promised to work it out, but I'll feel better when I have a collar with Sabrina's phone number on it.

Jaycee refuses to come out of her room the entire day. I stick by her side, refusing to eat and holding my bladder until it feels like it will burst.

Sabrina pokes her head in three hours into Jaycee's stakeout. "The dog needs to go out."

"I'm good," I breath from Jaycee's lap, though I don't know how I'll move without an accident.

Jaycee squeezes me and I nearly lose it.

Sabrina carefully leans over and plucks me from her lap.

I squat directly outside the door and panic when I turn to see Sabrina gone. Racing to Jaycee's window, I jump, trying to see inside. I bark wildly until the curtain opens and my girls stare at me. At least they're smiling, I think as I continue my awkward leaping. Sabrina disappears and the back door opens. I dart to it and slide my wet paws on the tile, making my way back to Jaycee.

Sabrina stands in the doorway, her arms crossed over her chest. "How about we go ice skating?"

The words are like a knife in my chest.

Jaycee shakes her head. "I just want to play with the puppy." Her eyes lift toward her mom and they suddenly fill with anger. "Since you're sending him away."

"We've talked about this."

Jaycee scowls. "No. *You*'ve talked about it." She clutches me onto her lap. "Please go."

Sabrina quietly closes the door behind her. I let Jaycee brush my hair but draw the line when she tries to put tiny bows in my fur. She sneaks to the kitchen and brings back a handful of dog biscuits. For the next hour she works to teach me simple commands, which I naturally pick up quickly. Sabrina interrupts our lesson with an attempt to draw Jaycee out of her room to make cookies. Jaycee firmly declines but an hour later Sabrina is back with a plate of snickerdoodles.

"I thought we could talk," she says, holding the peace offering out.

"Can we keep the dog?"

Sabrina drops her gaze. "No."

Jaycee turns her back.

I wag my tail at Sabrina's feet. "She'll come around. I hope you do too."

Sabrina scoops me up and deposits me outside. I race to Jaycee's window. After an embarrassing squat near the back deck, Sabrina sighs, letting me back inside.

Jaycee feeds me one of the cookies Sabrina left and we curl up on the floor for a nap. Afterward, we play hide-and-seek and when she gets bored with that, a short game of peek-a-boo. It's the first time I remember spending an entire afternoon alone with my daughter. Jaycee refuses to come out for dinner and it's well past dark when Sabrina tries to enter again.

She takes a seat on the bed. "Let's talk," she says, folding her hands on her lap.

"I don't have anything to say. I'm mad at you."

Sabrina tries for a hug, but Jaycee pulls away. "I think you're mad your dad is gone."

I sit between them, wagging my tail. "But I'm right here."

Sabrina strokes my head. "Give me your best argument for why the dog should stay."

Jaycee lifts her head. "You got Bobbi when you were sad. Why can't I get a puppy when I'm sad?"

Sabrina bites her lip. "That was different."

I place my paws on my wife's lap. "It's really not."

Jaycee shakes her head. "Seems the same to me. You lost your baby and got a cat. I lost my dad. Do you know what that feels like?"

"A puppy isn't going to replace him."

Jaycee pulls me into her lap. "I know that. But I love him. If you send him away, I'll cry for a thousand years." Tears well in her eyes.

"A thousand years?"

I peer up at Sabrina, remembering her words in the height of our fertility troubles. 'If I live to one hundred, I'll still have tears to cry for our babies.'

"I have too much love with no place to go," Jaycee whispers.

I slurp my tongue against her cheek, wondering when she got so wise.

A tear rolls down Sabrina's cheek. She'd said those exact words to me after our third miscarriage.

"And you think you could give that love to this puppy?"

Jaycee nods.

"Then you'd better decide what we're calling him."

I slide from Jaycee's lap as she lurches for Sabrina.

"Huck," she chirps. "His name is Huck."

I couldn't be happier to share a name with Sabrina's favorite literary character.

Chapter 9

Sabrina cracks the door to Jaycee's room early the next morning. "It's time to get ready for church."

After a quick trip outside to share the good news with Oakley, I tug on one of the outfits Jaycee placed on the bed, making sure my teeth don't go through the material.

"I think that's a good choice, too," Jaycee whispers, patting my head.

I slip out of the room so she can change in private. Ten minutes later, I'm in the living room, waiting, chewing on the rope toy. "Did it always take this long to get ready?"

"Five minutes, Jaycee," Sabrina calls as if I hadn't just asked a question as she passed.

"I can't find my hairbrush," Jaycee screams from her room.

"Use the one in my bathroom," Sabrina instructs.

"I don't like that one!" Jaycee's voice cracks and I race into her room to help.

A blue skirt splays around her on the floor as she sits with her face in her hands.

"If you'd put things away when you're done with them, you'd know where they are when you need them again," I senselessly bark, although I know right where she left the item for once.

She looks up, her wild brown hair still a tangled mess around her shoulders. "Do you know where my brush is?"

I poke my nose into her toy box, smelling a bone she'd hidden in there. "You threw it in the closet after you brushed me with it yesterday."

Jaycee's hand runs along my back as I move to check underneath her bed for more hidden treats. "I don't want to go to church," she whispers.

"Sunday is God's day," I yap.

She nods, pulling me to her chest. "I know Sunday is God's day." I stare into her watery eyes. Did she understand me? "Today is going to be the first time I won't get to sit between my mom *and* dad."

48

I swear tears pool in my eyes, but...can dogs even cry? "I know this is harder for you than it is me, but I promise it will get easier."

"I can't do it," she whines. "When I was little, my dad would always take my hand and make motions during the song like I was conducting the choir. When I got old enough to sing, he bounced his finger along the words in the book like a sing-along, and I don't think I'll get the songs right without that."

I whimper as she breaks down in tears. Not knowing what else to do, I lick them away and nudge her chin up with my nose.

"I wish you could go with me," she sobs.

Sabrina's heels clack down the hall and she pokes her head inside the door. Once she sees Jaycee curled up next to me, she steps inside and sits on the bed.

"We need to leave in two minutes."

Jaycee shakes her head, blowing a fresh dose of morning breath into my face. "Who's going to collect God's money?"

Sabrina cocks her head, massaging a muscle in her shoulder. "The ushers."

Jaycee's lip quivers. "But they're short one."

Sabrina slips onto the floor and wraps her arm around Jaycee. "You're thinking about the empty seat."

Jaycee nods. "I've been pretending Daddy is at work, but if we go to church, it makes it...real."

Sabrina's hand flies to her mouth. "I thought we'd start the new week on our regular schedule but you're not ready." She embraces our daughter. "I'm not either."

Jaycee sniffles and, before I know it, Sabrina's cheeks are damp. Within minutes, they're both sobbing.

I dart between them with no clue how to help. Resorting to a neutral position, I lie my head on my paws and whimper. "I hate that I did this to you."

Sabrina wipes her eyes. "Why don't we skip church? We'll grab a pizza for lunch later and we can spend the morning watching movies."

Chapter 10

My bladder pulls me from a deep sleep, one I hadn't meant to enter. I had wanted to stay up all night with Sabrina like we did when we first started dating...well, sort of like that, but her affections lulled me to sleep before I was ready. I slip away from her side and pounce over the cat who has taken up residence at the foot of the bed. Maybe I can figure out how to use the toilet. I laugh at the idea. But, on second thought, once I learn how to hike my leg, maybe peeing outside will be just as much fun as it was when I was a kid and tried to make funny designs with my stream. I'll have to try that I decide as I plod with determination to the back of the house.

Jaycee stares at the drab clothing laid out on her bed. The alarm clock screeches. She smacks it harder than necessary.

"You're not entering that 'goth' phase, are you?" I cock my head, wondering if 'goth' is the term being used these days. "You're too young for teenage hormones, right?"

My daughter rushes to me with open arms. She cups my snout and forces me to stare at the outfits. "I don't know what to wear to school. Which one says 'I just lost my dad so don't come at me with your attitude?'" She steps in front of each one, holding me over it a second before moving to the next.

"I really need to pee," I yip. "Why are you going to school so soon anyway?"

She's probably a nervous wreck.

"Yeah, I don't like that one either," she whispers, throwing the outfit in front of us over her shoulder. "How about this one?"

I wriggle in her arms. "You'll be wearing my doggie pee if you don't take me outside."

She picks up the dress she'd stopped in front of and holds it up. "This is too fancy. I don't want anyone to think I'm happy." Her morning breath seeps into my nose as she presses her face against my ear. "What am I going to do?"

She loosens her grasp and I leap from her arms. Taking a seat on her bed, she buries her face in her hands.

"Listen, I want to help you but, right now, I have to figure out how to get you to let me out," I whimper, spinning in small circles. My bladder begs to be emptied. I'd be crossing my legs if I were in human form and that's saying a lot coming from a grown man.

"Now there are four kids in my class who have lost a parent," she says, nearing tears.

I try crouching, leaving my hind quarters in the air. It does nothing for the twisting in my lower region. Maybe if I sit. Nope. Still there.

"We could start a club," she suggests, her lips forming a tight line.

I place my front paws on the edge of the bed. "Jaycee, I promise you, I'll get you through this. You just have to take me outside real fast."

She scratches behind my ear. "I bet you miss your parents too."

"Everybody I need is right here in this house."

"We can help each other. I'll help you to not miss your parents so much and you can help me to not miss my dad so much." She scoops me into her arms and squeezes so tightly it takes everything I have not to cover her in pee. "I'll bet you had lots of brothers and sisters. I always wanted a sister. But I would've taken a brother, too."

I wish I could've given that to her. I distract myself by slobbering all over her face. She smiles and puts me on the floor. My bladder refuses to hold on and I find myself creating a puddle on her carpet.

"Oh dear," Jaycee mutters, taking the tone of an eighty-year-old woman.

"It's going to be okay," I tell her in my chirpy bark.

She places her hands on her hips and wrinkles her brow like she's again trying to figure out the look her mother perfected.

I race to Oakley when she insists I go outside despite my empty bladder. "Is today the day you tell me who you are?"

"Soon enough," he mutters, munching the oats in his bucket.

"You're a little impossible."

"My wife used to say the same thing."

"I know I know you from somewhere."

The back door opens. "Huck!" Sabrina's voice beckons me.

"We aren't done talking about this," I say, running off.

Jaycee lugs a backpack down the hall. "Come watch me get on the bus, Huck."

She's calm and collected on the outside, but I sense a nervousness inside her. I give her extra kisses on her cheek when she picks me up. We stand on the front porch and wait for the bus. It's the first time I remember the three of us doing this and I wish I'd had the sense to do it sooner.

Chapter 11

The days drift by, most of them spent in the same way. I'd eat scraps of breakfast slipped under the table, Sabrina and I would wait for the bus with Jaycee, then I'd take a nap. The rest of the day I'd spend following Sabrina around, eager to see what she was up to. By the time night fell, I'd find myself curled up for a story on Jaycee's bed and I'd stay with Sabrina through her toughest hours. Sometimes we'd just lie there, other times she'd talk to me, telling me stories of things she and I had done together. I actually learned a few things I'd been too dense to pick up on. Last night she'd told me about the dreams she'd had for the future and had used my fur to soak her tears when she talked about not being able to do them.

I wake depressed and full of guilt. The energy in the house is different this morning and it takes me a long time to figure out why. I chase Bobbi around the house, hoping Sabrina notices how I'm trying to stay out of the way. It isn't until I go to check on Sabrina that I realize it's Sunday again and that's why they're getting dressed up. They're going to church. She wears a simple black dress with a gray cardigan. It looks lovely, but I wonder why she stopped wearing colors...then I remember my vision isn't the same. The dark blue walls in the kitchen are now a shade of violet I never would've allowed.

"Time is so weird now," I tell her as I sit at her feet while she applies makeup.

"We're going to church," she says, patting my head.

"You can't leave me alone with Bobbi," I yap, running off with one of her shoes. This is not the way to do things, I chide myself. She used to say she couldn't stand dogs who chewed on shoes. Take it back!

She catches me as I settle down to gnaw it. "Bad dog." She smacks my rear and my ears perk.

"Don't try to get frisky. I'm a dog now," I tell her, wagging my tail.

She wipes slobber from the shiny black heeled shoe with her hand as she retreats to the bedroom.

I chase after her. "I'm sorry. I don't know what comes over me sometimes. It must be something in the puppy DNA because I really can't help myself."

She slips the shoes on and brushes a tear from beneath her eye. "I never got the chance to tell Jason these had been in the back of the closet for ages and I didn't go shopping...again."

I cock my head. "Wait...what?"

She bends to pet me before going over to the full-length mirror. "It's not my fault if he didn't notice I'd never worn something before, right?"

I sit beside her. "Is it my fault those shoes look exactly like the ten other pairs in your closet?"

She smooths her blouse and pulls a necklace from her jewelry box. "Should I feel like I'm about to be ambushed?"

"At church?"

"Tell me it won't be that bad."

I lick her hand as she picks me up. "I wish I could. I remember the first time I went to church after my grandpa died. Staring at an empty place in a pew is hard." I wiggle against her. "Where are we going?"

She places me on the floor in the bathroom. "You're going to have to stay in here, that way if you have an accident, it will be easier to clean. And you won't be able to chew on anything you shouldn't. Be good," she says, shutting the door behind her.

"Wait!" I claw at the door. "Sabrina! Let me out!"

A full minute passes as I scratch at the door she'd worked so hard to refinish.

Light filters in the dark room and Jaycee pokes her head in. She flips on the light. "I brought you a ball. We'll be back right after lunch."

"I'll give you ten dollars if you leave the door cracked," I bargain.

"Don't worry, I'm gonna have a chat with Pastor Clifford before the service and tell him not to talk so much today."

I laugh, slightly relieved I don't have to listen to another long-winded sermon. It wasn't so much that they were bad, it was more that the message was already delivered and Pastor Clifford insisted on seeing how many times he could reword it in one go-round.

"What the hell am I supposed to do until lunch? And, speaking of lunch, you're going to bring me back some, right?"

The front door closes with a loud thud and I realize I'm alone, barking at no one.

"Bobbi?" Does she answer by her human name too or just her feline one now? "Audra!"

Silence.

"Great." I kick the ball with my front paw, moving it mere inches. "Right, I'm a dog and my body doesn't work like I'm used to."

I spend a long time getting a feel for the mechanics of my new limbs. Sometimes the ball skids across the floor and other times, it barely moves. I sit on the floor and try to pick it up as if my front paws are arms. They ache by the time I give that up. I try kicking from behind like a horse. It works...when my aim is accurate. Mostly I miss. I try to bounce it and end up knocking myself in the jaw on the only occasion it remotely comes off the floor. Frustrated, I chomp onto it and fling it with my mouth. It bounces off the wall. I dodge it and watch as it skips across the tile.

"I guess this is fun," I mutter and repeat my actions over and over. "Okay, surely they're into the second analogy of how the Bible lesson fits into modern day life." The ball hits the toilet seat. "I wonder if I can use that still."

I climb onto the lid, my paws sliding on the porcelain surface. In my clumsy attempt to sit, I accidentally flush the stool. Satisfied, I hop down and use my nose to lift the seat. It raises halfway and falls onto my snout, water filling the fresh bowl. "Hmm. Doesn't smell as bad as I imagined. But at least I flushed it."

"There has to be something else I can do." Spying one of Sabrina's hairs dangling over the vanity, I make my way to it. Using the handles on the drawers as steps, I climb onto the counter.

Items scatter as my front feet search for traction on the slippery surface. My back paw lands on the tube of toothpaste as I scamper the rest of the way up. A heavy whiff of mint fills my nostrils and one of my paws smears the sticky substance across the counter. I twist my body to see what I already know—Sabrina left the cap off the toothpaste. Again. A large pool of it covers the counter and now both my back paws and my tail. I yank the hand towel from the holder and toss it to the floor. The hair dryer and three makeup brushes tumble down with me. I spend the next hour wagging my tail over the fabric, alternating it with dabbing my feet on it.

After what feels like an entire morning working on cleaning myself, I realize the toothpaste is matted into my fur. "This is worse than when Jaycee used peanut butter for hair gel." I lick and lick, thankful for the strong mintiness to cover the taste of fur, dirt, and dog that would otherwise plague my tongue.

I yawn, giving up on the task. "What now?"

I stare at the door, whimpering. "Church should've been over hours ago. What's keeping you? I'm all sticky. Send help."

I make a circle, wondering if I have time to clean up *and* take a nap. "I'm not sure I can help with the mess, so I'll just sleep until you get back."

I wake refreshed and scratch at the door. Surely, they're home now. Maybe they forgot about me, I panic. I bark loudly. "I'm in here!"

"Would you shut up," the cat calls from the other side of the wood.

"Audra! Hey, I think they forgot to open the door after church."

"Church hasn't started yet."

I back into the wall. "Wh-at?!"

"I'm just kidding. It's 10:30." Church starts at 10:00.

I blink in confusion. "That's impossible. They left hours ago."

"Time works differently now. It takes forever to get used to."

"Can you let me out?"

"Not without thumbs. That takes even longer to get used to."

I try to kick the ball again. "What are we supposed to do until they get back?"

"I like to sleep. But that's hard to do when you're making so much racket."

"I'm sorry."

Her claws tap at the door the way she used to do her nails against the table—or anything really—when she'd be waiting for someone to answer a question she thought required less thought than it was being given. "I really don't think you are."

"I'm bored."

"Lick your balls," she says and I imagine her inspecting her outstretched claws.

"I can't—oh wait, dogs *can*."

"That should keep you busy for a while."

"I'm not doing that."

"Well, find something to do quietly. You're giving me a headache."

My ears flop as I shake my head. "Cats can't get headaches, can they?"

"Not without a dog."

I scratch my head with a back paw. "Hey, can I ask you a question?" I wait for a response. "Audra?" I call her by her cat name twice before realizing she left, presumably to take a nap somewhere on the other side of the house.

I've seen dogs lick themselves many times, but maybe I should give it a try to see what all the fuss is about.

I consider chasing my tail, but I know how that one ends. I pace the small bathroom. When my foot hits the large makeup brush, I stop. "Maybe I can be the first canine Picasso." The pencil-like handle is harder to pick up than expected, but I eventually get it. "Now for some paint."

I glare up at the counter, knowing her makeup bag contains useful tools. If I can knock the bag down, maybe something will open when it hits the floor. I work my way back up and shove the open bag. The contents clang to the tile but none of the powdery canisters break.

"Good thing I've got teeth." I grab a palette of colorful eyeshadow and easily crunch it apart. "What's in this stuff?" I run my tongue against the roof of my mouth and over my left paw, eager to eradicate the gritty substance and foul flavor. With my head cocked to the side, I dip the brush at a shade of blue Sabrina never wears. On the third attempt, I make contact and move to the side to begin my masterpiece. "I don't know if this is ocean or sky."

When the color fades from the brush, I search for something to resemble ground. "Everything is brown." I bite into a large round container with powder I plan to use as sand. My back teeth bite into it, and it breaks open, sending a cloud wafting over me. I sneeze into it and stick my tongue out, trying to get the particles out of my mouth. "Ugh. I really wish they would've left me some water." I turn and glance toward the toilet, thinking even that doesn't seem like such a terrible idea. This stuff tastes horrible. Worse than dog food. I curl into a ball and lick the remnants of mint toothpaste from my fur. With a thick coat of minty, chalky, fur-like residue in my mouth, I reach again for the brush.

My painting is now an ocean scene in the middle of a dust storm. "Lipstick," I shout, spying a deep burgundy inside the foundation tornado.

"Maybe I can write Sabrina a note, telling her it's me!" I pounce on the tube, carefully cracking it open so that I don't have a repeat of the tan twister.

I purse my lips and suck in the end, trying to grasp it without having to tilt my head. Squiggly lines cover the floor as I attempt to master the art of writing with my mouth. I finally get the lipstick in position and make my first move. The end breaks off as I hop backward to form the first *I*.

"Okay, no big deal," I cheerlead myself, reaching for the chunk of wax. Half of it falls to the tile with my bite. The other half sticks to my teeth. I move my tongue in and out but fail to remove it. With my paw, I bat at it until it plops to the floor. Lipstick streaks the side of one paw while blue and brown tint the bottoms of my feet.

"This was a bad idea." My heart races as I realize Sabrina won't be happy when she returns. "If only I had something to clean it up."

My eyes dart immediately to the toilet paper. I tenderly grab the flap hanging down and drag it to the mess. "This is going to take forever," I groan at the smeared floor. I yank harder on the roll and the strand breaks. "If only I could wad it all together."

I race to the roll and paw angrily at it. The thin paper shreds beneath my claws but I don't stop until there is nothing left.

"I'll be in the doghouse over this," I mutter, nearly laughing at the irony.

Curling up inside the tub, I wait for the worst.

Chapter 12

The key turns in the lock. Jaycee's boots slap the tile as she races toward the bathroom.

"Change your clothes before you play with the dog." Sabrina's orders send the boot clacking in the other direction.

I position myself right in front of the door, tail wagging, even though I know there's no room for the door to open and that I should be cowering in a corner. My heart races as her heels tap toward me.

"I'll bet you need to go out," Sabrina says, turning the knob.

I carefully avoid her gaze, instead focusing on her feet where I should be groveling. "I can explain. I got bored. I tried to play basketball, but the tub isn't much of a hoop." She dodges as I jump onto her legs. "I saw the paint—makeup—brush and wanted to paint you a picture. Actually, I was trying to tell you it's me. Please don't send me away."

I wag my tail and dare a look at her face. She's not happy. The last time I saw that expression, I had spent four thousand dollars on a new stove for the restaurant without consulting her.

She taps the toe of her new shoes. "Jaycee! You wanted a dog? Now's the time to prove it!"

She slams the door, her clacking footsteps pounding all the way to the living room.

"Oh, puppy," Jaycee cries in a fit of giggles as she stands over me.

I cover her in kisses when she bends to my level. "Gary didn't listen, did he? That's the longest sermon he's ever done. What was it about? Did you learn anything? Do I smell pizza? Did you bring me some?"

She giggles some more. "Mom's not happy."

I lick the invisible pizza sauce from her face. "You could have at least left some on your chin for me."

Water gushes down the drain, creating a hollow noise that brings the hairs on the back of my neck to full attention. "You need a bath."

I dig my paws into the floor, wishing there was something to grab hold of. I'm not about to get a bath from my daughter.

She points to the water. "Get in."

I dig my nails into the floor. "Not gonna happen."

Jaycee claps her hands. "Come here, Huck-a-doodle."

I stand my ground.

She presses her lips together and lunges at me, grabbing me around the waist. I wiggle in protest but still end up ankle deep in warm water.

"Mom will start talking about sending you away again if you do crap like this."

I stare up at her, my eyes full of sorrow. "Now you know how she feels when you make a huge mess in your room." I try to smile because I'm joking and I'm relieved she can't understand me because I quickly realize it's not a fair comparison.

Jaycee drenches me with water.

I shake. "This is for the time I gave you a bath when you were three and I ended up having to change my clothes after you splashed water everywhere."

Jaycee bonks me on the head with the empty cup she'd used to dump water over me. "Stop that."

"This is as bad as that time we went to the water park and you made me stand under that awful monkey who dumped the barrel of water over us," I grumble, remembering how she made us wait in the middle of a wade pool until the large bucket tipped.

"You did this to yourself," she scolds, reaching for my bottle of body wash.

She pours nearly half the container over me before returning it to the edge of the tub. "Be careful where you touch," I instruct as she rubs the suds into my fur.

"You smell like Dad," she whispers, stopping to pout. "It's nice."

I savor the moment, trying to shove the guilt out of my mind.

"Be careful back there," I yelp when her hand runs down my back leg. "There are places you shouldn't touch."

The cup comes for my head and I brace myself. A dozen times she dumps water over me until I feel like a waterboarded rat.

She pulls the plug and goes for a towel. The room is already a mess, so I shake, sending water flying onto the adjacent wall.

"You're lucky you're cute," she says, coming back to dry me off.

I shake again when she sets me on the floor.

She laughs until she sees I'm standing in the middle of a pile of toilet paper. "Better get you out of here or I'll have a bigger mess."

Dabs of paper stick to my feet as I make my dash for freedom when she opens the door. I race across the bed, losing most of the bits. After rolling across the comforter, I dart into the living room to see Sabrina. She's curled up on the couch with her nose in a book. I hop up to join her.

"No!" She shoves me to the floor. "Wet dogs aren't allowed on the couch!"

I try again. "What about mostly dry dogs?"

She shoves me again. "Down!"

"Hold that thought." I race through the house, hoping the air will dry me quicker this way. I hop beside her again, this time staying off the couch and covering her lap.

Her hand falls to my head. "Trying to beat the system?"

"You know it." I lick her cheek.

"You smell like Jason...and wet dog." She places her book on the end table. "I'm not sure how I feel about that."

"I *am* Jason." I peer up at her with what I hope is a smile.

"I'm still mad at you." She strokes my back, a sure sign she's on her way to forgiving me...I hope. "I probably have time to read another chapter before Jaycee finishes with that mess." She picks up her book.

I rest my head on her legs. "Better make it two."

Chapter 13

Oakley stares at me from the doorway of his shed, watching as I pee right there by the door early the next morning when Jaycee shoves me outside. She's learned to do that first thing, thankfully.

"Hey, Huck," he bellows.

I leap through the snow, running so fast that I trip over my feet and roll to a stop in front of him. "Hey," I pant.

He nods toward the house. "How's it going in there?"

I sniff his muzzle and work my way to both left feet. "Why do I smell Old Spice? Are you wearing cologne?"

He laughs, showing his flat teeth. "Not since that time Jaycee sprayed me with your Axe."

I cock my head and flick the snow from my ears. "She did *what?*"

"She said she didn't like the way donkeys smelled."

Concerned I might meet the same fate, I bury my face into my armpit—if that's even what it's still called—and sniff, the smell of wet dog filling my nostrils. "Wait...what? You said she snuck *my* Axe out. You know who I am?"

With his muzzle close to the snow, he raises his head and sprays me with powder. "I do."

I motion to the house. "Is there any way to get them to know that?"

He shakes his head. "'Fraid not."

"There has to be a way."

"I've been trying since you brought me home."

I slowly slink into the snow. First, I find out my mother-in-law is the cat we adopted and now I learn our donkey *is* someone else I know. A squirrel runs down the large pine, pausing at the bottom where he spots us, and darts toward the far end of the yard to the oak tree. My canine instincts grab ahold, forcing my curiosity of Oakley's identity to the backburner. I bound in and out of snow drifts toward the large rodent.

"I don't know why I'm doing this," I yell in loud barks as the squirrel perches just out of my grasp.

"You're part puppy now."

With my paws as high on the bark as I can reach, I freeze, mouth gaping open. "You can talk too?"

The creature climbs higher and circles around, retreating to face me. "I can do a great many things."

I drop to my haunches. "What in the Southern Mississippi is going on here?"

Oakley kicks his ball underneath the pine as if he's trying to hide his eavesdropping.

"I thought I'd drop in to see how you were adjusting," says the squirrel.

"Jesus?" There's a slight nod. "Shouldn't you know?"

"I wanted to hear it from you. Jaycee has told me all about you."

I beam with pride. "Please tell me I'm going to wake up in the hospital. Any minute now, I hope."

His tail twitches and his head shakes slightly. "I'm afraid that's not possible."

"You just said you can do a great many things."

"Your body was broken. I gave you a new one. That's what you wanted."

"You could have fixed it," I argue.

"Are you implying I don't know what's best for you?"

"This isn't what I had in mind."

"And yet, I have a plan." He flicks his tail.

I lie down, overwhelmed with the revelation that I'm stuck here...in a dog's body. This isn't a dream. I'm not going to wake up and resume my life. But at least I get to stay with my family. It will take time to come to terms with it all, but I know I will.

I glance toward the house. "You mind explaining why my mother-in-law is our cat?"

He chatters in a noise I'm not sure I've ever heard a real squirrel make. "When you were going through all those miscarriages you prayed for comfort for your wife."

I lunge at the tree. "So you sent her a cat who is really her mother?" The words come out so harshly I actually cower, afraid I'll be struck by a lightning bolt from the cloudless sky.

"Prayers are not always answered in the way you think is best."

I glare toward the donkey who amuses himself with that damn ball. "If you tell me Oakley is my childhood bully, I'm—"

He chatters some more. "Any time you want out, all you have to do is say the word."

"You mean I can go to Heaven with you any time I like?"

"That's right."

I stare at the house, knowing my family is inside hurting. "If I stay, they'll never know the truth, will they?"

He shakes his head. "It's your decision."

"But I'll get to stay and watch Jaycee grow up?"

"That's the deal."

I flop onto my belly, resting my head on my paws. "No work, no chores, just playing with Jaycee...and endless naps. It almost sounds like a dream come true."

"Don't forget about the cat."

My hind leg twitches, begging to scratch a spot behind my ears. "She has to stay? Can't I take over and you take her with you?"

"She's part of the deal. As is Oakley."

I inch back up the tree. "Any chance you could tell me who he is?"

"Just because you're a dog, doesn't mean you are going to stop learning. Oakley is here to help with that. Trust me, you'll need him." He scampers around the tree, sliding to the base. "What's it going to be?"

I stare at my stubborn donkey and turn to check the house. "I can't leave them now. I'll stay as long as you let me."

"Good dog." He smiles and I instantly know the other shoe is about to drop. "One more thing—"

I shake falling snow from my coat. "What's that?"

"I want you to find Sabrina's next husband."

Chapter 14

The weight of Jesus' statement bears down on me and my eyes bulge. "Excuse me?" My hind legs drop and my chest aches like someone sucked all the air from my lungs. I can't believe the words I'd just heard. It's hard enough to grasp the fact that I'm talking to Jesus in the form of a squirrel. *You have to find Sabrina's next husband.* The words echo in my brain. I can barely fathom that I'd died, spent a day in Heaven, and returned to earth with four legs and a tail.

"I know it's soon but, eventually, Sabrina will want a companion," the squirrel chirps.

I cock my head. "I thought that's what I was for."

"I don't have to tell you dogs don't live forever or that it's not the same as a human counterpart."

I'd like to punch a wall, but there's no wall and I don't have fists. So I dig into the snow in front of me. "And you want me to—"

He angrily chatters at an approaching squirrel in some sort of native tongue until the other rodent darts away. "I want you to steer her in the right direction."

"How am I supposed to do that?"

"I'm sure you can figure out how to drive away the men who aren't suitable or don't have pure intentions." I want to argue about modern times and intentions, but my instincts tell me to keep quiet. "If she finds someone you approve of, all you have to do is make sure their love blossoms."

My stomach flops and out comes my breakfast...and the plastic foot of Rockstar Barbie. "Can't she stay single?"

"I think we both know that isn't fair to her. Don't you want her to be happy?"

I hang my head in shame. "Of course."

"Trust in my timing."

Knowing how His timing works, I don't like the sound of what I'm in store for.

"I'll give you some time to think about it." He scampers up a tree. "I'll check in later to see what your answer is. In the meantime, stay away from snowplows. You're 0-1 with them." With that he slips into the branches and disappears.

After a long game of ball and chase with Oakley, he leads me inside his shed.

Motioning me inside his stall, he says, "I thought you might be getting cold."

I leap into the Old Spice scented straw, wondering how on earth that's even possible. "I think my tail froze half an hour ago."

He kneels beside me. "I'm glad you decided to stay, Jaybird."

I poke my head through the mound of straw I'd buried myself in, my body shivering from the cold and my denseness. Only one person ever called me 'Jaybird'—the nickname I'd passed down a generation to my own daughter—my grandpa. I laugh at the revelation. "It all makes sense now."

"What does?"

"Why Jesus told me to tell you 'hi' right before he kicked me out of Heaven."

He flicks my ear with his nose. "He postponed your arrival."

With the energy of a little boy who hasn't seen his best friend in too long, I leap onto Oakley's back and spring to the other side. "I can't believe you're really here," I chatter, using him as a jungle gym like I did when I was little.

"It's been a long two years waiting to talk to you."

I kick straw all over the shed as I display my pleasure.

"You're messing up my bed."

"I'll put new straw down tomorrow," I say, briefly forgetting my circumstances. We laugh as I remember and roll over.

A thick coat of his bedding sticks to my wet fur as we settle in.

I yawn. "This is a lot to take in. First, I died. Then I go to Heaven and find out my halo has four legs and a tail. But now I'm here, right where I want to be and I learn I have to help my wife find a new husband."

With a snort, Oakley blows a dozen straw flakes off my back. "I think you're missing the important aspect that you still get to watch Jaycee grow up. Sure, it may not be the way anyone would like, but it's still a blessing most people don't get."

"How are you so positive?"

He haws loudly. "When you eat enough hay, you learn to see the positives. I had faith it was all for a reason. And I think you're the reason." He glances toward his food bucket. "If you ask me, it's been worth the hay."

"Have you tried dog food? It tastes like it *wants* to be food but can't quite figure out how."

He laughs. "At least you get food scraps."

"I brought you treats."

"And you don't know how much I appreciated that."

I nuzzle into his side, wondering if it's weird for a grown man to be cuddling with his grandpa. "I don't know how I'm going to do this."

"One day at a time."

I hang my head. "The thought of Sabrina being with anyone else makes me sick."

He hangs his head over my back. "But you're forgetting one important detail."

Inhaling the dust I'd stirred up, I sneeze, following it with another yawn. "What's that?"

"A dog's love is better than a human's. You'll see."

His words bring little hope to my situation.

Chapter 15

My ears perk at the sound of a Chevy engine pulling in the drive. The vehicle door shuts and a moment later the doorbell rings. I race Sabrina to see who it is. My tail wags as I wait for her to let our guest in.

Kelley, one of my closest friends, stands on the porch, hands shoved deep in his coat pockets. The ballcap he'd started wearing a few years ago when he noticed his receding hairline rests on his head.

I immediately jump on him when Sabrina ushers him through the door. "Hey, Buddy, what's new?"

"Well, hi there, little—" he looks in my personal area to determine the end to his sentence. "—guy. When did you get a dog?"

"The day of Jason's funeral. It's a long story. But it looks like we have a dog now. He's a menace."

Kelley bends to pet me. "You're not a menace, are you?" His tone is thick with a childish accent he hasn't used since his twins were in diapers.

I back away. "Don't talk to me like that. What are you doing here?"

He shoves his hands back in his pockets. "I happened to be out this way and thought I'd stop by to see how you and 'lil Jay are doing."

I wag my tail at the reference to my daughter's nickname. Kelley had been the one who started the 'Big Jay' and 'Little Jay' pet names for us among my group of friends.

Sabrina sets the book she'd carried in on the desk. "As well as can be expected. That's what I'm supposed to say, right?" She nervously laughs. "The dog has kept Jaycee occupied, so I guess he's good for something."

"Sounds like it." He shrugs.

"Not if he's going to keep eating my makeup."

I press my paw into her thigh. "How long are you going to hold that against me?"

Kelley laughs, his grin plastered to his face long after the moment passes. He removes his hands but doesn't seem to know what to do with them so he awkwardly shoves them back into his pockets.

A weird silence hangs over the room for a long minute and I'm compelled to, once again, ask "Why are you here, Kelley? What do you want?"

He stares at the snow dripping from his boots. "How's school going for Jaycee?"

"Okay so far. I think it's good for her to stay busy."

Kelley nods. "Have you been to work?"

"No. I can't bring myself to go to the restaurant. Lauren has been great though."

"How's she holding up?"

"She's doing what needs to be done she says."

"Good." He shifts awkwardly on his feet. "Well, if you need anything, I'm off the next four days."

Sabrina smiles sincerely. "Thank you."

"And if you need anything here...you know, man stuff that needs done, you've got my number."

As he's saying the words, it dawns on me that he's recently divorced. "You son of a bitch," I growl. "I've barely been dead for...not long enough."

I latch onto the hem of his jeans.

Sabrina scoops me up around the middle. "I don't know what got into him. He's never done that to anyone."

Kelley ruffles the fur between my ears. "I'm sure he was just playing."

Sabrina turns her head at the sound of glass shattering in the kitchen. "I'd better go check that out."

"Let me know if you need anything."

"Thanks for stopping by."

I growl in Sabrina's arms as she shuts the door behind him. She furrows her brow, scowling at me. Instead of checking on Jaycee, she heads to the back door and deposits me outside.

I race around the side of the house to watch Kelley's truck leave the drive. Fueled by anger, I zip along the perimeter of the yard.

Oakley steps into my path on my second go-round. "What's gotten into you?"

"Logically, I know Kelley was just being nice. If his wife had died, I would've done the same thing. But he's divorced and something about the way he acted felt like he was testing the waters. No. I have to be wrong." I circle Oakley, sniffing the ground as if I'll find answers buried in the powder.

Oakley stomps the ground. "Jaybird, what's going on?"

"My friend, Kelley, stopped by."

"That was nice."

"You should have seen him. He was all 'I have the next four days off if you need anything." I leap from one spot to another like a boxer waiting to pounce.

"That's the sort of thing people do when someone dies."

"Grandpa, he's been checking Sabrina out in front of me for years. He and his wife split a year ago and now that I'm gone—"

"You think he's going to swoop in."

"He certainly acted like it."

"You're going through quite an adjustment right now. I don't know Sabrina all that well, but I know you. And I know you wouldn't choose a wife who jumped into bed with the first person to come along. It's too soon."

I plop into the snow. *You want to be with your family as they grow and that means finding Sabrina's next husband.* Could that be Kelley? I hang my head onto the cold powder. "How long do you think it will be?"

"It's different for everyone. I've had friends over the years who've lost spouses. Some moved on quickly—too quickly, I thought—but others took years. Some never did."

"Which do you think Sabrina will be?"

"There's no way to tell."

"You don't think it's going to be with one of my friends, do you?"

He picks up the ball. "How about a game to get your mind off it?"

He flings the ball and I chase it, making a mental list of my friends who may try to make a move. "Maybe she'll become a crazy cat lady," I offer, waiting for him to toss the ball again.

"You'd rather be in the middle of *that*?"

I duck as he chucks the ball a second time. "At least there won't be someone in my side of the bed."

"Jason, I know you don't want Sabrina to spend the rest of her life alone."

"She's got Jaycee."

Another throw. "It's not the same."

"I know. You're right. I don't want her to be alone. I just want to be the one with her."

"And you will be. Every step of the way. You still get to be her best friend. But one day, she'll need something more. It's okay to not be okay with that right now, but if you're going to do this, you'll need to be willing to be okay with it when the time comes."

"I think I need some time alone," I say and slink into his shed.

I curl into a ball in the corner of his stall.

A tiny mouse pokes out of the straw. "It's cold out there today. Maybe I should turn the heat up."

I snort, sending pieces of straw floating into the air. "I suppose you think you're funny. I didn't expect a front row seat to watch my wife fall in love with one of my friends."

The mouse scampers to me, taking a seat between my paws. "You're the one who asked to come back."

"I didn't mean 'give me four legs and a tail,'" I nearly snarl, but quickly remember who I'm talking to.

"If we're being honest, dogs are one of my best creations." I open my mouth to object but realize I can't. "You should be honored."

"It's hard to share your enthusiasm when I know my wife is going to move on. I didn't expect to be so close to the action."

"You act as though she's on Tinder as we speak."

I bug my eyes. "Is she?"

He laughs. "Of course not. She won't swipe right until she goes out with Candace and they drink too much wine." I leap to my feet. "Relax. She deletes her account the next morning."

I sit. "I always knew Candace was bad news."

He scampers to the railing. "Have some faith in Sabrina. She won't easily forget you. But she won't move on without your help."

"That sounds like an oxymoron."

"You still have free will. You can leave any time you like."

"I can't do that. My buddy is already trying to move in."

"Come on, you can easily laugh at that, right? We both know why Kelley's marriage ended."

I blink heavily. "Because his parents wanted to move in with them so they could save money to travel." I scratch my ear. "Funny they never seemed to go anywhere."

"Don't pretend it isn't deeper than that."

"Was it the moving of the furniture? Kelley said at least once a month he'd come home to a completely rearranged room." He gnaws on the railing with his tiny teeth. "Do you mind? I spent half a day working on that."

"I spent longer," He replies.

"At least be careful not to nibble the entire shed down. Oakley needs a place to sleep. You know Sabrina won't let him inside. I've tried. Hey, maybe you can change her mind on that too. It's pretty cold out here. Actually, she'd probably be okay if you'd just make it summer year-round."

"Let's get back to Kelley."

I spin in a circle. "Is he back?"

"No. My point is, they allowed their situation to come between them."

I dig in the straw. "Kind of like how the restaurant was starting to come between me and Sabrina?"

"I think you're starting to understand."

"Okay, but that doesn't make me feel any better about my buddy making a move on my wife."

"You need to trust in my timing."

"Sometimes I think the watch you're using for that is broken."

He laughs. "For there is a proper time and procedure for every matter, though a person may be weighed down by misery."

"Ecclesiastes 8:6. Sabrina made a sign with that verse and hung it over our bed after the third or fourth miscarriage."

He jumps into the straw and comes out on a tiny mound that makes him appear to be standing behind a pulpit. "It was the third. That one was rough."

"We made it to twenty-two weeks that time. We really thought we'd made it." I rest my head on my paws, remembering that pain. "Can I ask why? What did we do to deserve so much pain? And why let us bring a child into the world if you were going to let her grow up without a father?"

Giggles erupt outside the shed as Jaycee tromps off the deck.

Jesus pauses, an act I view as avoiding my questions. She barges in and I leap closer to the mouse, hoping to hear an answer before her chatter drowns everything else out. "At least tell me who Sabrina ends up with."

"When it's time, you'll know," Jesus answers, his eyes darting for an escape.

"Seriously? That's your answer?"

"I promise you'll both be ready when it happens," Jesus replies and dives into the straw.

I leap after him. "You're not all that helpful sometimes, you know that?"

"Trust." I feel the word more than I hear it, but I know he's gone.

Chapter 16

Two weeks pass. My days are spent following Sabrina around the house as she deep cleans every square inch. I don't think she appreciates our closeness as much as I do. I curl up on the bathroom floor while she showers, eager to catch a glimpse of her beautiful body. I can tell it annoys her to have me underfoot in the bathroom, but I can't stand to be away from her. It's hard not to return to work and I practically beg her to take me to the restaurant, but she doesn't understand my actions. When she gets fed up with me being in her way, she sends me outdoors to Oakley. He and I have the best time catching up. He reminds me how I held my faith during Sabrina's miscarriages and I know I need to be patient.

I wake to a dark house, curled up on the couch where I'd fallen asleep. Feet thunder toward me and whiz by. I open my eyes to see Audra zip by. She skids to a stop and turns, racing past me again. With one eye open, I watch her speed past twice more. Somewhere along the way, she collects a tiny ball with a bell in it. It rattles as she chases it across the living room.

"There are people trying to sleep," I mutter as she bats it off the baseboard. "What happened to quiet hours?"

She pauses to glare at me. "Got to get my exercise."

I bury my head underneath one of Sabrina's stupid throw pillows. "Pick a reasonable time to play your dumb game."

"Cats are nocturnal."

"You're not a cat."

She pushes the ball back and forth between her paws, creating an irritating rapid jingle. "Your grandpa is a donkey." She laughs at her comment.

I shove the pillow off the couch. "Leave him out of this."

"I don't even know why he's here." She leaps onto the coffee table.

I stretch out, claiming as much couch real estate as my tiny body will allow. "Probably the same reason you and I are."

She spreads her claws, licking between the wide space in two of them. "That's laughable."

"How so?"

She stops mid lick and slowly reels her tongue in. "For starters, *I* have a purpose."

I spring to my feet. "Oh yeah? What's that?"

"*I* am a comfort to Sabrina. Have you forgotten about how and when I arrived? It wasn't a coincidence. Nothing seems to be."

I sit and stare at the ceiling, remembering the day we stumbled into the animal shelter where Sabrina's friend worked. We were immediately warned about this cat they'd just picked up. Nobody could get close to it without wearing gloves and watching their back around it. They all said the thing was wilder than a bobcat. The way Sabrina tells the story, once she walked into the room, the cat stopped hissing and wound itself around her legs. Everyone was amazed and Sabrina called them all liars. It didn't happen too far off from that, I think, recalling how it had gotten loose and clung to Sabrina in an attempt to avoid a cage. Her friend told her it was a sign, but Sabrina was reluctant until they admitted they would have to euthanize it because it—seriously—was the most evil cat any of them had seen. *Of course. It all makes sense now. My first impression of Audra was much like the workers' at the shelter. Plus, if I'd just been turned into a dog and dumped at a pound, I'd probably be pissed too.* And it all happened six months after her mom had died, eight months after our last miscarriage, and two weeks after we found out Sabrina was pregnant again. We made it to five months with that pregnancy. She had spent a week in bed, curled up with the cat, not wanting to see me or anyone else.

I consider *my* purpose. There's no way I'm going to divulge that information. Not just yet.

Bobbi jumps onto the couch, sprawling too close for my comfort.

I wiggle my back end away from her, not trusting her talons.

She extends her claws. "After all Sabrina went through to carry your child to term, you still couldn't make it home before bedtime."

My upper lip curls, a low growl escaping. "You act like I didn't go through the miscarriages with her and that couldn't be farther from the truth. I held her hand when the doctors told her there was no heartbeat. I dried her tears. I steered her away from pregnant women when we were out because I could feel the pain it caused her to see them. *You* weren't there. Each time I would proudly paint the nursery a different color—because each pregnancy felt like *the one* to her. I put up the crib. Then I'd take it down again because she couldn't bear to look at it. You don't know how badly I wished I could make that stupid room disappear. But now it's Jaycee's room. So, I guess maybe the most important thing I did during that time was pray. I prayed for Sabrina. I prayed for Jaycee. But mostly, I prayed that no matter what, I would have the strength to carry your daughter through it. And, let me tell you, there were days I didn't know how to get through it myself. But I did. And I helped her get through it, long before you came back."

She jumps to the coffee table. "Don't try to tug at my heartstrings. I heard all about the late-night feedings you missed and the dirty diapers you didn't change."

"What should I have done—gotten up and put the baby on Sabrina's chest?"

"Yes," she snaps with a curt nod.

"Jaycee slept three feet from the bed."

She licks the length of her front leg. "Beside the point."

"You're impossible."

"It just seems like you thought your job stopped as soon as Sabrina was safely in the thirty-six-week range."

I clumsily leap onto the table beside her. "Wow. It's too bad Sabrina can't see you for who you really are."

She taps a single claw on my nose. I refuse to flinch. "I've been telling her the same thing about you for years."

I snap at her arm. She yanks it away. "Maybe that's the difference between us. I kept my opinions to myself."

She leaps to the floor. "How noble."

"Did you ever think that maybe I'm here for...Jaycee?"

She opens her mouth in a wide yawn. "Funny that you never were before."

I jump down and stare her in the face. "You act like I'm some deadbeat who walked out on her."

She turns and swats her tail in my face. "Might as well have. You were always at that stupid restaurant."

I laugh and step in front of her. "As in the place that provided us with income?"

"That's another thing I don't understand. Sabrina shouldn't have been working. She dreamt of being a mother for so long but refused to give up her job after finally giving birth."

I thump a paw to the floor. "There's no reason she can't be a mother *and* have a career."

"Thanks to you, she doesn't have a choice."

I want words that sting as much as hers do but, just for a moment, I pause. "She enjoys working. The home décor she designs for the restaurant is selling well. We even opened an online shop."

"I know. She told me."

I roll my eyes. Of course my wife talks to her cat like she's a person. I cock my head, shaking the confusion of the situation out. "Then why argue about it?"

She leaps onto the end table and stares at the cup Jaycee left out. As if she can't resist, she bats it until it topples over the edge.

"Dammit, Bobbi, you're going to ruin the floor."

"Don't call me that," she hisses.

"Bobbi? That's your name." I laugh. The idea that she hates it gives me more pleasure than if I'd punched her in the gut.

"Call me Audra."

I wag my tail. "I've called you Bobbi for so long I probably won't be able to change now." I lap my tongue over my nose for effect.

"Try."

With a sleepy yawn, I say, "I think Bobbi fits you better."

She prances over, glares at me a second, and bats me once with each paw, her claws digging into the sensitive skin near my eyes.

"Living up to your bobcat kin, I see."

"I'll run you off this time. Just you wait."

"Good luck," I turn and slip into the bedroom, leaving her alone in the living room.

Sabrina lifts her head off the pillow. "You want to sleep on my bed?"

I stretch against the mattress and she hoists me up. Sniffing the exposed side of her face, I wrinkle my nose. Does her moisturizer need to smell that way? Detecting a hint of salt, I consider the options—facial scrub or tears. My guess is the latter. I bury my nose in her coconut shampoo scented hair until I feel her cheeks raise in a smile. I scamper to my pillow and make a circle on it. *Why do I do that?*

"This is mine." She yanks it from under me and firmly claims my half of the bed, sprawling out to cover as much ground as possible.

I sniff her pillow, faint shampoo and fresh tears mingling alongside remnants of her perfume. Sabrina watches me search for the perfect spot, a loneliness I've never seen clouding her eyes. I stop to stare, wondering how many times she's hidden the same expression from me. I've got to do better. *But I'm a dog.* I tilt my head to the side. Is that an advantage or disadvantage? The first time I saw a look like this on her face was two weeks after the doctors told us we may never carry a child to term. She sat across the kitchen table from me with tears in her eyes and told me she would support me if I wanted to divorce her then argued with me when I confessed my love and said we'd get through it together. I suggested adopting, she suggested an attorney, conceding the house and everything in it. I recited our marriage vows and took her to bed. I smile to myself. If we can get through miscarriages, we can get through this. And it's up to me to figure out how. I nuzzle into her side and close my eyes with her arm draped over me.

Chapter 17

The alarm clock buzzes at 6:15. Sabrina groans and slaps the snooze button. She's never been a morning person. I sniff her face, backing away at her morning breath.

"It's time to get up," I tell her. She pulls the covers over her head. "Come on, we've got work...or school...or something."

I dance on top of the blanket to no avail. She's not getting up. Putting a corner of the fabric in my mouth, I tug. I'd always been the one out of bed on the first alarm but she'd always needed at least two snooze cycles. We'd argued about it more times than I could count.

"Just set the alarm for the time you need to get up," I repeat, yanking harder.

She fights just as hard. I retreat to her feet and burrow my way under the comforter. Finding my way to her arm, I gently clamp my teeth around her wrist.

"What if I tell you I have to pee?"

Her eyes bolt open. "You're going to pee somewhere if I don't get up right this second, aren't you?"

I drop her arm. "Can you understand me?"

She runs her hand lazily down my back. "Do you need to go out?"

"Now that you mention it—" I slurp a kiss across her cheek.

She yawns, dousing me in her dragon breath. "Come on."

I race her to the door and we discover a fresh coating of snow. Oakley waits in front of the shed. I spritz patches of snow all the way to him.

"I hope you're warm enough in there," I say almost apologetically.

He haws loudly. "Not sure what you'd do about it if I weren't, but I'm fine."

I laugh. "You have a point."

"How's it going in there?"

"Oh, you know Audra." Unable to contain my energy, I circle around him.

The back door flings open and Jaycee pops her head out. "Huck! Come walk me to the bus!"

I jump into the air. "I've got a job to do," I yell to Oakley, taking off in a sprint toward the deck.

Jaycee crouches to greet me, dressed in jeans and a gray shirt with a sequined unicorn. Her hair is done in a long braid that I bite at when she picks me up.

Sabrina ushers us to the front porch where we stand to wait for the bus. The moment it is out of sight, Sabrina looks down at me. "Today's the day. Guess it's time to figure out what to do with you while I work."

I spin a circle at her feet. "It's about time. Lauren probably has questions. I hope she hasn't been having problems in my absence." I pad beside her as she retreats to our bedroom to change.

She slides her pajama pants off. "I can't bring myself to lock you in a kennel all day."

"I'm going with you."

She pulls a fresh pair of jeans out of the closet. "Maybe I could lock you in the shed with Oakley...but that hardly seems like a nice thing to do to him."

I scratch at her foot. "That would beat spending the day with your mother, but I need to see my employees." I scratch again, hoping she'll see the desperation in my eyes. "I need to know how Lauren is doing." I settle to the ground, my heart suddenly heavy with guilt. Lauren must be a wreck. Panic overcomes me at the notion and I leap up, barking wildly.

"You have to take me," I plead. "I need to apologize to Lauren."

She peels her shirt over her head. I stop to stare. She takes a seat on the bed and fiddles with a bra she spent too much money on. I scramble up the mattress and plop down across her lap, hoping to keep her from donning a shirt for a moment longer.

"Maybe I should just take you," she sighs. "I could keep an eye on you in my shop. I guess that's our only option right now."

I lurch to lick her face. "Yes! Do that!"

She covers her torso with a yellow shirt I don't remember ever seeing her wear. "Well, come on then."

Sabrina throws the truck in park at the restaurant, her left hand clutching the wheel. Her right hand shakes as she runs it through her hair. She stares at the building like it's a battlefield.

I clamber onto the console. "This must be hard. I didn't think of that."

She turns to face me, tears welling in her eyes. "I can't do this."

I rest my paw on her arm. "It's okay if it's too soon. But would you mind letting me out so I can check on a few things?" I just need to observe for a few minutes, get a feel for how things are going.

Her lip quivers and I inch my way to her lap.

Sabrina inhales a shaky breath. "I don't think I can do this yet." She reaches for her phone. Dialing a number, she places it to her ear. "Hi, Lauren, it's Sabrina. I was planning to come in today, but I'm sitting here in the parking lot and I just can't make myself get out of the truck."

"I totally understand," Lauren comforts from inside the building. "We have everything under control."

"Are you sure? I know inventory needs to be done and orders need placed."

"Sabrina, you just lost your husband, take all the time you need. Jason showed me how to do everything."

"I...thanks. I'm really sorry."

"There's nothing to be sorry about." It pains me to hear the guilt in Lauren's voice. She feels responsible.

Sabrina nods, muttering a cordial goodbye. Her hand continues to shake long after she backs out of the parking lot. Instead of taking the quickest route home, she meanders through the country. I'm not surprised when she turns into her friend, Angela's, driveway.

She opens the door and I leap out over her, running to mark new territory on the closest tree.

I follow her to the door and wait for it to be opened. A deep bark resounds from the inside and Angela soon swings the door into the foyer.

"Sabrina." Her arms encompass my wife. "How are you?"

A giant nose scans my fur starting at my head and working toward my tail. "Stop that," I object when he gets close to my backside.

"If you're going to be in my house, you're going to have to introduce yourself." I jump backward at the intrusion to an area that has never been sniffed by anyone other than me since I learned I could reach.

"Well then, just ask."

"What's your name, kid?"

"Huck. Who are you?"

He follows Sabrina and Angela into the kitchen. "Kylo."

I roll my eyes. "Gene and Angela are Star Wars fans, huh?"

He whips his head around. "What the heck does that mean?"

I scurry under the table. "Star Wars...the movie?"

"I have no idea what either of those things are."

I cock my head. How does he not know what a movie is? "You know—the big box in the living room that people stare at?" He shoves his nose in Sabrina's crotch. "Hey! Knock it off!"

Angela shoves him away and offers Sabrina a mug of coffee.

"Oh, the picture player," Kylo nods. "My dad likes to watch people throw balls."

Dad? Does he mean human or canine? All I know is Sabrina better not start referring to herself as my mom.

I pick a sunny spot close to where Kylo has chosen to lie, but not too close, and curl up. The sun warms me against the cool tile. "So, did you used to be a human too?"

He lifts his head and blinks slowly. "I used to be a lawyer, but then I realized dogs don't wear suits and scam people out of money."

I roll away from him, soaking in his response. Angela's husband, Gene, is a defense attorney and even I had heard him talk about the high-priced lawyers he thought took advantage of people. Flopping over again, I try a different approach. "Did God send you to Angela and Gene for a reason?"

He yawns, stretching his tongue way out. "Yeah. They wanted a dog."

"Are you related to them somehow?"

Kylo stands, moves two tiles to the left, and flops back down. "I think Gene is my second cousin twice removed on my mother's side."

It takes me a minute to absorb the sarcasm in his voice. "I was Sabrina's husband before I died. God let me come back so I could find her a new husband. I only ask about you because our cat is Sabrina's mom." A laugh echoes across the room. The women ignore the sound so I continue. "And our donkey is my grandpa. Are you sure you aren't like a favorite uncle or something?"

"Kid, you've lost it. I think your mom should've eaten you at birth. There's something wrong up here," he says, scratching his head.

"I can see you don't believe me."

He stretches his legs, nearly hitting me with his giant paws. "I'd love to continue this bizarre conversation, but the sun only stays in this spot for so long."

I rest my head on the floor and listen to Sabrina and Angela talk at the table.

"Every day is a nightmare I keep hoping to wake up from. It's been less than a month but it feels like yesterday and ten years all at the same time," Sabrina confesses.

"It will get easier," Angela offers.

"I can't bear to go into the restaurant and the only reason I can walk through the house is because Jaycee is there to distract me. I can't even move the stupid jacket he insisted on keeping over the back of the kitchen chair. It's such a ridiculous place for it—as if we don't have a coat rack—but now I can't move it." She chuckles. "I hated that thing being there. I was always stepping on it and asking him to put it away. And now I can't bring myself to move it."

"Give it time."

Sabrina stifles a sob. "I know, but it's just one more reminder that he isn't coming home, that I can't ask him to move it for the millionth time."

"Have you tried talking to Pastor Clifford?"

Sabrina forces air through clenched teeth. "They convinced me to take a dog home."

"Afraid they'll talk you into a monkey or something?"

Sabrina laughs. "Kind of."

I yawn as Angela skillfully turns the conversation to Jaycee. My eyelids droop despite my interest in hearing how Sabrina thinks our daughter is handling my death and I'm powerless to stop sleep.

I wake upon hearing my human name.

"Maybe take it one step at a time," Angela suggests. "Sit in the parking lot for as long as you can handle then head home. Once you're comfortable there, head inside. Nobody is expecting you to work. Just sit in your shop for an hour or so."

"I don't know. What if they need something?"

"Tell Lauren up front that you aren't there to work, that you can handle emergencies only."

"I don't think I'm up for emergencies."

"So be honest with her and tell her what you need. Everyone is there to work with you. And if you need extra help, I'm available."

Sabrina steps in front of me, hoists me against her chest, and walks to the door. "I appreciate that," she says, tossing me outside.

From high in a tree, a bird makes an awful racket. I scan the empty branches until I find the culprit. I sniff the snow, picking up whiffs of Kylo, a stray cat, and two squirrels.

"Learning how to use your nose?" I whip around, looking for the source of the creature talking to me. "Up here."

"You can still pray for her, you know." The bird caws when I ignore the question.

I playfully pounce toward him, excited at the prospect of his words. "I can?"

"Well sure."

"I don't know what she needs."

He flutters onto a branch, away from my rambunctiousness. "I know."

I leap for the tree. "What is it?"

"I've already taken care of it."

"But she's still having a rough time," I argue.

"Her husband died a month ago."

"I wish there was something I could do...could we just turn back time?"

He squawks loudly. "If I had a nickel for every time I've heard that—"

"So that's out of the question?" The bird nods. "I didn't think I'd have to *watch* her grieve."

"You're the one who asked to come back." That's not what I meant and you know it, I muse. "I work in mysterious ways. Learn to trust them."

"It would be easier if she knew *why* you took me from her. Can't you at least tell her that? I know it's eating her alive. She couldn't understand her mother's death when she was going through the roughest patch in her own life. I know she's reliving that now."

He picks at his feathers with his beak. "Remember how you got fired right after Sabrina's first miscarriage? You thought the world was against you, but I foresaw the months of savings dwindle as you struggled to find work. It wasn't the right time to bring a child into the world. You wouldn't have been able to provide."

"We would've found a way," I argue.

"You spent an entire winter with the thermostat set to fifty-eight. That wouldn't have worked with a baby."

"I suppose not."

"You also would've found an eviction notice on your door." I cock my head, contemplating the scenario. It was possible. "If you remember correctly, you didn't get another positive pregnancy test until after you got a better job."

"Yet we miscarried again."

"Travis didn't deserve the way the world would have treated him." I scratch my head. "His body works perfectly in Heaven."

My heart aches at the thought. "What did Sabrina do to deserve this?"

"Nothing."

"I suppose it's better for me to leave one child behind instead of the small herd she'd hoped for."

Sabrina calls to me from the door. I turn and stare at her but make no move. "What can I do for her?"

"Be there when she needs you. That's why I sent you."

"Huck!" I turn at the sound of Sabrina's demanding shout.

"Follow her lead and you'll know what to do," the bird offers and flies away.

I bide my time and wait for Sabrina's cue. It doesn't come until the next morning after Jaycee boards the bus. She takes Angela's advice and drives back to the restaurant. Ten minutes drag on as we sit in the truck staring at the building. I crawl into her lap to let her know I'm on her side, but she puts the truck in reverse and we head back home. Four days pass before she's able to turn the ignition off while we sit. I try licking her hand and getting in her face, but we end up back home less than an hour after leaving the house. After a weekend of intense family time, a few tears from her and Jaycee, we approach the situation again on Monday. This time I spend the whole ride staring out the window, praying. I ask for guidance on getting Sabrina over this obstacle. She parks in her spot and turns the ignition off, her hands no longer shaking. I lie on her lap, waiting with her. If she doesn't gain courage today, we'll do it again tomorrow, I resolve.

Her hand waivers over the door handle. She bows her head and when her eyes spring open, she flicks the door wide against its hinges.

"It's not going to get any easier," she says, waving me out.

I leap onto the cold pavement into a fresh sprinkling of salt and snow.

The walls of Sabrina's shop are a soft yellow now, not the taupe we painted them. Stacks of wooden planks gather in the corner. The long work bench along one side is cluttered with an assortment of paints and trinkets she likes to call 'bedazzlers.' Another long table on the opposite wall holds a tray of ribbons, rope, and string. Plastic bins line yet another wall holding all the miscellaneous items she needs to create her custom designs for home décor.

"I need to get to work," she says, quietly staring at the project she'd left unfinished—the one she'd been working on the day before Jaycee's recital. She clutches a wooden sign to her chest a long minute before discarding it to the scrap pile near the door. It clatters to the floor, displaying the words she'd carefully painted nearly a month ago—Home is where the family is.

"Sabrina," I mutter, but I don't know what else to say so I sniff items near the floor, unable to control the urge to smell *everything*.

I chew on the edge of the discarded sign, hoping to draw Sabrina's attention back to it, but she busies herself with a new project and I soon grow bored. With a lazy yawn, I curl up beside her feet.

I wake to the smell of burnt wood and fresh stain. Sabrina hums a soft tune.

"If it's not too much trouble, I need to go out." I prance around the room, bumping into her leg. "Sabrina." She continues her work. "Sabrina. This is humiliating enough, having to ask to go to the bathroom, but...Sabrina," I yap, a little sharper this time.

She turns. "What?"

"I'll pee all over this floor; don't think I won't."

"You're probably hungry. And I didn't pack any food. Maybe Lauren will have some scraps you can have."

She leaps from the table when my bladder refuses to hold out any longer. "Oh, Huck."

I tuck my tail. "I tried to tell you."

She mops the mess with paper towel and connects me to a leash. "Not that this will do any good now."

Dennis and Layla emerge from a car, heading inside for their shifts. I pull on the leash, eager to see how they're doing.

"Hi, Mrs.—" Layla blows a puff of frozen air above her head as if she'd spoken a forbidden word. "—Parker. How are you?"

Sabrina leads me to the edge of the parking lot where snow covers the grass. "Just trying to stay busy."

Layla points to me. "Looks like you got a new friend."

"A little privacy," I beseech in a squat. Seeing that I won't be getting it, I hold my urge. "I'll give you a raise if you smuggle me into the kitchen," I beg of Layla.

She takes a step back. "Lively fellow. What's his name?"

"Huck."

We walk as far as the kitchen door. I salivate at the buffet of smells slipping through the crack. I tug forcefully on the leash at the rear kitchen entrance, but Sabrina has a firm grip. I relinquish my fight when Layla slips into the kitchen and pokes a small plate of scraps onto the ground outside the door. I gobble the chicken pieces and burnt meatloaf bits, all covered with two kinds of gravy, before anyone can take it away.

At the end of the day, as Sabrina puts her supplies away, she talks out loud. "I don't know if I can come here every day and not see you. Hell, I didn't even eat lunch today because you weren't here to share it with," she mumbles, slamming a hammer onto the edge of a paint can. "You cover every inch of this place."

"Still right here," I tell her.

She wipes her hands on her jeans and holds up the only thing she'd made all day—a sign with a white painted background and letters she'd burned onto it that read 'What God Brings You To, He Will Bring You Through.' The letters have a deep brown stain over it and the look on her face says she'll never part with it.

She reaches for a hammer. "I think this one I'm supposed to keep. These words kept ringing in my head all morning."

We're loading into the truck when Dennis emerges from the rear door of the kitchen. His arms circle a large paper sack. "We thought you might like dinner."

Sabrina opens the passenger door, her eyes studying me. "That's very thoughtful. I haven't felt much like cooking lately."

Dennis pats my head. "There's even a little something in there for Huck."

I lick his hand. It makes me feel a little dirty, but the smell of mashed potatoes, pork tenderloin, and mixed vegetables drives me wild. The fragrant aroma is even worse in the truck. The only thing stopping me from ripping into the bag is the thought of Jaycee and Sabrina going without as a result of my actions.

Chapter 18

We are barely home from our third day in a row at the restaurant when Jaycee bursts into tears at the dinner table.

"Some kid laughed at me because my dad died," she admits after much prompting from Sabrina.

I listen to the details from beneath the table.

"Might as well stop growling," Bobbi hisses, coming to sit beside me.

I snap in her direction. "I'm going to tear that kid to shreds."

She bats a paw at me. "I guess that's one way to get rid of you. They'll put you down for sure if you attack a child."

I puff my chest out and take a step toward her. "I will not let anyone treat Jaycee that way."

She prances around the table leg while Sabrina works to comfort our daughter. "Have you forgotten you have four legs and a tail?"

I snap at her again. "I haven't forgotten shit!" Her tail flicks as she sits out of reach on the other side of the chair. "But I have to do something to help."

"Good luck with that."

"Come on, you've been doing this longer than I have. What's the trick?"

She yawns, clearly enjoying this moment. Or so I assume. "Curl up on her lap and be there for her."

"That's not *doing* anything," I growl. "How is that supposed to help?"

"Don't be dense. I know you had a dog once upon a time, Jason. Didn't he—or she—get you through some tough days?"

I remember Falcon and hope he understands why I had to come back. "I guess so."

She bats at a mysterious floating object. "Just think about that and do whatever it was that made you feel better."

I consider her words a moment. "Why are you helping me?"

She moves to her water dish, taking her time to get a drink before answering me. "I love her, too, and I don't want to see her upset."

I nod. "Thank you for the suggestion."

She waltzes off, leaving me to the drama.

I lick Jaycee's bare toes until she notices me. Between sobs, she scoots her chair back and scoops me onto her lap. "Will you bite Liam for me, Huck?"

"Jaycee," Sabrina scolds.

"I'll rip the scrawny punk in two," I bark.

Sabrina pulls me from Jaycee's lap. "Let's leave the dishes for tomorrow and go watch a movie."

Two hours later, dishes still scatter the table, teeth are unbrushed, her bath is skipped, and homework is left incomplete. I whimper as someone rolls onto my hind leg. Kicking my way out of the covers that have gathered over our bodies, I land quietly on the floor. I wish I had a camera to take a picture of the sight before me. Jaycee's head rests softly on Sabrina's chest and her hand covers the side of her mother's cheek.

I'm still staring when Sabrina stirs, her gaze catching mine. She carefully slips away from our sleeping child. "You need to go out?"

I wag my tail.

A frigid freezing rain falls and I find myself taking care of business rather quickly. After a short check-in with Oakley, I stand at the back door and bark softly. Sabrina opens it and I keep her company in the kitchen while she cleans. Sadness radiates from her body as she moves around, dumping leftover food and washing dishes. I eagerly take the scraps she offers and try my best to stay out of her way. I fail miserably, of course, my desire to be close overriding practicality. She laughs and pats my head each time she almost trips over me and I feel like the distraction I provide keeps her from breaking down. It might be wishful thinking, I know, but when she heads to bed, she carries me with her. Bobbi lifts her head from her spot on Sabrina's pillow when the light flicks on in the bedroom. I dance around on the comforter while Sabrina slips her bra off and flings it toward the hamper. Desire courses through me as she slips off her jeans. Is it normal for me to feel passion for someone who isn't currently the same species? She flips the light off while I admire the view. Before I can rationalize my urges, Sabrina pulls the covers over my head. Okay, not tonight, I laugh to myself and scurry from the blanket to meet her on the sheet.

On her back, she reaches one hand over to pet Bobbi and another over to pet me. I freeze when she rolls to the side facing me. So many nights she'd done the opposite when we had gone to bed together. I joked on many occasions how the cat got more snuggles than I did. I curl in beside her and she wraps her arms around me. She places a quick kiss on the top of my head.

Chapter 19

The weeks turn into months, the snow melts, creating a soggy mess in what I can only guess is early April. Sabrina had taken me to the vet for my shots—I won't fall for that trick again (even though she got me with it three different times already)—and life somehow starts to feel normal for my family once more. At least from what I can tell. The tears for my absence became less of a nightly thing and are now triggered randomly. I've been doing my best to provide comfort when it happens and find I'm actually thankful they're getting along okay without me. Sabrina now manages the managers at the restaurant even though she still mostly keeps to herself in her crafting shed. I spend most days curled up at her feet, having proven I won't chew on any scraps of wood she doesn't hand me. The employees in the kitchen started a 'Huck plate' which consists of scraps that would otherwise be thrown away. Sabrina likes to tease them about fattening me up, but it doesn't stop them from tossing me a chicken tender that dropped to the floor. Kelley had been by a few times to check in and each time I had growled until Sabrina locked me in the bedroom.

Everyone is in the back yard picking up sticks after a storm the night before when Kelley's truck rumbles into the drive.

"Jason, remember to be nice," Oakley tells me when I drop the ball we'd been playing with. "He was your best friend."

"That was before he started making moves on my wife."

"We're back here," Sabrina calls.

"In all fairness," Oakley continues, "he didn't make a move while you were alive."

"Don't go being all technical." I race around the house to give Kelley another warning.

Seeing me, he produces a Kong ball. "I brought a peace offering." He shakes it near my nose. The smell of bacon grabs my attention. It's mixed with peanut butter. An odd combination, I think, but the prospect of bacon captivates me. He throws the ball and I chase after it, despite my desire to run him off.

"Thanks for coming," Sabrina says.

"Glad to help. I hope you don't mind if Amber drops the twins off here in a couple hours. She's getting her hair done."

"That'll be fine. I'm sure Jaycee will like the company."

I dig my tongue into the center of the ball, trying to pull a soft treat from the hole.

"Where's this limb you need cut up?" Kelley laughs, playing oblivious to the tree that's split in two ten feet to his left.

Sabrina chuckles. "I was going to try it myself, but I don't want to do anything stupid and end up cutting my leg off."

Kelley pulls work gloves from his back pocket, I notice, keeping a close eye on him in my peripheral vision. "I'm happy to help. I told you that." He nods to me as they pass. "Looks like my distraction technique worked."

"You may win him over yet."

"Don't count on it," I bark, carrying my toy toward them. "I'm watching you."

Kelley fires up the chainsaw and motions Sabrina away. I dart into Oakley's shed to avoid the deafening noise.

"When did chainsaws get so loud?"

Oakley pokes his head inside. "It's amazing how sensitive our hearing is now, isn't it?"

"I'd rather have opposable thumbs instead of supersonic eardrums." Oakley laughs and shakes a fly off his ear. "Do you ever get used to it?"

"It takes time."

"Still rather have thumbs."

Oakley scratches the ground with one hoof. "You can want in one hand—paw—" he switches hooves and scratches again. "—and poop in another and see which gets filled first."

"Still using that old line?"

"It's a classic."

Jaycee dashes through the shed, nearly crashing into Oakley on her way out the other side. I follow behind to see what's going on.

The sight of Sabrina watching Kelley stops me in my tracks.

"He knows how to run a chainsaw. You don't have to stand there and make sure he's doing it right," I yell, hoping to be heard over the noise.

She rushes to me as if I might decide I want a front row seat to the worst rock concert ever. "Do you want to go inside?"

I bolt away from her, heading for the branches on the ground. "Just because I'm a dog doesn't mean I can't pull my weight around here."

I clamp down and pull. Kelley pauses to watch before cutting away another section of the splintered trunk.

"Why is this so heavy?" I growl, frustrated again at my situation.

Sabrina yanks my collar, dragging me over to Jaycee. "Keep him out of the way until Kelley is done using the saw."

Half an hour later, Kelley shuts the chainsaw off and takes a seat on a log he'd created. "Where would you like these stacked?"

My ears perk as Sabrina joins him. "We can take care of that. You've already done enough."

"You can't move some of these. When they dry out, I'll come back and split them."

"I can't ask you to do that."

He removes his gloves and slaps them against his knee. "You're not asking. I'm telling you I'll do it."

"Really, Kelley, I can do it."

A car door slams in the driveway. I race to the front of the house with Jaycee chasing behind.

I hurry to sniff the newcomers. Thad and Cora, Amber and Kelley's eight-year-old twins, bend to pet me as the adults gather at the hood of Amber's car.

"His name is Huck," Jaycee boasts.

I sniff Cora's jeans. "I see you still have that Yorkie."

"We got a goldfish," Thad replies proudly.

Sabrina hugs Amber. "It's good to see you again."

"How're you doing?"

"Things are starting to get back to normal. I think."

"Good. We'll have to catch up sometime."

Sabrina nods.

Kelley lifts two bags from the back seat of her car. "What time should I have them home tomorrow?"

"Before dinner is fine."

Goodbyes are said and the kids race to the backyard.

With an increase in the number of kids, I have a hard time overhearing the conversation between Kelley and Sabrina as they stack wood in a pile near the shed.

"Watch this," Jaycee tells the twins, taking Oakley's ball to him.

He ignores it, preferring to nibble the fresh grass poking up.

"Come on, Oakley, they want a show," I urge. "Besides, I need something to keep my mind off Kelbrina."

He slowly lifts his head. "Kelbrina?"

I jump, landing in a firm stance an inch closer to him. "You really are an old man. You know, Kelley and Sabrina. You mash their names together into something ridiculous."

"I've told you before and I'll tell you again, Kelley doesn't stand a chance."

"I know that. But seeing him try makes me think about someone who *does* have a chance. And I'm not ready for her to be ready for that yet."

"He's only helping out. You're reading too much into it."

"Sure, he's only helping out...today. Tomorrow he's going to be asking her out. It's like when you take a baby home from the hospital. You know one day you'll watch their car leave the drive with all their stuff packed inside. It's gonna happen."

"Relax and enjoy the day."

I bark, letting out a frustrated huff of air. I don't know whether to focus my emotions on anger at my best friend or sadness that one day I really will be gone. "Throw the ball or I'm gonna bite your ankle."

"You wouldn't dare."

I pounce toward him again. "Remember that time I was standing on the dock and you said you would push me in if I didn't jump?"

Oakley grabs the ball and throws it. "I'm only doing this for the kids."

I chase the ball and lug it as far as I can manage, the kids racing after me. Thankfully, it's gotten a little lighter and less awkward to carry.

Thad and Cora work together to block me while Jaycee comes from the back to catch me.

My heart soars as we spend the afternoon playing. I finally tire out and slip under the deck to take a nap. When I wake, it's quiet except for a handful of birds calling to each other from the trees.

"They went inside for a snack," Oakley tells me.

"How am I supposed to keep an eye on them from out here?"

"Are you referring to the kids or the adults?"

I step up to a tree and empty my bladder. I'm slowly getting the hang of hiking my leg. "Very funny."

"You worry too much. It's going to be a long time before Sabrina is ready to move on. She's got a lot on her plate already."

Sabrina's soft laugh fills the air as the door opens and the budding couple emerges.

"Are you sure about that?"

I bound to them, circling Sabrina's feet, trying to read the expression on her face. There is no sign of the flirtatious smile she'd hooked me with so many years ago. Kelley picks up a few straggling sticks from the fallen tree and tosses them onto the burn pile. He'd positioned three stumps around it and they take a seat.

"I want to thank you again," Sabrina says, sipping from the glass of wine she'd carried out.

Kelley cracks his beer. "Jason would've done the same for Amber if the situation were reversed."

"But you're divorced." The words hold a hint of confusion.

"Don't mean anything. I helped Amber with a plumbing issue last weekend."

Sabrina nods. "It's good that you have a healthy relationship with Amber."

"It wouldn't do the kids any good to see us fighting. That's the reason we got divorced and I don't see how it would make sense to keep them in a broken home even after we split."

"I guess you're right."

"I'm happy to fill Jason's shoes until some man comes along and takes his place."

I snarl at Kelley as I move toward Sabrina.

"Huck, bad dog," she scolds.

"Tell him he's not taking my place," I snarl.

She bonks me on the head. "I appreciate that, but you should know I'm not looking to fill Jason's shoes any time soon."

I lift my head to lick her hand. "Tell him there's not a single man worthy of having you," I beg.

My words hit me in the gut. While I whole-heartedly agree with what I just said, I know I want Sabrina to be happy and, at some point, that's going to mean finding someone to love. Jealousy overtakes me and I saunter off to the shed to deal with my conflicting emotions.

Chapter 20

Summer passes in a blur of long strolls down our gravel road and endless games of tug-o-war followed by evenings sitting on the porch watching Jaycee play. Sabrina always built up a surplus of décor for the restaurant so she could take summers off to spend with Jaycee and this one was no different. I find myself caring less and less about what once nearly consumed me. How could I ever have been so blind to what was really important?

Kelley's visits become more frequent, an excuse for every occurrence. By Thanksgiving, he's bringing over a turkey he claims he doesn't know how to cook and for Christmas he suggests a meal at his place so I wasn't surprised when he showed up for New Year's Eve. I have a new strategy this time to fight the advances Kelley is making. I welcome him in like an old friend. Keep your friends close and your enemies closer, that's my new motto.

I follow Sabrina around the house, practically glued to her hip, as she vacuums and dusts on the morning of New Year's Eve. Kelley and his kids are expected by early evening.

"There's still time to call it off," I say, prancing along as she pulls the broom from the closet. "Tell him you're not feeling well."

"Blame it on Jaycee. Tell him she isn't ready," I suggest as she sweeps a load of my hair and dirt into the dustpan.

"Hell, tell him you've changed your mind," I offer as she reaches for the mop. "*Anybody* but Kelley."

"Huck, you're being extra...*extra* today. Why don't you go run off some of that energy with Oakley?" She swings the back door open and nearly kicks me outside.

I saunter over to my grandpa who makes his rounds along the perimeter. "She's really going to do it."

Oakley stops. "Do what?"

"Sabrina's going to have a date. With Kelley. In my house." He ambles on as if my words are nothing of consequence. "Well? Say something."

"Jason, it's been almost a year."

I lower myself to my haunches. "That doesn't make it any easier for me to sit back and watch. Put yourself in my shoes for a minute."

He comes to a stop by the swing set. "I know it's hard. I couldn't imagine having to watch your grandma with another man. But wouldn't it be better for her to date someone you know than a complete stranger?"

I silently consider his words. In theory, he's right, but Kelley is all wrong for her.

"Look at it this way," Oakley suggests. "You get to watch Jaycee grow up *and* make sure Sabrina ends up with a good guy."

I snort. "I don't see how I have any say in the matter."

"I've known more than one dog who ended relationships."

"Really?"

Oakley nods. "I know a guy who broke up with his girlfriend because her dog kept peeing on the floor during the night so he would step in it when he got out of bed in the morning. And I know another guy who said he briefly dated a woman who wouldn't let him sleep in her bed because that was where her dog slept. It was a teacup something-or-other."

I cock my head. "You're making this up."

"I don't remember the details, but you're smart, you can figure it out if she ends up with someone who isn't good for her or Jaycee."

I scratch my ear. "I suppose you're right."

He steps closer. "But you must let her move on, to try to be happy. Unless he treats her badly, you shouldn't interfere."

"Has anyone ever told you, you don't have to be right all the time?"

"Your grandma reminded me once or twice."

I laugh. "Right. Like you didn't learn all this good advice from her."

"And you can't tell a soul." He chuckles and turns to face the field behind us. "How about a game of ball?" Using his hind legs, he kicks the ball.

I remind myself that Kelley and I are old friends as I race to the door to give him and his twins a grand welcome.

Jaycee grabs Thad and Cora in the living room and whisks them away to the back of the house. I follow Kelley and Sabrina into the kitchen, positioning myself affectionately between them.

Kelley opens the refrigerator to deposit a bottle of sparkling juice for the kids. "How are things at Jaybird's?" He pulls out a beer and takes it to the table.

"To tell the truth, I've been forced to spend more time than I'd like inside the restaurant," Sabrina reveals.

Kelley's hand brushes my jacket that still hangs over the side of my chair. "Why is that?"

"We recently had to fire a waitress for stealing tips off other servers' tables."

Instantly beside her, I jump, landing my feet at her waist as she tries to move toward the sink. "You never told me that. Who was it? How much did she take?"

Sabrina shoves my nose downward until my paws hit the floor. "And I guess I just want to make sure everything is running smoothly. I feel like Jason would want that."

Kelley sips from a Busch Lite can and I wish I could still kid him about his choice in beer. "Don't you have a manager to do that for you?"

Sabrina stops peeling potatoes to smile at him. "If Jason were here, that's exactly what I'd ask him."

"But you think the rules are different for you?"

"It's just that, aside from Jaycee, the restaurant is all I have left of Jason. Sometimes—"

I perk my ears from the corner where I'm biding my time until she breaks out the good food.

"Sometimes what?" Kelley twists the can in his hands.

Sabrina shifts so that her back is to him. "Sometimes...I get lonely in my shop, that's all."

Kelley digs his fingertips into the scruff on his chin. "Sabrina, I've known you a long time and I've never known you to be lonely. Hell, Jason used to tell me how he'd practically have to bribe you to get you out of the house." He laughs and takes a long pull. "I remember the day he discovered how well using ice cream as bait worked. He acted like he'd cracked some ancient code."

I move to Sabrina's side to see her expression, although I'm not sure what to make of the small smile. "I guess I did tend to stick to the house when I wasn't in the shop. It's not because I don't like people though." Sabrina slides a baking dish into the oven. "I just got so used to hiding from everyone, I guess I became a recluse."

I want to bite the sympathetic look off Kelley's face, but I stick close to Sabrina instead.

"I hid from the pain, but Jason found comfort around people."

At this, Kelley nods slowly.

Bobbi strolls through the kitchen as if she owns the place, prancing underneath the table, weaving between Kelley's legs.

I dive at the two of them, snapping at her but catching Kelley's ankle.

"Ow!"

Sabrina spins to find me at his feet. "Huck! Come on, out you go!"

Chair legs screech on the floor as Kelley stands. "It wasn't his fault. The cat was there too. I think she must have swatted at him and he got me by mistake."

Sabrina stands between us. "Are you covering for him?"

Kelley scratches my head. "It was an accident."

I give his hand a lick and march down the hall to see what the kids are up to before Sabrina can make good on her threat to throw me out.

Jaycee and Cora replicate dance moves they've seen on something called *Tik Tok* and they look pretty ridiculous if you ask me. In true dad fashion, I get right in the middle of the action, acting as silly as possible. Thad thinks I'm hilarious, but the girls do not. They kick me out and shut the door. I stroll to the living room where Kelley and Sabrina lounge on the couch, waiting for supper to bake.

"So he's got this big 'ole gash on his leg from the bumper," Kelley says, wearing a smile that covers his entire face.

I roll my eyes. I've heard this one. More than once. I slide onto the couch, shoving my hind-end into Kelley's thigh. I cringe slightly as I nuzzle into him, but if I fall asleep with my head on his lap, he's unable to scoot closer to my wife. I settle in for another exaggerated retelling of the time Kelley sewed up our buddy Lance's leg after a night of drunken off-roading when we were all barely legal drinking age. The story is worse when Lance is around. He shows off the scar like a prized battle wound. I know Sabrina has heard the story from both parties, but she giggles as he recants it again. I close my eyes to drown them out. The smell of overcooked pork lifts me from my nap.

I yawn. "Would anyone care to know that dinner is burning?"

As I say the words, the hum of a remote-control car grabs my attention. It races across the tile with three sets of feet chasing after it. I leap down to chase it as it passes.

"It's like a mechanical bunny," I bark, hopping in its path.

"Huck!" Jaycee steers the car to the left. I jerk after it, only to be wrestled to the ground by Cora.

"No, no, no!" Sabrina's shriek stops everyone in their tracks. I hadn't even realized she'd gotten off the couch.

I wander into the kitchen, hoping to get a ruined meal. She displays a pork chop on a fork.

"I forgot to turn the burner on so now we have potatoes that aren't cooked and meat that's too done to eat."

Kelley places his hand on her shoulder. "I've had worse." This does little to remove the frustration from Sabrina's face. "Amber was a terrible cook."

Sabrina playfully taps his chest. "I've had her cooking. It was good."

He shakes his head. "You had carryout. From your restaurant."

Sabrina's eyes reveal the secret she'd known for years and they share a laugh.

"Do I get that or not?" I sit at her feet, patiently waiting.

Kelley plucks the chop from the fork and tosses it to me. "Oh, I'm sorry. I should've asked."

"Thanks," I tell him after nearly swallowing it whole. Even burnt it takes better than dog food.

Sabrina waves her hand. "Jaycee does it all the time." She places the remaining pork on a plate. "I'll cube them later and he can have them as treats."

"Let me," he says, taking the plate and grabbing a knife from the block.

"I've ruined dinner," Sabrina complains.

"Nonsense. Cook the potatoes, slap cheese slices over them and put it in the oven. We can top it with bacon bits."

I cock my head and notice Sabrina doing the same. "Bacon? Sounds good to me."

"We're not in college anymore," she says with a laugh.

Kelley chuckles. "And you're not exactly a bachelor cooking for one."

I turn at the sound of thumping against the floor and realize my tail is wagging. "Bacon?"

"Or frozen pizza works, too," Kelley suggests.

"Pizza is good," I yap.

Kelley reaches down and scratches my head. "We have one vote for pizza."

"They're in the freezer in the garage. I'll get them," Sabrina offers.

"I'll cube the meat while you do that."

The second she's out of the room, Kelley tosses me a chunk of burned pork.

I sit by his feet, smelling the dog poop he stepped in roughly three days ago and gobbling as many treats as he can offer before the garage door opens again.

With less than an hour to go before the new year, the children take up a computer game. Finding it as boring as I would've as a human, I slink into the living room. I want to be there when the ball drops.

Kelley hands Sabrina a glass of wine and opens his beer. "Did you make a resolution?"

"They're overrated."

"I always make one regarding the kids. A few years ago, I vowed to read more bedtime stories. That was before Amber and I split. Last year I made an effort to have a better relationship with her so the kids wouldn't continue to deal with the fighting we put them through before we divorced."

Sabrina nearly beams. "I like that idea. So what about this year?"

He takes a sip and laughs. "I think I'm going to learn how to cook."

"I have a position open at the restaurant."

At this, I'm on her lap. "Did you finally have enough of Tommy's shit? Or maybe it was the new guy on days...tell me what happened."

Kelley laughs and kicks his feet up on the coffee table. "I think I'll just look on YouTube or what's that one you women are always raving about?"

"I can send you some simple recipes if you like."

"That would be nice." He places his beer on a coaster. "You never told me about your resolution."

Sabrina glances at the clock. "Kids," she hollers. "It's almost midnight!"

"We're in the middle of a round," Jaycee screams back.

"You're going to miss the ball drop," Kelley yells.

"It's okay; we'll drop a ball later," Thad returns.

Kelley and Sabrina laugh, standing to watch as the countdown begins.

"Don't you get any ideas about kissing," I order, jumping on Sabrina.

"Five...four...three..." They turn awkwardly toward each other. "Two...Happy New Year!"

Auld Lang Syne plays in the background as Kelley and Sabrina hesitate to move. Kelley gingerly leans over and pecks Sabrina's cheek.

Her hand softly rubs where his lips touched and she leads him back to the couch. "Kelley, I—"

"I'm sorry if I was out of line."

She shakes her head. "Not at all. It's just that you were Jason's friend and it's a little weird. I thought I could get over it. I know you've been wanting this for a while and, I'm not gonna lie, I invited you here thinking it would be an easy way to dip my toe in the water, but now I don't know. I think it's me, not you. Oh man, that's cliché. I mean, I don't know what I'm ready for and I honestly don't know if I could date you. I'm sorry if I led you on."

I slide to the corner of the room where I don't have to see the embarrassment on either of their faces.

"Listen, Sabrina, it's totally fine. If one of the guys started dating Amber, I think I'd be a little weirded out, so I get where you're coming from. I'd like to think, in time, it won't be so weird. And, if you're willing, I'm okay with waiting until you are ready. Even if you never are, that's okay too. I just want you to be happy. Jason would've wanted me to look out for you, so I'm taking it upon myself to see that you don't become a spinster."

Sabrina's laughs echoes into the hall. "I want you to do me a favor, Kelley."

"Name it."

"If a nice girl comes along and grabs your attention, go after her with everything you have. Don't waste an opportunity because you're waiting for me to come out of the dark cloak I've wrapped myself in."

"On the condition that you do me a favor," he says.

"What's that?"

"Take off the cloak. You are beautiful inside and out and the world deserves to see it."

I jump to my feet to step between them. "Okay, pal, you heard what she said a minute ago. Stop trying to wear her down with all that gushy romantic talk."

"I think your dog is telling me it's time to go. Maybe I should've filled my pockets with burnt pork," Kelley says with a chuckle.

Sabrina taps my nose. "Huck, be nice."

"Kids," Kelley calls. "Huck says it's past bedtime and we need to go home."

Chapter 21

The anniversary of my death comes with a solid reminder that I still have work to do. Instead of curling up on the couch for another *Friends* rerun after tucking Jaycee in bed, Sabrina slinks to the kitchen. Her hand lingers over the jacket I'd left hanging on the chair. With a heavy sigh, she lifts it gently and brings it to her nose. A tear slips down her cheek as she slips it on and heads to our room. I follow behind, curious about her unusual activity. She pulls out a box of pictures from the back of the closet and surrounds herself in them on the floor. I lie just outside her circle, watching. She plucks one up and studies it a minute, a smile growing on her face. Before long, her lap is covered in memories. Sadness pours out of her despite the happiness she shows when touching the images. A tear trickles down her cheek as she proudly shows me a picture of the three of us in front of the tree on our last Christmas together. She tells me stories about several photos, showing them to me. The most recent ones pain me the most. I know I should be in them, but I'd gained a tail by then.

Her trip down memory lane lasts well into the night before she gathers the pictures and stacks them back into the box. She shrugs off the shirt and folds it neatly on top of the box.

"I'll never be able to move on with my life if I don't take the first step," she says, fiddling with her wedding ring.

I whimper at her feet, afraid of what she's about to do.

She slowly crawls into bed and waits for me to get comfortable beside her.

"Tomorrow we start a new chapter," she whispers.

With a shaky hand, she removes the ring and places it on the nightstand. Her arms clutch around me as the tears pour out.

"One last pity party," she sobs.

I lick the salty droplets from her face and curl into her. "I never should've taken you for granted. From now on, my only job is making sure you and Jaycee are happy."

My heart aches at her pain and the realization that I'll do my part to make her happy, even if that means letting someone else love her.

The first half of the year passes quietly. I'm pleased to see Sabrina's smile has returned with almost the same zest it once held. Life is as perfect as it can be with me being a dog. I get daily restaurant reports from Lauren when she talks to Sabrina before each shift. Sabrina and I spend the evenings curled up on the couch watching Netflix and Jaycee takes me everywhere she goes where dogs are allowed. Oakley and I enjoy quiet mornings together and Bobbi has resorted to making herself scarce when I'm around. And, to top it all off, I haven't been pressured to hold up my end of the return-from-Heaven bargain. Kelley still drops by about once a month, but I no longer fear his intentions. By the time the holidays roll around again, he's reconciled with Amber after her parents have moved to Florida.

I almost relax on the whole issue of finding Sabrina a new husband when the second anniversary of my death rolls around. So when Candace calls out of the blue, I'm caught completely off guard.

"I'm getting married," she shrieks into Sabrina's ear.

"That's great." My wife's voice sounds joyful to the untrained ear, but I know her better. Sadness hides in her words.

I take my place by her side and lick her hand. "It's her third marriage," I remind her.

Candace married right out of high school, divorced two years later, and married her second husband the same year Sabrina and I married. They divorced within six months. Candace was convinced every guy she dated was her 'soul mate' though she couldn't seem to stick with any one guy to watch two consecutive Olympic games. Without having to be told, I feel certain the groom isn't the same person we saw her with last winter.

"I'd like you to be a bridesmaid," Candace tells her.

"I'd be honored."

"Mike's brother is single," she says after babbling on about arrangements and venues for a good twenty minutes.

Sabrina places a brush in a bowl of water and cocks her head. "Mike?"

"My fiancé, silly."

I lie down in front of Sabrina, not wanting to miss any of this show.

Sabrina swirls her brush. "I thought you were talking about Vance."

Candace giggles. "No, no. Vance is long gone. I met Mike a few months ago and the sparks just flew."

"Here we go," I tell Sabrina, following her to the table where her recently finished work dries. "It was love at first sight," I mock.

"We've been inseparable ever since. I can't wait for you to meet him."

"When's the wedding?"

"A month from today."

"Oh." There is no hiding the surprise in her voice.

"I'm sending you an itinerary. This weekend we need to pick out dresses—I hope you don't have anything planned—and in two weeks we're doing the bachelorette party. Please tell me you're free."

Sabrina sighs, shuffling supplies around on her desk. "Candace, I literally split my time between home and the restaurant. Jaycee isn't doing any activities."

I hang my head at the reminder that my daughter had quit dance after my death and refused to take up anything new.

"Maybe we can change that. Mike's brother is recently divorced," Candace chirps.

"Jaycee isn't old enough to date."

Candace laughs. "Obviously. I meant for you."

"I'm not looking to be fixed up, especially not with someone who is on the rebound."

"We'll see," Candace smugly responds. "I'm sending you the dates now. See you Saturday."

I spend most of my evening sleeping and chasing Bobbi into hiding. When the key jiggles in the lock, I race to the front door. Sabrina had gone to Candace's bachelorette party and Jaycee was spending the night with Kelley and Amber. Anxious about her being out with Candace—thanks to the forewarning that she'd 'swipe right' after a night out—I bolt to her. My feet skid to a halt upon seeing an unfamiliar man handing Sabrina her keys.

I sniff his ankles, then his hand. "Who are you? What are you doing here? Get your hands off my wife," I order.

He steadies Sabrina as she sways in the doorway. "Hey, doggie."

I sneeze into his hand. "Doggie? Seriously?"

"Thanks for bringing me home, Steve," Sabrina says.

I look up at Steve. "You can go now."

"Would you like me to get you a glass of water or something?"

Sabrina shakes her head. "I'm good. You can go."

I lick her hand, my eyes fixated on the man next to her. "What she said."

"Let me at least help you to the couch or something," he offers.

I step between them. "I know what you're thinking."

Sabrina nods. I guard the bedroom door while he guides her to the couch.

"Lock the door behind you," she says after he deposits her on the sofa.

"Sure thing. Are you sure I can't get you some water?"

"Cabinet to the left of the sink," she offers and he returns a minute later with a glass. "Thanks."

"No problem."

I follow him back to the door to ensure he locks it and leap onto the couch beside Sabrina.

She groans. "I'm so happy to be back here with my favorite guy," she whispers, patting my head. "What a joke."

I cock my head. "Me?"

"When Candace wasn't going on and on about how lucky she was to find Lance...Vance...Mike. I think his name is Mike this time. Anyway, she decided she was going to fix me up. Made it her personal mission."

I nuzzle next to her. "I never really liked Candace."

Sabrina's laugh echoes into the room. "That was Steve." She waves her hand toward the front door. "He's the brother. Vance, no—Mike's—brother. He was so conveniently there to watch the band his buddy plays drums for."

"Nice."

She taps a finger to my nose. "But I think he was there because Candace's new fiancé has heard how loosey-goosey she is. Perhaps he figured I was the same." She laughs again. "Look at me, I've turned into a ninety-year-old church lady. Good grief. Maybe I do need to get out more. Do you think it's time?"

I lift my head and slather a slobbery kiss on her cheek. "Time for bed. This will all look better in the morning. You're sad for what you don't have. I get that, but it's important to remember what you *do* have."

"Anyway, luckily, I already knew Steve. I wouldn't let a stranger drive me home." Her head falls back against the couch. I jump when she snaps her fingers. "He has a son in Jaycee's class and I'd met him on that field trip I chaperoned last year."

"That should make the next school outing a hoot."

"Oh no," she cries. "I just remembered Candace insisted I sign up for a dating app. I told some guy I would love to have a drink. I think we're supposed to meet for lunch on Wednesday."

I nuzzle my nose into her abdomen. "It's okay, tomorrow you'll delete the app. Don't worry about it."

She grabs my ears and pulls them out like wings. "I should cancel, right? But what if he's a nice guy?"

"I'll get you a date if that's what you want," I offer, my heart heavy at the thought.

Her soft snoring ends the conversation. I lie my head on her lap and close my eyes, though I don't know if I'll get any sleep. My wife appears to be ready to move on and I don't know how I'm going to handle that.

The day before the wedding, Sabrina wipes away secret tears, not that Jaycee would notice. She's too busy trying on outfits and playing with her hair. I mope around the house next to Sabrina, wondering how the air is filled with emptiness. I had done my best to bring love to my family, and yet, palpable sadness consumes my wife. On a trip outside, Oakley had told me the time was drawing near for Sabrina to start dating and reminded me again of my pact with God. As much as I want to hold on to the notion that things can stay as they are, I know they are coming to an end.

Chapter 22

I think the ordeal with Candace scared Sabrina away from dating even more and yet another year passes before she broaches the thought again. It starts when Lauren asks her to double date because she's anxious about her personal life after acquiring her nieces. Sabrina quietly arranges for Jaycee to stay the night with Kelley and Amber and agrees to help Lauren out.

I pace nervously around the house while she's gone, anxious she'll soon be bringing someone home. Bobbi gloats about the prospect, talking nearly nonstop about what he might be like. We're both disappointed when Sabrina returns. Bobbi hates that there won't be a second date while I am despondent over what happens next.

Sabrina dives into a series of first dates, all taking place during school hours where I am forced to stay in her shop for an hour, usually about twice a week, while she meets someone for lunch. It's painful that she seems to be looking so hard even though she tries even harder to find excuses to avoid a second date. She keeps Jaycee out of the loop and I assume that's the same reason for stalling the process of moving on. Of course I hope I have something to do with it, but I remember I have a job to do. I still don't know how I'm supposed to help her find a husband when I'm locked in here, but I'm keeping my eye open for opportunity. Nearly a year later, I see my chance to get her a second date.

I perk my ears and turn toward the door of Sabrina's shop before the knock interrupts her.

"Levi says he needs to discuss something with you," Lauren announces. "It's a scheduling issue and I told him I'd pass the message along, but he insists."

She glances up from her table. "It's fine. I'll be right there."

"Sorry to bother you. I can send him up here if you like."

Her ponytail bobs as she shakes her head. "It's a nice day and I've been cooped up in here far too long. Come on, Huck. You probably need to pee anyway."

The three of us head toward the restaurant. Levi stands beside the Jackson Food Services box truck. Lauren keeps walking and Sabrina slows to a casual stroll, watching me dart off to water a nearby tree.

"Hi," he says. "Hope I'm not disturbing you."

Sabrina wipes her hands on paint splattered jeans. "Not at all. Had to take the dog out anyway."

"Good. There's been an increase in some prices. I left a sheet with Lauren but I wanted to let you know." His gaze travels to the back of the building. "And, also, that I really enjoyed bumping into you the other day. I was wondering if you might want to go out for dinner sometime...you know, intentionally."

Sabrina bites her lip. "Oh."

I race to Sabrina's side, seeing an opportunity.

He fiddles with a clipboard in his hands. "If you need more time, I totally understand."

She tucks a stray whisp of hair behind her ear. "I'll have to check my schedule."

I groan, staring up at her. That line has always been her go-to for escaping commitments.

He shuffles his feet. "Of course. You have my number."

She nods. "I'll get back to you."

I sit on her feet. "At some point you'll have to break down and give someone a second date." I yawn loudly. "I don't mind if you want to wait a decade or so, though."

He smiles, climbing in his truck like a deflated balloon. Suddenly I'm hit with the reminder of how I felt all those years ago when Sabrina had pulled the same crappy line on me. Now I'm rooting for the man. He deserves a little help.

When Sabrina turns and starts back toward her shop, I take three steps and plant myself in front of his truck. There's no way he can get through unless I move.

Levi rolls down his window. "Sabrina, I seem to have a roadblock."

"Huck." She pats her hand onto her thigh.

"Give him a chance," I tell her.

I refuse to budge even when Levi lays on his horn.

Sabrina returns to my side, yanking my collar in her direction.

I dig in my heels. "Not until you agree to a date."

Levi steps out of the cab. "I wonder what his problem is."

Sabrina shakes her head. "I have no idea. He never acts like this."

I open my mouth and take her hand. She allows me to lead her closer to Levi.

Levi scratches his hand. "What's he doing?"

Releasing her hand, I trot to Levi and pull on his khaki trousers. He clumsily steps to Sabrina. Poised between them, I stare from one to the other.

Levi pats my head. "I've got deliveries to make, Huck. Would you mind letting me pass?"

Sabrina squats and her arms encircle my body. When she stands, I'm pressed against her chest.

"If you drop me, I'm going to make you feel bad for an entire year. I'll walk with a limp and you'll have to tell people you broke me," I threaten.

Levi places his hands on his hips, amused. "You got him?"

"Yep," Sabrina breathes.

She takes a tentative step, then another until we're safely closed inside the paint-fumigated room.

"That wasn't very nice," she scolds.

"I don't understand why you won't go out with him. We've known him since we started the restaurant. He's a good guy."

Returning to her work, she smiles at some thought known only to her. Reaching for her phone, she pauses her finger over the screen and sets it down. "Levi and I bumped into each other at the coffee shop a few weeks ago. Somehow, we ended up not taking our coffee to go and visited before work. It was nice."

She raises the sign she's working on and turns to me. "What color do you think this should be?"

I slowly open my mouth in a wide yawn. "You know I have limited color vision, right?"

She nods as if I provided a useful answer. "I was thinking green as well."

My eyelids droop as she pulls a brush from a can. When it tings against the tin again, I slowly stretch and stand.

She displays the work as if I hadn't seen the same thing a dozen times—a *P* in the middle of a circle with vines twisted around it. The letters vary but it's a popular creation.

Biting her lip, she places it on a separate table to dry. Glancing at the clock, I realize it's time to clean up. Jaycee freaks out if Sabrina isn't home when she gets off the bus. We'd learned that the hard way late last spring. A train held us up and we found Jaycee crying hysterically on the porch. She thought Sabrina had been in an accident and wasn't coming home. From then on, Sabrina allowed extra time for travel.

She reaches for her phone again. "I'm thinking about calling him." I wag my tail for encouragement. "Should I?"

"Do it," I bark.

She nods. "What can one dinner hurt?" She scratches my ears. "This is going to be our secret. I'll arrange a sleepover somewhere for Jaycee."

Chapter 23

Sabrina quietly closes the truck door in the dark driveway. It had started raining an hour ago and she quickly darts up the walk while I watch from the window. Her key enters the lock.

"You're back earlier than I expected," I whisper while waiting impatiently for the door to open.

She shakes her coat off and slips her shoes off on the rug. "Hey, Huck. Man am I glad to see you."

I sniff her ankles, working my way up her calves. "You went to Bud's BBQ? I know we don't have many options, but he could've at least taken you to Burlington."

"No, I didn't see any other dogs," she says, stroking my head.

I stick close to her as she slinks into the bedroom. "Tell me about your date."

The zipper to her sleek red dress slides down to her waist. "What a waste of three hours. I could've spent the evening finishing my book."

My tongue hangs as she stands nearly naked in front of the mirror, grabbing pajamas from a drawer. I wonder if I'm drooling and it dawns on me this is exactly how I felt every time I saw Sabrina in this state of dress when I was able to reach out and caress her curves. They haven't changed much in nearly fifteen years, I notice, admiring the extra pounds she put on after her hysterectomy. She'd hated the extra weight, of course, and finally gave up the fight on losing them shortly after I grew a tail.

Grabbing the remote, she plops onto the couch and pats the seat beside her. A small laugh slips through her lips. "I wish Jason were here. He would *not* believe what I found out about Levi. We've known him since we opened Jaybird's and I never would've guessed he's a hardcore gamer. What'd he call it? There's a name for whatever it is he does." She shakes her head in confusion.

Bobbi appears from behind the couch and plops onto Sabrina's lap. "How was the date?"

"I'd rather bring the stinking donkey in the house than go on another date. From now on, I'm hanging out with my kid and my pets," she says, placing a hand on each of our heads.

"Ditch the two asses and it sounds like a good time," Bobbi purrs.

"Is that supposed to upset me?" I place my head on Sabrina's lap, shooting an annoyed glare at the cat. "Can you turn that off?"

She purrs louder. "And not irritate you? Not a chance."

"I can't think with all that racket so close to my head."

"Nobody said you had to be on the couch."

"Come on, stop it. We have to figure out how to get her to date again."

She licks her paw and scrapes it across the back of her head. "Leave it to me."

"How are you going to fit that into your sleep schedule?"

"You have no idea what I do all day."

I yawn, stretching my tongue out. "I know you don't want her to end up alone."

She flexes her claws. "No, but I don't want her to bring home some guy like you."

Sabrina giggles at a couple on TV.

"Well, it's my job to make sure she picks out the right one," I boast. "That's why I'm here. God said so." I feel childish at my words, but important, nonetheless.

"He wouldn't send a man to do a woman's job. Better let me handle it."

"Not a chance."

"Then I'm going to help. I don't want her ending up with another person who doesn't value her."

"This is *my* job. I can't afford to screw up this time."

"I won't let you."

I yawn and turn my attention to the television, pretending to be interested in the rom-com Sabrina is invested in. My eyelids droop out of boredom and the next thing I know Sabrina is trying to slip off the couch without disturbing my nap. I lazily lob off the couch and follow her into the bedroom.

She crawls into bed and pats the pillow beside her. Her gaze travels to the ceiling. "Jason, if you're up there watching, I could really use a sign regarding this whole dating thing. I'm not sure I'm ready and I'd really like to know that I have your approval."

I lick her hand. "Let's work on that together."

Chapter 24

Somehow, we make it to Jaycee's fifteenth birthday in the blink of an eye. It seems like we just celebrated twelve. As the candles burn atop her cake, I study the changes in my daughter since I came to her as a dog. She's grown more than a foot and the freckles on her cheeks have quadrupled in numbers. Her hair has gone from long to short and back again. Her style in clothing has matured as well, not that I approve of the drab colors she now chooses. And her demeanor reminds me of Sabrina during what we jokingly referred to as 'the dark years'—the time we spent grieving over lost babies and praying for a family. She's depressed to the point that Sabrina considers counseling. As she blows out the candles, I silently wish for her to have a life-changing year.

Jaycee isn't the only one whose appearance changed. My wife has gained a few wrinkles, not that I would ever mention that to her, and I even spotted a few gray hairs when we were snuggled in bed the other night.

The kitchen is full of family and friends and the noise is almost more than I can bear. But I don't want to miss a second of the action. I bounce around the room, grabbing the occasional head pat and stroke down my back, but when a curious toddler pulls my tail, I slink off to the quiet of my bedroom for a nap.

"Oh, great," I mutter upon seeing Bobbi curled up on my pillow.

Her eyes flicker open and shut at my arrival. I leap up and take a spot at the foot of the bed. When I close my eyes for a nap, the image of Jaycee's sad face fills my mind. I stand, circle, and flop down again.

"Would you get comfortable already," Bobbi complains when I move positions for the third time.

"I can't help it. You should've seen her face. She's so...sad."

"Sabrina's fine. Birthdays just make her weepy. She'll spend all evening crying because there will never be another fifteenth birthday. Remember how upset she was on Jaycee's fifth birthday?"

I pause at the memory. Sabrina cried the entire week leading up to it. By then we knew we'd only get to celebrate one child's birthday every year. I tried to make her see the bright side—that we'd been blessed with a child at all—but it did little good. She also cried at the end of each season while she was putting clothes away, knowing they would never be passed down to a sibling. It was a time I dreaded. I dig a tiny ball of mud from my paw. "Not Sabrina. Jaycee. Why is she so sad all the time?"

"She's a teenager."

I run my tongue against my teeth to remove a muddy clump. "I think it's more than that. You were a teenage girl once; what's it like?"

Bobbi slowly rises to her feet and stretches. "She's going through a rough patch, but she'll come out on the other side."

"When will it be over?"

"It's hard to say. She's been through so much already."

"I want to help."

She strolls by me, flicking her tail. "You can't do that by avoiding her like you have been. Don't think I haven't noticed."

I sit to scratch with my hind leg. "How on earth do you even know what's going on? You only come out of hiding at night when all the chaos is gone." I snort as she leaps off the bed. She's right though. I have kept my distance from her. "She's always shoving me to the side or slamming doors in my face. It's difficult, but don't you dare act like I don't try."

"You're giving up too easily, Jason."

I stare into her yellow eyes for a long minute, knowing the next words out of my mouth might be as dangerous as drawing a gun in an old west duel. "What should I do?"

Bobbi extends her claws and retracts them several times before turning to me with an almost evil smirk that softens just before she answers. "Keep trying. And don't take 'no' for an answer."

"Do you think it will work?"

She slips underneath the bed, her voice nearly a whisper when she replies. "It has to. I know you can get through to her."

I cock my head. "How do you know?"

"Because I know why she's sad and angry," she says softly as if she's nearly asleep.

My ears perk. "Why?"

"She wants her daddy. You've got this, Huck."

"Thanks, Audra."

The noise level finally drops to a normal level—which isn't exactly 'Quiet Time' at Church Camp—and Sabrina takes a seat beside me on the bed.

"Did the party wear you out too, Huck?" I raise my head and lick her hand. "I think Jaycee had an okay time. I just wish I knew how to bring back the girl she buried beneath all that hostility."

"I know I haven't been doing my part," I tell her. "But that's going to change."

I follow her into the kitchen where it appears a streamer tornado has blown through.

Forgotten balloons litter the floor and I see no better way to share my joy than by popping the suckers. Jaycee jumps as the first one bursts beneath my teeth. She shoots me a dirty look when I chase after the second. By the third, she's heading for the knife block. The flimsy shred of latex clings to my tongue as I race to the closest one before Jaycee reaches it. She beats me to it, kicking it away to stab with a large knife.

"Fine, be a buzz kill," I grumble, pawing at the plastic flake on my tongue.

Sabrina swings the back door open. "How about a potty break?"

I barrel through the opening, a gray streamer tagging along on my back paw.

Oakley gallops toward me. "Bring me a party favor?"

I sit to tug the thing off. "When did they start making these things so dull?" The thin paper sticks to the roof of my mouth and I shove my tongue out to discard it the way Jaycee did the first time she tasted peas nearly fourteen and a half years ago.

"In case you've forgotten, we don't see colors the same way we used to. It's one of the things I miss most."

I pluck the final remnants off my fur. "I feel like I've been a dog longer than I was a person. I know it's not possible because Jaycee just turned fifteen, but it seems like I've been on four legs for decades."

He laughs. "In dog years, you have."

A fly lands on my nose as I consider this. "I'm middle-aged again."

"I guess you're too old for a game of ball," Oakley challenges.

"Not a chance."

We race toward the toy. I reach it first and start a game of keep away.

"This isn't fishing, but it's a hell of a way to pass time," I say, setting it down to wait for Oakley to get close enough before I snatch it away again.

He trots lazily after me. "It's not about what you're doing."

"It's about who you're with," I finish for him, this time giving him some distance so he can kick the ball.

"That's right."

I chase after it. "How do we get Sabrina to the lake? You know what I would give to smell the air there?"

"You know your sense of smell is far greater now. Imagine the fish guts."

Forgetting the ball, I lie down and dream out loud. "Imagine the plunk of the lure hitting the water...the screech of the reel as it winds the line back in...maybe a purring Evinrude...and, most importantly, the plop of the fish as it breaks the surface."

"Stop it. You're depressing an old man."

The fly buzzes around my head and lands on my ear. I flick my head and snap. "I'm gonna get that stupid fly."

"Wouldn't get you if you were moving."

Oakley positions himself in front of the ball and kicks it directly at my head. I dart out of the way just in time.

"So that's how we're playing now," I mutter through clenched teeth.

"Just teaching an old dog new tricks."

"Know any for dealing with teenagers?"

"Take her fishing. I solved many a problem with a line in the water."

I drop the ball. "Always was hard to get your mind off fish."

"I don't see the problem."

"Won't work in this situation."

"Find something she can't turn down."

"How am I supposed to do that?"

The back door creaks halfway open, the smell of pizza topped with pepperoni and sausage lingers, though I know there will only be scraps remaining. "Huck!"

My tail wags at the mention of my name.

"Hope they saved you a slice of pizza," Oakley calls as I race to Sabrina.

"Keep thinking about how I can help Jaycee," I yell, putting distance between us.

Looking around, I'm amazed to find the mess gone. Had I been outside that long? Another damn fly buzzes my head as I turn from the living room doorway. Bobbi is there somewhere and I'm in no mood to deal with her. I snap at the fly, missing miserably. Thankfully, the statistics on dogs catching them are low—I think—or I might be embarrassed.

"Sometimes if you slow down and listen, you'll learn something valuable." The voice is soft, as if coming from the house itself.

I spin in a circle. The fly buzzes inches from my nose. I snap again. And miss again.

"Don't ask a question if you aren't prepared for the answer."

I spin again, searching high and low for the source. "Where are you?"

"I am here. Settle yourself so I may speak to you." Instantly understanding, I sit, ready to listen. The fly lands on my nose. "I have been trying to get your attention all evening," he says.

Feeling foolish, I bow my head. "I didn't know it was you."

"That is what happens when you stray. My voice floats away on the wind because you do not recognize it. I am still here for you, Jason."

He drops to the floor and I crouch, waiting for his words.

"You're forgetting what I told you that day at the lake," the fly says.

The lake?

He continues as if I had spoken the words aloud. "I told you things would change when Jaycee picked up soccer."

I tilt my head. Oh yes, the day I died and begged to be sent back. He *had* mentioned soccer.

"I'm not sure I understand."

"Follow me." His tiny wings buzz across the room and he lands on a black and white ball. "Do you see now?"

"I think I'm starting to. But how do I—"

"You know your daughter, Jason. I know you can do it."

"I'll need your help," I admit.

"I'll always answer when you call," he says and is suddenly gone.

What am I supposed to do now? The ball is still in a box.

"A little help here," I say, gritting my teeth against the cardboard. I rip tiny pieces from the package. "Can you take this to Jaycee's room for me?"

Jaycee, having come out of her room, rolls her eyes.

"I hate to be rude—" I try to fit the ball into my mouth. "—but this is what's going to change your life." I bark at the ball. "I don't know how I'm going to pull this off."

Jaycee picks it up in what's left of the box. Leaping wildly, I follow her as she takes it to her room. I crouch in a playful position, urging Jaycee to open the package. She does, but instead of playing, she tosses it to the back of her closet and slams the door.

And that's where the ball stays the entire summer. I grumble to Oakley until he's sick of hearing about it. He urges me to pray then insists I wait for the answer. When I complain about the response time, he lectures me about patience.

I race across yellowing grass one afternoon, irritated by being left outside in the scorching heat.

"It's got to rain soon," Oakley comments, searching for a fresh patch of greenery to munch.

The yard is covered in tiny bare spots from his snacks, but I pay little attention to him or the concrete dirt. Today is the day I'm finally going to find what creature Jesus is camouflaged as. I know He's around here somewhere. I've been looking for weeks, but He refuses to show himself. Sniffing around the shed, I scope out every insect I can find. None of them are talkative so I move on to the woodpile. Beneath a pile of last year's leaves, I sniff out a shrew.

"How do I get Jaycee to pick up the soccer ball?" I dig ferociously, trying to force an answer from something that only screams in response.

"Jaybird, you've got to quit this and wait until the time is right," Oakley says, coming to investigate the small hole I'd dug.

"He has to be here somewhere," I growl.

A sparrow flutters overhead. I chase after it, calling for it to stop. Skidding to a halt as it climbs high into the sky, I slowly inhale a new scent.

"Jaybird, no! Leave that one alone," Oakley shouts, frozen where I left him. I inch my way to the bush Sabrina and I planted the year we moved in. Somewhere in there is an animal. I crouch and crawl my way inside. "Huck!"

Two beady eyes stare back at me. With one final step, my eyes bulge. "Well, shit," I mutter, coming face-to-face with a skunk. "I suppose you aren't going to tell me how to get Jaycee to play soccer."

I shimmy backward, a quick prayer rolling off my tongue. The skunk scampers away.

I turn my eyes upward. "I'm not even going to complain that you answered *that* prayer."

Oakley laughs, plopping down on the grass. "Dogs are supposed to have good noses."

I charge toward him. "I didn't think it was a *real* skunk."

"You thought divine intervention would come in the form of a skunk?"

I roll on to my back. "I dunno. Maybe. I just don't know how to get Jaycee on the path she's supposed to be on."

"You can't stop God's will."

I roll back over. "See, that's where it doesn't make sense. Soccer is supposed to change Jaycee's life and He told me I am supposed to pick out Sabrina's next husband but how am I supposed to do that if I can't—"

"Relax. You're here to enjoy the ride. When it's time for action, you'll know."

"How?"

"Watch for the signs. You might have to wait for Jaycee to clean her room and realize she's got a ball she's never played with. Or maybe Sabrina can't help but smile when someone's name comes up, then you'll know to nudge them together."

I sit to scratch my shoulder. "You act like I'll actually have the power to do that."

"You'll find a way."

"What I'm hearing is that the mystery man is like a bottle of cheap whiskey and Sabrina is the teenage kid—I'm the older brother who hooks the two together."

Oakley cocks his head. "Weird analogy."

"And it still doesn't tell me how to do it."

"It's like fishing. Right now, your girls are too afraid to put the worm on the hook. If you're patient enough, they'll get over their fears and throw the line out. Then all you have to do is watch for the bopper to go down."

I spring to my feet. "Why didn't you say that in the first place?"

He shakes his head. "I thought I did."

"So basically, I'm just taking the fish off the hook?"

"No," he snorts. "You're the net. You make sure the fish gets in the boat. They can take it from there."

"I don't like this analogy anymore."

"Jaybird, you don't have much of a choice."

"I hate it when you're right."

He shakes a fly from the tip of his ear. "Make sure you don't drop the net this time," he teases.

I paw at his hoof. "One time. I did that *one* time."

"Yeah. You did that the one time I took you out before church."

I roll my eyes, knowing a story is coming. "Here we go."

"You fell overboard...in your Sunday clothes," he adds. "I thought your mom and grandma were going to fillet us both."

I laugh. "Grandma was mad because we had slipped out the back door while she helped Mom fix the heel on her shoe."

His neck stretches taut until his mouth is next to my ear. "Wanna hear a secret? I think your mom broke her heel on purpose."

I blow a puff of air through my nose and pull into a seated position. "What?"

Oakley nods. "Don't you remember how you'd gone out the day before and caught all those nightcrawlers? Plus, you stood in front of the TV and commented about how the weather would be perfect right smack dab in the middle of church? You talked for half an hour about what spots the fish would be at—and you were correct. After you went to bed, I was interrogated, but I confirmed you were right on the money. I don't think your mom could take that away from you."

"But she was mad," I note.

"Not really. She was pretending so Gramma didn't lecture her."

I laugh. "What were you going to do if I hadn't fallen overboard?"

"Push you in myself, I reckon," he chuckles.

I curl into the side of him. "Remember how you told them both we didn't really miss church because you told the story of Jesus feeding the five thousand?"

"I remember." He tucks his head around me. "I don't know if I've ever told you this or not, but you're only given so many perfect days, and that was one of them."

"I can still hear Gramma chewing us out," I say, a smile plastered to my face.

"It was worth it."

I blink heavily. "I miss those days."

"I miss talking about those days."

Lifting my head, I crane my neck to look him in the eye. "Remember how we used to sneak into the kitchen after Mom and Gramma were asleep? I wish we could do that again."

"Sabrina will kill us both if she finds us sitting at the table eating the last of the chocolate cake."

A memory flashes through my brain of the time he and I were caught doing that after Gramma's 70th birthday party. Mom had switched on the light, gotten a glass of water, and left the room as if she hadn't seen a thing. The next morning, he told Gramma raccoons raided the kitchen. Gramma's only comment was, 'It's funny that coons are capable of unlocking doors and using forks but not able to load dishwashers.'

"I could spend the night out here with you," I suggest.

"Don't you want to be inside with your wife?"

"Just a night or two, for old time's sake."

Oakley smiles. "I'd like that."

"We need a plan to make it happen."

"Want me to call the skunk back?"

"I want you to think long and hard about the answer to that," I chuckle. Inhaling deeply, I point my nose to the woods. "There's something dead back there. A deer, maybe."

Oakley climbs to his feet. "Can't you just refuse to go in?"

I shake my head. "Sabrina won't hear of that."

His gaze falls to the dropping sun in the western sky. "You'd better get going. I'll stand watch."

I slip through the hole in the fence and race to the woods past the field behind our house. I have no idea how I'll bring myself to cover my fur in decaying matter, but once I sniff out the carcass, I find I can't help but roll in it. Once I'm convinced Sabrina will never let me in the house, I race back to Oakley. Within ten minutes Jaycee calls me inside for the night. She takes one whiff of me and tells Sabrina I'm not allowed in until I've had a bath. Sabrina confirms Jaycee's diagnosis, leaving Oakley and I alone for the night.

I chase Oakley around the yard. "Worked like a charm."

"I'm having second thoughts," he yells, running from me. "You really bring down the value of this place," Oakley teases as we lie inside the shed, me on one end and him on the other.

"You know you're gonna miss these nights one of these days."

He settles into the straw. "There's no doubt about that."

"When I was a kid, I remember adults would say stuff like that all the time and I never realized how true it was until—"

"Understanding comes with age."

I laugh. "I guess I *am* getting old. I would give anything to go back to those sleepless nights when Jaycee was a baby." I rest my head on my paws, the weight of my words heavy in my heart.

"I'd like another afternoon sitting on the porch, watching traffic with your grandma. We used to laugh and say we'd never do that but now that's what I'd give anything for. Did she ever tell you about the old lady across the street from her when she was a kid?" I shake my head. "She came out at the same time every day and sat for precisely two hours on her porch. Your grandma said she always wondered what on earth she was looking at. It took me fifty years—give or take—to grasp the story to that."

I lift my head, curious as to how he'd know the reasoning behind the actions of someone he'd never met. "What was that?"

"The lady lost her husband and her kids had all moved away. She came out just before your grandma and her sisters got home from school. Then she spent two hours watching them play outside because it reminded her of a time from her past. That's all. It was rather sweet."

"How do you know that?"

"I put it together from listening to the stories your grandma would tell."

"But you didn't have neighbors to watch. What were you doing on the porch?"

"Waiting to see if there was anything Gramma had to say."

I cock my head. "Did she have a secret you expected her to tell?"

He snorts. "There wasn't anything your grandma and I didn't know about one another."

"What were you waiting on her to say?"

"Absolutely nothing. I was content to just be next to her. But, if she had wanted to argue about the thermostat setting, I would've happily bantered with her...and changed the temperature."

"That's a story for the ages," I whisper, feeling robbed of my own.

We lie silently for a bit, listening to the crickets and bull frogs from the neighbor's pond.

"They sure make a lot of racket," I comment.

Oakley yawns. "It sounds beautiful to me."

"Just a bunch of noise."

"Listen closely."

I close my eyes and consider his words but it might as well be highway traffic as far as I'm concerned. Don't they know people are trying to sleep?

Chapter 25

Over the next few months, I tried to give Sabrina signs that she should move on, but she didn't seem interested anymore. For three weeks we spent our lunch breaks walking a dog with Mrs. Harbison's grandson, Rusty. Mrs. H, as everyone called her, fell and broke her hip after tripping over her Yorkshire Terrier and now Rusty had to stop by before his second-shift job to run some energy out of the dog, despite the cold weather. I thought things were heading in the right direction, but when Mrs. H was sent to assisted living, Rusty decided to take the dog to live with him in Burlington. Sabrina retreated to her shop after that and was content to do so. Jaycee's teenage hormones raged and Sabrina said on more than one occasion she didn't need to mix dating into *that* mess. And that was okay with me. Sabrina developed a system for dealing with Jaycee's moodiness—if the morning was rough, we'd stay at the shop late and bring supper home from the restaurant. Of course, some days something would happen at school and we'd be ambushed in the afternoon, but we all did the best we could. I had no idea that on an unseasonably warm Tuesday afternoon in early spring, my world would be turned upside down.

Sabrina had left me at home because she needed to do inventory at the restaurant and I was all too happy to spend the day with Oakley instead of locked in a room by myself.

I race to the road when the bus is two stops away. My tail beats into the soggy ground. A bath is in my near future and I already dread it.

"Traffic flies down this road." I turn to find Oakley standing behind me. "You act like a kid who's had too many yoo-hoos for breakfast."

"This is the best part of my day."

"You have a lot of 'best parts of the day'—eating scraps from the table, watching your wife take a shower, farting next to the cat—"

The mom down the road at the stop before ours, greets her kindergartner with a 'how was your day?' I inch closer so I'm front and center when Jaycee arrives.

Jaycee bounces off the bus and the look on her face stops me in my tracks. She nearly skips past me and hurries into the house.

Oakley and I stare at each other dumbfoundedly. "Was that a smile? On my daughter's face?"

He swings his head toward the house. "Get in there and find out what's going on. I want a full report."

I scratch at the door until she returns to let me in. After giving her a proper welcome home, I follow her to the kitchen, leaving a trail of muddy prints behind me. She tosses me a strip of leftover bacon as she makes herself a sandwich, a goofy smile plastered to her face. It's a good look on her. She reaches for her tablet. Her eyes light up as she peers at the screen. This can only mean one thing—a boy.

She takes the device and her plate to her room. I hop onto the bed and lie beside her, trying to see what's causing her giddiness. Stretching my paw out, I cover the screen with a leg. Instead of yelling at me, she rolls over and types something. I reach for her arm and she pulls me into a hug.

"Want to play?"

I wag my tail as she hops off the bed. To my surprise, she digs inside her closet and pulls out the soccer ball I'd nearly given up hope on.

I bound down the hall and follow her outside. She kicks the ball off the deck. I glance at her before racing after it.

"Oakley! She got the ball out," I call, bringing him out of his shed with my words.

"So she did." He smiles.

I turn to watch Jaycee—make sure this isn't a trick—and my feet stumble over the ball. I tuck and roll, happy to be the source of my daughter's giggles.

Jaycee joins me, picking up the ball and trying to bounce it on her knee. It wobbles off to the side.

"What brought this on?" I bark as I scamper to collect the ball.

"I'm thinking about playing soccer this year," she says.

I circle her, wondering again if she can understand me. "That would be great."

She dribbles the ball sloppily around the shed.

I follow, barking out questions that go unanswered. She tries the knee thing again and I chase the ball under the deck.

"Be a pal and get that for me, Huck," Jaycee pleads.

Struggling to get a good grip, I lie down behind it.

"Huck, please," she begs.

I snap at the ball again, moving it less than an inch in her direction. "I really wish I could help you out."

Jaycee crouches, peering at me with dread at the prospect of crawling under the deck. She slowly works her way in far enough to barely touch the ball.

I smile, assuming a playful position. "What's his name?"

She works the ball toward her with extended fingertips. Taking it, she plops onto a stair and clutches it on her lap. "Reese has been playing since middle school. I'll look like a fool in front of him."

I take a seat beside her. "Reese? Isn't that a candy?"

"I told him I'd been practicing since last summer," she laments.

"Never mind that. Let's talk about what you're doing conversing with members of the opposite sex."

"He helps out with the girls' soccer team, and I just know he's going to laugh at me. Maybe I should just be his lab partner for Chemistry and leave it at that." She pauses to pat my head. "He's so cute though."

"No. There will be none of that talk."

"But if I play soccer, we can spend more time together. Maybe he'll even help me practice. He said he would. I don't know what I'm thinking," she rattles. "He's a junior. And junior girls have boobs. I'm barely an A cup."

"I'll rip his head off!"

"Calm down, Cujo," Oakley calls.

"She's talking about her boobs," I scream.

"At least she's talking to you," he offers.

Jaycee twirls the ball on her finger, catching it when it falls. "He might be the kind of boy who doesn't care about that...who am I kidding? All boys care about is one thing. At least that's what Mom keeps saying."

"And she's right. Stay away from boys." I lie my head on her lap. "You know, I'm picking out a new boyfriend for your mom. I could arrange something for you too...in about ten years."

Oakley laughs from his patch of grass two feet from us. "I don't think you have ten years left."

"Shut it!" I force the sinking feeling into the pit of my stomach. Is my time really running that short?

Jaycee bolts upright, tossing me off her. She darts inside and returns with her tablet and a bag of carrots. Oakley's ears perk and she holds a treat out to him. Her fingers dance across the screen and she pulls up a picture of a kid with a pile of hair twisted in a knot at the back of the head. The soccer uniform doesn't reveal any form fitting clues to gender and I'm genuinely confused at what I'm looking at. I stick my nose on the screen, hoping to get a better idea.

"Is that a moustache? On a girl?"

The back door opens and Sabrina joins us on the top step. Jaycee hits a button and the screen goes black.

I pounce on Sabrina. "You're back! How did inventory go? Are the sales up for the last quarter? Did you remember to check competitor's prices to make sure we're getting the best deals?"

Sabrina latches her arms around me. "I missed you, too, Huck."

I sniff her blouse and work my way down to her calves. A hint of grease and fried food fills my nostrils, mixing with the vague scent of the usual co-workers I'm used to smelling. But there's something new. I sniff again, drawing out a strange scent of testosterone-laced sweat. No, the sweat is hers, I deduce upon further sniffing. The testosterone belongs to someone different. "Want to tell me what that's all about? I mean, it's bad enough I had to hear my daughter talking about boobs, but now I find out you're rubbing against someone with...strong...urges." She pushes me to the side. I fight my way back. "I leave you alone for one day and this is what happens? You know I'm supposed to—" I pluck the bag of carrots from the deck and race around the shed, circling back toward Oakley.

Both my girls wear the same goofy grin. I drop the bag at the donkey's feet. "Someone might as well have a good day," I say.

"Come inside please," Sabrina says to Jaycee. "There's something I want to talk to you about."

"I have to hear this," I say, bidding Oakley a farewell.

"Something happened today," she starts. "I know we haven't talked about it much...or ever, but I think it's time we should."

Jaycee stares longingly at the soccer ball she dropped at the door.

"Your dad has been gone six years and—"

"I'm right here." I pounce, shoving my nose in her lap.

"It's been rough. But I don't have to tell you that." She twists a lock of hair. "There's going to come a day when you will be all grown up and—"

"Will you get on with it?" I shove my nose father up her chest. "Why do girls have to dance around things? Just say it!"

"I don't know how to say this—I've been asked out," she says, slowly lifting her eyes to our daughter. I race around the table, studying the look on Jaycee's face. "I wanted to talk to you—to see how you felt about it—before I gave an answer."

I shove my nose in Sabrina's lap. "So you're just going to act like you haven't been out on a date already? What about all those lunch 'meetings?'" I fall to my haunches. This one is serious.

Jaycee's chair legs screech on the tile as she throws the chair backward. "Do whatever you like," she grumbles, taking the soccer ball back outside.

I stand awkwardly in the middle of the room, unsure if I should follow Jaycee out the door she'd left cracked or stay near Sabrina.

Sabrina pats my head. "Jaycee isn't ready."

I stick to Sabrina's heels as she follows Jaycee outside. "I think there's something bothering you besides the issue of me dating," she says after calling our daughter over to the deck. "Talk to me."

Jaycee's brow softens but anger dances in her eyes. I take a seat between them on the top step in case they resort to fighting.

Jaycee tosses the ball into the yard, narrowly missing Oakley. "How come you're getting asked out but I'm not?"

"I didn't realize you'd given it thought."

"Well, I have," she barks, storming into the house.

Her bedroom door slams.

Sabrina slumps her shoulders. "Maybe it's too soon."

Chapter 26

Jaycee spends a long week actively avoiding Sabrina. I divide my time between the two, trying my best to get them in the same room. Jaycee switches between sulking and chattering away about Reese while she kicks the soccer ball around the yard. Sabrina starts more than a dozen conversations, each met with a one-word answer.

"You need to patch things up with your mom," I tell her as we chase the ball that refuses to go where she wants it. She's set up five-gallon buckets in various places and aims for them as we run up and down the yard. I assume she's practicing passes, but she's yet to hit her mark so I can't be sure.

"Ugh," she growls, missing again. "I'm never going to make the team this way." She slams her foot into the ball, sending it pounding into the side of the shed.

I sit, fuming at the fact that I can't chew her out for her behavior. "Not with that attitude."

She marches to the deck and reaches for her phone. Her finger runs up the screen so many times I question how long it will be before she ends up with carpel tunnel. A smile spreads across her face and she stops the scrolling nonsense.

"I've got it!" She races inside and comes back out with a tripod. She's changed into a form-fitting gray tank top and tight shorts and her hair no longer displays the stray whisps from her previous exercise. She places the phone on the tripod, testing angles.

I waltz over, sticking my nose up to the screen. "Whatcha doin'?"
She shoves me away. "Huck, stop."
I nuzzle my head in the crook of her elbow. "I've seen that look before."
"Seriously, Huck."
"I don't like where this is heading." I turn, wagging my tail over the phone, knocking it off the stand.
"Do you mind? I'm trying to make a video."

"Wipe that grin off your face." I slather her with kisses. "Infatuation is not a good look on my teenage daughter."

"She's growing up, Jason," Oakley calls from the safety of the shed.

"Whose side are you on?"

"Soccer is supposed to be the thing that changes her life. Why are you trying to interfere?"

Jaycee reaches for a nearby stick and flings it across the yard. I consider Oakley's words as I sprint away from her. Maybe he's got a point. Jaycee hurries to finish the setup while I'm distracted.

"Give her a chance," Oakley suggests while she races for the ball.

"She'd better be the next big soccer star," I mutter, watching her take the ball and kick it toward the first bucket.

"What are you doing?" Oakley calls as I race after her.

"This has something to do with a boy and he needs to know her father is watching," I yell, darting out of the ball's path.

Jaycee turns and kicks the ball back toward the target, shooting it wide again. Oakley runs at me as if we're suddenly playing a game of chicken.

I lunge to the left, making contact with Jaycee's leg. She barrel-rolls over me and smacks into the bucket. The girl I've lived with for the last few years would've picked the bucket up and thrown it at me. The one in front of me jumps to her feet and takes a bow. She even bends to hug me when I check to see if she's okay.

"See? I need help," she says, and races to the device.

After an awkward supper where Sabrina's questions are ignored, I seek Bobbi out.

"I think Jaycee has a pretty big crush on some boy," I tell her when I find her sleeping on Sabrina's pillow.

"She's not the only one."

My back foot slips off the bed and I scramble closer to the cat. "What's that supposed to mean?"

"Sabrina is ready to date. Finally."

I snort. "How do you know that?"

Bobbi yawns dramatically. "She talks to me. You've been so preoccupied with Jaycee and that damn donkey, you're forgetting your wife. No surprise there, though."

First she thinks I'm ignoring Jaycee and now she thinks I'm ignoring Sabrina. I can't win.

"I could say the same about you. You have no idea what's going on with Jaycee because you're too busy sleeping. At least I'm interacting with her."

She extends her claws. "I put in my time with Jaycee when she was little and wanted to chase me around the house. Now that she's older, she couldn't care less about where I am. Sometimes I think she doesn't even know I'm here."

I inhale deeply, almost feeling sorry for my mother-in-law. "Look, I didn't come in here to fight. I came because I've seen too many times how moms get so invested in their own dating lives that they don't see warning signs from their kids. And boys only have one thing on their minds, let's not forget that."

She licks her forearm. "I remember the day I found out about Sabrina's first love. His name was Blaine. It lasted two months. You have nothing to worry about."

Relaxing, I flop down. I'd heard about Blaine. Nothing more than a young crush. "You're sure?"

"You'll know when to worry when you see that look in her eyes."

"What look?"

She stares past me as if she can't bear to meet my eyes as she says the words. "The look Sabrina had on her face when she looked at you. It never went away. And believe me, I tried to make it disappear."

My heart soars. "I was there," I say coolly.

"Just watch for that. That's when you know you're in trouble."

"Thanks." I leap from the bed.

"Don't you want to talk about Sabrina's dating?"

"I think that will all work out the way it's supposed to." I stop at the door. "I'm more worried about making sure Sabrina knows Jaycee is ready to date." I nearly choke on the words.

"We'll just have to make sure we show her the signs. She's so busy being the sole provider now," she spits as if my hard work had nothing to do with paying the bills.

"Right." I step out of the room before the urge to rip her to shreds overtakes me.

Slipping down the hall, I hop onto Jaycee's bed.

"Your mom is on the couch watching a *Friends* rerun. It might be a good time to have a chat with her. You know how Monica and Chandler always put her in a good mood."

She points to her tablet, showing me words beneath a picture. "Are you asking for help with soccer or your dog," the text reads, followed by a smiley face with tears popping out of the eyes.

She rolls over, pulling me into a full body hug. "He's actually talking to me," she squeals.

I groan, pulling out of her grasp. "He clearly only has one thing on his mind."

"The dog is a lost cause, I'm afraid. And I won't be far behind at the rate I'm going. L-O-L," she says, her fingers typing as she talks.

"That's flirting. Before we brought you home from the hospital your mother and I told you that was not allowed."

"Jealous already, Huck?" She scratches the place on my back that sends me in to gleeful submission. "Oh look, he's already responded."

"What's so great about Candy Pants anyway?" I whimper, but she pays no attention.

"He wants to come over Monday after school to help." She squeals again, a sound that pierces my ears.

"Would you mind taking it down a decibel?"

"Me or the dog?" She whispers, typing.

Is this the look that means trouble, I wonder, watching a brief exchange of their plans.

She smiles, her eyes sparkling in a way I haven't seen since before my accident. But as suddenly as the giddiness appeared, it vanishes.

I lurch into her lap. "What's wrong?"

She crosses her arms, her lips drooping in a pout. "I have to talk to Mom."

My tail pounds the bed. "At least some good comes from this nonsense boy business."

Chapter 27

I pace the floor anxiously on Monday, waiting for the bus to arrive. Sabrina had taken half the day off to tidy up the house for company even though she keeps the place nearly spotless these days.

After being scolded for getting in the way too many times, she sends me outside.

"That boy is coming over today," I tell Oakley. "You have to help me run him off."

"Why? You eager to meet the next one?" I clamp a nearby stick with my teeth and grind until it splits in two. "You know there will be more."

"Not if I snap his pretty little neck. Maybe I'll drag him around by that man-bun she likes so much. I don't know who came up with that, but someone should pull his man card."

"Man bun? Does he carry around a large sandwich?"

I dig a hole to ease my frustration. "Picture Bea Ratcliff from church. Now imagine her hair on a man's head."

He snorts. "That's the most ridiculous thing I've ever heard."

"Tell me about it."

The bus doors open and Jaycee's feet skip across the gravel drive.

I glance at the front yard, wondering if I should race around the house to see for myself that she is alone. "Maybe he's decided not to come after all."

"That's not good."

I stop mid-dig. "How is that not good? Isn't that what we want?"

Oakley takes a dump where he stands and I consider scolding him for being inconsiderate, but I remind myself he's still an old man at heart and they tend to act however they want. "I know you're rusty to the whole teenage dating drama," he says when he's finished. "You didn't have sisters, but teenage heartbreaks are harder on girls. If this boy has hurt her, you'll hear about him far more than you already have."

Curse words escape my lips in a censored bark that makes me laugh. Apparently, I'm not allowed certain phrases. "I don't see how that's possible. That's literally all she talked about yesterday."

"Would you rather they were tears? Because that will be the case if this boy changed his mind about coming over."

"I'm going to see if I can find out what's going on." I race to the door and peer inside. Jaycee hunches over a textbook at the table. She twirls her hair. Sabrina scrubs cabinet doors. "Everything looks normal," I report.

"Then he's still coming."

The downshift of a Mustang engine grabs my attention as it crunches gravel in our drive.

"Huck, stay," Oakley orders, halting my sprinting stance.

"I need to see who's here," I argue.

"Wait for her to introduce you."

I turn and stare at him. "Seriously?"

"If you play your cards right, you can keep an eye on them, but if you mess up early, they'll lock you in the bedroom for sure and you'll never know what's going on."

"You have a point."

"If you're lucky, one day you'll be old and wise like me."

I laugh. "I'm like seventy in dog years."

"Seventy is not too young to learn something new but you've got a few years before you reach that ripe old age."

"I'm going to watch from the window." I race to the door and press my nose against it. "He brought donuts! And coffee for Sabrina. What a suck-up," I yell.

"I think your dog wants in," the boy says, his smile trained on me.

"Be nice. Remember your manners," Oakley instructs.

"Right. Introductions first, pounding second."

"Jason."

"Leave him outside," Sabrina says. "He's been driving me nuts all afternoon. Maybe you can wear him out so he'll be calmer this evening."

Jaycee turns on her heel and returns to her seat. Candy Pants shrugs, sliding a book onto the table.

"*Pride and Prejudice.* I remember this. Real snooze fest."

Jaycee laughs. "Maybe you can tell me how it ends and spare me." Sabrina whips around, shooting our daughter a glare. "I don't see the point in torturing us with stuff that puts us to sleep."

When Sabrina's back is turned, Reese leans over and whispers, "Get the audiobook."

"Thanks," Jaycee mouths, shoving her mouth full of a chocolate-covered donut.

"These are delicious," Sabrina says, cupping a large fritter.

"I'll let my mom know you like them." Sabrina lifts an eyebrow. "She runs the coffee shop on the corner of Main and Earl—The Caffeinator."

"I haven't been there since my pregnancy cravings with Jaycee. I'll bet I gained an extra twenty pounds, thanks to these donuts."

Jaycee rolls her eyes. "Mo-om."

Reese laughs, patting his non-existent gut. "I know the feeling. I had to join soccer just to keep the weight off. I was chunky all through elementary. Mom was always bringing stuff home and I finally figured out if I was at practice, I wouldn't be around to eat everything."

Sabrina pours a glass of milk. "Tell her she can bring leftovers here any time she likes."

Reese chuckles, shoving his hair out of his face. He pulls it back into a ponytail, revealing a shaved portion near his neck. "I'm going to polish off the box if we don't get outside soon."

Jaycee scoots her chair back. "I'll go change."

While she's gone, Sabrina questions Reese about school, learning he's two grades ahead of Jaycee and he hopes to get a soccer scholarship but he's undecided as to what he'll actually study.

I leap onto Jaycee the second the door opens. "He's too old for you. He'll be off to college soon and you know what that means—frat parties and girls. Do you think you can trust him with that?"

"You're a bit ahead of yourself, Jaybird," Oakley croons from the grass.

"Fine." I shove my nose at Reese's shoes and ankles. "What are your intentions with my daughter?"

He bends to stroke my fur. "You must be Oakley. No, Huck. Man, I can't remember." He turns to Jaycee for help.

"Huck. Oakley is the donkey."

"Right." He holds his hand out for me to shake. As much as I hate it, I can't refuse. "Nice to meet you, Huck."

"The donkey doesn't shake," Jaycee teases as Reese moves to greet Oakley. We all laugh.

"Maybe we could teach you," I smirk.

Jaycee hands Reese the ball.

"I assume the buckets are your teammates?" Jaycee bites her lip, color flushing her cheeks. "Okay. That's a good start. I couldn't tell much from the video besides your dog plays for the opposing team."

Jaycee giggles. "It was the bipods versus quadpods." She swipes the ball from his hands. "I'm not sure that's a word."

Reese laughs. "I like it." He knocks the ball from her hands, takes a few steps back, and kicks it to her. It whizzes past her foot.

"I was supposed to stop that, wasn't I?"

He shrugs.

I sprint for it. "Too much talking going on here. Just kick the ball. That's what you came here for, right? Right?"

Jaycee plucks it away from me and kicks it back. It veers to the side, but Reese's quick feet block its path.

"Watch this," he says, nudging the ball with his foot.

He rambles pointers as he guides it skillfully down the yard, around the buckets, and back to Jaycee. I follow along trying to best him, but he's good enough to avoid my tactics.

"Watch out for poop," Jaycee calls.

He laughs but the ball stays with him until the final stretch where he gives it a hard kick, directed straight to Jaycee. She jumps out of the way rather than stopping it with her shins.

"Wow," she marvels. "How did you do that?"

"Donuts." She cocks her head. "More like avoiding donuts. Spent hours outside just so I didn't have to smell them."

He puts her through a series of drills until I'm bored out of my mind. Talk turns strictly to soccer and I no longer feel the need to be in the midst of the action. I join Oakley a safe distance away and watch.

"Seems like a good kid," Oakley comments.

"The jury's still out."

"Give him a chance."

I poke at a grasshopper, sending it fluttering away. Lowering myself to the ground, I close my eyes and resort to listening to the soft punting of the ball and Reese's instructions. Every time Jaycee speaks, I lift a lid to determine if she's giving that look I'm supposed to be scared of. Finally, Reese says he should be getting home for supper. I instantly leap to my feet.

"You were a perfect angel today," he says, patting my head.

Jaycee giggles. "You don't know him very well."

They start for the driveway with me positioned between them.

Oakley sidles up beside me. "Where do you think you're going?"

"I'm going to go check out his car."

"Right." He pulls a chunk of grass with his teeth. "Do *not* pee on the tires," he orders.

"I make no promises."

In the driveway, Jaycee peers inside the front window. "Wow, fully loaded, it looks like."

He nods. "My step-dad works at a dealership. I wanted a new model but, hey, it gets me from A to B."

I scratch Jaycee's leg, demanding attention. "Try not to be too impressed by a kid with a car he isn't paying for."

"Maybe he can hook me up. I start driver's ed in a few months."

"I'll bet he could find something perfect for you. Should I have him look?"

Jaycee shakes her head. "I'd better talk to my mom first."

"Let me know." He turns to her, a charming smile plastered to his face.

Her foot dances on the gravel. "I think I might need more lessons before tryouts."

"I'm free tomorrow."

"That's it. I'm sorry but I can't hold it any longer." I park myself next to his tire and spray my scent over it. "That tree was too far away," I explain, looking toward the maple in the yard.

"Huck!" Jaycee bolts toward me. "I'm so sorry."

Reese laughs. "It's okay." He opens the car door. "Same time tomorrow?"

She nods and they wave to each other as he pulls out of the drive.

Chapter 28

Oakley and I lie side by side watching Reese and Jaycee practice. The clouds overhead threaten rain, but Reese doesn't seem to notice anything but the soccer ball. Jaycee's eyes focus on the boy beside her.

"I'm less worried now than I was two weeks ago when they started these lessons," I tell Oakley.

"While it *does* look like you're going to avoid a relationship, it doesn't look like she's going to avoid being crushed when she realizes he only wants to play soccer."

"That's when I'll drag him around by the hair."

"Sooner or later, you're going to have to get used to the idea of her dating."

My ears perk at the sound of water bottles opening. "Break time. Gotta go," I say, leaping to my feet. I plant myself between them on the top step of the deck.

Jaycee's arm slips over me. "Can I ask you something?"

I cock my head in her direction. "Oh, you're not talking to me."

"You mentioned your step-parents." Reese waits for the question to follow. "Is it weird?" She tugs at the end of her ponytail.

I flop onto her lap. "Welp, this is awkward."

He loosens his own ponytail, scratching his head. "Is what weird, exactly?"

"Was it weird when your mom started dating?"

He takes a swig of water. "It was at first. I guess you kind of get used to it."

"How does it work?"

He cocks his head. "What do you mean?"

"Like did your mom just start going out with a new guy every weekend? Did they expect you to come along on the dates or was she just gone all the time? Was it like you got shoved to the back burner or like they tried too hard to make sure you were included? Because I don't really feel like being a third wheel while someone's all kissy face with my mom."

Reese raises his hand like he's about to comfort her with a gentle touch. He waivers it near her arm and drops it to his side. "Your mom is dating?"

Jaycee shrugs. "Some guy asked her out. I think she blew him off because of the way I acted when she brought it up. It's not that I don't want her to date. I just didn't know she was interested. It's not like she has a lot of time for that sort of thing. Or, at least, that's what I thought. I mean, I want her to be happy, but I'd just rather she skipped the whole dating thing. I'm supposed to be the one bringing strange boys home." Color flushes her cheeks. "I don't mean *strange* boys. But, you know, she's not supposed to be introducing me to her dates. It should be the other way around."

I cover my face with my paw. "Why do girls ramble on and on?" I hide my eyes to help absorb the honesty my daughter spews onto her crush. I wish there was a way to pass this on to Sabrina.

Reese runs a palm over the stubble he calls facial hair and turns to Jaycee with a sincere smile. "I think the first thing to know is, you've seen too many movies. It almost never happens exactly the way you're describing."

Jaycee's fingers draw circles over my fur. "Tell me how it works then."

He sighs. "Well, my dad met my step-mom on a dating app. They went out a few times then decided they wanted us kids to meet."

Jaycee falls back onto the deck. "I didn't even think of that! I don't want more siblings. What if we hate each other?"

Reese laughs and takes her hand, pulling her upright. "Again. Too much TV. Although, there's a good chance you may not get along at first. God knows Devon and I didn't like each other for a long time. But Karma and I hit it off from the start. Granted, she was three at the time so it was hard to dislike someone who thought I was cool because I could do armpit farts."

Jaycee cackles at the image. "How old were you?"

"Nine."

"What about your mom?"

"I met a few of the guys she dated. Some I liked, some I didn't."

"And your step-dad? Was he one you liked?"

Reese scoops up the soccer ball and spins it on his finger. "By the time he came along, I stopped caring. I tried not to get attached because I felt like he was just going to leave too."

Jaycee nods. "I bet that was hard."

"Yeah, but I'll never forget the night I knew he was the one." He lets out a small laugh at the memory. "My mom had a doctor's appointment in Milwaukee and on the way home there was an accident that closed the interstate for hours. I had a soccer game that night and Bill came alone. He sat beside my dad and cheered louder than anyone when I scored my first goal."

"That's really cool."

"It was. I told him I wanted him to drive me home instead of my dad and the look on his face as he recapped the whole game for my mom said it all."

"I'm glad it worked out for you. All my friends hate their step-parents."

"Don't get me wrong, I hated my step-mom at first, too. It was fine while they were dating, but when she moved in, she had all these new rules, and my dad expected us to follow them. I didn't like it. But it was just the change that bothered me. You'll get used to it." He hops to his feet. "I should be going. My sister could take her first steps any second and I don't want to miss it."

"I'm confused."

Reese smiles. "My other sister—my mom and Bill's daughter."

The color drains from Jaycee's face. "They had a baby?"

He leads the way around the house. "Two, actually. My little brother is four."

"Oh goodness that's a lot of siblings."

"I wouldn't trade any of them for the world."

As Jaycee watches him leave, I see the gears turning in her head. Once he's out of sight, she heads in to find Sabrina.

"I have questions," she starts.

For the next twenty minutes, she grills her mom about her intentions with dating. Sabrina assures her she won't be adding additional children to the mix, thanks to an emergency hysterectomy—a detail Jaycee seemed to have forgotten. That appears to ease Jaycee's concerns slightly, though Sabrina makes it clear she has no control over step-siblings. The conversation ends with Jaycee's approval, leaving me feeling torn. I want my wife to be happy, but part of me wishes no man will be able to fill my shoes.

Chapter 29

I stare at a spider spinning a web in the corner of our living room.

"We've given Jaycee time to come around. Jason, it's time for you to let your wife live the rest of her life," it says.

I jump backward at the unexpected voice. "Didn't expect to find you back here."

His tiny legs work quickly to create another layer of web. "You never know where you'll find me."

I sneeze at the dust bunnies hiding behind the couch. "Hey, while I've got you, can you tell me how worried I should be about this Reese character?"

"I *can*. But I'm not going to."

I sniff at a stale chip lodged somewhere in the couch, wondering if I should investigate it. "Oh, come on. As one father to another?"

"How will you ever learn trust if I tell you how it ends?"

"How about a hint?"

"Raging waters are no match for a dingy."

Instinctively, I lurch forward, ready for attack. "Are you calling my daughter a—"

A cramp in my hind quarters pulls me into submission.

"Only time will tell who jumps overboard." I shake my head at the riddle. "I came here to talk about Sabrina."

Having regained use of my back end, I lower myself to the safety of a peaceful position. "Is she okay?"

Continuing work on the web, Jesus speaks softly. "I've been generous with the task I've given you. You're taking your time."

I rest my head between my paws. "I don't think you know what you're asking. First of all, it's impossible for me to set up a date." I lift my head. "Unless you'll allow me to talk to her."

He rubs two of his front legs together. "You know I can't do that."

"Sure you can. It would make this all so much easier."

"All you have to do is introduce her to him."

I cock my head in disbelief. "How am I supposed to do that?"

"A dog's nose is a powerful thing." *Great. More riddles.* "All will be revealed when the time is right."

Did he just read my mind? That's helpful.

"Maybe this will be helpful—if Sabrina doesn't meet him before you die, she'll spend the rest of her life broken and, ultimately, alone."

My jaw flops open and I suck in a dust bunny. Coughing, I soak in the words. Could he be serious? Surely not. Recovering, I peer into the corner. All traces of the web are gone.

"Bobbi!" I race through the house, sniffing out my mother-in-law. Her scent is everywhere. "Audra! We have a problem!"

I skid to a halt, picking up a new trail at the corner of the hallway. "Bobbi! Can you hear me?"

I find her lying in a laundry basket next to the dryer. Normally I'd yell at her for getting hair all over the clean clothes but there isn't time for that.

She yawns, blinking her eyes open. "Do you mind? I'm working on my beauty sleep."

I shake my head to clear the snarky comment building in my brain. "I need your help."

She stretches. "Need me to shove Jaycee's plate off the table again?" While that's a tempting option—she *had* left the crust of her PB&J sitting on the counter—I have more pressing concerns. "Sabrina should make her clean up after herself. She was never allowed to leave her plates sitting around. As soon as she was done eating, her dishes always went straight to the sink."

"Bobbi—Audra—I need your help. It's about Sabrina. I haven't been completely honest with you."

She shoves her nose inside her tiny food dish. "Well that's a shocker."

I slam my paw into the dish, flipping it over and scattering food across the floor. "This is serious. And, if you'd shut up and listen, I think you'll enjoy helping me."

She crunches on a stray bit of food. "Why would I help you?"

"Because it means Sabrina might get the son-in-law you always wanted."

She perks her ears. "I'm listening."

"I was sent here to introduce Sabrina to her next husband. And I have no idea how to make it happen."

A smile plays on Bobbi's lips. "I like where this is heading." Her tail flicks as she sits in front of me. "But I don't have faith that you'll pull it off."

"I have to."

Bobbi runs her tongue over her forearm and drags it across the top of her head. "You'll find a way."

I beat my tail into the side of the washer, creating a loud thud that makes the cat jump. "If I fail, Sabrina will end up alone."

She runs her tongue over a paw. "I know my daughter hasn't been all that interested in dating, though I don't see why. It's been six years. Nobody would judge her for moving on. But I doubt that your failure would cause her to be alone the rest of her life."

"Do you really think I would be asking for your help if I were lying?"

Bobbi pauses, paw over her ear. "Hmm. I suppose not. Do you have a plan?"

I drop my head. "Not exactly."

"Sounds like you want me to do all the work."

I lift my lips in a snarl. "You know what, never mind. I don't need your help after all."

I turn to leave, my pride beaten over the task at hand and Bobbi's demeanor about it all.

"Wait," she whispers. Bobbi's paw moves toward mine. It hovers and settles on my fur. "I know exactly how you're feeling. When Tom remarried, I felt the same way. At least I didn't have to watch him fall in love with someone else. God spared me of that. And they don't visit often since they're two hours away."

Filled with compassion, I nod. Tom had met his new wife two years after Audra's death and moved to Green Bay and now they don't visit except on holidays.

"It hurt to know he found happiness with someone else, but I'm glad he did. I would rather he have a partner for the last stage in life than to think of him going through it alone. Life is too short to live it halfway."

Tears build in my eyes. She's completely right. I force my emotions deep inside. "I think I need a few minutes alone."

"Take all the time you need."

I wander the house, studying all the places special to me—my recliner where I relaxed after work every evening, the bed Sabrina and I shared, the closet where we'd hide to eat cookies when Jaycee was little. Finally, I settle onto the floor, nestling against the wall in the dining room that Sabrina had insisted on painting with her body instead of the traditional brush and roller method. My heart swells at the memory of her youthful giddiness as her body glided across the drywall. She had sworn me to secrecy on the story concerning the wall, joking that she wanted me to think of that day while we hosted family dinners. Her plan worked. I never looked at that wall and thought of anything else, even after the color changed several times. Now as I stare blankly at it, I see her smile, the way she'd felt so confident and free pressing her body over and over against it while I watched. I yearn for the remnants buried under layers of paint and the realization I might as well be a train colliding with my body.

I don't want to rob her of that joy. And, more importantly, I don't want to rob the right person of knowing what it is to love her. She's too special to keep to herself.

Chapter 30

After the dance recital disaster that landed me with extra legs, there's no way I'm missing Jaycee's first soccer game. On the drive to school, I find myself quietly thanking Reese for the inspiration to get Jaycee on the field. It's not baseball, but I'll take it. Sabrina sets up her lawn chair near the bleachers where our team is seated. Jaycee rushes over when she sees us.

I leap onto her, my paws reaching her shoulders. "Good luck."

"I can't believe you brought him," she scowls at her mother.

Sabrina lifts a shoulder. "He wouldn't get out of my way. You should have seen him. I thought I was going to break a leg. He kept tripping me. And when I opened the door, he was out before I could grab him." Jaycee pats my head, but her lips press tightly together. "He ran to the truck and sat there wagging his tail. It was adorable."

"He'd better not run onto the field."

Sabrina waves at Reese.

He jogs over. "Hello, Mrs. Parker."

Sabrina blinks her long eyelashes dramatically. "It's Sabrina. You know that."

"Right." He taps Jaycee on the shoulder. "I just found out their best player twisted her ankle at practice earlier this week."

I sniff Reese's shoes. He stepped in nacho cheese sauce. "Where did you find that? Is there any left?"

He strokes my back. "Now we have a chance. Northview is the best school in our district."

Jaycee laughs. "That doesn't help my nerves."

I slather my tongue across her arm. "You'll do fine."

"We'd better get over there," Reese suggests.

"Good luck," Sabrina and I yell.

The ref blows a whistle and the teams line up. I watch the ball dance from player to player, up and down the field. Jaycee chases it nervously, as if she's unsure what to do if it comes to her. By the second quarter, she relaxes some and manages to make a kick to a teammate. In the third quarter, she misses a block, allowing the opponents to score a goal. Reese cheers the team on from the sideline, high-fiving the girls who score. The coach calls them all together before the last quarter, giving them a pep talk to raise their spirits. They are down four goals and it's obvious they are discouraged. Jaycee dribbles the ball halfway across the field before it's stolen from her and Northview scores again. The seconds tick away, but we manage to make a goal before the whistle blows to end the game.

"That was embarrassing," Jaycee grumbles on the ride home.

"You all played really hard," Sabrina consoles. "Besides, you heard Reese; Northview is the best team in the district."

I slide my head onto Jaycee's lap. "You'll get better with practice."

"They didn't even have their best player," she grumbles.

"I'll bet the next time you play them you'll be so good they won't know what hit them."

Jaycee silently stares out the window. We're nearly home before Sabrina broaches a different subject.

"I almost forgot. Would you be interested in babysitting this summer?"

Jaycee tilts her head. "I don't know. Apparently, I'm going to be busy practicing soccer."

"It's a paying gig. Five days a week."

"I guess I'm listening."

"There's a customer at the restaurant who is new to town. He has a ten-year-old son. The place where he's going after school doesn't have any availability for all day care and, somehow, he heard I have a teenage daughter who might be interested in the job."

Jaycee shakes her head. "Were *you* the one who put that idea in his head?"

"It's either that or bussing tables. Choice is yours."

Jaycee blinks incredulously. "Is he a brat?"

"He offered to set up a meeting at Flater's Dairy Corner so we can all see if the chemistry is good."

I thump my tail against the seat at the prospect of tagging along for ice cream.

"Fine," Jaycee agrees. "But I'd rather clean the grease trap than wipe boogers from some kid who doesn't know how to wipe his own butt."

Sabrina cocks her head. "He's ten. Pretty sure you don't have to worry about at least one of those."

"I said fine."

Chapter 31

Jaycee groans as Sabrina wakes her up the first day of her summer vacation. "Why can't Deacon start work at noon?"

Sabrina flings the comforter from the bed. "Get up. He'll be dropping Finn off in half an hour."

I leap onto the bed. "The sun has been up for nearly two hours. Up and at 'em!"

Jaycee reaches blindly for the covers. "I can sleep another twenty minutes," she groans.

"Come on, I have to leave and I don't want Deacon to think he made a mistake."

"Ten minutes?"

I lick her face. "I have the whole day planned! First, we're going to play fetch with a stick. But I'll eventually shred it until there's nothing left. Then we're going to eat. No, first we'll eat. Then we'll play fetch. Then we'll eat again. After that, we'll need to splash in the water at the creek. I'll probably need a nap after that. Then we can play ball and chase Oakley around. Come on! There are so many things to do." I take her arm gently in my mouth.

Sabrina laughs. "Someone is excited."

Jaycee groans. "That's because he's a morning dog."

"Maybe Deacon should've hired Huck to babysit."

"Let's go," I bark.

Half an hour later a blond-haired boy sits on the floor stroking my back while he waits for Jaycee to stop staring at the TV.

His eyes wander toward the bookshelf. "Can I read a book?"

Jaycee shrugs. I follow him to inspect the covers, surprised to see a shelf still holding children's books. His fingers brush the spines and he plucks a small book as if he'd just picked the greatest treasure.

Flopping down on the floor, he motions me over. I oblige, remembering the days of listening to Jaycee read. The story is about a talking dog who helps a boy with bullies. I'm impressed with how easily the words flow from him.

He even uses funny voices for the characters, explaining that's how his dad reads to him. When the dog is thrown in the pound, Finn throws his arm protectively around my middle. I lean into him and wait to see how the story plays out. All is well in the end, of course, and Finn replaces the book.

He stares at Jaycee, a hint of disgust tinging his face. "What can we do now?"

Jaycee waves him to move out of the way of the screen. "I dunno."

"Can we go outside?"

"Maybe later," she groans.

"Are you planning on sitting in front of the drool box all day? Jaycee," I bark.

"Read another book," she suggests.

So we do. This time about a cat who gets lost.

Finn flops onto the couch. "How about now?"

"How about now, what?"

"Can we go outside?"

She flips off the TV. "Sure."

I race to Oakley. "This is Finn," I say, nodding to the freckled boy beside me.

"Nice to meet you."

"Finn, I'd like you to meet Oakley."

Finn turns to Jaycee who has taken up residence on the top porch step with her phone. "What's his name?"

"The donkey? Oakley."

Finn pats Oakley's head. "Hi, Oakley."

I spot a tennis ball near the shed and retrieve it. "Want to play ball?" I drop it at his feet.

He stoops and tosses it awkwardly. "Fetch!"

"We're gonna have to work on your form," I tell him, dropping it again at his feet.

He throws again.

"Pull your arm in some," I coach, racing to retrieve it.

He tosses it farther this time.

"Better," I yell, chasing after it.

I'll bet an hour passes as we play, Jaycee happily looking up from her screen from time to time. When she finally puts her device down, we watch her curiously as she goes into the shed.

She returns with a faded leash. "Want to see something funny?" I race to Jaycee's side. She attaches the leash and hands the end to Finn. "Take off walking."

I prance eagerly alongside the boy until Oakley joins our stride.

Jaycee guides the end of the leash over until Oakley carefully bites it. "Let go," she tells Finn.

Finn does as instructed, then laughs heartily as Oakley parades me around. When we've made a few laps, Oakley drops his end and munches a mouthful of grass.

"Let's go in and find something to eat," Jaycee suggests.

"Do you have chicken nuggets?"

I race them to the door and wag my tail until Jaycee opens it.

"We have chicken tenders," she tells him.

He shakes his head. "I only like the ones shaped like dinosaurs."

"Do you like pizza?"

"If it's plain."

Jaycee opens the freezer door. "We have pepperoni. I can pick those off for you."

"I'll eat the pepperoni," I offer.

Finn shakes his head. "It will have meat juice on it still."

Jaycee laughs. "Meat juice?" Finn shrugs. "What about peanut butter and jelly?"

"The stuff in a jar?" Jaycee plucks a jar from the pantry. He shakes his head. "It has to come together. In the same jar."

Jaycee throws out a few more suggestions, but each is turned down for one ridiculous reason or another. Finally. Jaycee takes a seat at the table. "How about toast?"

I lie down to wait this out as he refuses that offer based on the time of day. Jaycee tells him to open cabinets and find something he'd like to eat.

"Maybe he likes dog food," I suggest with a yawn.

Drifting off, I nap peacefully until the smell of powdered cheese and milk fill the kitchen. Mac and cheese, I realize, scooting myself under the table for any possible handouts.

"Here's your mac without the cheese," Jaycee comments, a bowl smacking the table maybe a little too forcefully.

With lunch out of the way, Finn begs to be entertained. Jaycee digs out board games and manages to keep her screen time to a minimum while they play the games that had been buried in a closet for way too long.

Bobbi strolls out of hiding midway through a game of Clue and plops herself down right on the middle of the board. "Man, it's been a long time since I've done this."

Jaycee scoops her up and places her to the side.

"Wait ten seconds and do it again," I urge. "This is taking forever."

Bobbi yawns. "I think he's about to figure out whodunit," she says. "Who is this kid anyway?"

I scratch my ear. "His name is Finn. Jaycee is babysitting him this summer while his dad works."

"What about his mom?"

I move on to my back, scratching it a minute before answering. "Not really sure."

A spark ignites in the cat's eyes. "Maybe this is what we've been waiting for."

I drop my tongue from my mouth, making a goofy face. "Sabrina isn't going to marry a child. That's still against the law."

"It takes a special kind of stupid to think that's what I meant," she mutters.

"I doubt she's going to wait for him to grow up. That would be—" I shake my head in disgust.

"The father, you twit."

Finn jumps to his feet. "It's Mr. Green!"

Jaycee urges him to sit. "You still have to find out where he did it," she explains. "And how."

"Oh yeah."

Bobbi, obviously proud of the thought she'd planted, steps to the middle of the board.

Jaycee removes the cat three times in a row before her next move. "How about if I share the weapon with you and we guess on the room?"

Finn nods. "I think it's the library."

She gasps. "Not the library."

He giggles.

"So, we know it's Mr. Green with a candlestick. Let's see where he committed this gruesome act." She pulls the cards from the envelope. "The conservatory," she ends dramatically.

He scrunches his nose. "What's a conversatory?"

Jaycee laughs. "Con-serv-a-tory. And...I don't know. A room for rich people, I reckon."

Finn nods, handing her game pieces that Bobbi scattered. "Hmm. When I grow up, I think I want a conv-conser-a what?"

"Conservatory."

"Yep, that's what I want."

Jaycee stacks the boxes of games. "What are you going to put in your conservatory?"

Finn places his hands on his hips, deep in thought. "Puppies!"

Jaycee nods. "That seems like a good place to keep puppies. How many puppies?"

"Seven," he says matter-of-factly.

"Seven? Wow. What kinds?"

He inches to me on his knees and throws his arms around my neck. "The kinds at the shelter."

Jaycee stops her cleanup. "That's awfully sweet of you."

Finn's arms tighten around my neck. "We had a dog once."

"Oh?"

A hint of saltiness grabs my attention. I swipe my tongue across his face, hoping to keep the tears from coming.

Sensing this, Jaycee sets the games down and comes to us. "What happened to your dog?"

His bottom lip quivers. "Dad took him to the pound. I'm going to rescue him when I'm older."

My heart sinks at his words. Jaycee tenses. Even if I could talk, I'm not sure what I'd say to this poor boy.

Jaycee's arm slides around him and he curls into her. "I'm sure he didn't have a choice," she consoles.

Finn shakes his head. "When my mom left, there was nobody to feed the dog, he said. But that was my job. I fed him. I promise, I did."

Jaycee strokes his hair. "I believe you. You don't look like the kind of person who wouldn't feed a dog. Especially when you want seven for your conservatory."

He nods. "I fed him every day."

"What was he like?"

This brings a smile to the boy's face. "He was a good dog. He barked at everything though. It made my dad mad."

"Sometimes Huck barks a lot. And at nothing, too."

Finn giggles. "Scout barked at squirrels. And if you walked by him too quickly. He didn't like that."

"Maybe he thought you saw a squirrel he didn't know about," Jaycee suggests.

"He couldn't see," he explains softly.

"Was he old?"

Finn nods. "I don't think he could hear either because when Dad would yell at him to shuddup, he wouldn't listen."

Jaycee laughs but quickly stops herself. "You know, I hear there is a special shelter where you can take your dog when they get old and it makes them all better." Finn's ears perk up. "But there's a catch."

"What's that?"

"They have to stay there. It's the only way the magic works."

Finn cocks his head. "I think I'd like to stay there, too, then."

Jaycee shakes her head. "Oh no, that's part of the fine print."

"What's fine print?"

"It's...well, it's usually a trick. Always remember to look for it before signing anything." He nods. "I'll bet your dad didn't know about that. But, even if he did, and it were the only way to save Scout, you'd want that, right?"

"I guess so."

Jaycee rubs his back. "Of course you would. Because, you see, when you go to this special shelter, the old becomes new."

"So, Scout is a puppy again?"

Jaycee points her finger. "Yes. *But* he has to stay there."

"That's not fair."

"It's really not. Although, if you stop and think about it, it's the best thing for Scout, don't you agree?"

Finn considers this. "Do you think he's happy without me, though?"

Jaycee's breath catches. "He misses you, sure, but he knows one day you'll be coming to pick him up from that shelter."

His eyes sparkle. "When I have my conservastory?"

Jaycee smiles at his mispronunciation. "He's waiting until you're ready for him."

Finn taps his chin with a tiny finger, a smile growing. "What's the name of the place? So I'll know where to look when I go to pick him up."

Jaycee stalls him with a lingering hug. Leaning in, she whispers, "Pearly Gate Estates."

"That's clever," I admit.

That brings a smile to the boy's face and, thankfully, the conversation ends because I feel myself choking up.

When Deacon arrives, he's immediately questioned about Pearly Gate Estates. I'm guessing Jaycee had somehow filled him in using her phone because he plays right into the charade.

The next few weeks pass in nearly the same manner. Finn brings along toys now and he and I spend the mornings playing in the house while Jaycee taps away on her tablet. Then there's the fight over what to each for lunch, which usually results in the dinosaur nuggets Sabrina had picked up for him. Afterward, we play ball outside or soak ourselves in a sprinkler until late in the afternoon. Then we wait for Deacon to call with some excuse or another and ask if Finn can stay later. Sabrina enjoys doting over him in the evenings and I know Jaycee would never admit it, but she's growing fond of the kid. That becomes very clear at lunch today.

After spending the morning chasing a remote-control truck, Jaycee calls us inside to eat. Expecting a fight, I curl up smack in the middle of the kitchen where I'll be handy should my services be needed.

"I'm going to make a deal with you today," Jaycee says, crossing her arms.

Finn groans. "What are you going to try to make me eat?"

"Grilled cheese."

He shakes his head. "I don't like cheese."

"Have you ever had grilled cheese?"

His eyes study the floor. "No."

I lift my head. "How have you not had grilled cheese? Are you sure you're American?"

"You haven't heard my deal," Jaycee states.

"I want nuggets."

"Hear me out. Have you ever thrown rocks in a creek?"

He raises an eyebrow at the seemingly strange question. "Why would I do that?"

"It's quite fun. You've never done it?" Another headshake. "Well you're missing out on one of the best parts of being a kid."

This time his lip raises. "I am?"

"I used to do it sometimes with my dad. He was always busy with work so we didn't go often, but it's one of my favorite memories of him."

"It doesn't sound all that exciting."

"Don't knock it 'til you try it," she says. "I promise it will be fun. I'll even show you how to skip a rock."

He laughs. "That sounds funny."

"What do you say?"

"I'd rather have nuggets."

For three days they have this argument. Finally, Jaycee hypes it up enough that he gives in and tries a bite of the gooey sandwich. I nearly trample onto his lap when he eats the required half a sandwich so we can go to the creek.

Jaycee leads him down the lane by our house which takes us to the creek that runs behind the cornfield past the edge of our property. I race along the path, circling back when I get too far ahead. Finn giggles at my antics.

I bark at their heels. "Can't you guys walk any faster? You act like you only have two legs or something."

Finn crouches and darts off in a sprint. "Come on, Jaycee. Huck wants to race."

"Atta boy," I bark.

Jaycee joins, passing Finn. She lets him catch up and whiz by her. She's panting by the time we reach the water's edge. "You beat me."

"And I'll beat you on the way back too," he giggles.

I leap into the creek, splashing water on the two of them.

Finn jumps backward and stares at Jaycee. "How do we do this?"

Upon hearing his question, I make my way toward them and shake. "Have you been living under a rock?"

Jaycee scowls at me. She picks up a stick, knowing I won't be able to resist. I take off after it, thankful there's no current to speak of. A rock plops into the water.

"Like this," Jaycee says, tossing another.

"That's it?"

"That's it."

He gives it a try. And another. And another. "It's okay. I guess."

"What?!"

"I don't get what all the fuss is about."

She takes a seat and motions for him to do the same. "The first time I was here with my dad, I bet him we couldn't fill the creek in with rocks so we could walk across it." She laughs at the memory.

He rolls his eyes. "I think you lost."

She laughs. "We had fun trying though. One time it was so low, we almost made it." She tosses a rock nearly halfway across. "We got to about there. If you look closely, you'll see a big rock near the middle. My dad rolled it all the way from other there." She points to a large tree.

I stop near the rock she speaks of, enjoying hearing the story from her perspective.

"You could see the top of it all that summer. We didn't get much rain that year," she explains. "That was the year before he died," she whispers.

Finn sneaks a glance at her but decides to throw a handful of rocks in the water. They fan out in a shower of pebbles, creating ripples. I bite at them, hoping to lighten the mood.

He slowly flings rocks one at a time, his eyes glued to the water. "At least you know where he is."

Jaycee cocks her head. "What do you mean?"

"My mom left. I have no idea where she is."

"Do you want to talk about it? Sometimes it helps me," she offers.

He clambers to his feet. "Can we skip rocks now?"

"Of course."

I run to the bank, scouring for the perfect rock. My nose is to the ground but I'm lost in a memory of the children I left behind so I could be here today. I wonder if they're skipping rocks in Heaven. A piece of me wishes I could combine the two worlds, but I figure that day will come when it comes. For now, I must focus on Jaycee.

The lesson is instructed nearly how I conducted it years ago, with my daughter playing my role. She does a great job and Finn soon skips rocks left and right. Most of them only make two brushes over the water before sinking, but his chest sticks farther out each time he accomplishes the feat.

"One of the kids in my class has a boat," he suddenly announces. "His dad takes him fishing every weekend."

Jaycee hands him a smooth stone. "That sounds like fun."

"I tried to be friends with him, but he doesn't like me."

"How could anyone not like you? Did you tell him you're fun to hang out with?"

"No." He plucks a rock from her hand.

She nods. "Who needs a boat, anyway?"

Finn throws a stick, grabbing my attention. I paddle out to it and bring it back. Within ten minutes it's nothing but splinters. I still can't explain why I chew the things to shreds.

Jaycee picks up a large rock and throws it high into the air, creating a plume of water straight up. Finn immediately rushes to try his hand.

I lap water several feet away, waiting for the madness to stop. Hearing Jaycee sneak up behind me, I know she's up to a trick she'd learned from me, but I play the part. Unmoving, I wait for the rock to land so near me that water splashes over me. Finn's giggles are reward enough.

Jaycee sticks her toes in the creek and swishes them around. "You know what I wonder? Why adults are always asking what we want to do when we grow up. I don't know about you, but I don't have the slightest clue."

Finn jumps into the water next to her. "I want to be a Blue Angel."

I dart for him, nearly knocking him over as I barrel into him.

"Sorry," I say, shaking it off. "I was going for a high-five but forgot I can't really do that these days. That's cool kid."

"That's probably one of the most awesome jobs ever," Jaycee says.

Finn raises his arms and swoops around like a plane. I chase him along the bank.

"We should be heading back," Jaycee says, holding her arm out to stop him.

"Can we come back tomorrow?"

"Are you going to eat what I make for lunch?"

"I'll think about it."

She throws her arm over his shoulder. "Then I'll think about bringing you back."

Chapter 32

The humid summer air hangs heavy around us as Finn, Jaycee, and I wait for Deacon on the porch. He's late. Again. This time he claims to be behind on a contract he's working on for a ghostwriting deal. I lift my head at Finn's tiny confession.

"I don't think my dad likes me," he whispers.

My heartstrings tug me to my feet and I lie down beside him, panting drops of drool on his bare leg.

Jaycee wraps her arm around his shoulder. "What makes you say that?"

"He doesn't want to hang out with me."

"Of course he does. He's just busy with work."

Finn's shoulders droop. "Other kids get to go camping and stuff with their dads. He never wants to do anything with just *me*."

"Have you tried talking to him?"

Finn shakes his head. "He doesn't want to talk. Unless it's about his book."

"Maybe he doesn't know how you feel."

Finn leans over to hug me. "What was your dad like?"

Jaycee leans back, propping herself on her elbows. "He was busy a lot, and sometimes I felt invisible to him, too."

I clamber across Finn's body and lick Jaycee's nose. "I never meant to make you feel that way. I wish I could make it right."

"I'm sorry he died," Finn says quietly.

"Me too. He was a good dad. Mom said that sometimes life gets in the way of what's really important and people forget what it's all about."

He slowly strokes my fur. "I think that's what happened to my mom. She left one day and didn't come back. Dad says she has problems."

"She must if she left you behind."

"I wish she had taken me with her."

Jaycee squeezes his hand. "Maybe she couldn't."

"Dad says it's better this way, but I'm not so sure. I feel like I don't have any parents."

"Well, you have me. And I'm not going anywhere."

He smiles but it fades quickly. "I wish I could stay here forever."

Jaycee sits silently for a minute. "Have you tried getting your dad to do things with you in the evenings after he picks you up?"

He nods. "He doesn't want to do the things I want."

Jaycee tugs Finn's arm until they're both standing. "Follow me!"

Not wanting to miss whatever they're up to, I race inside behind them. "Go into my closet and dig out the nerf guns. I'm sure they're in there somewhere."

She rushes to the desk and scribbles something on a piece of paper while I chase Finn to her room.

He throws shoes and purses out of the way in a dash to find the toys. "Bullets," he mumbles, sliding three guns to the middle of the floor.

I scoot in beside him. "I may have eaten them all," I mention nervously.

Somehow, he finds a dozen darts beneath the clutter and a few minutes later he lugs it all back to Jaycee. She tapes the note to the door and props a gun against the house.

"Find us before we find you," it says, a smiley face at the bottom.

"Now we hide," she tells Finn and they take off running.

Finn points behind the shed. "There?"

Jaycee shakes her head. "That'll be the first place he looks."

They run around the yard until finally settling on the large pine tree. When they dip into the branches, I slip in beside them. "You'd be better off splitting up and taking him from both sides."

"Huck's going to give us away," Finn whispers.

Oakley meanders over, sticking his nose in the pine needles. "What are you doing?"

"Botching an ambush on Deacon," I offer.

A car door slams shut in the driveway. Finn's eyes grow wide in anticipation.

"I don't have time for this," Deacon's voice booms. "Come on, I have a deadline to meet."

Finn's smile disappears.

I lick his face. "I'll go out and see if I can help."

Deacon is in the backyard by the time I meet him.

"I don't think you understand the game," I tell him. "Where's your gun?"

He ignores me, yelling for Finn to get his things.

"Five minutes, Deacon. Can't you spare that?"

"Go, go, go!" The call comes from Jaycee as the two of them charge from their spot, peppering Deacon with a shower of foam darts.

"Okay, you got me," he says. "Now we have to go."

Finn's gun thuds to the grass. I run to him, afraid he may cry. Instead, he clings to Jaycee's side.

"It was a nice idea," he whispers.

Jaycee drapes her arm over him. "Run inside and get your things before you get in trouble."

He does as he's told and Jaycee takes stride beside Deacon. "He was just trying to have some fun with you," she says.

"I know. And I'm sorry, but I've got a lot of work to finish before midnight."

"One of these days you're going to regret choosing work over your kid. You may think I'm just a teenager who doesn't know anything, but I'll tell you you're wrong. Two weeks before my dad died, he asked me if I wanted to build a snowman. I told him no because I wanted to watch YouTube. YouTube. I thought there would be plenty of days we could do things together, but I was very wrong."

"I'm terribly sorry that happened to you."

She crosses her arms as they turn the corner of the house. "Finn will probably give you another chance. I suggest you take it."

Finn waves meekly at us as Deacon ushers him to the car.

Chapter 33

"I can't believe you're getting him to try new food," Deacon tells Jaycee on Friday evening. "How'd you do it?"

Jaycee shrugs. "Something I like to call 'creek magic.'"

Deacon laughs. "I don't believe I've heard of that."

Sabrina steps beside Jaycee. "It's powerful stuff. Maybe Jaycee can show you how to use it."

Jaycee leans over, hiding her mouth with her hand. "It's worked three days this week. Stupid rain got in the way yesterday."

Sabrina steals a glance at me and Finn wrestling in the living room. "Maybe the two of you could come over tomorrow for an early supper," she suggests. "I know the weeknight evenings are hectic for you."

Deacon rubs a muscle in his neck.

Finn, having overhead the conversation as well, rushes in. "Please? Puh-lease?" He drops to his knees and throws his hands together.

"It would be our pleasure," Sabrina nudges.

Deacon scratches his temple. "I feel like I'm already imposing."

I make my way to him for a thorough inspection. I'd done a quick one when he first walked in, but if he's eating dinner in my house, I want to know everything possible. Had fast food for lunch. Most likely Arby's. Spilled coffee on his pants and tried to clean it. I'm sure it tricked the humans, but not me. Antibacterial soap. At least he washes his hands, I think, turning to wag my tail at Finn.

"If it makes you feel better, I can grab takeout from the restaurant," Sabrina offers. "That way you know we aren't going to any trouble."

Deacon is on the spot and he knows it. "Can I buy?"

Sabrina laughs. "At the restaurant I own?"

"I guess that does sound silly."

Finn yanks at his father's khakis. "Can we?"

Deacon gives in with a smile. "It's been a long time since we've eaten something besides frozen dinners."

"It's settled then," Jaycee says, high-fiving Finn.

She turns to Sabrina the moment they are out the door. "You're cooking, aren't you?"

"How can I not?"

Jaycee's smile fades. "I completely forgot. I'm supposed to go to Reese's tomorrow."

Sabrina sighs. "See if he can come over here instead?"

Chapter 34

I dance around the front door, wagging my tail while I wait for Jaycee or Sabrina to make their way from the kitchen to answer the knock that will happen just as soon as Deacon and Finn get up the steps. I throw in a bark for good measure. Reese had shown up hours ago and I'm eager for Finn's distraction to keep my mind off the teenage romance.

"What's taking so long?" I jump against the door to peer out the glass. "You brought me something? Are those cupcakes?"

Jaycee nudges me out of the way as Deacon's knuckles rap on the wood.

Finn steps inside, his hands clinging tightly to a stuffed dog toy shaped like a dead duck and an apple.

He bends to pet my head. "The apple is for Oakley."

"That was sweet of you." I lick his face. "You stuck your finger in the icing, didn't you?" He giggles and tries to step around me. I block his path.

Deacon offers the cupcakes and a sheepish smile at the frozen dinner hidden beneath. "We brought dessert. There's chocolate and vanilla in there. And I brought back-up."

"Neither were necessary," Jaycee says, holding the treats above my head when I leap into the air for an inspection. "But thanks for the cupcakes. Mom is on this health kick so she made raspberry sorbet for dessert. I'm not sure if that qualifies as healthy, but these will pair nicely with it. Thanks."

"I need to see if they have the good icing," I beg. "The boy over here won't even let me lick his dirty hand. I should warn you, he recently picked a booger."

"Please, come in." Jaycee leads the way to the kitchen.

Deacon shoves his hands in the pockets of his crisp jeans. "I would say you have a lovely home—which you do, of course—but that feels like a formality and that's not my nature. Plus, I've been here before."

Sabrina wipes her hands on a dish towel and offers a smile. "Please, sit. We'll talk about the weather."

Deacon looks out the window over the sink.

"It's gonna rain," I tell him, tugging the duck away from Finn. "In about ten minutes."

"Looks like it might rain," Deacon offers.

Sabrina opens the oven door, sending a waft of eggs, potatoes, ham, onions, bacon, and cheese into the kitchen. I clamp my teeth into the duck, squeaking it half a dozen times.

I shake my head like I'm making sure the duck is dead, waving it in Finn's face. "If you drop some food on the floor, I won't be mad."

Deacon scratches his head. "I thought you were ordering from the restaurant?"

Sabrina shrugs. "I was planning on it, but I stopped at the store and inspiration struck. We're looking for new menu items and I thought maybe I could test this recipe out on you. It's a breakfast casserole." She bites her lip as she waits for his reaction.

I park myself in front of her. "What's wrong with the menu?"

"Happy to be a guinea pig," he says.

"Glad to hear it. I've been on the internet all day and I have a list."

He laughs, his eyes following her around the kitchen. I turn my head and squeak the duck at him. "I'm watching you."

He extends his legs and his boots nearly touch my feet. "Those are awfully clean boots," I grumble. "Either they're new or you don't work hard enough."

Sabrina lifts a sheet of paper from the counter. "Actually, there's something else you could help me with, if you don't mind." Deacon nods. "I'm thinking about starting the breakfast shift back up and I want to revamp the old menu. Could you look this over for me?"

Deacon taps his finger against the paper. "Half this stuff needs to go."

Sabrina cocks her head. "Really?"

"You want to stick to the classics—B's and G's, omelets, waffles, now that's where you can mix it up a little—but some of this stuff is off the wall. Oatmeal cupcakes? That *has* to go. And breakfast cookies? I don't know about that."

"I was on the fence with that one. I thought maybe a quick and healthy option. Maybe I can introduce that later."

"I'd stick to what you know first and roll out fancier options later."

I dart out of her way as she moves to open the cabinet where the plates are kept.

"Thanks," she says, placing a stack of plates on the table.

The clouds open up as Sabrina removes breakfast—dinner—from the oven and a torrent of rain pours down, though I don't think they notice.

A crack of thunder booms and the wind picks up, all going unobserved by the people in my house. I make my way to the back door.

Finn takes a seat beside me. "You don't want to go out in this, boy."

Jaycee stands at the refrigerator, dumping ice into glasses. "Open the door and he'll realize that."

Finn does as instructed.

I stick my nose into the air, sniffing the enhanced smell of fresh water hitting the earth. "You okay out there, Grandpa?"

"You're letting the cold air out," he haws from the shed.

Rolling my eyes, I step backward. Leave it to him to scold me for standing in the doorway of my own house with the door open.

Finn shrugs and closes the door.

"Time to eat," Sabrina announces.

Deacon rubs his hands together. "Smells delicious."

Sabrina places the meal on the table as everyone takes their seats. "Thank you."

Finn stares out the window while Jaycee scoops a small serving onto his plate.

Deacon passes a pile of pancakes to Finn. "So how does this work?"

Finn hands the plate to Reese without taking one. "It's raining," he whispers.

Jaycee's lips form a tight line when Finn glances to the freezer and the meal his dad brought. "Finn, you're going to eat what's in front of you. That's the deal."

"But it's raining," he argues.

Reese whips out his phone and pulls up a radar. "Looks like it might last a while."

Jaycee furrows her brow at him. "You're not helping." She turns to Finn. "We had a deal."

"It's okay. I brought one of his favorites," Deacon offers.

Jaycee shakes her head. "Finn told me you two mostly eat frozen dinners and there's no sense in letting him get away with it when Mom made a perfectly good meal."

"Jaycee, this isn't our business," Sabrina scolds.

"But it's the whole reason they're here. I changed my plans for it," she argues.

"That's enough." Sabrina's tone is sharp.

Reese pours syrup onto a stack of pancakes and hands it to Finn. "Maybe it will stop raining in time," he says, melting the hurt from Jaycee's words off the boy's face. "But you still have to eat everything on your plate."

Finn's eyes sparkle with worry. "What if it keeps raining?"

Reese looks around for approval but continues without receiving it. "If it rains too long, I have another idea. It will depend on how long you can stay though." He glances to Deacon. "It has to get dark first."

As if on cue, the lights go out. Sabrina rushes to get candles despite light filtering in through the window. "This is...intimate," she says, placing them around the kitchen.

Deacon scoops a generous helping of the casserole onto his plate. "Let me check my itinerary for the night." With a smile, he taps the screen on his phone. "Yep, it's clear."

Everyone laughs. After a few moments of silence, Sabrina takes the focus off Finn who nibbles around the egg on his plate. "How's...work?"

My ears perk at the hesitant tone of my wife's voice. Why did she say 'work' like that? Is he hiding something?

Deacon takes a sip of water. "That depends on if we're talking about the business or pleasure aspect of it," he admits with a laugh.

"Tell me about both," she suggests.

Reese and Jaycee strike up a conversation about Reese's summer job detailing cars at the dealership, making it hard for me to concentrate on Deacon's words. I slip to Sabrina's feet and lie down near her chair to better hear their chatter.

"I can't go over the details until publication," Deacon offers. I consider moving from my perch to see what expression his face holds. "Personally, I'm working on a story about a man who basically kidnaps his daughter to escape his powerful ex-wife when he discovers...something." He claps his hands together. I slip to the space near the stove where I can monitor the entire table.

Sabrina's fork clinks her plate. "*Something*? That's vague. Tell me more."

He laughs. "I don't know more."

"How do you not know more? You're the writer."

I collapse heavily onto the floor.

Deacon reaches for a second helping from the pan in the center of the table. "True, but it's not my story to tell."

Sabrina sips her water, confusion filling her eyes. "That doesn't make any sense."

"I'm telling the story, but my characters decide what happens."

"The characters *you* made up?"

He nods. "It's a symbiotic relationship. I need the characters for the story, and they need me to tell it."

She shakes her head. "I don't follow."

"Maybe it's better you don't. You might think I'm crazy if you did."

Reese nudges Finn, drawing Sabrina and Deacon's attention to the end of the table. "If you eat everything on your plate, I'll take you fishing with me next weekend." He glances up at the boy's father. "If it's okay with your dad."

I poke my head between them. "I'll eat everything on *all* the plates if I can come too."

Jaycee nibbles on her casserole. "If I eat everything on my plate, can I come?"

Reese laughs. "You want to go fishing?"

Sabrina opens her mouth to object but stops when Finn shovels three bites quickly into his mouth.

Reese turns to Deacon with an apologetic shrug. "Looks like you might need to check your itinerary for next weekend."

The clock on the oven and microwave beep as power is restored to the house.

Finn nearly knocks his chair over as he races to the window. "It's still raining," he pouts.

Sabrina steps beside him, her eyes straining toward the rain gauge on the corner of the porch. "Looks like we got two inches so far. We're going to have to postpone that trip to the creek even if it stops raining now."

Finn's bottom lip juts out. He points to his empty plate at the table.

Deacon's mouth drops open. "Did you feed the dog your dinner?"

"I understand the accusations, but I'm innocent," I bark.

Deacon points to the empty plate, at me, then to Finn. "You really ate that?"

"I want to go fishing. And I want everyone to come so you'd all better eat your dinner."

Reese ruffles Finn's blonde hair. "You've got it."

Finn forces a smile. "Can we have cupcakes now?"

In one swift swoop, Jaycee glides the dessert onto the table. "Let's do it!"

Sabrina hurries to clear dishes. "Remember there's sorbet in the freezer. Which really doesn't go with breakfast. I should've thought about that."

"Thanks, Mrs. P, but I think we're good with the cupcakes," Reese chuckles.

Deacon grabs the main dish as hands go flying toward the chocolate section of the container he'd brought. "I wouldn't mind sorbet. Raspberry, was it?"

Sabrina smiles. "You don't have to have pity sorbet."

I leap to my feet when his hand rests on her shoulder.

"I've never had pity sorbet. What does it taste like, do you think?"

Rolling her eyes, she moves to the freezer. "Raspberry."

He smiles. "My favorite berry."

"Is he flirting with my wife? Wait. Is she flirting back?" I turn in a circle and bark, not knowing what else to do.

She scoops two helpings into the fancy dishes I'd claimed she'd never use and, up to this point, I'd been right. She motions to the living room.

"Pity tastes delicious," he says after an awkward silence between them.

They sit on opposite ends of the couch. I slip against the wall where I can keep an eye on them while keeping watch on the shenanigans in the kitchen. Sabrina has no idea those kids are on their third cupcake each.

"Better than revenge pie," Sabrina teases.

Deacon holds up a finger. "I think I read that in a book."

"I saw it in a movie." Crossing her legs, Sabrina laughs. "I hope I never reach Minny Jackson angry."

"Minny Jackson? Who's that?" I cock my head, wracking my brain. Revenge pie. Movie. Minny Jackson. "Oh, the lady from *The Help* who baked her shit into a pie and served it to her former employers."

"I guess I'm not that creative," she laments.

Deacon holds the spoon to his mouth. "That's not true. I've seen your work. It's amazing." His eyes twinkle mischievously. He may not tell her, but he's not fooling me. He bought some of her work.

"Thank you." She clinks her spoon into the empty dish.

Reese pokes his head into the room. "It's dark enough to go nightcrawler hunting," he says.

Deacon crinkles his forehead. "Y'all will hunt anything around here."

Sabrina leans in to whisper in Deacon's ear. "We're starting you out easy. When you're ready we'll take you snipe huntin'."

A grin grows on Reese's face. "Snipe hunting is only for the most skilled hunters. Let's see if they can catch the elusive nightcrawler first," he says with a wink toward Sabrina.

"I can't believe you're passing up this golden opportunity," I grumble, prancing over to join in the excitement.

Once outside, armed with flashlights and plastic containers, the two teenagers show Finn where to look.

Deacon nervously approaches my grandfather. I get the impression he's never been this close to a large animal. "I always thought you had to live on a farm to have horses and such." He laughs.

Sabrina pats Oakley's rear to move him out of his stall. "This is *not* a farm. But that doesn't mean we can't keep livestock. Technically we have enough land to raise one cow. Or half a dozen pigs. And don't get me started on the number of chickens. All fun facts my husband used against me when I tried to find some sort of zoning law forbidding us to have equestrian animals. Apparently, there are no such laws here."

Deacon stares at the tack on the walls. "Interesting. So, how did you end up with him?"

Sabrina grabs a pitchfork and mucks the stall. "Jason's grandmother."

"Did she live on a farm?"

"I have a feeling you're going to like this story."

Deacon runs his hands over the halters hanging on the wall. "Let's hear it then."

"Jason's grandfather died when Jason was young. His grandmother never remarried. She said she had one great love and that was Ward. Jason and his mother tried to convince her to get a pet for a companion, but she was allergic to cats and said dogs were too high maintenance."

"But a donkey is not? Isn't it easier to let a dog outside than to constantly muck a stall?"

"I haven't got to the best part yet. Jason basically became her pet, always doting after her. But before he left for college, he was worried about what his absence would do to her. I guess you would have to know Jason to really appreciate this next part. In late July of that year, our town was hosting a fundraiser for a local farmer's wife who had recently been diagnosed with cancer. There was a raffle for a donkey to help with medical bills. Ten bucks got your name thrown in a bucket."

Deacon nods. "You got a donkey for ten bucks? I don't know much about this stuff, but I'd say that's a good deal. Kind of weird, though."

Sabrina smiles, her finger held up to stop his assumptions. "That's not really the way things work around here. The farmer's wife had cancer. Everyone chipped in. I don't know a single person who was there that night who didn't have at least five entries in that bucket. Heck, the sixth-grade class had thirty tickets."

Deacon laughs. "What would a bunch of twelve-year-olds do with a donkey? Take turns having him on the weekend?" He gasps lightly. "Remind me to circle back to that idea later."

Sabrina chuckles. "They were quite disappointed they lost. Anyway, like I said, everyone had multiple tickets. Jason was no different." Her eyes glisten, though I'm sure Deacon doesn't pick up on the extra moisture that my superior eyesight detects. "He'd worked all summer to save enough so he would only have to work weekends while he was in school. When the news broke about Lisa's diagnosis...he dropped his whole savings into that bucket. He lived to help people."

Deacon blinks heavily. "How many tickets did he end up with?"

"A lot. Except he didn't want anyone to know how much he donated so he bought them in batches from different volunteers." A single tear slips down Sabrina's cheek. "He wrote the farmer's name on every ticket except one."

Deacon smiles. "Let me guess—the other ticket had his grandma's name on it?"

"Lucky guess." She reaches over to stroke Oakley. "Rumor has it that over ninety percent of the tickets had Farmer McClaskey's name on them."

"Now that's the kind of story you don't get in the city."

"Here, like this," she says, taking his hand and showing him how to give Oakley the apple without getting bit. "It wasn't until his grandma died that we learned the truth. Lisa McClaskey—fully recovered—came to help us bring Oakley from his grandma's to here and she told us her husband had learned what was going on with the raffle. Truth was, he couldn't afford the extra mouth to feed, though he appreciated the gesture. Her eyes lit up as she recalled him seeing those sixth graders line up for the raffle. None of them could keep quiet about their tickets. The whole town knew how hard they had worked to earn the money for them."

"I'm kind of sad they lost. No offense."

Sabrina spreads fresh straw into the stall. "I was too. But, after seeing Jason's grandma with Oakley, I'm glad she won. Turns out, the ticket with her name was on top and Farmer McClaskey used a slight of hand trick to pull it from the bottom of the bucket."

"I'm not sure I understand."

"I saw that spark of creativity in your eyes a moment ago. Play it out and you'll know why he chose to not let it become a school pet."

Deacon studies Oakley intently.

"It's funny, I haven't thought about this story in a long time," I admit. "It's even better now that I fully understand."

"It's one of my favorites," Oakley whispers.

Sabrina fills him in on how my grandma used to sit for hours with Oakley in their back yard as if they were old friends—which, of course, they were.

Sabrina moves outside and fondly watches the activities in the grass. "Where is it you said you're from?"

"Saint Louis."

"What brought you to Union Grove?"

"I can write from anywhere and it was getting expensive living in a big city," he says, the words clearly rehearsed.

"You're not fooling me," I bark, knowing there's more to the story than what he admits.

Sabrina laughs. "You're a writer and that's the best you could come up with?"

Deacon shrugs "What did you expect?"

"I don't know. Something a little less bland, I guess."

Oakley shoves his head under Deacon's arm and munches on fresh hay.

Sabrina runs a brush down Oakley's back. "Maybe a powerful ex-wife and something to hide?"

Deacon's body tenses. "The biological father. Maybe that's the secret. I could work with that," Deacon whispers his notions into the wind.

Sabrina turns her head at the sound of giggling behind the shed. "What?"

Deacon waves his hand. "I think you just became my muse for the book I'm working on."

"I thought he kidnapped his own child?"

"That's not really kidnapping. This works better. If he's not really the biological father...I think that will make a good plot twist. I'm going to run with it."

Sabrina slaps his shoulder. "Sounds like you owe me some inspiration."

Reese claps his hands, leading the group into the shed. "I think we have enough."

Finn's cheeks are smudge with dirt and his grin proves the night was not a total loss even though he didn't get to go to the creek.

Deacon rustles his hair. "It's time for us to get scootin' anyway."

Reese bends to Finn's level. "The real fun is next weekend."

Finn smiles and makes his rounds saying goodbye.

"Glad you got to see me," I say on my turn.

Chapter 35

Finn bounds in the door bright and early Thursday morning. "Two more sleeps until we go fishing!"

I leap at his feet, jumping to lick his face. "Two?! Surely, it's Saturday by now. Check the calendar again," I tell him.

"You don't have to do the countdown every morning, Finn," Deacon playfully groans.

Jaycee rubs sleep from her eyes. "I think he's excited."

Finn dodges my tongue, giggling as he dances around the room. "I've never been fishing."

I prance my way around him. "We're going to catch bluegill, crappie, and if you're lucky, maybe some bass. It's going to be great!"

"I'll try to be in early tonight," Deacon says, though we all know he's going to call late in the afternoon and promise to be here 'after the next chapter.'

Finn looks longingly at Jaycee after his dad closes the door. "How do you make time go faster?"

Jaycee makes her way to the kitchen. "Like I told you yesterday and the day before—stop thinking about fishing."

He slaps his palm to his forehead as she pours two bowls of cereal. "I don't know how."

"Try."

He slips into my chair at the table and digs his spoon into his Lucky Charms. "What's it like?"

"What's what like?"

"Fishing."

"Eat your breakfast and I'll tell you."

Finn dips his fingers into the milk, picking the marshmallows out one by one and taps his feet until Jaycee is finished. After taking the bowls to the sink, Jaycee leads the way to the TV and switches on the gaming console.

A few minutes pass and she hands him the controller. "Maybe you can get some practice."

I stare up at a fishing game she pulled up. "Seriously? You can't call this 'practice.'"

"I wish I would've thought of this days ago," Jaycee mumbles, taking a seat on the couch.

He's still playing the game at lunch and Jaycee uses it to her advantage, offering him more gaming time if he eats the ravioli she prepared. To our surprise, it works like a charm and he eats every bite.

As expected, Deacon postpones pickup time, but Finn uses it to practice casting.

The moment Reese arrives on Saturday, I plaster myself to his side, knowing he won't let me get left behind.

"We won't need half this stuff," Reese comments, rifling through my old tacklebox.

"What do you mean?" I growl.

He plucks a frog lure and dances it toward my face. "Would you eat this?"

"If I were a Muskie or a Largemouth," I snap, careful to miss the jig.

Jaycee toys with a Savage duck lure. "We're *not* using this. Who could eat a precious little duck?"

I race a circle around them. "It's not real," I admonish. "Pike love it."

Finn's tiny knock on the door interrupts Reese's criticism of my tackle.

"Whatever. We'll just take it all," Reese suggests. "I've got a good setup so this can be extra."

Finn eagerly knocks again.

I block his path to the door. "I've got everything all set up. It's July so you'll need everything in the middle rack on the left side. In about two weeks you'll want to switch to the right side. Have you checked the forecast for today? If it's going to be over seventy, you'll want to look in the weed beds."

Jaycee clamps the box shut. "We've got at least fifteen poles in the garage. I don't know if they still work."

I slip in front of Reese before he can make it to the door. "You'll want to get the Ugly Stik with that reel Sabrina got me for Christmas. And the one that looks just like it with the bait caster. Here, I'll show you." I grab Reese's arm and pull him toward the garage.

"Come in," he yells with an exasperated sigh.

Finn bursts through the door.

Deacon lifts a tumbler of coffee. "He's been up since five. I couldn't hold him back any longer. He's driving me nuts."

I slather kisses over Finn's face. "I have been waiting for this day for *so* long."

"Must be in the air," Reese says. "The dog's been driving me nuts since I got here. I almost feel like he's bossing me around."

Deacon laughs.

I pull Reese's arm again. "Let's make sure you get the right poles."

"I'm making sandwiches," Sabrina calls from the kitchen.

I sniff the air. Ham, turkey, cheese, and mayo, but no mustard. I always have mustard on my deli sandwiches. I wag my tail anyway. "I'll take three!"

Jaycee gives Finn a quick hug. "I made sure to get you the peanut butter and jelly stuff you like," she whispers.

Half an hour later, the cooler and gear are packed. The ride to the lake is filled with a hundred questions from Finn. I'm proud of his knowledgeable inquiries. Deacon explains he'd found a YouTube channel about fishing and had consumed himself with it the last few evenings.

I plan to get right to the water when the truck stops but an unnatural instinct takes over as soon as my paws hit the ground.

"They'll let anyone in here," I grumble, sniffing the scent of a chihuahua. "Uck. Geese galore." My nose is overwhelmed with smells. A dead fish on the bank. Diesel exhaust from the truck that just pulled in. Cigarette smoke. Worms. An infant who needs a diaper change. A little bit of B.O. And my personal favorite—a golden retriever in heat.

I wonder what our children will look like as I race in her direction.

"Huck!" Sabrina's tone cuts through my strange desires, reminding me she's the only woman I want to chase.

I turn and gallop toward her. "I wasn't checking her out. I thought she had a squirrel in her...pocket." Geesh. I'm glad that wasn't in English. How lame.

She points with an arm full of poles. "We're going this way."

"Be careful with those," I instruct, following closely on her heels. "I don't think you know how much money you've got right there."

Sabrina carefully leads the way past several small groups, including the chihuahua and his parents. Poor thing is convinced he can take me, he claims as we pass.

"Keegan Alexander says we should go for the weeds," Finn announces, formally claiming the spot beside me.

"Who?" The response comes in unison from the group.

"The YouTuber," Finn explains.

"He's right," Reese says. "This time of year, that's where we'll find 'em."

Finn reaches for a pole, eager to get his line wet. Deacon awkwardly takes it from him and stares deep into my tackle box. The hair on the back of my neck is alert, as if ready to stand at attention if I give the word. I was less worried when I caught my mom snooping under my bed where I hid my *Playboys* when I was fifteen.

"You've got a nice collection," Deacon offers with a small laugh. "Jason must've been quite the fisherman."

My first instinct is disgust at my name on his tongue, but I'll take the compliment.

"He loved fishing and was always looking to add new lures. Each one had a story when he'd bring it home." She leans over and points to a polished silver spoon. "This one he had to have because it was just like the one his grandpa gave him on their first fishing trip."

"I wish Finn could have stories like that," he whispers, fingering through the box.

"Try this one," I say, poking my nose over a red and white spoon. "I think I just realized why I had to buy it. I guess it's been waiting for Finn to use."

"I think Huck is pointing to that one," Finn says, gently removing the Johnson Silver Minnow.

Deacon laughs. "He's just sniffing."

Sabrina leans over. "Ah. Jason bought that one with our last five bucks. It's a funny story now, but I was pissed at the time. The restaurant was just starting to make enough to cover expenses. Our first month in the black and he buys a stinking fishing lure to celebrate."

Reese's line hits the water. "Are we gonna fish or you girls gonna gossip all day?"

Finn waves his hands, motioning Deacon to hurry up.

"He never used it," Sabrina continues, working her own line. "Said it was going to be his son's first lure."

Deacon leads Finn to the water, awkward confusion seeping out of him. "You don't have a son." Panic fills his eyes and he steps in front of Finn before he can cast. "Let's find a different lure. We're being disrespectful."

Sabrina turns, beaming. "I may not have a son, but Jason would absolutely love that lure being used for a boy's first big fish."

Deacon looks skeptical. "Are you sure?"

"He would insist."

Jaycee swoops over and ushers Finn to the water. "He'd be honored." She zips her line into the water. "I'm using the last one he ever used."

I creep to her side. "I don't even know which one that is." I sit as it dawns on me she's saying the words for his benefit.

Deacon steps into the mix, his eyes questioning the sanity of the situation. Jaycee reels the line in twice before he puts words to his thoughts. "Jaycee, I hope you don't mind my request, but would you please use another lure? If I know me—and I think I do—I'll have to go diving for that thing if it gets lost. And I didn't bring a change of clothes."

She laughs. "He's got three more just like this. It's really no big deal."

He places his hand on her shoulder. "It is. It's a sentimental piece and you should cherish it."

Jaycee appeases him by swapping lures even though she made the story up.

"I see this is the old people section," Deacon says, setting up his spot next to Sabrina.

"Who you calling 'old?' We'll let Reese deal with the hang-ups," Sabrina whispers. "It'll be good for him."

Deacon swings his pole back. "Who's gonna deal with mine?"

"I've got ya." Sabrina casts her line.

After twenty minutes with no bites, the gang launches into serious chatter. On my left, Reese and Jaycee make up stories with Finn about a fish who flies into outer space and on my right, Deacon and Sabrina chat about...work.

"The bank is one of those sacred places where work doesn't belong," I tell them.

They don't listen. I lean in closer to get the latest update on the restaurant, though I'm surprised by how little it stirs the workaholic in me.

I plop down a safe distance from Deacon's unskilled casting and enjoy their banter.

"And the fish circles the moon," Finn chirps. "But that's not where he wants to live either."

"He should fly through a meteor shower," Reese suggests.

"Maybe his ship gets busted and he has to repair it on the fly," Deacon boldly offers.

Finn quickly reels his line in. "He doesn't have a ship, Dad."

"My bad," Deacon replies, casting his line out.

"It's my story," Finn gripes.

"Sorry. I'll stay out of it."

Sabrina switches lures. "So, how's the book coming?"

Deacon sighs heavily. "Slow. I'm working on the foreshadowing to give the reader clues that the main character isn't the biological father but I'm not sure how to do that."

"Hmm. Maybe bring up some sort of discipline issue where he's afraid to dole out a punishment because he doesn't feel like it's his...responsibility isn't the right word."

"He feels like he doesn't have the authority."

"Exactly."

Deacon inspects his lure as if it's the reason the fish aren't biting. "I should warn you that bringing up my writing can result in lengthy conversations, half of which won't make much sense to you. You'll become a sounding board and I'll suddenly go quiet when it finally clicks."

"I don't mind that."

Deacon changes lures and casts directly into the weeds. "I'd rather talk about your work."

"I don't mind listening to you talk things out if it's helpful."

He waves his hand. "I'm good right now. That could change soon though. I may have to take you up on that offer."

"Feel free."

"What about you? What was work like this week?"

She laughs. "I filled in for our manager one day because she had a sick kid. Of course it was the day she had three interviews scheduled for a cook. I've never given an interview."

Deacon yanks his line. "I think I've got one!"

I leap to the water, glancing from it to the man holding the pole. It takes three seconds to figure out what has happened. "You're stuck on a log."

Finn rushes over, Reese and Jaycee not far behind. "Bring it in! Come on, Dad!"

Deacon furrows his brow as he yanks his line. "I...can't."

Sabrina sets her pole down. "I think you've caught a log-fish."

Finn's eyes turn to saucers. "What's that?!" Reese leans over and whispers the truth in his ear. "Oh." Finn slinks back to his spot, disappointed.

"Think you'll keep it?" I bark, bouncing like a maniac. Sabrina's skillful nature of removing the hook, stops me from getting too mean about his mishap. "I'm seriously impressed," I tell her, licking her hand.

"Here ya go." She hands the pole over.

"That was embarrassing."

She throws her line back out. "Wait until you hear my story about the interviews today."

"That bad?"

"The first one went okay. The girl was a little quiet, but I liked her. The second one though, that was a doozie. It was a guy—keep in mind we're hiring for a line cook and someone to do prep work—he was something else. First of all, he's got a degree in culinary arts, has experience doing elaborate desserts, and has ten years of experience."

"No offense, but what was he doing applying at a place like Jaybird's?"

She yanks her pole, her lips tightening as the fish gets away. "That's what I asked. He wants to revamp my menu. Says it's his dream to turn a small restaurant into a large chain. It was rather insulting."

"Wow."

"I told him I wasn't interested and he should take his talents to Milwaukee. He slammed his portfolio closed, looked at me, and said, 'Well, if the job's off the table, can I ask you out?'"

Deacon fumbles his cast and the lure drops at his feet. "He *what?*" I still don't understand how I can sense emotions, but I swear he's a little jealous right now. His chest tightens and he almost...*smells*...mad.

"Right? I was so flabbergasted, I called the next interviewee—another man—and rescheduled."

"I got one!" Finn's tiny voice bellows.

Reese helps him reel in a nice three-pound Muskie. Pictures are taken and the fish released. The excitement over, I close my eyes to nap in the warm sun.

Chapter 36

"I always dreamt of having a son," I tell Oakley one afternoon after our third Saturday fishing expedition in a row. "And now I think I've gotten a glimpse of what it would be like. Finn has talked about nothing but fishing for days. First it was all about how he couldn't wait to go and, for the last two days, it's been about how he caught the biggest fish of the day...and how excited he is to go again."

Oakley laughs. "I know. I heard all about him catching more fish than Reese."

"That boy would tell a fence post about his catch, I think." I scratch my neck. "Reese spent more time showing him *again* how to change lures than he did fishing. And I can't tell you the number of times he stopped to untangle line."

"You know that's not the important thing about fishing."

"Somebody needs to give that memo to Deacon."

Oakley flicks a fly off his ear with a shake of his head. "What do you mean?"

"He's been bringing his computer. Says he 'feels inspiration near the water.' Sabrina had to make him stop writing."

"I don't understand that man. He leaves his child in the care of a teenager for roughly ten hours a day and, on the weekend, he still doesn't spend quality time with him?"

"I know I have no room to talk—I spent long hours away from my own child, a regret I'll harbor until the end of time."

Oakley swipes his tongue across the top of my head. "One of life's hardest lessons is learning to forgive yourself. We're only human." We break into a fit of laughter at his statement. "What I mean is...you've changed."

I prance a circle around him. "You could say that."

He nips at my tail as I pass. "You know what I mean. On the inside."

"But Jaycee will never know that."

"Jaycee may not know her dad was there during her late childhood years, but she'll never forget the dog who curled up beside her because the thunder was terrifying or the time he ran onto the soccer field to stop the opposing team from scoring a goal."

I cover my face with my paw. "She told you about that?"

"Oh yeah," he haws. "Laughing the whole time."

I remove my cover. "She was so mad."

"For a minute. But she said you looked so proud of yourself for tripping the other team's player that she couldn't be too mad."

"Okay, first of all, I didn't mean to trip her. I just didn't realize she was running so fast."

"You need to focus on knowing that one day you'll be reunited and you can tell her everything."

I leap toward him. "I like the way you think." The phone rings inside the house, grabbing my attention when Sabrina yells down the hallway, inquiring about a fishing trip tomorrow.

"See if I can come," Oakley suggests.

"Shh." *Dammit. What'd I miss? Sabrina said Jaycee could go out with Reese tomorrow? Alone?!* "I gotta go."

I scratch at the back door until an annoyed Sabrina swings it open. "We agreed no dating until she's learned to juggle six eggs for no shorter than fourteen minutes without dropping one." Normally, I'd laugh at the ridiculous request we were to make of our daughter. It was something we concocted over too many cocktails the night we started 'trying.' "I know it's been a long time, but how could you forget *that?*"

"It's supposed to storm in the morning and Jaycee has a date in the evening," she says into the phone. "We'll go next weekend. Maybe we can rent a boat, spend the day away from everyone else."

"I'm sure Finn would love that. I just don't know how to entertain him tomorrow. He's going to be so bummed." The voice belongs to Deacon.

I jump at Sabrina's feet. "Hey, Jaycee isn't old enough to date. We need to talk about this."

She shoves me away. "Maybe he can come over here and entertain Huck. He drives me nuts when he's cooped up in the house too long."

"Thanks for the offer, but I'm sure I can find some way to keep him busy. He's been asking to have a friend over. Maybe we'll do that."

I bat Sabrina's calf. "We need to talk."

"Mom!" Jaycee shrieks from her room.

"That sounds like a plan. I have to go. Girl trouble." Sabrina ends the call and makes quick strides to Jaycee's room.

Half of Jaycee's closet lies piled on her bed. "I have nothing to wear," she laments, flinging dresses onto the bed.

Sabrina pats her back. "Where's he taking you?"

"Dinner and a movie."

I leap onto the bed, rooting deep into the pile. "No. Not a dark theatre."

Hangers rustle as Sabrina searches. "Calm down. That sounds casual."

I poke my head up, a shirt dangling over my ears. "What are you looking for in there—Narnia? Wear what you have on," I suggest, leaping off the bed. "Your shorts could be longer. That shirt is perfect," I say of the baggy material that's tied neatly in the middle of her back.

"Great. Now he's keeping it casual. Doesn't he want to show me off?"

Sabrina laughs and takes our daughter's hand. "Casual dates are the best. It means he wants to get to know you. It's intimate."

I lurch off the bed and wiggle my way between them. "Don't use words like 'intimate' when talking about our daughter with some boy."

"He's embarrassed by me? Doesn't want his friends to see?"

Sabrina shakes her head. "It's not that at all. He'd rather spend time with you. Alone. There will be plenty of times he'll want to show you off, but right now he doesn't want to share you with anyone."

Jaycee throws herself onto the bed. "I guess you might be right. But what do I wear? If I get too dressed up, I'll look foolish. If I don't dress up enough, he'll think I'm not interested."

Sabrina sifts through the items on the bed, receiving a turned-up lip from Jaycee at every choice. "Let's go shopping."

Jaycee smiles. "Really?"

"Every girl deserves a new outfit for her first date."

I block the path as they move toward the door. "Wait a minute."

A firm tug on my collar proves they won't be stopped. I race to the back door, pretending to need out.

"You just came in," Sabrina says with a scowl. "We won't be gone long."

In a matter of two minutes, they are out the door and there's nothing I can do about it.

"I need to stop this," I mutter, pacing around the house. "But how? Maybe I can chew some wires on Reese's car so he can't drive it. How will I get to his house though? What if...I eat something that makes me terribly sick and they have to rush me to the hospital?"

Bobbi steps into my path, appearing from nowhere as I turn a corner. "What if you stop being a grinch and let your daughter be a teenager?"

My lips curl back as I prepare to snarl, but a single thought stops me. She's been through this before. "How did you survive when Sabrina went on her first date? How old was she? Did you want to rip his head off?"

She swats at my face, claws retracted, thankfully. "Breathe. Your emotions are perfectly rational. Tom was a nervous wreck the night Sabrina went out for the first time."

I slowly lower myself to the ground. "Tell me about it?" I'm sure she's about to tell me the story about Eric Hewitt, her Spanish tutor freshman year. He was two years older and they went to the county fair where they discovered all they had in common was Spanish.

She sits inches away from my face, the stale stench of vanilla lingering about her. "Right before middle school, she had the biggest crush on this kid name Houston. He was moving away over the summer and Sabrina said she'd just die if she didn't get to go on at least one date with him." I blink. How had I never heard this story? "We were friends with his parents so we all went to the bowling alley and let them hang out while we chatted in the bar. They thought it was cool."

I sneeze at a dust bunny on the floor. "The bar is attached to the bowling alley."

"Yep. We'd peek out at them after each drink. But made them happy. They thought they were alone, but we had a pretty good eye on them the whole time."

"Is that really a date?"

She laughs. "It was to her."

I cover my head with a paw. "That doesn't help me at all. What if Reese breaks Jaycee's heart?"

"We'll all be here to put the pieces back together."

A low growl escapes. "Who's going to put *his* pieces back together?"

"You know, you and Tom are more alike than I may want to admit." I cock my head. Is she giving me a compliment or insulting me? "Not too long before you came along, some boy stood her up and I had to stop Tom from going to his house to demand an explanation."

"Is that unreasonable?"

She licks her paw and runs it over her ear. "Didn't stop him from announcing it to a handful of people when he realized the boy was the cashier at our grocery store. Everyone in a long line found out what the kid had done."

"That's awesome!" I yawn, drooping my tongue out. I'd heard that story before, but it's still one of my favorite Tom moments. "I don't like the idea of my little girl going out alone with a boy."

"She's sixteen, Jason."

I stare at my paws, trying to add the years on my toenails. "I guess time gets away from you."

"She's going to be moving away in a few years."

I puff out my chest. "Stop."

"Huck, I'm only trying to point out that time is running out."

"I don't need this right now," I snap, and slink to the bed I shared with my wife. I need to think.

Chapter 37

I press my nose into Sabrina's side. She sleeps peacefully in the middle of our king size bed, clinging to a pillow. Her hand falls over my back. I rest my head on her side, staring at the empty space I used to fill.

"We need to talk about Jaycee dating," I whimper, nudging my nose into the bend of her elbow.

She stirs softly, rolling to her back. I reposition myself across her chest. "She's too young. You think you know Reese, but I promise you he only has one thing on his mind. He's a good kid, I'll give you that. But I need to know if Jaycee is strong enough to stick to the convictions you've instilled in her." I whisper the words to my wife, but somehow my conversation turns to God.

Please give us strength. Help Sabrina make wise decisions when it comes to our daughter and help me be at peace with them. Give Jaycee strength to stick to her guns if Reese pressures her to do what she knows isn't what's in her heart. I don't know why it's taken me this long to realize I should also be asking for guidance for the man You have picked out for her. I don't know if that's Reese or not, but I'm trusting You to lead him to her. I pray he walks by Your side and she'll recognize him when the time is right.

Sabrina's eyes flutter open. I stretch my neck forward, licking her face.

"No wonder I felt like I was sleeping under a ton of bricks," she whispers, her hot morning breath tickling my nostrils.

I wiggle up her body. "Are you calling me fat?"

"Huck," she groans. "Get off me."

I beat my tail against her legs, wiggling upward until my head fits nicely in the crook of her shoulder. "I know you hate to be bothered in the mornings, but I can't help myself." I slather kisses over her cheeks. "One day I'll do this for the last time and I don't know when that day is coming so I can't let a single opportunity pass. I hope you understand."

Her brow relaxes and a smile spreads across her face. "It's Saturday, Huck. Let me sleep."

"The day's a'wastin'." I leap off the bed. "Great. I'm turning in to my grandfather."

She pretends to sleep, adding a fake snore for good measure.

I nudge her arm and take it gently in my mouth. "Get up, get up, get up. It's time to get up," I belt out the made-up tune my mom used on me when I was a teen.

Sabrina groans. "Who needs an alarm clock when you have a dog?" She slips on a robe and pads to the kitchen.

Thunder booms and rain pelts against the house but I still race to Oakley when she opens the door. "Good news. I've decided not to worry about Jaycee's date. If Sabrina thinks it's okay, I'm on board. Candy Pants is a good kid."

He laps water from his bucket, eyes studying mine as if he's waiting for the punchline. "Someone had a good night's sleep," he says upon discovering my sincerity.

"Did some prayin'."

"That'll do it."

I follow him around the perimeter while he performs his morning ritual of making sure nothing changed overnight.

"I'm kind of sad Finn won't be dragging us to the lake today," I admit.

"Don't brag," Oakley scolds.

"I'm not meaning to. It's just that I've gotten used to having someone to play with again. Jaycee is getting to the point where she doesn't even pick up a stick when I bring it to her. She's always staring at a phone."

"She's at that age."

"I reckon. Pretty soon I'll only get her attention in passing."

"It's a phase, Jason."

"How long do those last?"

Oakley stops when a bunny appears in the far corner of the yard. "You had a phase where the only meat you ate was ham. It lasted six months."

I shake the water from my back. "That's because I was afraid I was going to get Mad Cow Disease."

"Remember the night you almost cried because you thought your hamburger was cow?" I glare at him as he laughs. "Grandma saved dinner because she told you it was called *ham*-burger because it was made with ham and the 'burger' was because it was shaped in a patty."

I sit, staring at the bunny who has spotted us. "And I asked why it wasn't called a 'ham patty.'"

"You *do* remember." He laughs. "You gonna chase that thing or do I have to?"

I quickly glance at him and bolt toward the frightened bunny. "I should've brought some salt," I yell.

He haws in the background and I'm not sure if he's cheering me on or reminiscing about the summer I carried a salt shaker around after he told me the way to catch a bunny was to put salt on its tail.

When the bunny seeks shelter in a bush, I head back to Oakley. "You know," I pant. "I was sixteen when I realized why you told me that about the salt." He cocks his head. "I remember because I was driving down 600 South when I saw a bunny sitting in the middle of the road. I don't know why but I thought of that summer. You had bet me five bucks I couldn't catch one."

"And you never claimed the prize."

"I'm sure I could now," I wager.

He looks toward his hind quarters. "I left my wallet in my other pants."

"Would you let me finish my story?" He swoops his head, motioning me to finish. "I came to a stop because I was afraid I'd run over the poor thing. We sat there for nearly two full minutes and it dawned on me that if I could get close enough to put salt on its tail, I'd be close enough to catch it."

He drops to the ground and rolls on his back, laughing. "That's the best story I've heard in a long time."

I take a bow. "I'm here all day."

"I can't believe it took you that long to make the connection."

"Okay, you've got your laugh. I'm getting out of this rain."

"I wish I had someone to tell that story to. Send the cat out," he chuckles.

I turn to face him. "I'm going to drink a lot of water and when I come back out, I'm going to pee on *all* the grass."

The afternoon activity in the house has me walking a mile from Jaycee's room to Sabrina's and back while she gets ready for her date. By the time she asks Sabrina which hairstyle she should do for the billionth time, I'm exhausted. I collapse at her feet as she sits in front of the mirror to finally put on makeup and trudge behind her when she returns to her mom's room for a different necklace, only to fall at her feet again when she decides to finally finish her look.

"Oh no," I say after seeing her completed ensemble. "You're not wearing that."

She twirls in front of her mirror. "How do I look, Huck?"

"Where did *those* come from?" I bury my head at the sight of cleavage on my teenage daughter. "Take them back. You don't need 'em."

Sabrina appears in the doorway. "You look beautiful."

Jaycee smiles into her mirror, ignoring the compliment. "I've been thinking...do you think you could talk to Deacon?"

Sabrina raises her eyebrow. "About?"

"Finn really wants to spend more time with him. I hate seeing him missing someone who is right *here*." I nuzzle into my girl's side. "I guess it's just hard watching Finn struggle to get his dad's attention, knowing they're lucky to have each other when my dad is the one thing I want, but can't have."

Sabrina throws her arms around our daughter. "You are so much like your dad. Always wanting to help people. You should be focusing on this date, not worrying about other people's trouble. Be careful that it doesn't become a curse."

Jaycee smiles. "I just wish they were closer."

"I'll talk to Deacon when the time is right."

"Thanks. It would mean a lot to me. And I know it would to Finn, too."

She jabs her finger in my direction. "He doesn't think so."

Jaycee's smile quickly fades. "Crap. I'm ready and he's not even here yet."

I brush against her bare leg. "A girl after my own heart."

"You are your father's daughter," Sabrina whispers as the doorbell rings. "Make your bed or something. I'll tell him you'll be a few minutes."

I race to the door. "You'd better be on your best behavior tonight," I bark, beginning my lecture before Sabrina can let him in. "The number one rule is keep your hands to yourself."

"Hi, Reese. You look handsome," she says. "Jaycee will be out shortly."

I sniff his khakis and wonder why he's chosen a gray polo to pair with them before remembering my color vision is not what it used to be. "Why do you have a candy bar in your pocket? Don't you know it will melt?" I inhale deeper and discover it's only an empty wrapper.

"I'll have her home by eleven," he says. "If that's still okay."

Jaycee slowly emerges, waiting to be noticed. Loose curls fall over her shoulders and her skirt sways as she walks. I wonder if we have time to sew a few inches to the bottom. As Reese's eyes land on her, new concerns overcome me. I vow to chew all her pushup bras to shreds but the idea quickly sickens me.

I circle Reese. "New rule number one. Rule number one is you wear a blindfold. Except when you're driving. There will be no kissing so get that out of your head right now. Actually, go back to the first time you thought about kissing my daughter and unthink it."

"You look—"

She closes the distance between them. "If you say 'amazing,' I'm going to kick you in the shin."

I dart around them. "That's my girl."

He chuckles. "I was going to say, 'like a girl.' But I realized how dumb it would sound. I've never seen you dressed up."

She waves her hand across her body. "This is what it looks like."

"I like it." He steals a glance at Sabrina.

I step between them. "I thought this was supposed to be casual."

She smiles. "Are you going to stand here and be awkward around each other all night or you going to go have fun?"

Reese nods. "Right."

Sabrina opens the door. "Get out of here."

Without waiting to be told twice, I bolt outside. Reese's car reeks of fresh wax and tire shine despite the rainfall this morning. "Nothing fixes that like dog pee," I mumble, lifting my leg on the rear tire.

"Huck," Reese scolds. "I waited all morning for it to stop raining so I could wash the car. If I'd needed your help, I would've asked."

"It's the price you pay for dating my daughter," I tell him and hurry to mark the front tire.

He meets Jaycee at the passenger door. His hand slides to the small of her back as he opens the door.

"That's it," I bark, leaping inside. "You're getting a chaperone."

Sabrina watches the teenagers in amusement, Jaycee looking to her for help.

Everyone calls my name, patting their thighs, pretending to throw balls or pull imaginary treats from nonexistent pockets. I hold my ground. I figure a little stubbornness on my end is warranted.

"Mo-om, can you help?" Jaycee tugs on my collar. "Reese?"

I smile at her frustration. Sabrina stands beside Reese, assessing the situation. I dig into the cloth seats with all my might when she yanks my collar. Reese's arms open wide as if he's going to try picking me up. I growl.

He throws his hands in the air. "Let's take him."

Jaycee's skimpy skirt blows in the breeze as she turns to face him. "You can't be serious."

"If you go change, I'll move. That outfit is way too revealing," I bark.

"Why not? He clearly wants to go for a ride," Reese says.

Jaycee sends her mom a questioning look.

"I don't think you have a choice," Sabrina admits.

"See if you can get in there. Maybe he'll move over," Reese suggests.

Jaycee crams into the seat, covering my body. "If you think I'm going to let you sit here so you can hold hands, you've got another thing coming. The last thing I want is a distracted teenage boy behind the wheel," I groan.

Jaycee pulls herself off me and slaps her hands on her hips. "I'm *not* sitting in the back seat on my first date," she whines.

Sabrina leans over, whispering in Jaycee's ear. "I know it's not the way you pictured it, but some of the best memories come out of unexpected circumstances. I'll bet you look back on this one day and laugh."

Jaycee scrunches her face and shoots me an evil glare. "I'm going to be covered in dog hair."

Reese takes her hand. "I promise we'll have fun."

Jaycee smacks her purse on the seat beside her. "This is not how this was supposed to go."

Reese rolls down my window as he puts the car in reverse. They wave to Sabrina in the driveway. I stick my head out the window, grateful someone understands the need for wind in your face. Sabrina always complains about the noise it makes having the passenger window down and not the driver's window as well so she only allows me this pleasure on the way home from work if the weather isn't too hot or too cold.

Jaycee crosses her arms, pouting. "What are we going to do about dinner?"

Reese glances at her in the rearview. "I have an idea."

"I don't see how we're going to be able to have dinner with Huck tagging along. Unless you want to do drive-thru."

Reese's hand reaches through the space between the seats. "Let me worry about it, won't you?"

"And we'll have to cancel the movie. I was really looking forward to seeing it too."

My ears flap, creating a weird numbing sensation on my head. I smile into the humid air, cooled by acceleration of the car. A bug attaches itself to my tongue, but few things give me the feeling of being utterly free like the wind in my face. Jaycee continues to grumble as Reese takes the highway out of town. Wondering what tricks he has up his sleeve, I lean over him to check the speedometer.

"Huck, do you mind? I'm trying to drive here."

Jaycee leans forward, shoving me back toward my own seat. "He's drooling all over your car!"

Reese places a hand on my back. "It'll dry."

Twenty minutes later, we're in the traffic of Burlington. We stop for a red light and Reese turns to the back seat.

I clamber onto the console. "No funny business. You're still manning a missile with my daughter in it. Eyes on the road," I scold.

I stumble when his foot hits the gas. After a few more turns, he pulls into Echo's parking lot and takes a space next to a red corvette. Hanging halfway out the window, I admire the machine parked next to us.

"This is embarrassing," Jaycee whines, staring at the menu out the window.

"Let me help." I release my best dog fart to date.

Jaycee's eyes grow wide in horror. Laughing, Reese hangs his head out the window.

The smell finally dissipates and Reese smiles softly, squeezing her hand. They order a few minutes later and he climbs into the back seat with her. "Better?"

She leans into him.

"I think I'll sit back here now," I announce, leaping onto their laps.

Reese laughs. "Someone is jealous."

Jaycee smiles for the first time since we'd left the house. "Apparently so."

Reese settles for scratching my ear. "What classes are you taking next year?"

I turn and slop my tongue over his face. "I'm so glad you asked. I'll be studying how to run off boys who get ideas about kissing my daughter. I'm a little worried about it, but I'll bet I'm a natural."

For ten minutes I listen to stories about teachers Jaycee can expect next year and what they like and don't like. There's even a bonus tidbit that if you have Mr. Jacobsen first period, he won't count you late if you tell him you had car trouble—even if you do it more than once a trimester.

"Please tell me you ordered me a cheeseburger," I say when the overwhelming smell works its way toward the car. "You aren't going to make me sit here and watch you eat, are you? I need to eat, too," I plead, climbing my way to the front seat.

A few minutes later, a waiter places a tray on the cracked window. Reese unwraps my burgers and holds them out for me. I gobble them up before he decides he wants them for himself.

Reese and Jaycee slowly enjoy their meal, chattering about past soccer games and kids on their teams. Finally, Reese returns to the driver's seat and Jaycee fights me for Shotgun. She loses.

"Want to take Huck to the park? There's a nice one down the road," Reese suggests.

"There's not much else we can do with him," she mutters.

Shortly before dusk we finish our walk through the park and Reese leads us back to the car. They seemed to have a nice time. I even let them walk side by side—a reward to Reese for his cautious driving. I still claim the front seat, hopping in before Jaycee has a chance.

"I'm enrolling this dog in obedience school first thing Monday morning," she grumbles.

Reese reaches over. "Nah. He's a good dog. Bill is allergic and my dad says we don't have time for a dog since I insist on playing sports. You're lucky. I'm stuck with a hamster. It's actually my sister's, but the stupid thing always runs on its wheel in the middle of the night. I can hear it across the hall."

"Maybe the hamster needs obedience school."

He laughs. "I'll look into that."

Instead of turning toward home, Reese steers the car through town, driving down a lane between a row of pine trees. He pays a man at a gate and we enter a grassy parking lot. Pressing my nose against the glass, I immediately recognize the spot—Mack's Drive-In.

"I haven't been here since I was your age," I say, climbing onto Reese's lap for a better view.

"I looked this place up while you were in the bathroom earlier," he says. "It's not the new superhero movie, but it's the best we can do...unless you want to sit on a couch at my house and have two toddlers smooshed between us."

Jaycee smiles. "This is perfect."

I sniff the blanket he pulls from the trunk. It smells of stale grass with a hint of Little Debbie. Thankfully, there's no perfume to be found. "Mind telling me why you have a blanket just waiting in the trunk? What exactly do you keep it on hand for?"

He shakes it out and spreads it on the ground in front of the car. "My mom left this in my car after a soccer game last season. Watch where you sit because my brother takes snacks everywhere he goes."

Jaycee checks a corner, kicks off her sandals, and sits on her knees. "Brothers," she says with a chuckle.

He takes a seat beside her. "Right?"

I make a circle and plop down at their feet.

"What movie's playing?"

Reese forces a laugh. "*Sing 2* and the new Matrix."

"Nice."

"Would you like some popcorn?"

Jaycee nods. "I'll go with you."

He stands, shaking his head. "You stay here with Huck. Last thing I need is him asking for a hot dog."

She laughs, patting my head. Reese returns ten minutes later with a bucket of popcorn, two drinks, and a hot dog.

"The lady at the counter dropped it on the floor so I told her I had a dog that would dispose of it for her. You know, so it didn't go to waste."

Jaycee beams at the gesture. Reese hands her the drinks and slips me the hot dog. It's gone in two bites.

"Okay, Reese, you've got your brownie points. Don't push your luck," I order, noting the lack of dirt on my snack.

The previews end and I settle in for a nap, sticking close so I can be alert the instant he makes a move.

Halfway through he gets a jacket from the car and slides it around Jaycee's shoulders. She slips her head on his shoulder.

"I've seen that move," I whisper, a knot growing in my stomach. "I can fix it," I say, ripping an SBD.

Jaycee's nose wrinkles. Reese jabs a finger in my direction.

"Huck, you're gross!" Jaycee plugs her nose, waving a hand across her face.

By the time the second movie starts, she's moved to a lying position, her head on his lap.

"I texted your mom to see about an extension on your curfew," he says, twisting a section of her hair around his finger.

"Oh?"

"Yeah. This movie ends about the time she wanted you home. I told her we'd be straight back afterward and she agreed."

"Smart kid," I say and move to nestle myself next to Jaycee.

True to his word, we head home the minute the credits roll and I'm nice enough to stretch out in the back seat this time.

I busy myself watering a tree while Reese walks Jaycee to the door.

"I'm sorry tonight didn't turn out the way we planned."

Jaycee runs a finger under the strap of her top. "It was better...after I stopped grumbling about the dog tagging along."

"I had a lot of fun."

I leap onto the porch, awkwardly standing behind them. "Maybe Oakley can join us next time," I suggest, laughing at my own joke.

"I suppose you'll want to bring the donkey next time," Jaycee teases.

"Heck, let's bring the cat too," he suggests.

Jaycee giggles. "Can you picture them all crammed in your back seat?"

He laughs. "How about I just take *you* out next time?"

"Sounds good to me," she beams. "I'll lock the dog up before you come."

I step up to the door and whine. Jaycee twists the knob and I slip inside to report to Sabrina, leaving my daughter privacy to enjoy her first kiss.

Chapter 38

Summer lingers on in long, slow days filled with sprinklers and naps under the shade tree. Deacon drops Finn off early one rainy morning. According to the news Sabrina turned on, it's supposed to rain all day. And if I know anything about boys and rain, it's either going to be a great day or an incredibly boring one. Jaycee confirms the latter by stating up front that they are staying inside until the rain stops. That makes my decision to hitch a ride with Sabrina easier.

I enjoy my quiet morning curled up underneath the table she's working at in her shop. My slumber is soon interrupted by a ringing phone.

"Are you busy?" My ears perk at Deacon's voice on the other end.

"Not terribly. What's up?"

"I thought you might like to do some book research with me."

She glances in my direction. "What kind of research? I have Huck with me."

"He can come. I just need to take a drive."

"A drive?"

"I'll explain when I get there," he says and ends the call.

Ten minutes later, he's standing in the doorway, humid air blowing in from the sun that's decided to come out after all.

I stretch. "Well, one thing's not changed—the weatherman still doesn't know what to predict."

Sabrina locks up and heads to Deacon's sedan.

"I was hoping you could drive, actually," he admits. Sabrina moves to our truck and opens the door for me to hop in the back. "I need to pay attention to the surroundings."

She turns the key. "Where are we going?"

I poke my head between them.

Deacon grins as if he's about to say something incredibly stupid. "I was hoping you'd know. I've got this scene...just drive and I'll try to explain."

Sabrina waves to a customer as she pulls out of the parking lot. "I'm like your free Uber driver." She laughs.

His hand reaches for hers but he pulls back. My spark of hope quickly flickers out as he changes his mind. "I don't want you to think I'm taking advantage."

"It was a joke. Where would you like to go?"

He sighs. "The middle of nowhere?"

I rest my chin on the console between them. "What do you want to do there?"

"I know right where that is," Sabrina chuckles.

"Great. I need to see it."

"There's nothing there," I tell him. "Except maybe some trees or a field."

Sabrina flips on her blinker and makes the first turn out of town. "How lost do you want to get?"

"If you wanted to dump a body where it wouldn't be found, where would you go?"

"That's two counties over, is that okay?"

Deacon whips his head in her direction, a tinge of fear emanating from his body, though I'm certain Sabrina doesn't pick up on it. "Are you serious?"

She laughs. "No. But you should see the look on your face." He relaxes. "Though I once worked with a woman who used to live in Indiana and she said there was this highway where they were always finding bodies."

"That sounds like a story I need to hear."

"I can't remember exactly, but it had something to do with Chicago. I guess it was a matter of location. They found several bodies along the same stretch over the years. One of them was in a suitcase and another in a box. The farmer would find them during planting or harvest. Her husband was a journalist and covered many of the stories."

"I think I just got an idea for a book."

"You can call it 'Body Dump Road.'"

He laughs. "Highway to Decay."

She shakes her head. "Maybe we should keep working on that."

"I could have the main character be a detective and his—*her*—love interest be involved in the murders," he announces excitedly.

"Maybe someone in the town can be an accomplice...like her brother!"

Deacon rubs his hands together. "This is why you're my muse."

She flicks her hair over her shoulder to be funny, but I feel the flirtation there. "I feel so important."

Deacon's gaze slips to the window and the farm houses slowly passing by. Sabrina makes several turns, heading north toward Caplinger's land.

"There's been talk of putting wind farms all along here," Sabrina offers, motioning to a patch of fields.

Deacon scowls. "Why ruin a perfectly good landscape?"

Sabrina smiles. "It's been a huge debate for a few years. Doubt it's anything to worry about."

"Good. No need to insult God's work."

"We call this 'Caplinger County,'" Sabrina says, sloshing a tire through a puddle on the gravel road.

"Why?"

"The whole northwest corner of the county is owned by the Caplinger family. Two hundred years ago a man named Donald Caplinger struck it rich in the Gold Rush out in California. He'd left his wife, Eliza, behind and came back after six years, hoping to live out his days like a king. Except she had died of cholera. Her sister had taken over the raising of their kids—all six of them."

Deacon's eyes spark with interest in a story I've heard a thousand times. "Wow. That must've been rough."

Sabrina shrugs. "I'm sure it was. But the sister was an awful woman. Long story short—"

He waves his hand to stop her. "I want the long version."

"Okay, the short long version. The sister was very attractive, but no suitor would take her because of the kids. Nobody wanted a brood that belonged to neither of them. Which I don't understand because, in that time, it was the same as free labor. Anyway, when Donald Caplinger returned, she found out how rich he was. She claimed it was his fault she was an old maid—at twenty-four. So he agreed to take her as his wife."

"Wait. That would've made her eighteen at the time he left. Why wasn't she married then?"

Sabrina holds up a finger. "She was something of a wild child. Rumor had it that she was going around town seducing married men."

"This is juicy."

"Donald and the sister—Martina—fought like crazy. They had four kids of their own. The kids couldn't stand their cousin-siblings." She makes a face at the technical relation term for the combined children. "He died first and she made sure his first six children got next to nothing."

"How'd she do that?"

"Blackmail from what I hear. But that depends on who you ask." She goes on to tell how, for decades, we had our very own version of the Hatfields and McCoys. The oldest group fighting for what was rightfully theirs and the younger trying to claim their share.

"Fast forward a few generations and the four children he had with the sister sold off hundreds of acres due to bad crop years and such. The whole thing reeks of a Netflix documentary."

"How do you know so much about this?"

She turns onto a gravel road between fields. "I guess it's local legend or something. This all belongs to the bloodline of Caplinger's second brood. They own about six country blocks."

"You'll want to turn left up here," I mutter, bored with the conversation.

"What does that mean?"

She continues straight, motioning to the stop sign up ahead. "From this stop sign to the next is one block."

Deacon turns his head to the back window. "That's like a mile long block."

She laughs. "Now you understand the phrase 'a country mile.'"

"I think I have another book idea."

Sabrina stops dead in the middle of the road. "Here we are."

He opens the truck door and steps out. Sabrina follows suit, letting me out as well. "It's not what I expected," he admits.

She leans against the bed of the truck. "What did you think you'd find?"

He bends, studying the few rocks left on a once gravel road. "I don't know. A crumbling barn or something. What do you call this road?"

She points to the distance. "That's Caplinger's Corner."

He shakes his head. "No. I mean, is this a gravel road or like the last dirt road in the Midwest?"

She laughs again. "It doesn't get enough traffic to put fresh gravel down. And that's a good thing. It's basically a field access road. The nearest house is two roads over."

He nods. "Okay. Well, what do you do in the middle of nowhere?"

She motions to the truck. "Get in." She stops at Caplinger's Corner, pulling off the road in a grassy area big enough for a tractor. "On hot summer nights this is a good place to find teenagers hanging out."

A crease forms in his brow. "What do they do here?" She bites her lip, a smile giving her away. "I'm guessing you've been here before."

"Once or twice."

He smiles. "Was this your drinking spot?"

I join them on the tailgate. "That's not all it was."

"Sometimes."

He turns and stares deep into the cove of trees. "Is this like a make-out spot?"

She lifts a shoulder. "For some. I preferred a different spot though."

"Mind showing me?"

I leap out of the bed and wait for the door to be opened, eager to see the place where Sabrina and I shared our first kiss.

Five minutes later, we're another road over, tucked into a real dirt road between two rows of cornfields.

"When I was a teenager, there wasn't much to do for entertainment, so my friends and I played hide and seek in our cars."

Deacon scratches his chin. "I'm not sure I know what that means."

"We'd all meet up in town and then we'd split up in teams. One vehicle would be 'it' and everyone else would drive around looking for a place to hide. Normally, we'd stick to the city limits, but sometimes when we were really bored, we'd go out in the country looking for a place nobody would find us. This was our go-to spot for those nights. Nobody ever found us."

"Who is 'us?'"

"Jason was always my partner. Sometimes we'd have a car full but most times it was me and him. This is where we kissed the first time."

I leap onto her lap, slathering her with wet kisses.

"I'm sorry," he says. "I wouldn't have asked if I had known."

"It's okay. I need a trip down memory lane every once in a while."

"So, you and Jason were high school sweethearts?"

"We broke up before college but found our way back to each other shortly after."

"That's nice."

"What about you?" She points a finger at his chest. "Did you have a high school sweetheart?"

He blows out a hard puff of air. "Hardly. I was too...well, I couldn't narrow it down to one girl. In fact, I didn't have a steady girlfriend until Finn's mom."

"I see."

"Not really, you don't. I only attract women who are completely crazy." He lists off examples to prove his theory.

"I'm not sure that makes you some sort of magnet for women with issues," Sabrina argues.

"I don't know, but I'm done trying."

Sabrina tenderly reaches over and rests her hand on his shoulder. "What if you miss out on the love of your life because you gave up too early?"

"I'm not hiding from the love of my life, but I'm not looking for her, either."

"I guess that gives you time to focus on Finn. Boys need their dads at his age."

"Finn and I don't have anything in common."

"I think all parents feel that way at some point," Sabrina says softly.

"I feel silly saying this, but sometimes I think I keep my distance so that if I mess it up, it won't hurt him so badly."

She rubs his arm gently. "You won't mess it up. Give it a try. Come snipe hunting with us tomorrow, maybe you'll find some common ground in the woods." She laughs. "We all know you didn't find it at the lake."

He laughs and rubs his hands together, but I feel his desperation to change the subject. "How about we work on the second part of my scene?"

Sabrina sighs. "What's that?"

"I need to see if I can get us home."

She claps her hands together. "This should be fun."

I watch her type a quick message to Jaycee telling her to set up the festivities for the next evening. I hope it works.

Chapter 39

Finn clutches a pillowcase with a superhero I've never seen on it. "Is it time?"

I spin a circle around him, nipping at the corner of the fabric. "Please say it's time. He's driving me nuts with all his bouncing."

Reese studies his phone and glances at Sabrina and Deacon. Sabrina nods, letting Reese take the lead on our adventure.

"The conditions are favorable for catching snipes," Reese announces, pretending to check his phone. "But don't worry if you don't catch anything on your first time."

Finn nods and everyone picks up a pillowcase from the deck railing.

I leap off the porch. "You're gonna have a blast!"

As we head for the woods behind the house, walking around the field still full of six-foot corn, Reese lays out the strategy for catching the elusive snipe.

"They're rather quick," Sabrina offers.

Deacon cocks his head, questioning our endeavor. "What exactly do they look like?"

"You'll know when you see one," Jaycee chimes in.

Finn tugs her hand. "How will we know if we've never seen one?"

Sabrina tickles his ribs. "They're like nothing you've ever seen."

Reese chokes back a laugh. "So, when you see one of the little boogers, you open your bag wide." He motions with his own pillowcase. "And you swoop like this."

I bark at his theatrics. "You're a natural."

The sun slides past the trees on the horizon, leaving about an hour of daylight.

Deacon scratches his head, studying Sabrina heavily. "You do this often?"

Sabrina nods, a sparkle gleaming in her eyes. "Every chance we get."

"What do you do with them when you catch them? Can you eat them?"

Terror washes over Finn's face.

Reese turns the corner and we step onto the gravel lane. "Sure. If you catch about fifty."

Sabrina laughs. "You might have a snack."

"I don't get the point," Deacon argues. "If you don't eat them, why hunt them?"

Jaycee shrugs. "Because it's fun."

Finn practices his swooping snatch. "I want to take one home as a pet."

Reese waves a finger in his direction. "Oh no. You can't keep them in a cage. They'll die."

Finn's eyes widen. "Why?"

"Nobody knows. They just do."

We finally make it to the woods and Reese gives the final order. "You must be quiet. Snipes scare easily."

Finn nods, pressing his lips tightly together. We wander through the woods aimlessly for what feels like an hour.

Sabrina points between two trees. "There was one," she whispers.

Finn and Deacon freeze, eyes glued to the spot she'd pointed out. Reese and Jaycee join in, pointing out the creature.

"I'm gonna sniff one out," I bark, earning a stern scolding look from Finn.

"Quiet, Huck, you're gonna scare them away." He jumps around a tree, bag poised. "I think I see one!"

"Get it," Reese orders.

Deacon folds his hands on his hips. "I don't see anything."

"They're everywhere, Dad," Finn beams, running off. He swoops his bag closed and peers inside. "Missed again."

My nose to the ground, I pretend to have a lead but, really, I'm sniffing a raccoon mother and her babies who passed by shortly before we arrived. Sabrina points for Deacon, using my tactic to her advantage. "Follow Huck."

Deacon hesitantly swoops his bag to the ground.

"It takes some practice," Sabrina offers, peering inside his empty bag.

Jaycee and Reese take up the charade and soon Deacon and Finn are talking strategy. They plan to entrap the creatures by Finn scaring the snipe straight into Deacon's bag as they stand opposite each other. They fail several times but keep at it. I hear three sets of footsteps growing fainter as Jaycee, Reese, and Sabrina slip away. Nobody told me what to do at this point of the game so I wait to see if they notice. Completely caught up in their hunt, I realize the master plan of this escapade and sneak out to join the others in the cornfield.

"I'm not sure Deacon is falling for it one hundred percent," Sabrina whispers. "We may have left too soon."

"I think we'll be fine," Reese says, motioning them to head toward the house.

Each taking our own row between itchy cornstalks, we zig zag our way back.

"I'll bet we don't make it to the house before we hear them calling us," Jaycee says.

Sabrina pauses. "What are we betting?"

Reese bends a stalk for Jaycee to slip through the row. "Losers wash the winner's car?"

As they lay out the terms of the bet and discuss how far they think they can get, I turn my attention to the conversation coming from the woods.

"I'll run real fast and scare them all up and you catch them," Finn suggests to his father.

Try as they might, the next ten minutes prove unfruitful for the team and Deacon finally mentions they're alone.

"They left us?" Finn's voice cracks and I suddenly feel terribly sorry for him.

"I think they're playing a joke on us."

Finn sighs heavily. "Why would they do that?"

"I suppose they think it's funny."

"You know the way back, right?"

"If you can get us out of the woods, I'll get us back to the house," Deacon teases.

"What about the snipes?"

"I don't think they exist."

"You don't?"

"I have no idea what we've been chasing all night," Deacon offers. "But I haven't seen anything unusual."

"Me either." Finn laments. "I was just pretending because I thought everyone else could see them. I didn't want to disappoint you."

"Why would that disappoint me? Being honest is something very valuable."

"I didn't want Jaycee and Reese to laugh at me."

"Well, they probably are. I think we've been pranked."

"We'll have to prank them back then," Finn says.

"What do you have in mind?"

"I dunno. You're the writer. Think of something."

"I'll do that."

Their voices grow faint for a few minutes as they head in the opposite direction, but just as quickly, they return and steadily gain clarity as they approach the edge of the woods. We're almost to the yard and Reese questions the activities of the pair left in the woods. While they debate on that, I listen intently to make sure they're finding their way back.

"Dad," Finn says. "You said being honest is good, right?"

"Mhmm."

"Then I want you to be honest with me."

Gravel crunches under their feet as they take the long way back.

"About what?"

Finn clears his throat. "Do you like me?"

Deacon's feet stop moving. "What kind of question is that? Of course I do."

"You work all the time."

"Somebody has to pay the bills. Unless you want to get a job?"

"If I get a job, will you spend more time with me?"

Deacon starts walking again. "So that's what this is about?"

"You don't have time for me."

"Of course I do."

Finn kicks some rocks. "When we're around Sabrina and Jaycee. But you never want to do anything just me and you."

Fabric rustles together as I assume they embrace. "Can I be honest?" There's a pause then he adds, "I'm scared."

"Why?"

Their feet scuffle along the road for a bit before either of them says another word. I silently plead with Deacon not to miss his chance. As they turn into the grass ditch that leads back to our house, he offers an explanation.

"I've never been good at relationships. As dumb as it sounds, I thought if I never got close to you, I wouldn't fail at fatherhood," Deacon admits.

I lie down, covering my head with my paw in embarrassment for the poor man.

"That doesn't make sense," Finn whispers.

"Every single one of my girlfriends dumped me...including your mom. She chose...things she thought were more important over me."

"I'm your *kid.*"

"Yeah."

"You can't quit on your kids."

He sighs heavily. "But kids can quit on their parents."

Finn's feet stop moving again. "They can?"

Deacon cracks his knuckles. "I know you're not old enough to understand this, but sometimes when kids grow up, they decide they don't like their parents anymore."

"And you think I won't like you when I'm big?"

"Something like that."

"That's silly." Finn's feet move again, slower as they get closer.

"Not really. Not to me. I did it to my parents."

Finn gasps. "Why?"

"You might be too young for this story, but I'll tell you anyway. When I graduated high school, I told my parents I wanted to go to college to study Creative Writing. Told them I wanted to write books. They told me that wasn't a 'real job' and refused to help pay for schooling."

"But you're a writer." Confusion fills Finn's words.

"Yes, but not like I want to be. I'm still working as an editor and ghostwriting. I want to be a novelist."

"You're writing a book," Finn argues.

"Yes...It's all pretty complicated. But, when I walked out the door, I told my parents I wouldn't speak to them again until I proved them wrong."

"That's why you work so hard."

"Partly. I love what I do, but I also want to prove that I can do it—that I can make a living selling books."

"I know you can do it," Finn encourages.

"I think I just realized my dreams aren't as important as the story my life tells."

"What does that mean?"

"It means the fictional characters I create might live on forever, but I won't. And I don't want the people in my life thinking they mean less to me than the ones living in my head."

Finn slaps his hand against his face. A mosquito, I imagine. "Okay."

"It means, I see now that I love you more than I love writing. I'm sorry I was afraid to admit that sooner."

I bark as their figures enter the yard.

"Things will be different now," Deacon says, throwing his arm around Finn's shoulder.

I race to greet them. "Congratulations," I say, dumbly. "You fell right into our trap."

Jaycee, Sabrina, and Reese share a laugh with them on the porch. The kids all disappear inside when Jaycee says cookies are waiting on the table. I follow them to the kitchen, hoping to snag one myself.

Deacon and Sabrina remain on the porch. I lie under the table, waiting for crumbs, and listen to the conversation outside.

"That was a dirty trick," Deacon says. "I'm going to use it in a book."

Sabrina laughs. "See? I'm a helpful muse."

"Thanks. Thanks a lot." The crickets make their awful racket in the silence between them. "Actually, Finn and I had a good talk." He recants the story, adding details about struggling for several years during and after college and about how he's certain writing is what drove women away. He'd spent so much time consumed in his stories that he was sure the women couldn't handle it. The conversation returns to snipe hunting and Sabrina shares her experience.

"My dad waited until I had a big slumber party. There were six of us. I think we were thirteen. He must have gotten tired of the noise because he asked if any of us had been snipe hunting. None of us had and we were thrilled to be let out of the house at night. Armed with flashlights, we took off for the woods. I'll bet we spent half an hour out there before we figured it out."

"Did you feel as foolish as I do right now?"

"We had so much fun we didn't care."

"I hope Finn looks back one day on this memory with as much fondness as you have of your experience."

"I'm sure he will."

They smile at each other...and there's *the look* I've been waiting for.

Chapter 40

The next morning, Jaycee reminds Sabrina she needs to be home before Deacon arrives. I'm not sure what's up her sleeve, but I spend the next hour following her around the house, eager to find out.

She cleans the kitchen while Finn eats his cereal.

Bobbi stretches out in the middle of the living room rug. "Have you seen the way Deacon has been looking at Sabrina? He might be *the one.*"

"I haven't noticed anything," I snarl. Though I have seen the sparkle in his eye when he's near my wife.

She leaps over the edge of the couch, disappearing into the darkness. "He only stays for dinner when she's around. He lingers close to her when they're in the same room."

"That doesn't mean a thing."

"You're dense as ever, Jason," she says and slips into the kitchen, curling up near Finn's feet.

I follow Jaycee to the trash can where she dumps a dustpan filled with my hair. "What's going on? I can keep a secret." When she removes the bag and takes it outside, I am inches from her heels. "Do you think Deacon is sweet on your mom like Bobbi suggests?"

"Huck, I'm just going to the bathroom," she tells me, coming back inside.

Finally, after lunch, I get the scoop. Jaycee throws three packages of water balloons onto the table. "Are you ready to set the battlefield?"

Finn tosses me the last bite of his peanut butter sandwich.

"Thank-sh," I mutter, working my tongue to unstick the glob from the roof of my mouth.

Jaycee bangs cabinet doors open, removing several large bowls. "We've got work to do."

Together we go outside and huddle around the garden hose. Jaycee shows Finn how to fill the balloons and she ties them. He overfills the first one and it splatters on the ground.

I stretch and flop down in the shade. "Mind if I nap while you do all the hard work?"

Soft giggling fills the air as I close my eyes. When I wake, the bowls are filled. Jaycee has one in her hands and Finn works to keep another one from overfilling.

I shove my nose in the bowl nearest me. "Quality work, Finn."

He lifts his head and calls my name. I glance up in time to see a yellow ball flying at my face. I snap my jaws around it, sending water spraying. Finn bursts into laughter and tosses another.

"Finn, you're wasting ammo on the dog," Jaycee scolds.

He shrugs and grabs the bowl. I follow them around the yard, watching in confusion as they leave the bowls scattered along the property.

Finn brushes his hands on his shirt. "How long until they get here?"

"A couple hours."

"Can't we play with some of them now?"

Jaycee tousles his hair. "I'm on *your* side, remember?"

He turns to me. "We can throw them at Huck."

Jaycee shakes her head. "No targeting unarmed creatures."

"Boo."

"Okay, now we have to go inside and make dessert. I assume you'll be staying for dinner, and we have to do something to make up for the assault we're going to lay down."

Finn restlessly checks the window every five minutes until Jaycee sets a timer on her phone. "I told them to be here promptly at six because I had an engagement this evening."

Finn frowns, crossing his arms. "What about the water balloon fight?"

"That *is* the engagement," she explains.

Oakley brays outside as Finn's smile returns. "Hey! Can I ride Oakley? I can be like a soldier from long ago!"

Jaycee giggles. "No. That would be awesome, but Oakley wouldn't like it. Besides, I don't know a single soldier who rode a donkey."

He pouts. "Every good soldier needs a valiant steed."

I stop and stare at him. "Where'd you learn that word?"

Jaycee ruffles his hair. "Valiant steed. Hmm. Do you even know what that means?" He nods proudly. "Oakley is not valiant."

I whip my head around to face her. "Watch your mouth."

Finn nods again. "He is so." His fingers drum on the tip of his chin. "Well, Jesus rode a donkey," he proclaims.

Jaycee laughs. "Jesus wasn't armed with water balloons."

"If it's good enough for Jesus, it's good enough for me."

"He's got you there," I tell Jaycee.

"You're not riding Oakley," she states.

"You're no fun." Finn stomps to the living room, his footsteps feigning anger.

Sabrina drops her purse to the floor and runs both hands along my body. "At least somebody missed me."

"Keep doing that. A little to the left," I order when she scratches my shoulder.

She straightens herself and nods to the porch. "I'll man this battle station. You two take your places and we'll attack shortly," she says to Jaycee and Finn.

I run to the back with the kids, eager to see where they choose to hide.

"We didn't plan a strategy," Finn shrieks.

"But we know where the ammo is hidden," Jaycee offers.

"Right." Confusion sweeps Finn's face as he spins in a circle. "Where?"

Jaycee points to several locations and bends to whisper in his ear like she's sharing top secret information. "Plus, I've hidden small piles underneath some of the plants along the house."

"Good thinking," Finn beams.

They settle into their hideout, leaving me to quickly grow bored. I decide to go check on Sabrina. She tosses a blue balloon from one hand to the other.

"The kids are really excited," I say, sitting beside her. "Makes me sad that we only had one child. I guess I understand why now, but it's sad that we'll never get to watch the bond between siblings grow. Look at me, I'm babbling," I mutter.

"I wonder what's keeping him."

A car speeds down the road. I leap to my feet. "Where's the fire?"

"I'm sure he'll be here soon."

A few minutes later a Camaro flies past. "Hey! Didn't anyone teach you about speed limits?"

"Lauren is getting married," Sabrina casually tells me.

I nuzzle her chest. "I hope he's good to those kids," I say, silently wondering how her nieces are doing.

"He's a good man. Loves those kids and wants to have a dozen more." She laughs at the thought.

Another car screams down the road. "This isn't a drag strip," I bark at the small sedan.

"The wedding is in September."

I relax next to her again. "I'm happy for her."

Twenty minutes pass and I point out every vehicle traveling over the speed limit. Finally, Deacon's car approaches.

I stand, ready to chew him out.

Sabrina tosses a water balloon into the air, catching it while staring Deacon down. "Think I should pelt him before I say hello?"

I race toward him. "Those kids have been waiting for you," I scold, but the scent of something grabs my attention. "Is that...a German Shepherd? In heat? Wow. Some nerve."

I turn to give Sabrina the order to fire but her arms are behind her back.

"I swear I would've been here on time, but there was a dog in the road and I was afraid she was going to get hit. Luckily, she had a collar on and I was able to call her owner. Had to wait ten minutes for them to arrive."

She brings her arms around and displays the water balloon. "I thought I was going to have to go into battle by myself. The enemy is staking out my backyard."

He tilts his head. "I thought Jaycee had plans."

Sabrina points to the balloons on the porch. "Yeah...to soak us."

He smiles. "They're on!"

She leads the way to the bowl on the porch and dishes out their weapons. "You go one way and I'll go the other."

He stares at the two balloons in his hands. "These aren't grenades. We don't have enough ammo for this fight."

"This battlefield has convenient reloading stations. Try to stay dry."

He raises his hand to his temple, saluting. "Aye, Captain."

I dart toward the backyard, taking alliance with Jaycee and Finn. "The British are coming! The British are coming!"

Oakley haws from his shed. "Is that the best warning you could come up with?"

I pause by his shed. "It worked for Paul Revere. Besides, 'the adults are coming,' doesn't quite have the same ring."

"It's not like they can understand you anyway."

"Then what's the point of making fun of what I say?"

He hangs his head over the half-door. "Because *I* can understand you."

Finn giggles as Deacon pretends not to see him crouched behind the pine tree. He lunges and throws his bomb, smacking his dad in the side. Deacon retaliates by launching both his balloons at his son, one of which Finn dodges.

"Reload," I yell, crossing Deacon's path so Finn can reach the bowl first.

Sabrina pummels Jaycee with two balloons while her back is turned. Deacon takes the brunt of a balloon to the chest. The chaos quickly becomes too much for me to keep up with and I find myself barking wildly, cheering on an assortment of attackers. As the ammo winds down, I notice Jaycee and Finn strategically plotting. I stick close to them, careful to dodge when Deacon or Sabrina gets too close. Finally, the bowls are all empty and the group forms a large circle in the back yard. Balloons fly in all directions as they empty their gathered supply.

"Truce," I yell.

Sabrina laughs, wringing water from the end of her shirt. Deacon carefully picks bits of colorful plastic from her hair. I tense. Finn and Jaycee quietly slip off, the adults caught in a moment I'm uncomfortable witnessing. The flowerbeds. They still hide balloons. The surprise of the attack doesn't last long, thanks in part to Finn's giggles. Armed with two balloons each, they chase Deacon and Sabrina around the shed and across the yard. Jaycee gets a direct hit on Deacon, but the rest miss their targets. After reloading twice more, Sabrina stops them.

"Okay, how many did you hide?"

Jaycee tosses a balloon in the air, catching it. "That's for us to know and you to find out."

Sabrina and Deacon flee again. When Jaycee and Finn go to reload, the adults make their getaway for the house. The door closes before I can slide in. I hear the lock click but the pair stands waving as I stand guard. Finn's shoulders slump upon realizing his targets escaped. With a mischievous smile, he turns on Jaycee. She retaliates. Pretty soon they take a seat on the deck, their ammo depleted.

Chapter 41

Reese and Jaycee spend the last days of summer vacation together and, by the time fall rolls around, I'm nervous they're about to take their relationship to the next level. I bring my concerns to Sabrina the week of Fall Break. Jaycee is spending the night with a friend, leaving Sabrina and me alone.

"I think it's time you had 'the talk' with Jaycee," I say as she unrolls her yoga mat.

Bobbi stops her stroll to check her food dish. "Really, Huck? Why do you keep talking to her as if she can hold a conversation with you? You don't speak the same language."

I plop myself onto her mat. "Sabrina and I share a deep connection. Besides, I have to try."

"Sabrina can handle it. You should be more worried about finding her a date than what Jaycee is doing on hers."

"I don't think teenage pregnancy is what this family needs," I snort.

"If she waits too long, we'll never see any grandchildren."

I roll to the side as Sabrina forces herself into my space. "As long as Sabrina is around to spoil them, I'm okay with that. Jaycee has dreams. I'd hate if all that changes because she isn't careful."

She twists her head around, looking about the room. "How noble."

I scratch at Sabrina's leg as she crouches in some weird bird-like position. "As I was saying," I begin. "Jaycee and Reese have been spending a lot of time together. I don't have to tell you how teenage hormones work. Maybe it's time to put Jaycee on The Pill."

Bobbi slinks in from the kitchen and leaps onto the back of the couch. "Wish I had some popcorn."

"Stop it," I say in a low growl.

The phone rings, distracting us all.

"Mom, I'm not feeling well," Jaycee whispers from the other end of the line. "Can you come get me? Aubrey threw up and I'm worried we ate something that made us sick."

"Uh. Sure. Give me five minutes."

I turn to Bobbi. "Sound like morning sickness to you?"

Bobbi's mouth gapes open in a dramatic yawn. "It's ten o'clock at night."

"Sabrina's morning sickness was at night with Jaycee," I argue.

"You're overreacting."

I leap off the couch and meet Sabrina in the hallway where she's slipping on her shoes. "I'm going with you. I'd like to know what the girls ate."

Sabrina grabs her keys and I race to the door, determined not to let her out without me. She opens the door and I bolt onto the porch before she can scoot around me. She sighs and lets me in the truck. I pounce on the seat and across the console. Aubrey lives straight across the cornfield from us and it takes three minutes to drive around it and pull into her drive.

The girls are on the porch when we arrive. Sabrina rolls down her window as they approach.

Aubrey clutches her stomach, her face pale. "I'm sorry to drag you out."

"You just ate a cupcake," I tell her, sniffing her breath. "Chocolate with buttercream icing. And sprinkles. No way you just threw up."

"It's no problem," Sabrina says. "I'm sure you'll both be better by tomorrow. What did you eat?"

Jaycee groans. "Chocolate."

Aubrey bites her lip. "We started making cake, but let's just say they never made it to the oven."

"Yep, that'll do it."

"Liar," I bark as Jaycee opens the back door.

She buckles the seatbelt and waves to Aubrey. "Sorry to end the sleepover early. Maybe we can try again next weekend?"

Aubrey nods. "Hope you get to feeling better."

"Me too. And you too," she babbles. "We'd better hurry. That batter could come up any minute now."

I sit on her lap as Sabrina backs out of the drive. "I don't know why you lied, but I plan to get to the bottom of it."

I stay by Jaycee's side long after Sabrina puts her to bed and places a bucket on the floor. The moment we're alone, she opens her phone. For three hours a string of short vibrations signals incoming messages as she chats with Reese and Aubrey. I practically clobber her to find out more, but she's become expert at dodging my nosey affections and all I can deduce are the names on the screen.

A slow, gentle creak pulls me from a restless sleep. I open my eyes to find Jaycee slipping her leg out the window.

"Where do you think you are going, young lady?"

She places a finger over her lips. "Shh. I'll be back soon," she whispers, patting my head.

I poke my nose out the window. "Get back here!"

She shoves me back inside and slides the window so it's cracked only an inch.

I dart to the door to alert Sabrina, but Jaycee was careful enough to close me in her room.

"Not going to stop me from barking," I yell.

I scratch wildly. "Can anyone hear me? I need some assistance in here! Sabrina!"

Bobbi somehow manages to work the door open from the outside.

I quickly bound to the bedroom where Sabrina rests undisturbed. I sit on the floor next to the bed, my face inches from hers.

Bobbi moves from the foot of the bed to Sabrina's pillow. "Stop being creepy."

"Hey," I whisper. "Did Sabrina ever sneak out as a teenager?"

She eyes me suspiciously. "Do you mind? Some of us are trying to sleep. I should've left you locked in that room."

I extend my neck so that my hot breath is heavy on her face. "Only asking because Jaycee has left the house." Bobbi pulls herself into a seated position. "Help me wake Sabrina."

"Huck, Jaycee is a teenager. They do that sort of thing. She'll be back by morning."

"What if she's not?"

She curls into a ball against Sabrina's chest. "What do you plan to do—sniff her out?"

"Yes."

"Come on, Huck, let the girl have one night. If it becomes a problem, then we can bring it to Sabrina's attention."

I perk my ears, listening to the outside as I consider her words. "Maybe you're right."

"I am," she yawns.

"Fine. But if she isn't back, this is on you."

I quietly slip back to Jaycee's room to wait.

Chapter 42

Aside from the night Jaycee was born, it was the longest night of my life. I spent the endless hours contemplating ravaging her belongings to see what else she was hiding, but finally decided to just wait. The window creaked open again an hour before dawn, just as I was dozing off. I acted like a fool, greeting her as if she had come back solely for my benefit. Looking back, I imagine I was just relieved nothing terrible happened on her adventure. It was a short-lived feeling, the anger quickly resurfacing at the worry she'd caused me. I snubbed her for days, not that she noticed. Her every waking focus was on Reese. It was literally all she talked about. Another month passed before Sabrina made an appointment to ensure graduation came before grandchildren but, by the next spring, it turned out to not matter anyway. Reese suffered an injury two games into the soccer season, shattering his chances at ever playing the sport again and that meant no college scholarship. He was devastated and his disappointment trickled into his relationship with Jaycee. They ended things in a rather heated fight on our front lawn and, last Sabrina dared to ask, Jaycee was concerned Reese was abusing pain killers. The school year ended with Jaycee speaking only when forced with a direct question. I spent most of the summer outside with Oakley and Finn. For some reason Finn was the only person who made Jaycee act normally. He and Deacon were around a lot that summer and, by the time school started again, I felt pretty confident in Sabrina's friendship with Deacon. The emotions coming from the two of them when they were together gave me hope. If anyone is going to take my place, I want it to be Deacon. I realized this the winter of Jaycee's senior year of high school. But, if they're going to end up together, it really does look like it's up to me to make it happen.

Turkey, mashed potatoes, dressing, noodles, all the traditional Thanksgiving dishes line the counter. My mouth salivates as I plop myself in the middle of the kitchen floor, begging anyone who walks by to drop me a bite. Jaycee has a new boy over. He smells of pot and bad news. Deacon and Finn walk in the door, without knocking, I notice, bringing with them the smell of pecan pie and warm rolls. When chairs scoot back at the table, I crawl into the empty chair I always occupied and sit.

"I'll carve the bird," I say, per my usual Thanksgiving speech. "It *is* why we're gathered here today."

"They're never gonna let you at the turkey," Bobbi says, sauntering in. "Though it amazes me that you still try."

"Part of me still hopes one day they will see it's me."

She flicks her tail at Deacon. "I think you've been replaced."

"Not yet," I say, although I can't help but notice the looks Deacon gives Sabrina every chance he gets. I wonder if he'll ever make a move.

"Let's say Grace," Sabrina suggests, yanking my collar until I'm back on the floor.

Dishes clank and clatter after the prayer until everyone is served. Chatter picks up in the process and I sit faithfully at Finn's feet, knowing he'll slip me bites when nobody is looking.

"At school," Finn says, "we go around and say what we're thankful for. But this year, I want to make a Thanksgiving wish."

"We save wishes for Christmas," Deacon quietly admonishes. "Thanksgiving is a time to be thankful for what you have."

"I'd like to make a Thanksgiving wish," Jaycee states coolly.

Disapproval radiates off Sabrina as she undoubtedly stares across the table at our daughter.

"You have to share it," Finn chirps.

"I wish I can play soccer again without...being reminded of what happened last year."

The pot smoker, whose name I've learned is Lorne, casually asks about the events in question but Sabrina quickly diverts his attention.

"I wish Jaycee gets accepted into the college of her choice," Sabrina adds.

Deacon sighs. "Lorne, how 'bout you? You have a Thanksgiving wish?"

"I wish there's enough pie to go around."

The group laughs.

"That's one wish I don't think we'll have trouble fulfilling," Deacon says.

"Your turn," Finn prompts. "What's your wish?"

"I wish that you always know you're the most important person to me and that you can come to me for anything, at any time."

"Daaad," the boy whines.

"What? You wanted my wish and that's my wish."

"Whatever. It's my turn! I wish for a Christmas morning like they have in the movies."

For the rest of the course, Finn explains his desires, but the teenagers and adults describe movie scenario disasters that are the opposite of his wish.

I yawn, waiting for someone to drop food on the floor. Apparently, Finn has forgotten about me in all the excitement.

"I wish I'll have the courage to watch Sabrina fall in love," I mutter, drifting off.

Chapter 43

Three days before Christmas, I expect the mood in the house to be cheery, but it's not. Sabrina is exhausted from shopping, wrapping, decorating, and her normal duties. And apparently, Reese has a college girlfriend, which Jaycee isn't taking well. Thankfully, she sent Lorne packing the week after Thanksgiving, but it's only made her mood worse. She's been angry since, snapping at anyone who gets near her. For that reason, I've kept my distance. Finn has been getting off the bus at our house after school most days, so I spend my time helping him avoid homework. Deacon's been better about picking him up promptly and, even on the weekends where Jaycee is out with friends, he comes over to see me. Deacon and Sabrina give off an unusual smell when they're around each other and I do my best to ignore the growing feelings between them. Even if I wanted to investigate the depths of their relationship, I can't. Finn saw something on TV which suddenly made him build an obstacle course in our back yard and I can't let him down, especially since this is the wrong time of year for such a feat.

We are outside in a foot of snow tiptoeing over a three-foot beam he found somewhere when he skips half the course and takes a seat on the swing.

"You skipped the box and the tunnel," I say, staring at an empty old tote and the soggy cardboard box he'd cut the end out of to make me crawl through.

"I miss my mom," he whimpers, his gloved hand sliding down my back when I take a seat in front of him. "Do you think she'll ever come back? She probably doesn't know how to find me now."

"Oakley," I yell, drawing my grandpa out of his warm shed. "What do I do about this?"

"Just listen."

"He needs someone to talk to," I argue.

"He's got someone—you. Now if you don't mind, I'm going back inside where it's warm. Next time you disturb me, you'd better have something for me to eat."

With that, Finn and I are alone again.

"Dad says she didn't leave because she wanted to, but I don't understand that. If she didn't want to leave, why did she?"

"Adults are complicated."

"I can't even remember what she looks like. She could walk by me on the street and I wouldn't know."

"People like to say, 'it's their loss' in these situations, but it's really your loss too," I tell him. "You're missing out on having a mother. It's not fair to you either."

"It's not fair," he grumbles.

"Maybe she thought she was protecting you."

I steal a glance at the kitchen window, hoping someone inside will see I need help.

"I like living with my dad and all, but I wish I had a mom sometimes."

"I know what you mean. My dad was never around. He left when I was two and we lived with my grandparents after that."

He leans in close and flaps my ear open, letting in a brisk chill that runs to the center of my brain. "Maybe I could get a good step-mom. My friend has one and he really likes her. She adopted him last year."

"It doesn't take a piece of paper to treat someone like family."

"I know I'm a bit old for Santa, but I asked him for a new mom. If he doesn't bring her, I guess he's not real after all."

I droop my head between his legs. "That's not really how it works."

The back door opens, jerking my attention away from the boy. I race to Jaycee.

"Need your help over here," I say, leaping onto her.

"Huck, get down," she scolds.

Jaycee takes a seat in the swing beside Finn. "You got the Christmas Blues?"

"What are those?"

"It's where you get sad around the holidays. Used to happen to me every year."

"Really?"

She nods. "The first few years after my dad died were the hardest. I could be fine all year then Christmas would roll around and I'd just get blah."

"I think I'm blah."

She places a hand on his shoulder. "Why?"

"Other kids have two parents. Their mom *and* dad get to watch them unwrap presents. Some of them have Christmas at *two* houses. I feel left out."

"I used to feel the same way. On the last day of school before Winter Break the first year my dad was gone, Luna Hostetter's dad came home from Afghanistan. Surprised everyone in the gym during assembly. I remember being insanely jealous. I wished it could've been me instead of her. It wasn't fair."

"I wish my mom would come back," he whispers.

"I'm sure you miss her."

"I don't remember her at all."

"But your dad does. Maybe he'll share his memories with you."

He shakes his head. "He doesn't like to talk about her."

"Have you asked?"

He nods.

She leans over and kisses his forehead. "Someone once told me that it was easier that way. He said that way you can make up whatever you want about that person and it didn't hurt so badly."

I leap into her lap, knocking her back in the swing. "I said that! I said that's what I did about my dad. He was a charter captain who was lost at sea and that's why he never came around!" I drop to the ground. "Sounds pretty childish now," I admit.

"You see," Jaycee continues, "I know what I'm missing with my dad. It sucks. It sucks a lot. But my mom told me that he lives on inside me. She said I have his wit and I like to pout like he did when he didn't get his way." She scrunches her face at that and places a hand on his chest. "The important thing is you have lots of people who love you and are here for you."

Finn moves from the swing and into her arms. "I'm lucky to have you."

"I'm here any time you need anything. Let's go in. Mom's making hot chocolate."

Chapter 44

Jaycee pours a glass of milk and stirs chocolate syrup into it while Finn picks out the best of the sugar cookies they'd spent the day decorating. After touching nearly every one, he places a stocking, a tree, and a gingerbread man onto a Santa shaped plate. I wag my tail as he changes his mind, hoping he'll drop it on the floor. He swaps the stocking and the tree for a snowman and a star. My tail thumps excitedly, despite the lack of cookies tossed in my direction. It's been a long time since we've had a Santa believer in the house. I know he has his doubts, but he puts on a good show.

"If you don't get into bed soon, Santa won't come," Sabrina reminds them, winking at Jaycee.

Deacon stands awkwardly in the kitchen, knowing Finn's sleeping bag is on the floor in Jaycee's room.

"I can't thank you enough for doing this," he whispers to my wife.

"Are you kidding? This is a gift to me too," she tells him in a hushed tone. "I've dreamt of having a herd of kids opening presents on Christmas morning."

"Well Finn's only *one* kid," he says, glancing toward the tree. "But, judging by the gifts under that tree, you're expecting a few dozen to arrive overnight."

She presses her fingers close together. "I may have gone a tad overboard."

Finn dances Jaycee around the kitchen in their matching pajamas, sparking something inside Sabrina.

"I have to get a picture by the tree," she yells, clapping her hands together.

I jump into the middle of the action, tripping Jaycee on her path to the living room.

"This is perfect," I bark.

After performing a few photo bombs, I sit perfectly between them while Sabrina and Deacon snap their pictures. Then we're ushered to Jaycee's bed where everyone gathers for the reading of the Christmas Story in the Bible. Sabrina kisses them both goodnight.

"Really? You know you can't go to bed without reading *'Twas the Night Before Christmas*," I tease.

Jaycee clears her throat and produces a book from beneath her pillow. "Forgetting something?"

"Of course we aren't leaving Santa out," she says, settling back in.

"You have to do the voices like Dad did," she reminds her mother.

Sabrina's fingers linger over the inscription I'd written Jaycee's first Christmas. She throws a nervous glance Deacon's way. "I'm not as good as Jason was at doing voices. Please forgive me."

Jaycee leans into her mom's side. "I still hear his voice when you read it."

I crawl up from the foot of the bed and lie across the three of them. I can't help but think how lucky I am as I listen to her read. Even if I have to go to the bathroom outside and eat the same food every day, it's worth it to be around for every moment like this.

Half an hour later, after kisses and countless trips to see where Santa is on the app Sabrina downloaded, the kids are finally asleep.

"Thank you again," Deacon says, sitting next to her on the couch.

"The pleasure is mine."

I wonder what's in the packages beneath the tree and contemplate ripping one open to find out. I'd already discovered there's a rawhide bone with my name on it.

"I guess I'll be as surprised about the rest of them as I was when I was alive," I mutter.

Deacon strokes my back. "You know, I think Finn might be putting on a show where the Santa thing is concerned. Last year he seemed skeptical and this year I have a feeling his believing is all for my benefit."

Sabrina places her hand over his on my back. "He's at that age, but I'm sure you'll find a way to keep the magic alive somehow."

"I've been asking my friends how they handled it when their kids stopped believing and they all have different answers."

"Maybe it's best to just go along with it."

He groans. "I think so, too. He wrote Santa a letter and asked him to find me a girlfriend."

I perk my ears at the sound of her soft laugh.

"Jaycee did that once."

"How did you handle it?"

Sabrina fiddles with the remote, pulling up a new screen on the TV. "I told her that was Cupid's department and the only way to get a message to him was to make a valentine, turn it to confetti, and throw it into the air."

He raises an eyebrow. "Did she do it?"

Sabrina's eyes light up at the memory. "Of course. But she was rather upset to learn that Cupid had to piece the confetti together before he could read her request. We're still waiting on his response," she chuckles. "I made sure we used a hole punch for the confetti."

"That's brilliant!"

She shrugs. "I didn't know what else to do. I wasn't ready to date."

Sweat seeps from his pores. "Are you ready now?"

I reach up to lick her face. "I think he's going to ask you out and I want you to know whatever you say is fine with me."

"If the right person comes along, I'd consider it."

Disappointment washes over him and, I admit, over me too. "I'm sure it will happen when the time is right."

I throw my arm over my face. "You two are going to friend-zone each other. How lame."

I yawn as Sabrina drags her nails over my back. Nothing has ever felt so wonderful.

Deacon reaches for the remote and pauses over the Play button on the screen. "Okay, *Die Hard*—Christmas movie or not?"

Sabrina and I whip our heads toward him at the exact same moment. "Yes!"

I bark my objection. "It's *not* a Christmas movie," I huff. "Just because it happens at Christmastime, doesn't make it a Christmas movie."

"Jason said it had nothing to do with Christmas and if it were a Christmas movie, it would be in the Christmas section in the stores, and it's not, so it's clearly *not* a Christmas movie."

I roll so she can rub my belly. "Sounds like good logic to me."

Her nails dig into my armpit. "But he's wrong."

If her touch didn't feel so good, I'd be arguing my point a little stronger.

Deacon smiles. "If someone says 'Merry Christmas' in the movie, that makes it a Christmas movie. Or something like that."

"I'm not watching any Hallmark movie. I've seen one of them."

"And they're all the same, right?"

"Exactly." She points a finger at him. "Star Wars or Star Trek?"

He shakes his head. "Neither."

She snaps her fingers. "Same here!"

"Vampires or Zombies?"

She sticks out her tongue. "Yuck."

He rubs his hands together. "Okay, the real test—Marvel or DC?"

"Am I supposed to know what that means?"

"I'll give you a pass on that one. The correct answer is both."

I yawn as I wait for someone to start the movie. Instead, they continue their game of comparing likes and dislikes. It doesn't take me long to realize how compatible these two are...maybe even more so than she and I were.

"If you're not watching the movie, I'm going to bed," I announce, slipping into the bedroom.

Chapter 45

Thankfully Sabrina had come to bed alone. I hadn't decided how I'd handle the moment when she didn't, but I'm glad I have more time to figure it out. This is a strange new feeling for me, going back and forth from wanting her to go forward to wanting things to stay the same. I know I'm supposed to be helping her move on, but I don't know how.

The room is still encased in darkness when Jaycee and Finn creep in. Sabrina plays her part, groaning and pretending to be sound asleep as Jaycee gently shakes her. And two hours before her normal wakeup, I don't imagine it's a hard part to play. When that doesn't work, Jaycee motions to Finn who bounces his behind on the edge of the bed. Barking once, I nuzzle my head, followed by the rest of my body, underneath Sabrina's arm.

"You might as well give it up," I tell her, anxious to see what the kids are so excited for. I had tried to help wrap so I could see what their gifts were, but Sabrina had locked me in the bedroom for being in the way and I didn't get to see anything.

Jaycee and Finn's pleas for her to get up drown out Sabrina's groan. I smile at the eagerness in Jaycee that I haven't seen in many years. Taking Sabrina's arm in my mouth, I gently tug, coaxing her up. "We want to see what's under the tree!"

"It's five o'clock," she mutters.

Panic overwhelms me and I jump from the bed to find Bobbi. "Bobbi, who got the presents for Sabrina?" Silence. I sniff under the bed and around the room until I find her curled up in a laundry basket still full of towels. "Bobbi, who got Sabrina's gifts? She has presents, right?"

The cat yawns as if she's only concerned with the five or ten minutes of extra sleep she can get while Sabrina gets coffee. "Jaycee is old enough to do it herself now."

I sit, wagging my tail. "Right. I forgot." We've been through this ritual every Christmas morning, even when Mrs. Clifford, the pastor's wife, was still taking Jaycee shopping.

"I'm glad Mrs. Clifford doesn't have to take her anymore," I mutter, remembering some of the awful gifts the elderly woman insisted on.

"Let me start the coffee," Sabrina grumbles. "Guess we're not waiting an extra hour for it to start itself."

"Already done," Deacon offers, handing her a mug as she shuffles into the kitchen.

She smiles at his thoughtfulness then runs a hand through her hair, suddenly anxious about her appearance.

He motions to the oven. "Breakfast will be ready in about twenty minutes."

"We may have to do Christmas more than once a year," she says, flashing a carefree smile.

"Wait," I say. "Was that a wink? Did you just wink at him, Sabrina?"

Ten minutes later, Sabrina sits on the couch with a mug and the kids perch as close to the tree as possible, noses stuck inches away from neatly wrapped boxes.

"What are you waiting for? Pass them out," Sabrina urges with a laugh.

"Who's that for?" I ask, bounding near Finn's legs as he starts a pile for himself across the room. "That smells like socks," I tease Jaycee as Finn places a package in her pile.

The next few minutes are chaos as the three of us move around each other. I continue to offer my suggestions as to what may be in boxes, but nobody seems to care.

I slip onto the couch to inspect Sabrina's gifts. "I'm sorry I didn't get you anything. I just didn't think you'd like donkey poop or busted dog toys. I guess I could've opted for a dead rodent but that doesn't sound like something you'd like either."

Sabrina places her hand on my head and slips it down my back, instantly calming my excitement. "Don't worry, there's one for you."

I slurp my tongue up her cheek. "Aw, you shouldn't have." Jaycee tosses a small present to Sabrina. "What is it? Tell me! Tell me!"

The gift she places before me isn't the bone I'm expecting. It's a softball from Finn and Deacon. The shape reveals that, but I can't get over the thrill of being included in such a human holiday. I know most families include their pets—and we always bought Bobbi and Oakley something—but every year the gift strikes me as incredibly thoughtful. And my nose tells me there's still a bone somewhere in all these gifts.

Sabrina motions with her hands for the kids to start unwrapping. "What did Santa bring you?"

I'm curious about that too, but I'm already on the floor scratching and biting the paper off my new favorite toy.

"I want to see what Huck got first," Finn whispers, his voice holding a hint of magic.

Sabrina chuckles. "It's a softball. You were there when we picked it out, remember?"

Finn lifts a shoulder. "Yeah, but he makes it look like so much fun."

"Almost there," I tell him eagerly. A sliver of paper sticks to my tongue and I run it across my teeth to remove it. Three licks later and I'm free. "It's a ball! Just what I've always wanted!" I deeply feel like this is the best thing anyone has ever given me.

"Yay!" Finn claps wildly, stroking my head.

I turn to show Jaycee but she's shredding paper from her own gifts. I watch wrapping paper fly and I'm soon covered with it. Finn reveals a remote-control car and Jaycee, a new jewelry box, hand crafted by Sabrina.

Deacon, whom I'd briefly forgotten was here, shreds paper from a box in front of him. "I love it," he says, displaying a leatherbound notebook with a *D* on it. No doubt Sabrina had done the fancy design bordering the edges.

Sabrina opens a gift from Deacon—a new brush set and paints.

"I would've bought you jewelry," I say, shaking the paper from my back to join her. "I didn't buy you enough when I was alive," I lament, though I know Sabrina would rather the money be spent on 'something useful' as she always said.

Bobbi strolls in as the excitement dies down. Making a lap around the living room, she checks out the presents and hops into an empty box.

I lie my head on Sabrina's lap. "I think they're happy."

Deacon slips quietly into the kitchen, returning with a plate of cinnamon rolls dripping with icing.

Sabrina takes it from him, eyeing the hand he holds behind his back.

I leap off the couch to investigate.

He slowly brings his arm around, dripping icing onto the floor.

Sabrina laughs. "Did you really put icing on a Milk Bone for the dog?"

"It's Christmas," he offers as reasoning.

I lick the spots on the floor and gobble the treat. "Surprisingly good," I mumble.

A remote-control car whizzes by me and I turn my attention to chasing it. Despite the chaos as Finn and I race through the living room, I notice a thump at the window. When the car passes by the couch again, I leap onto the sofa and shove the curtain away with my nose. Oakley stands smiling, watching the shenanigans from the split in the drapes.

"Merry Christmas, Jaybird," Oakley says cheerfully.

"Merry Christmas, Grandpa."

"Go play," he orders. "We'll talk when you need to take a leak."

I shove the curtain open and return to attack the car racing around the house. Sabrina and Deacon work on cleaning the mess of paper strewn about, though I catch them stopping to watch us...and chat about Oakley staring inside.

I wear out sooner than I expect but I find the only way to convince Finn I need a break is to stand at the back door until he reluctantly lets me out.

"Looks like you were having fun in there," Oakley says.

I pee on a tree and slip into the shed to lie down in his straw. "I'm beat."

"I got tired just watching you." He plops down beside me.

I snort a bit of straw from my nose. "This may be one of the best Christmases ever."

He smiles. "Does that mean you want Deacon and Finn to stick around?"

My eyelids droop and I whisper, "I think I do."

"Better make sure he doesn't let her get away then."

I groan an agreement and give way to the fatigue plaguing me.

Chapter 46

I made an elaborate plan to get Deacon and Sabrina to kiss on New Year's Eve, but Finn caught a stomach bug two days after Christmas and everyone was sick. I took it as a sign and decided to hold off on any further schemes. At least for a while. My hiatus lasted months and, before I knew it, Sabrina was getting ready for Jaycee's graduation.

Bobbi zips through the house, and I admit I'm impressed she can still move that fast at her age.

"Tom and Kay are coming for Jaycee's graduation," she explains, speeding from one end of the house to the other. Of course her former husband and his wife will be there.

"I know. Sabrina has been talking about it for weeks. She cleaned the house from top to bottom. But why are *you* racing around like a maniac?"

She makes another lap around the circle of the house, barely pausing to elaborate. "I should've thought ahead. I haven't seen Tom in a long time."

I howl with laughter. "Are you seriously trying to lose a few pounds for someone who only knows you as his daughter's cat?"

"I just want to look my best, okay?"

The doorbell rings and she zips out of sight.

I greet Kay and Tom as old friends, but it appears Tom has forgotten a few names. Kay takes him to the spare room where they will stay so he can rest.

"I hope tomorrow is a better day," Kay whispers to Sabrina. "I'd hate for him to not be lucid for Jaycee's graduation. He asked me thirteen times where we were going on the way here. It's a two-hour drive," she sighs.

Sabrina offers coffee. "I'm sorry. I'll try to get up that way to help more often."

Kay waves her hand. "He has a nurse who drops in for a few hours each week. We're still managing. You're more than welcome to come visit, though."

"You make sure you call me if you need anything."

Kay nods. "Tell me what's new with you. Is there a man in your life?"

Sabrina laughs. "Just jump right in."

"I'm sorry. Sometimes I forget my manners. I don't talk to many people these days. Besides your dad and the nurse, that is. And some days I spend most of my conversation pretending to be Audra. So much so that I don't know how to act anymore."

Sabrina stares out the window. "I'm sorry. That must be rough."

"I had some good years with Tom before Alzheimer's set in. I thank God for that."

"I thank God he has you."

Kay smiles. "Now, back to the man in your life..."

Sabrina laughs. "I'm busy with the restaurant. There's not much time to date."

"Make time. Jaycee will be off to college soon. Do you plan on spending all your time working?"

"I'm perfectly happy."

Kay rolls her eyes. "You need someone besides a dog to keep you company after Jaycee leaves."

She takes a seat at the table. "There's always Oakley and Bobbi."

"They won't live forever."

The thought rattles me so I slip off to find Bobbi. Her nervousness radiates heavily from behind the couch where I find her pacing in the darkness.

"I don't know why I'm so afraid to see him," she says. "I guess I'm worried it might be the last time."

I hang my head at the grimness everyone is spewing on what should be a happy reunion. "If it is, do you want to spend it hiding from him?"

"I wish he could somehow know it's me."

"I know the feeling. Just go be with him. That's all you can do."

Kay laughs at something Sabrina says.

"I miss him," she says quietly.

"Go to him."

With a nod, she saunters from behind the couch. I follow her at a distance to the room where he sleeps. I hear her leap onto the mattress and she's purring within seconds.

Tom comes out of the bedroom, Bobbi in his arms. His eyes bulge as he stops in front of the back door. "When did you get a donkey?"

"He belonged to Jason's grandmother before she died. We inherited him. His name's Oakley," Sabrina explains.

Tom wrinkles his brow. "Helen died?"

Kay guides him to a seat at the table. "Yes. She had a heart attack a long time ago. Years, actually."

"I won't offer my condolences to Jason, then." He strokes Bobbi's back and cranes his neck to the doorway of the living room. "Where is Jason anyway? I haven't seen him in ages."

Sabrina kneels in front of her father. "Daddy, there was a terrible accident and Jason was killed on impact."

Tom hangs his head. "Why didn't anyone tell me?"

Kay gently kisses his forehead. "Jaycee will be home soon. You know she's graduating tomorrow?"

The comment works to change the subject. Tom's eyes bulge. "Graduation?"

"Yep. Last year of high school. She heads off to college in the fall," Sabrina offers.

Kay points to Bobbi. "You hate cats."

Tom lifts an eyebrow. "I do?" Sabrina and Kay nod. "Well, I like this one."

Sabrina laughs. "She's not a likeable cat. The boy Jaycee babysits for has been trying for years to make her like him and Bobbi just doesn't like people. She seems smitten with you, though."

Bobbi stretches up to lick his face. "I'm glad you have Kay. I would never want you to face this alone." She turns to me. "Jason, all you can do is love someone in the time you're given and leave the rest to God. Not many men would've agreed to do what you did. Hell, if I had to sit back and watch Tom fall in love, I don't think I could've done it. Not from the same house. At least in my situation I don't have to see it day in and day out. You're a good man after all, Jason Parker."

Coming from my mother-in-law, that's about the best compliment I can get and I suddenly have a newfound desire to do what I'd been sent to do.

I had hated to miss graduation but was a little thankful they don't allow dogs at the ceremony. After last night, I'd gotten overwhelmingly sad that Jaycee's grown. That can only mean my time is winding down with her. And I still have a job to do. It's bound to be the hardest thing I've ever done but it's time to make sure my wife doesn't end up alone when I return to Heaven.

Chapter 47

I stick close to Finn after school lets out. Sadness grows inside him with each passing day. He hides it well, insisting on extra fishing trips and ice cream runs, but I can tell he's as upset about Jaycee's impending college departure as Sabrina and I are. When the day finally arrives, Jaycee throws her arms around me.

"You take care of Mom for me," she says. "And be nice to the cat."

"No partying," I tell her. "And come home at least once a month. Your mom needs to see your face."

She places a kiss on my head and scans the room for Bobbi.

"She's on the dryer," I offer.

Jaycee searches the house, looking for her missing pet.

Deacon's heavy footsteps pound through the house. "Truck's loaded." He heads to the kitchen and helps himself to a glass of water.

Finn pouts on the couch. "This is stupid."

I hear Jaycee in the laundry room talking to the cat. "You don't need to swat Huck *every* time he walks past. You're both getting too old for those games. How about you be nice to each other? I'll see you soon." She smooches the cat and steps into the hallway where she gets a clear shot of Finn's quivering lip.

"Hey," she says, taking a seat beside him. "I'll be home before you know it."

"What am I supposed to do after school?"

Jaycee lays her head on my back. "I think Huck will need you to come over and throw a ball sometimes." She steals a glance at Sabrina. "What do you think? Couple days a week at least."

Sabrina nods. "He will. My arm's not that good after using it all day. Do you think you could help us out?"

I beat my tail against the floor, stretching to slurp Finn's face. "She throws like a girl."

244

Finn smiles. "I'd be happy to help, but throwing balls makes me hungry." A twinkle flashes in his eyes and we all know what's coming.

"Then you'll have to stay for supper," Sabrina insists.

"If you guys are done bargaining, we need to get on the road," Deacon suggests.

Sabrina pats his arm. "Don't worry, you're invited to supper too."

Finn points at Sabrina. "Three school days and one weekend day. Huck needs exercise on weekends too."

Sabrina tousles his hair. "I'm glad you thought about the weekends. You know, I was thinking about doing all this fun stuff now that Jaycee won't be here to entertain me. I might do a lot of hiking and I'll need someone to make sure I don't get lost. Or I might decide I want to go skydiving and I'll need someone to stop me."

He raises his hand. "I made it home from snipe hunting so I think I can help with the hiking." He taps his finger to his chin. "But if you go skydiving, can I come?"

"Sounds like I need to come home often," Jaycee says. "Apparently I'm the only one who knows there's no reason to jump from a plane that isn't crashing."

Deacon pats my head as they pass. "I've got your back on that one."

"Thanks," she whispers as they slip out the door.

I lie inches from the door, head on my paws, pouting. "I can't believe she's all grown up." I'm torn between pride and sadness, knowing Jaycee won't be home for weeks, maybe even until the holidays.

My ears perk at the sound of footsteps on the porch. A key enters the lock, the knob twists and Jaycee nearly trips over me in her haste.

She bends to my level, throwing her arms around me. My tail beats against the floor and I raise my paws over her shoulders.

"I needed one more hug," she says.

"Not as much as I did."

Finn kept up his end of the deal and rode the bus to the house three days a week. On those days Sabrina left her shop early and met him on the porch. The three of us spent hours in the backyard. I helped Finn perfect his pitching arm, we dug for worms after a rain, and Sabrina let us video chat Jaycee after homework was done.

Chapter 48

Finn proudly holds my leash as Deacon leads the way along the trail. I smell water up ahead and it seems they're in more of a hurry to reach it than I am. Not that I'm not eager, but it's such a *long* way. I don't remember it ever taking this much time to reach the waterfall. If I didn't know any better, I'd think they'd regained some of their youthful energy, but it's time for me to face the fact that I'm not as young as I once was. We step aside for a couple trekking back and I'm all too happy for the brief break.

Sniffing the weeds lining the path, I find a toad seeking shelter. "Finn, over here." He yanks the leash as they continue on. "Oh, you don't want to catch toads today? I need to know these things."

"This would be a good time to work on your mission," the toad says as I pass. "I let you watch Jaycee grow up. Now it's time to focus on the next chapter of Sabrina's life. Time will be up before you know it."

A knot forms in my stomach as I step past the toad without a word. What can I say to that? No person—or dog—lives forever.

"Finn called Jaycee twenty-eight times this week," Deacon says with a laugh.

I mark a tree while Finn stops to defend himself. "I had things to tell her."

"I'm sure she needs to spend time studying, Finn," Deacon suggests.

"She said I could call whenever I wanted," Finn argues. "She even said she'd help me study for my English test next week."

Sabrina laughs.

He points a contented stare at Deacon. "See? She's still helping me with homework."

"As long as she isn't too busy."

"She said she wasn't."

I stop, my view suddenly a face full of stairs heading straight up. "Please tell me there's an elevator." The smirk on Sabrina's face tells me she's remembering the times I'd used that line. Or maybe she's enjoying the day and I'm reading too much into it.

Deacon motions for Finn to go ahead. "The view is going to be amazing." He waits for Sabrina to fall in line behind Finn.

"I see what you did there," I grumble, hearing his feet slap the boards at the tail end of the line. "Enjoy the show."

Part of me wants to be mad that he's staring at my wife's backside as she climbs the million stairs up the side of the canyon wall but, if I want her to be happy, I'm going to have to accept someone checking her out. And it might as well be Deacon. I'm too old to search for another love interest. She'll have to make do with this one. Besides, he's not so bad. He's always bringing over tiny crafty things that she seems to really love. Last week he found a mess of costume jewelry at a thrift store and showed her a post on social media about how she could repurpose it. Sabrina was tickled shitless. And the week before he pulled up a piece of driftwood from the lake and suggested she carve longitude and latitude coordinates into it. That was another winner in Sabrina's book. The piece now hangs proudly over the door at Jaybird's, or so she said. He seems to know the way to her heart without being overly obvious. Besides doing thoughtful things that touch her creative side, he likes to bring a gallon of milk over when he notices she's about out. He claims it's because Finn drinks it all, but he and I both know she'll forget to buy it until she's in the middle of a recipe and realizes it's not in the fridge. Maybe there's hope for them yet. Panting, I slow my pace, realizing my thoughts have carried me halfway to the top. My legs burn as I press on, wondering what else I like about Deacon. He's considerate of her feelings. He always turns down the heat in the car, even when he's still cold. And I don't think she's caught on to his dislike of spicy food. He eats it despite the obvious noise his stomach makes afterward that proves it doesn't like him very much. He always lets her have the cherry on his ice cream cone when they stop at Flater's Dairy Corner. My tongue hangs from my mouth from a mixture of delectable thoughts and exercise as I take the final steps to the top.

"Thank goodness. I was starting to think *I* had a crush on Deacon."

Deacon places his hands on his thighs. "That was a workout," he huffs.

Sabrina steps out of the way for a family of six heading down the stairs.

"Much easier going this way," the dad says, smiling at our group.

Deacon leads the way to a platform overlooking a waterfall. "Listen," he orders, staring into the lush forest.

An owl screeches in the distance and I'm certain I'm the only one who hears the Blue Heron snap a snack from the creek below. Two squirrels chatter from opposite trees and a chipmunk scurries away from a lone set of footsteps. A light breeze rustles the leaves as blackbirds sing. But none of it is as loud as the rushing water crashing into a pool at the bottom of the canyon. Not even the toddler screaming as he's removed from his play in the creek can quiet the force of nature before us.

Finn taps his foot anxiously. "Can we go now? I want to see the bottom."

Deacon smiles and leads the way to a bare path that curves gradually down the opposite side. "I found myself needing to connect to a scene and this is where I ended up," he tells Sabrina as Finn and I hurry ahead.

"Not too far," Sabrina cautions. "A hiking scene? Did one of them fall into a patch of poison ivy?"

"That's too cliché. I needed an epic proposal and the main character loves hiking."

"Please tell me you didn't write a Hallmark movie scene."

I slow down, keeping Finn from getting too far out of sight.

"Yuck. Of course not," Deacon says in disgust. "Well, crap. Maybe."

Sabrina claps. "Run it by me. You may have to change the whole thing."

He laughs. "I based the entire scene off this trail. It's nearing sunset and they have a romantic picnic where we just stopped on that overlook. Then he leads her down this way and at the waterfall there are candles all around." He holds out his hand to help her walk around a rocky patch. He walks a few more steps until he realizes he's still holding it and gently releases her.

"Candles? In the woods? Smokey the bear wouldn't like that." She tugs on her bottom lip with her teeth.

He fidgets with his hands, a smile forming, though I sense his nervousness. "Good point. I suppose they're the kind with the batteries in them. I'll have to make that distinction. Anyway, he leads her behind the waterfall where he's spelled out 'Will you marry me?' in rocks."

"On a scale of one-to-Hallmark movie, you're at a Nicholas Sparks novel."

He laughs. "I'll take that as a compliment."

"Wait. Is she wearing a white tank top? Do they end up all wet? Because that tips the scales."

"I'm sure they'll change her attire when the movie is made."

"Does she say 'yes?'"

"If I tell you, it'll ruin the ending."

She smiles. "Is this the book where the guy kidnaps the kid? The one with the powerful ex-wife?"

Deacon shakes his head. "No. I haven't finished that one yet. This other story wouldn't leave me alone. It just came to me."

I yank Finn forward, eager to get to the water that's come into view. "Sorry, Deacon, I'm afraid the only proposal I'm worried about is the one Sabrina has yet to accept. And since you're nowhere near uttering those words, I'd like to take a swim."

We're splashing in the cool water's edge when they finally make it around the bend. After getting the approval to remove his shoes, Finn joins me near the bottom of the waterfall. A German Shepherd stares timidly at the water from the other side of the pool. Kids splash around me, arms outstretched as I swim past. I dodge their reach, circling back to Finn.

"Don't get all wet," Deacon orders from the bank.

"I've got you," I say, standing in a foot of water near Finn. He laughs as I spray him with a quick shake.

"I wish Jaycee were here," he whispers, fingering a smooth rock perfect for skipping.

"Me too." I lunge at him as he takes a stance to fling the rock. He lands with a splash on the rocky bottom. "See? Now you'll be allowed to get wet."

Deacon groans but waves Finn on, okaying him to swim. As we chase each other around the other kids, I catch bits and pieces of Sabrina's conversation with Deacon.

"Maybe he needs a hobby to help him get over the change of Jaycee being gone," she suggests.

They have removed their own shoes and have their toes in the water. Finn finds a stick and tosses it away from the crowd. When the kids see that I retrieve it, they line up for a turn to toss it.

"A sport might do him good," Sabrina offers.

The smile on Finn's face draws me away from the conversation. I can see that I'm in the midst of a memory that will last a long time. We're the center of attention until a puppy arrives with a young couple. When the kids gravitate toward the pup, I take my exit from the water.

"I need a nap," I say, shaking next to Deacon. He crinkles his nose as I lie down beside him. "May I suggest you get the boy something with wheels? That's the only way to cure blues over a girl. And, trust me, it's only going to get worse. And more expensive."

Finn eagerly pets the puppy but returns to my side quicker than I expect.

"Can we take a picture? I want to send it to Jaycee," he says.

Sabrina stands. "I think she'd like that."

They position themselves near the waterfall after the young woman with the puppy agrees to take the photo. I wait until I'm called and take my place beside Finn. His hand rests on my head and the lady snaps a few pictures.

"I can hang out with Finn tomorrow if you want to get some writing done," Sabrina offers on the way back.

"Actually, we had plans to go fishing," Deacon says. "Would you like to join us?"

"I don't want to intrude on your guy time."

Finn yanks her arm. "Please come. We need someone who knows how to make the good sandwiches."

Sabrina smiles while Deacon pretends to be hurt. "Only if you still agree to take the fish off the hook for me."

"That's why you keep me around," Finn beams.

She tousles his wet hair. "It's not the only reason."

Chapter 49

Finn soon gets off the bus at our house every day and Sabrina twists Deacon's arm to stay for supper most evenings. We see them every weekend with a new outing each Saturday. Sometimes they leave me behind and I spend the day outside with Oakley. Finn dwindles his calls to Jaycee in half but still misses her immensely. Her visit over Labor Day helped but it's clear he needs something to ease his loneliness. Deacon says he doesn't have many friends his own age, that he'd rather hang out with a donkey and a dog than boys on a football field. That's why Sabrina, Finn, and I are standing in the driveway waiting for Deacon to arrive on the first Saturday in October. Apparently, he has a surprise and needs to borrow our garage for an extended period of time. I perk my ears as a truck engine revs over the crest of the hill half a mile away. Finn dances in place.

I run to get Oakley. "You want to see the surprise? Deacon is almost here!"

"I'll take a gander," he says, slowly making his way around the house.

Deacon's sedan pulls in the drive, followed by a truck with a trailer on the back.

Finn's eyes light up at the sight of a go-kart on the flatbed.

Deacon holds up his hand to stop him. "Don't get too excited. It doesn't run."

Finn beams. "Do you know how to fix that?"

Deacon laughs. "I'll need some help."

Oakley brays from the side of the garage. "Oh boy. What have you gotten yourself into?"

"A lot of nights at the track!" I turn to Deacon and Finn. "Right? We're going racing, right?"

Finn inspects the kart. "I'm going to be the next Dale Earnhardt!"

The man in the truck smiles. "In that case, I'm going to need your autograph." He pulls out a small notebook and pen as if he were prepared for such a statement.

Deacon holds out his hand to stop Finn from taking the paper. "I get the first autograph."

The man nods. "We'll need two autographs please."

Sabrina steps up. "Make that three."

Pride radiates off Finn as he scribbles his name on three sheets of paper.

"This is perfect," I say as if I had something to do with the project.

Chapter 50

The go-kart project takes Finn's full attention over the winter. He and Deacon spend many evenings and countless Saturdays working inside the garage so that by spring, the kart is running. It's another year before he's learned to control it and is begging to race. Deacon signs him up for every event in a hundred-mile radius that summer. He finishes in the top ten five times and comes in second twice. The last event is at a track half an hour from Union Grove, and he's invited everyone he knows to watch. Jaycee brings her new boyfriend who fails to impress me upon arrival. He doesn't have the man-bun Reese once sported, but he does have an arm full of tattoos and a mouth full of dip. My instincts tell me it won't last long. I don't sense any deep feelings with him, only obligation to tag along.

After watching Deacon inspect the kart, we head to our seats. My tail wags in excitement as we wait for them to take to the track. Finn's black kart starts in the middle of the pack, a Jaybird's Country Café sticker emblazoned on the side.

The noise is deafening to my sensitive ears, but I bark each time Finn makes a pass. A blue kart rubs him, sending him out of his line and up the track but he recovers well. Jaycee's boyfriend stares at his phone even as the final laps wind down. It isn't until Finn takes the checkered flag that he leaps to his feet and cheers like he has a clue that Finn won his first race. I dance around our group, boasting about the boy I suddenly realize is the son I never had. I couldn't be prouder if he were my flesh and blood and I can't wait to congratulate him. Judging by the cheers from Sabrina and Jaycee, I'd say they feel the same way. They snap a dozen or more pictures of him on the podium and Sabrina proudly shows them to the people standing beside her. I can't help but laugh and wonder if she knows the impact that boy has on her. When an elderly woman asks if Finn is her son, she embarks on a lengthy explanation over their relationship. That's when Deacon slips away to meet Finn. I follow him, anxious to see him myself. The two high five and quickly turn the greeting into a hug. Deacon spins him around, oblivious to my presence. I bark to alert them but the crowd drowns me out. I scoot out of the way of other parents who circle around the second and third place finishers. When a second bark doesn't work, I paw at Finn's leg. He bends to pet me, but I decide the event warrants a hug and leap onto him. He catches me and we dance a circle.

"I'm so proud of you," I yell, licking his face. "You did fantastic!"

Once everyone is done taking pictures of the winner and the winning kart, Deacon abandons it and leads Finn to the concession stand.

"How about a sno-cone for the winner?"

Finn shrugs. "I was hoping for a beer, but I guess a sno-cone will do."

Deacon laughs. "I'd buy you a beer, but that could put your chief mechanic in jail."

"Sno-cone it is."

I trail along, spying Kelley, Amber, and their twins standing off to the side of the concession stand. Kelley cocks his head as we approach. Thad, the older twin, calls to Finn and they share a high five. I stand in line beside Deacon, waiting for our turn to order.

"Three sno-cones," Deacon tells the girl behind the counter.

"Tiger's blood," I offer at Deacon's hesitation.

"One tiger's blood, one blue raspberry, and one grape," Deacon orders.

Three minutes later he's trying to figure out how to carry them all.

"Huck?"

I turn to find Kelley behind me.

Deacon passes the blue cone to Finn.

I sniff Kelley's outstretched hand. "Glad to see you and Amber worked things out. We should grab a beer and talk about it sometime." With a laugh, I slurp the back of his hand.

"Either I've got mustard on my hand from the hot dog earlier or you've decided to let loose of that grudge." He looks up at Deacon. "You must be with Sabrina."

Deacon's body goes rigid, his eyes staring at the treats in his hand. "I'm Deacon Howard," he says awkwardly.

"Kelley Barnes. I recognized Huck," he explains. "Jason and I were friends. Congratulations on the win, by the way."

"Thank you."

Amber steps beside Kelley. "How's the book coming?"

Kelley nods as if he expects her to already know Deacon.

Deacon laughs. "It's getting there. Thanks to your coffee."

I sit, wagging my tail as I watch the kids come up to Finn and congratulate him while Deacon and Amber chat about the potential of a novel being written inside her coffee shop. He promises to acknowledge it before publication, should that day ever come.

Red liquid drips down Deacon's hand. "I'd better get going before these melt all over me."

Kelley leans over me to offer advice to Deacon. "Sabrina is one-of-a-kind. If you know what's good for you, you won't let her get away."

Amber playfully slaps his arm. "Mind your business, Kelley."

They gossip about a budding love as we head back to our seats.

"Won't be long before the whole town is talking," I note, slipping out of the way of a rowdy group of teenage boys.

Chapter 51

I had thought for sure the rumor mill would kick Deacon and Sabrina into dating, but despite the chatter around town, the two laugh it off, telling people they are just friends. By the time winter rolls around, Deacon has saved enough money to buy a late model car for Finn. Naturally it's not in good working condition, but that makes for quality time in the garage for us boys. Finn shovels driveways to earn money to paint the car and scouts every local business to sponsor him. By spring we are ready for the first race.

When a wreck mid-season takes him out, we all think we are done for the year.

"I've already maxed out most of my credit cards," Deacon says to Sabrina on the front porch the night of the wreck. "And I've been working less so I can help get the car ready. I don't know what to do."

Metal clings to the concrete floor of the garage as Finn tears a dented fender from the machine.

"Let me help," Sabrina suggests, opening the door to a discussion I've heard a dozen times.

"You're putting a kid through college," Deacon argues.

"Jaybird's is a sponsor—"

I leap off the porch, sparing myself from another round of monetary responsibilities.

I enter the garage cautiously. There's enough anger flowing from Finn to fill the garage. Sweat pours off his forehead and grease streaks his cheeks and covers his hands. Blood dots his knuckles as he hammers dents out of a fender I know can't be saved. The grill crinkles into the hood, the smell of fluids leaking onto the concrete. I lie on the cool floor to watch Finn take out his frustrations. Deacon pokes his head in near midnight.

"I'm heading home if you want a ride."

Finn turns the wrench in his hand. "I'm not done yet."

"Sabrina has the bed in the guest room ready for you when you get tired. You're not going to fix this tonight."

"I need to be ready for Saturday's race."

Deacon places his hand on Finn's shoulder. "Things won't look so gloomy in the morning."

Finn ignores him and tosses a hose to the ground. Deacon's car pulls out of the drive, leaving us alone in the garage. The crickets and bull frogs from the neighbor's pond serenade us with their nightly song. I thump my tail against the floor, adding to the beat. Finn's grumbling creates the vocals.

"I admire your drive, but your dad is right—you aren't going to fix this tonight."

"If I can just get all the bad pieces off this stupid thing, I'll—" A hunk of metal lands on his foot. "—Shit!"

I ease my body off the floor and slip to his side. If I weren't looking at the lanky boy before me, I'd guess he were a middle-aged man, but the peach fuzz on his chin gives him away. He strokes my head and continues his work. Time slips by as he fiddles with the engine.

"You've got to take a break," I tell him after waking from a nap.

He cranks the engine, listening intently to the sound it makes.

"I reckon it won't do you any good for me to tell you what's wrong," I say, whining by the door.

His eyes meet mine and he kills the motor. "I guess you're right." He steps from the car. "It's time to call it quits."

"I have no doubt you'll get it back on the track," I tell him as he opens the door and follows me inside.

The clock on the stove says it's a quarter past three. He pours me a fresh bowl of water and gets himself a drink before showering and slipping into bed.

The smell of pancakes and bacon draws me from my place at the foot of Finn's bed. I decide to let him sleep and slink to the kitchen alone. Deacon is seated at the table while Sabrina mans the stove. He glances at her often while scrolling through something on the computer. He's reluctantly excited but Sabrina can barely contain her enthusiasm for whatever he's looking at.

She slides him a plate. "What do you think?"

He slips me a strip of bacon when she turns her back. "You organized a whole fundraiser while I was sleeping?"

She shrugs. "I was waiting for Finn to come inside. It gave me plenty of time."

"I can't believe you did this."

"Finn has talent, and he works hard. I'm happy to help."

Deacon pushes his chair back and catches her in a hug. Endorphins flow from their bodies as they embrace. For a second their eyes meet and I brace myself for a kiss. It doesn't come. I crawl underneath the table, slightly disappointed, and wait for another piece of bacon.

Chapter 52

The back parking lot for Jaybird's hosts the fundraiser with freewill buffet and silent auction. I zig zag my way through the tables, scarfing up bits of food dropped on the ground before sniffing out the baskets lining the table for the auction. Finn's mangled car sits on a trailer next to the restaurant and he stands beside it recanting the story of his wreck. I can't help but notice his embellishments to the event. It brings a smile to my face that can't be broken when I turn my gaze to Sabrina and Deacon working side by side to serve guests.

"Why can't they see they make a great pair? And, if they see it, what are they waiting for?"

Pastor Clifford drops money into the bucket near Sabrina. He leans over for a hug and whispers, "Jason would be proud."

"That's an odd thing to say," I mumble as a tiny girl toddles to me.

With so many voices mingling together, it's hard to focus on the ones I'm interested in hearing, but I know nobody wants a dog near the serving table so I find a place in the grass underneath the shade tree.

"I needed a nap anyway," I mutter, closing my eyes.

I wake in time for the 50/50 raffle, my stiff bones creaking as I clamber to my feet when Amber's name is drawn. She smiles as she hands her cash prize to Finn.

The crowd thins quickly after the auction winners are announced, but one face grabs my attention as he claims his beef jerky bouquet. I inch my way closer, wondering if my eyes are playing tricks on me. If they're not, I may have just lucked into a way of pushing Deacon and Sabrina together.

"Rodney?" He heads toward the far end of the parking lot. I bark to get his attention. "Rodney Summers?" I sit in front of him to block his path.

Sabrina stops wiping down tables and turns to us. "Rod?"

He smiles sheepishly. "I was going to say hi, but you looked busy."

She drops her rag and hurries over, wrapping her arms around his shoulders. "Haven't seen you in a while."

"It's been a few days."

She laughs. "Where've you been hiding?"

"Your dog?" He raises an eyebrow at me. "Why does he look like he wants to eat me?"

She points to the meat in his hands. "It's not you he's after. Right, Huck?" Her hand grazes my head.

She nods. "Where've you been the last...decade?"

"Hillbilly Hell."

She scrunches her face. "Is that a real place?"

"'Fraid so."

She laughs. "What does that make Union Grove?"

"I don't know. What would you call a suburb of Hell?"

She lightly smacks his arm. "We're not that bad."

I drop my tongue out of my mouth. "This may have been a bad idea."

"Thankfully, my being here is only temporary," Rod says.

Sabrina tilts her head. "Oh?"

"Oddly enough, I'm here on business. I work for WindTech."

She looks around. "Don't say that too loud. They'll run you out of town."

"Hopefully, I can change some minds. I'm giving a presentation at the town hall meeting next week."

"Save yourself the trouble. You know the folks around here," she says coolly.

"That's why I'm hoping they'll listen to me."

I turn my gaze to Sabrina. "Say the word and I'll chew his leg off right now. If I have to listen to a monstrous wind turbine in my backyard, I'll go mad. And, as far as my hearing is concerned, that's a huge back yard."

Finn steps beside Sabrina with an armload of chairs. "These go in the storage room, right?"

Sabrina stops him with a hand to his shoulder. "Rod, I'd like you to meet Finn Howard. He's the racer your beef sticks supported."

Finn and Rod share a laugh and a handshake.

"Thanks for your contribution," Finn says.

Rod holds up his basket. "Thank my weakness for jerky." He winks in Sabrina's direction.

"Welp, I'm already regretting this idea." I steal a glance at Deacon. He peers at us with curious eyes. "Okay, maybe not. I can smell his jealousy from here."

Rod sets his basket on a nearby table. "Would you like some help with the chairs?"

Finn happily hands over half a dozen and hurries to gather more. "Finn, you're not supposed to recruit the guests into working."

Rod lifts a shoulder. "Nonsense."

"Seriously, Rod, we've got this," she argues upon their return.

Chairs clang shut as he folds them up. "If you don't mind, I'm working a business proposal here."

"Oh no," she mutters as he makes his second trip to the restaurant.

When all the chairs are put away, Rod gathers his jerky and merely waves a goodbye across the parking lot to Sabrina.

I hurry to Finn. "Care to tell me what that was about?"

Choosing to ride home with Finn and Deacon rather than Sabrina, I anxiously wait for the beans to spill. It doesn't take long for Finn to confide in his dad.

"I may have lucked my way into a major sponsorship," he beams before making it out of the parking lot. "You saw the guy who helped me with the chairs? He gave me his card and wants to be at my next race."

"Who is he?"

Finn pulls a business card from his back pocket. "Rodney Summers. Works for WindTech. Says he wants to take some videos at the race to send to his bosses. He's going to try to get me some major funding."

I twist my head from Finn to see Deacon's reaction.

He scratches his jaw. "Wow. That's great."

I shove my face into Deacon's chest. "Are you kidding me?! 'Round here that will lose him a ton of respect, maybe fans. It'd be like putting a Confederate Flag on a car and racing the Indy 500. Some people won't care, but a great deal will have an issue with a sponsor like that. They'll think we support his business."

Deacon shoves me out of his way. "What does Sabrina think about it?"

"She doesn't know. He talked to me about it while we were putting the chairs away. Said he doesn't want anything said until after he sees me race and gets word from the big guys."

I nudge Finn's chin with my nose. "She won't be happy."

"I hate to keep her in the dark, but if it doesn't work out, I'll hate seeing the disappointment on her face even more."

Deacon nods. "Let's see how this plays out."

"On the plus side, I ran some estimates for repairs, and I think we'll have just enough to get back on the track in two weeks."

"That's what counts."

Chapter 53

Through a lot of hard work and long hours, the car is ready for the track after only missing one race.

I sit beside Sabrina as we wait for Deacon to join us in the stands, my eyes ever scanning the crowd for Rod. I smell him long before he sees us and greatly enjoy watching him pick us out like a hawk searching for a mouse in a field.

Sabrina stands when she sees him. "In a million years I'd never have guessed I'd be seeing you at a dirt track."

They share a brief hug and he motions with his chair, asking permission to set up camp beside her.

He eyeballs the empty lawn chair beside her. "I have a vested interest in this race."

"Why do I get the impression I'm not going to like this?"

He unfolds his chair and slinks into it. "Hear me out. I'm trying to bring awareness to this county about windfarms, right? What better way to do that than slap a giant turbine sticker onto the local track star? It will get people's attention and open their minds."

She shakes her head. "How do you figure?"

"I'll set up interviews with the local paper. It will combine something people love with something they—"

"Hate?"

He waves his finger.

I'd like to bite it off. "I'm sorry I pointed you out at the fundraiser. I should've let you go on your merry way."

"I don't see it that way. The uneducated can be persuaded to—"

"Uneducated? Put it that way and I have no issues. You'll be run out of town so fast the door won't have a chance to hit you on your way out."

He smiles smugly. "Bad choice of words." His eyes fall again on the empty chair. "If I'd known you brought me a chair, I wouldn't have bought this." He taps the arm where a tag still dangles.

"Don't worry, it will be filled soon enough."

"Boyfriend?" He bites his lip. "I couldn't help but notice the other day that you aren't wearing a ring."

Panic seeps from Sabrina, her eyes frozen to the empty seat. "The seat belongs to Finn's father."

Rod licks his lower lip. "Ah, it's starting to make sense now. But it doesn't answer my question."

"Yes. He's my boy...friend."

I sit on Sabrina's feet. "This could work out after all."

Cars take to the track and Deacon arrives moments later, confusion covering his face at seeing Rod next to Sabrina.

She jumps up to greet him with a peck on the cheek. "Honey, this is Rod, an acquaintance from college."

Rod stands, extending his hand. "By 'acquaintance' she means 'boyfriend.'"

Deacon nods. "Rod Summers?"

Sabrina cocks an eyebrow. "Do you two *know* each other?"

Rod shakes his head. "I'm assuming he's in on the topic we were just discussing. I also assume you have a name other than 'Honey.'"

"Deacon."

"Nice to meet you, Deacon. I'm sure we'll be getting to know each other all personal-like before long."

The green flag drops, drowning out any chance of real conversation. Rod videos snippets of the race.

Deacon leans over and tells Sabrina to remind him to tell Finn to gun it coming out of turn four in the next heat.

During the break, Deacon excuses himself to the pits, refusing Rod's inquiry about joining. That leaves me to endure small talk of Sabrina recanting her life after college, including my death. Rod explains how he's been a happy bachelor, traveling the country to decorate landscape with an energy source that 'is the way of the future.'

Sabrina casually drops her hand over the side of her chair and clasps Deacon's when he returns.

"He's starting fourth in the main. I think we have a shot," he whispers, awaiting the drop of the flag.

"If he wins, I'll have him a sponsor for sure," Rod says. "No offense to Jaybird's."

Sabrina glares at him. "Can't compete with 'big money.'"

Chapter 54

Finn tinkers under the hood, checking his phone like he's waiting for a girl to call. Except I know he's anxiously expecting Rod's number to flash across the screen. Rod had invited himself to celebrate with us in the pits after Saturday's race and it quickly turned into a conversation I fear gave the boy false hope. He was supposed to show the video to his bosses and get back with Finn by this afternoon. Finn goes over every detail of the car and pulls it into the driveway to wash. Not wanting to be splashed with the hose, I head to the back yard to find Sabrina and Deacon. They sit on the deck, her with a glass of wine and him with a beer.

"I'll give you five dollars for a sip," I say, taking a seat beside Deacon.

His arm falls over my back. "Finn driving you nuts, too, boy?"

Sabrina swirls the deep red liquid in her glass. "This is my fault. Rod only stopped by the fundraiser because of me."

Deacon's other hand slides to her knee. "There's something about him that rubs me wrong. No offense. I know he's your friend."

She waves her hand in the air. "I wouldn't call him that. We dated briefly in college. Looking back, I think I only agreed because we went to elementary together for a few years before his dad's job relocated him to Atlanta. It felt familiar. And being away from home, I guess I wanted something that connected me to my roots."

"Was he always so...pushy?"

She nods. "It's why we broke up, actually. He borders on the controlling side."

"I'll have to cut your tongue out if you tell this, but I hope his offer falls flat. I realize the burden that places on Finn, but I don't like the idea of working with this guy."

Sabrina's shoulders slump. "It would be nice to have the financial support. Are you really letting Finn make the decision?"

Deacon shrugs. "I can't make his decisions forever."

I perk my ears at the sound of Finn's phone ringing but make no move to investigate.

"I never got the chance to thank you for going along with the boyfriend act. He caught me off guard and I was afraid he was trying to ask me out. I didn't know what else to do," Sabrina says.

He leans over, nudging her with his shoulder. "It's my pleasure."

Her face flushes and a mixture of embarrassment and excitement spills out of her. Deacon smells of nervousness with a hint of lust. I drop my body to the deck, soaking in the musty oak fragrance of the boards, wondering if these two will ever come to terms with their feelings.

Oakley wanders over about the time Deacon finishes his beer. "I'll have an apple if you have any," he says.

Deacons stands, inspecting Sabrina's glass. "One banana for the donkey and a beer for me. Anything for you?"

I lift my head. "I'll take a beer."

Sabrina shakes her head.

"I ordered an apple," Oakley groans as Deacon opens the door. He returns with a beer, banana, and Milk Bone.

After dispersing the treats, he sits a little closer to Sabrina.

"He's getting closer," Oakley mumbles, his mouth full.

"They're fake dating now."

Oakley flicks his ear to send a fly packing. "In my day you were either dating or you weren't. What's this 'fake dating' shit?"

I leap from the porch and jog to his blue ball. "Do you remember Rodney Summers? The kid who set the clock half an hour fast on the last day of school?"

"I remember. You all had plans to pull that prank again."

"Yeah, it didn't work. Anyway, Sabrina ended up dating him for a few months in college."

Oakley snorts. "Why would she do that?"

I fling the ball. "I don't know. But Finn is on the phone with him as we speak. He wants to offer sponsorship with WindTech."

"I'll sponsor him myself before I let that happen!"

"What are you going to do, get a job?"

Oakley takes the handle of the ball in his mouth. "If I have to. We don't want those blasted things around here."

"It would take some stress off Deacon, but I can't say I would support the decision."

Finn races around the side of the house, grabbing our attention.

"He offered me a contract! I'm going to print some copies so we can all read it!"

"I swear I'm going to bite Rodney if I have to see more of him."

"You have my permission," Oakley says.

Chapter 55

Rodney shows up for the next few races and brings along two of his colleagues for the last one.

"We're going to have our answer next week," he tells his companions, slapping Finn on the back after the car is loaded on the trailer.

Deacon and Sabrina exchange a weary glance. It seems they are as sick of Rod as I am.

"We'll be in touch," Deacon says, slipping his arm over Sabrina's shoulder. "Now, if you don't mind, we have an hour's drive home and a fender to beat out."

Rod steps over to inspect the slight damage where Finn got too close to an opponent. "Look forward to welcoming you on board."

Deacon wastes no time broaching the topic once we're alone in the truck. "Have you finished making your pros versus cons list?"

"I keep adding to the cons, if that's what you mean."

Sabrina turns around and faces him in the back seat. "What are the pros?"

"We don't have to worry about money if I wreck."

Deacon laughs. "That's a big one."

Finn wrings his hands together. "Honestly, that's the only thing that has kept me from telling him to climb one of his stupid turbines and jump off. I'm all for green energy, but can you imagine what it would be like to be a bird and fly through an area cluttered with the monstrosities?"

Sabrina nods in agreement. "I'm glad you're looking at both sides of the fence."

"I just think there's a better way. Why not replace all roofs with solar panels?"

Deacon shrugs. "I think that's comparing apples and oranges."

Finn leans forward. "And what happens when one of the turbines stops working? I've seen countless broken ones—even one completely missing a propellor or whatever it's called. Can you imagine being in the way when that thing drops? You'll have a farmer running his combine and there'll be like a deer or something crushed by one of those things."

"You might be stretching on that one," Deacon suggests. "What's really holding you back on this decision?"

"You haven't told me to jump on it."

Deacon reaches his hand back and finds Finn's knee. "It's your decision. You're nearly fourteen; it's time for you to start making some hard choices."

"But this affects all of us. What do you think, Sabrina?"

"I'll support you no matter what."

"I know you will but I want to know what you think."

She twists in her seat. "I think if you take the sponsorship, people will automatically think you're for windfarms. Sure, there will be those who support that, but there will also be those who oppose the notion."

"Yeah," he mutters.

"What if Jaybird's was a dumpy establishment with unfair working conditions? Would you still allow its support even if the whole town knew what went on there?"

Finn sighs. "I feel like this is a no-win situation."

Deacon slows for a red light. "Bottom line is, we'll figure out how to keep you on the track either way. I don't want you to worry about that."

"I appreciate everything both of you have done for me," Finn says. "But, as much as we all despise Rod, I think it's the responsible thing to do for now."

Deacon taps his fingers on Sabrina's thigh. "Looks like we're going to continue fake dating."

She laughs. "The whole town is already on board with that theory."

I lie my head in Finn's lap. "Deacon may not write Hallmark movies, but it looks like he's living one."

I close my eyes for a nap. The excitement of the track has worn me out.

Chapter 56

A car door slams in the driveway, pulling me from a deep sleep. Finn is still in the spare room and Deacon is on the couch after they had spent a late night getting the car ready for the upcoming race. I dance at the front door waiting for Jaycee's key to turn in the lock.

My nose twitches as she turns the knob. "Reese?" She opens the door and, sure enough, Reese stands behind her.

"Hey, Huck, you remember Reese?"

I dance between them, sniffing their legs. "Did you get a cat?"

I follow them into the living room where Deacon rubs his eyes and slips his shirt on.

He greets her with a hug. "Is everything okay?"

She nods, a smile plastering her face. "I know it's early and you have a race tonight, but I couldn't wait to come over."

Deacon extends his hand to Reese. "Long time, no see."

I inhale my way up Reese's pant leg. "Seriously. Did you get a cat?"

He grazes my head. "You must smell my room-mate's cat. She's the devil."

I cock my head. "The cat or the room-mate?"

Jaycee glances to the bedroom where Sabrina still sleeps soundly. "Can you wake Finn? We have something we want to discuss with all of you."

Deacon nods and quietly slips to the back of the house while she hurries to wake her mom. I race around, taking turns in each room, not sure who to follow. Sabrina is concerned with her daughter's sudden appearance and the fact that she brought Reese, which is apparently reason for her to freshen up before entering the living room. Finn, on the other hand, is so eager to see Reese that he comes out in the basketball shorts he sleeps in to talk fishing to his old friend. Jaycee opens her computer and quickly prints several sheets.

"I've got time to throw a line out this afternoon, but I'm afraid we'll have to cut it short," Reese tells him. "I've got a race to attend tonight."

"Reese," Sabrina says, tying the sash on her robe as she comes out of her room. "I hope you brought donuts."

His face pales and his eyes dart to Jaycee.

"They're in the back seat," she tells him.

"I'll be right back."

Deacon pulls mugs out of the cabinet for coffee.

After everyone circles around the table with breakfast, Jaycee passes out the papers. "I know you have a deadline for the sponsorship with WindTech but Reese and I would like to make a proposal for your consideration."

Sabrina holds up her hand. "Hold up. It's too early for all this." She snatches everyone's papers. "Why don't we start with what brought the two of you here."

Jaycee reaches for the sheets but Sabrina proudly sits on them. "We're trying to tell you."

She shakes her head. "No. I mean, the two of you *together*. What's up with that?"

Reese blushes. "I realize I was a jerk to your daughter, and you probably aren't pleased with my presence."

Jaycee's hand slides to his. "I'm going to do this the quick way so we can get on with things. Reese had an interview in Appleton and he asked me to dinner."

"I wanted to apologize for the way things ended," he explains. "I was in a bad place and I'm not proud of my actions back then. I'm better now."

Jaycee squeezes his cheeks. "We're doing the Cliff's Notes version, okay? So, we went to dinner. He didn't get the job."

"I'm sorry," Sabrina offers.

"Mom. Quiet. It's good he didn't get the job."

"It is?"

Jaycee scowls. "Listen. My car was making a weird noise and I asked him to check it out."

Deacon raises his eyebrows. "Why didn't you call me?"

Reese laughs and grabs a donut. "I don't think we're getting away with Cliff's Notes."

For the next ten minutes they recount how they had rekindled their relationship over the last six months and decided to keep it a secret until they knew if it would be long term. From there, they move on to tell how Reese had been studying body work and collision repair for vehicles. Once satisfied with that, Jaycee demands the papers Sabrina sits on, but motions for Reese to take control of the conversation.

"Four of my buddies and I are going to open a repair shop in Burlington. Actually, we're buying out a dying business and are hoping to revamp it."

Worry seeps off Deacon. "That sounds like a lot to bite off for someone fresh out of college." I move beside him, though I don't know if it's to console him or myself. It sounds like Jaycee might get dragged deeper into this and neither of us want her to crash and burn beside him if he's not successful. It all hits too close to home for me. I stare at Sabrina. Her eyes refuse to meet theirs.

"We've got it all worked out," Reese insists.

We embark on another lengthy show of how the main supporter of the endeavor is a retired mechanic—and uncle—of one of the guys and he plans to help get them on their feet. Apparently, he even put up much of the collateral to get them started.

Reese takes the pages from Sabrina and passes out the papers with a sigh. "Now if we can get on to what brought us here—we want to sponsor you. And I'll tell you why."

Jaycee enthusiastically launches into her campaign, promising to offer free car repairs in exchange for their logo being plastered all over the car. The deal comes with requirements to be at the shop one day a month to talk to folks and do general PR stuff.

Reese and Jaycee stare at a stunned group when they are both done adding details.

Finn runs his hands through his hair. "You're telling me I can go out and Dale Earnhardt the car every week and not worry about it?"

Reese clenches his jaw. "We'd prefer you didn't, but, in a sense, yes. We won't pay you for advertising, but we'll fix you up when you need it."

Deacon reaches for a second donut. "I assume the plan is to promote yourself by showing your craftsmanship with his car?"

Reese nods. "Something like that. Would you take your car to a shop run by fresh-out-of-college kids when there's a more experienced place across town?"

Deacon takes a bite. "I suppose not."

I lick the crumbs that fall to the floor. "Maybe not a strong marketing plan, but I like it."

Sabrina refills her coffee cup and starts another pot. "I hate to burst the enthusiasm—this sounds like a great opportunity—but we need to know your guys are qualified."

Reese shuffles his feet. "We're putting together a list of certificates and all that stuff for everyone on the team. I can personally assure you we'll get the job done and you'll never know we don't have the experience of older mechanics." He sucks in a breath. "We have experience, of course."

Deacon stands. "I hope you're not wanting an answer on the spot."

Reese gathers empty plates and takes them to the sink. "Of course not. Think it over."

"What is there to think about?" Jaycee objects.

Finn takes another donut from the box. "We can still go fishing, right?"

Sabrina laughs. Deacon rolls his eyes, but Finn has already motioned for Reese to follow him to the garage.

"I'd better call Rod and tell him we have a new development and need an extension."

"Good idea," Sabrina agrees.

Chapter 57

"It was fun fake dating you while it lasted," Deacon says a week later as they sip nightcaps on the porch.

After hearing about Reese's offer, Rod countered with a deal that could put Finn through college. But Finn had already made up his mind. He wanted to work with Reese. And when the town voted against installing the turbines, Rod left with his tail tucked between his legs.

"Shame you never got to fake take me out," Sabrina hints.

I twist my head to stare up at her. Sure enough the disappointment in her eyes matches the longing pouring from her body.

Deacon's gaze slowly meets hers. "I would've loved fake taking you out. But Finn's so attached to you and Jaycee that I worry..." He takes a long pull from his beer.

"If it didn't work out—"

"Exactly." He inhales deeply. "Maybe if we'd given it a shot in the beginning," he offers.

"I wasn't ready to date then. Hell, I'm not so sure I'm ready now."

"See? Maybe it's all for the best this way."

She swirls the wine in her glass. "Maybe."

"You've got a lot to offer. Don't think there isn't someone out there who can make you happy again."

She nudges his leg with hers. "Same goes for you."

He excuses himself to get another beer and she wraps her body over mine, hugging me tightly.

"I've waited too long being afraid of replacing Jason that I wonder if I've missed my chance," she whispers. "Deacon is so worried about what would happen if things went wrong, but did he stop to think about things going *right*?"

I lick her hand. "Talk to him. I can *feel* the love between you. You have my blessing."

"You need to come here," Deacon says, door flung wide. She leaps to her feet. "I think there's something wrong with Bobbi."

I follow them inside, barely slipping in before the door closes. Sabrina hurries to the kitchen where Bobbi is curled up in the corner. Now attuned to the situation, I smell the sickness emanating from the tiny creature. Sabrina bends to do her own inspection.

"I tried to give her a treat and she barely lifted her head," Deacon whispers, worry heavy in his voice. "You know how she can't resist those things. Usually comes running any time she hears the Milk Bone box rattle when we give Huck a treat."

Sabrina nods. "We need to call the vet." She paces the kitchen, dialing a number on her phone. "I guess we'll have to see if we can get her in at the animal hospital in Burlington. Why can't this happen during business hours?"

I shove my nose gently into Bobbi's side. "You don't smell so good. What is it?"

She twitches her whiskers. "This is what the end smells like."

I lie down, resting my head next to hers. "It can't be. Sabrina and Deacon just affirmed they won't give dating a real shot. And you don't want me picking out her next husband alone, do you? You have to fight this. We can still get them together."

"Deacon has more brains than you; he'll come around." She pants heavily. "Had...to...get...one more...in."

"I wouldn't expect anything else."

Damn. What is that in my chest? Am I really upset to see her go?

Her heart rate drops slightly. "I believe in you, Huck. You can make them see."

A tear threatens to escape but Finn bustles in the room, cat carrier in hand. Deacon makes the call to Jaycee, giving her the address of the animal hospital.

Sabrina's shaking hands tenderly scoop Bobbi into the crate. Her eyes are already dotted red and my heart breaks for the tears I know will come.

"See you on the other side, Jason," Bobbi manages through struggled breath as they escort her out the door.

Chapter 58

Jaycee enters the house carrying a small cardboard box with Deacon, Sabrina, and Finn following.

"I'm so sorry," I say, brushing Jaycee's leg.

"Huck, don't."

I move to Sabrina and sniff her legs. "I wish she'd said something to me. I would've gotten your attention somehow," I tell her.

She shoves me away.

I calmly greet Deacon and Finn. "Thanks for being with my girls tonight."

Finn strokes my head. "Not right now, boy."

Deacon and Finn slip to the garage while Sabrina and Jaycee head straight for the back door. I follow them outside. Someone should warn Oakley. They take a seat on the top step, muffled sobs escaping them. I leave them to their grief and slip inside the shed.

Oakley's alert eyes greet me, his ears flicking like a satellite trying to pick up signal.

"Bobbi," I choke on my words, silently staring at him.

He strains his neck over mine, hugging the best way he can. "I know."

I nuzzle into his side. "I have a nose. And your face said it all when you walked in."

"After all these years we finally found a way to get along and now she's gone."

"That's what my brother said at his wife's funeral."

I manage a smile at his joke, though I know there's truth in it. Flopping into the straw, I sigh. "One day I'm afraid you'll see them put me in the ground."

"Asses do seem to live longer."

"I'm being serious."

"So am I. Donkeys have a longer life span than dogs or cats."

I curl up beside him. "I hate that you have to witness it."

"God won't leave me behind without purpose. *That* I know."

"I guess Bobbi had filled hers."

His ears stand erect. Bull frogs and crickets create a melody harmonized by a hoot owl. "Tonight they sing a sad song."

I pause a second to listen. "It sounds the same as last night."

"You're not listening correctly. Learn to be still."

Sabrina's voice breaks my concentration. "We were so busy going from the garage to the track and with work that we didn't notice Bobbi's odd behavior," she laments.

"I'm not going to try to make music out of a bunch of creatures," I whisper. "Not when my girls are so upset."

"Go. Be with them. That's your purpose," Oakley whispers.

I clamber to my feet, putting aside my own feelings.

Finn and Deacon slink around the side of the house with lights and shovels.

Deacon slips his hand around Sabrina's shoulders. "Where would you like to bury her?"

Sabrina turns to Jaycee. "I think she'd like it beneath the pine tree."

Jaycee nods in agreement. Finn and Deacon get to work while Jaycee consoles her mother over her guilt.

"They said these things can spring up suddenly," Jaycee offers. "Heck, I didn't notice anything when I was over."

"She was such a good cat. I can't believe she lived almost twenty years."

Jaycee leans into Sabrina. "She had a good life."

Sabrina wipes a streak of tears from her cheeks. "She helped me through my darkest days and I couldn't return the favor."

"Mom, don't beat yourself up. Even the vet said you were lucky you didn't just find her body worn out from age. Be thankful you got to say goodbye. It's a luxury we're not always afforded."

I lap the salty tears from her fingertips. "Wise girl, our daughter."

"You're right," Sabrina admits.

Attention turns to me as if we're all facing my mortality tonight.

"I don't mind the attention, but I have no plans of leaving you yet," I tell them.

"We're ready," Deacon says before any of us truly are.

Jaycee carries the box over to the hole and the group circles it. Oakley makes an appearance in the background, snorting his presence.

Deacon slips his hand into Sabrina's. "Care to say a few words?"

"Sometimes I think animals know us better than we know ourselves," she whispers. "When I first met Bobbi, everyone tried to talk me out of bringing her home. They said she was a wild beast that couldn't be tamed. But she got me. From first sight. It was like she knew I needed *her.* And I did. Oh how I did. There were so many nights I thought I'd never make it through, but she was right there as if to say, 'I need you too.' We *got* each other." She twists her head to stare at Oakley. A small laugh escapes her lips. "I think I finally understand why we have a donkey."

Her laugh grows until it turns to uncontrollable sobbing. "I understand."

Jaycee steps forward, placing the box in the hole. "Bobbi...well, what can we say...Bobbi never really cared for anyone but Mom. The rest of us just took up the time Mom should've been devoting to her."

They share a chuckle over Jaycee's words and Finn raises his hand a few inches until Sabrina nods for him to speak.

"I know Bobbi wasn't my cat, but it kind of felt like she was." His hand slips to my side and he turns to nod toward Oakley. "She tried to trip me enough times that I know I'm never getting a cat."

Deacon smiles, one that quickly fades as he places his hand on Sabrina's shoulder. He holds the shovel between them. "Shall I?"

She shakes her head, taking it from him. "I'll do it."

Deacon slaps his arm on Finn's back, motioning for them to leave the girls in peace.

I lie on the ground, knowing one day there will be a bigger grave beside this one. If I didn't know better, I'd swear I could hear *Swing Low Sweet Chariot,* in the background.

Chapter 59

There is a void in our days for many months, but time eases the wounds and before we know it, we're heading into the next racing season with The Grease Garage on the side of the car. I wish I could give him props on the name, but I'm still speaking a different language.

My aching joints tell me time is running out, but I have no idea how to bring Sabrina and Deacon together.

A ladybug lands on a nearby dandelion in the grass smashed by the hordes of people. "It's hard to change a man's mind."

I turn to see who had spoken but nobody is around. Sabrina and Jaycee had gone to the pits with Deacon and Reese, leaving me tied to a lawn chair. A few people smirk upon seeing me chained to the flimsy device, but I no longer care about proving anything to anyone.

I sniff the air. "Excuse me?"

The ladybug flutters to my paw. "Would you like some advice?"

"If I'm to succeed, I think you're the only one who can help. Where have you been, anyway? I don't see how I can do this without being able to communicate with my...Sabrina."

"I've never left your side. You're the one who got side-tracked."

I lie my head carefully between my paws, shame welling up inside me. "How's Bobbi?"

"She's loving on some grandkids who eagerly await your return. And I'm supposed to tell you she knows you'll get the job done."

My other kids. How could I have forgotten them so easily? My heart swells with guilt and a longing to see them again.

"Second Peter 3:8." He returns to the dandelion, giving it new zest amongst the trampled grass. "With the Lord a day is like a thousand years, and a thousand years are like a day."

His words give me comfort. "I haven't missed much."

"They're fishing at the lake."

"I hope they understand why I needed to come back."

"You have their full support."

I rest my head on my paws. "I can't go back to them a failure."

"How about that advice?"

I cover my eyes with a paw. "What happens if I can't make these two see how good they are together?"

"You know your wife better than anyone."

He flutters away at the return of Deacon and Sabrina.

I wag my tail but make no movement to greet them the way I once would have. "What am I supposed to do with that advice?" I strain my eyes, searching for the ladybug, or any other creature that might offer an explanation. But my vision is cloudy these days. I can't find scraps of food thrown to the floor at dinner so it's a miracle I saw the ladybug at all.

The cars speed around the track as fast as my mind works to form a plan. Finn suffers minor damage trying to block a pass but still finishes fifth. By the time we head home, I am no closer to figuring out how to bring two stubborn people together.

"This would be a lot easier if I were dealing with teenagers and reckless hormones," I tell them on the way home.

"I guess we get to see what kind of work Reese and his boys can do," Deacon says as he maneuvers the trailer onto the road.

"I think Reese is pretty excited about it," Sabrina says with a smile.

"I feel terrible about messing the car up on the first run," Finn mutters.

"You didn't do much damage. Should be able to knock it out in one day," Deacon offers.

Chapter 60

True to his word, Reese and his crew have the car looking good as new before the race the following weekend.

Somehow that summer turns out to be one of the best of my life. Finn meets a girl at the track and they are instantly inseparable. I leave Sabrina's feet at the shop to hang out wherever Finn and Evie are. We spend days at the lake, evenings on the tailgate of his '95 F-150, and nights curled up on the couch watching movies. Even when they hang out with friends, I'm allowed to tag along. Somewhere along the way, I find I can no longer jump into the cab of the truck as I used to. After watching me struggle to pull my back legs up, Finn started keeping a stool in the truck to aid me. When his buddies poked fun at us, Finn shot them a glare and coolly said, "You shouldn't have to lose your dignity when you get old." Tears slipped from my eyes the whole way home that day. By the time school starts that fall, Deacon and Sabrina are joking about living together. Neither can remember the last time they didn't spend the night under the same roof. They still sleep in separate rooms but, somehow, Deacon always managed to nod off during the movies Sabrina insisted he stay for after supper every night. There had been a few nights I thought she might drag him to bed with her, but something held her back. One morning the first week of school, Deacon thumps a thick bundle of computer paper on the table during breakfast.

He taps a red pen to his temple. "My home for the next week is in the editing trenches."

Sabrina giggles. "I'll try to keep the enemy from invading."

Deacon smiles. "By that I hope you mean you'll keep Finn from tearing up his car this weekend."

"He's had a rough season," Sabrina admits.

"I think Reese might be regretting his deal. He's certainly getting the short end of it."

"I don't think he minds. Besides, Finn is helping out. I think Reese might be getting himself an apprentice."

Deacon flips through the pages, worry lines covering his forehead. "I have to get this finished and I already feel like I've read it three hundred times. Just seems I've spent more time at the garage than working on what pays the bills."

Sabrina places a waffle in front of him and fills his mug with coffee. "Might help if you didn't play supervisor at the garage. Reese has already proven he's good at what he does."

He nods. "I know. I just feel like I should lend a hand."

While they banter back and forth over responsibilities and how tired they both are, an idea hits me. I wait for Deacon to remove his hand from his manuscript and clamp my teeth on it. Thankfully he'd left two inches hanging over the edge, but my muscles still ache at the sudden movement. They both shout my name and reach for it. I jerk out of their grasp, carefully moving so that Sabrina is the one to successfully take it from my mouth. When she tries to hand it back, I step between them and growl.

She passes it over my head. "What has gotten into you, Huck?"

Deacon wipes my saliva from the top sheet. "He's acting strange."

"Give it back," I bark. "You can thank me later."

He stares curiously at me. "It's like he's trying to tell us something."

"Remember that day you were stuck on a scene and you were telling me about how your characters were in love but they didn't know it?" I peer at him intensely, recalling the late-night session he'd had using me as a sounding board. If I can get Sabrina to read the words, maybe she'll see how he feels about her.

"Pass it back to me," Sabrina suggests.

He does. I sit, patiently waiting. When Sabrina hands it back, I growl.

"I think he wants you to have it," Deacon concludes. Sabrina shrugs. "I used the last of my paper to print that."

"I'll slip it back later when he's not looking."

"Read it," I snap.

Deacon laughs. "I think he wants you to do the editing."

"I wouldn't know how."

I press my paw to her shin. "Figure it out."

Deacon smirks. "You know, it wouldn't hurt to have some fresh eyes on the thing. I've covered the plot holes, so really all you'd have to do is read over it and see what jumps out at you...if you don't mind."

"I don't know what that means."

He reaches for it but I shove my body in his way. "Things like 'you' when it should say 'your.' Or if I say that a character has blue eyes in chapter one but in chapter nine they have brown eyes, that type of thing."

She nods. "I can do that. I was going to run errands today. If I give you the list, can you get the supplies I need?"

"I'd be more than happy to swap agendas."

Sabrina whips out her phone. Her fingers race across the screen. "There. Sent you the list. Happy shopping."

His phone pings. "Happy reading."

Sabrina grabs the manuscript, eyeing me as she takes it and a cup of coffee to the couch.

Deacon returns with an armload of supplies and sandwiches from Jaybird's three hours later.

"I'm fairly certain that was an even trade," he says, pouring two glasses of tea. "I officially hate shopping as much as I hate editing."

Sabrina laughs, clutching the manuscript to her chest. "I officially love editing as much as I love shopping. Well, at least this book. It's fantastic."

Color rushes to Deacon's cheeks as he slides a Styrofoam container to her. "You're biased."

"I swear I've been hooked since Holly slapped Zane at the kissing booth."

Pride shines in Deacon's eyes. "Well, you're not exactly supposed to slap the person who paid five dollars to kiss you."

"But he hasn't shown up again. Instead, she and her son are waiting for his friend to get back from vacation."

He nods. "Ah, good. Can I ask what your impression of that scene is?"

Sabrina plucks the tomato off her sandwich and passes it to Deacon. "I get the feeling Holly is eager. Like maybe she has a thing for the friend's dad...or mom." She takes a large bite and holds up her finger. "Is that why she slapped Zane? She's into women?"

Deacon tosses her a packet of mayo. "I can't tell you anything. I need your genuine reaction."

"Fine. I found a few typos and one place where you left out a word completely."

"I hope you remembered to mark them."

"With bright red ink."

With a mouth full of food, Deacon smiles. "What should I do with the rest of my day?"

"Oakley's stall needs mucked."

"Another chore more enjoyable than editing."

"You should probably plan to cook supper too. I think Evie is coming over with Finn today. They have a biology test tomorrow."

He laughs. "Why do they always study here? It's not like we don't have an empty apartment."

Sabrina slips me a scrap of ham from her sandwich. "My TV is bigger."

"Good enough, I guess."

"I'm taking this outside to read," Sabrina says after lunch.

I follow her outside and nap while she reads from the comfort of a lawn chair.

Deacon whistles from the shed as he fills manure into a wheelbarrow.

A few times Sabrina calls out to him, questioning incidents in the book, but Deacon refuses to give her any details. I shift positions and take another nap, hoping she reads fast enough to get to the good parts by evening.

Over dinner Sabrina explains my 'odd' behavior this morning and tells Finn and Evie how she'd come to read Deacon's latest project.

Evie passes Deacon a plate of burnt fried chicken. "What's the book about?"

Deacon bites his lip and turns to Sabrina. "Ask her."

"Well so far, we have two single parents who spend a lot of time together because their kids are best friends. I think the plot is that they're in love with each other but don't know it?"

Deacon shovels mashed potatoes onto his plate. "It's about them realizing what's in front of their faces."

Sabrina pours a glass of tea. "Yeah, but there's also this Zane guy. Holly—the mom—slapped him at the beginning of the book but now he's her son's teacher and he's just asked her out."

Deacon smiles. "That throws a wrench in things, huh?"

Finn points to Deacon and Sabrina. "Sounds familiar."

Deacon chokes on his water.

Denial is thick in Sabrina's voice when she adds, "But there's no Zane. This isn't us. Tell them, Deacon."

Deacon wipes gravy from the corner of his mouth. "I'm merely telling the story of two single parents. Everything else is coincidental."

Sabrina swirls her fork in a pool of gravy. "So, the Shetland pony is not based on Oakley?"

Deacon's knife scrapes against his plate. "You're reading too much into it."

"My English teacher says writers write what they know," Evie chimes in.

"That's not entirely true. I had to do research for one of the teenagers. There's no way he's based off anyone I knew prior to starting the book." His comment gains him curious stares. He stands. "Anyone want dessert? I made brownies."

Finn laughs. "It sounds like you wrote the story you're too afraid to live."

I smile, watching Deacon and Sabrina stare at each other like two kids caught coloring on the walls.

Deacon's phone rings. "It's Reese. I have to take this." He excuses himself to the other room.

"We have ice cream to go with the brownies if you want some," Sabrina offers.

"Reese needs to see me at the garage," Deacon says upon his return. Finn stands, but Deacons waves him off. "I can take care of it."

"If it's about the car, I should come."

"You have a test to study for. It's really no big deal."

Chapter 61

S abrina's eyes barely leave the pages in front of her even though the doorbell has rung twice. "They'll go away, right?"

I raise my head, no longer caring to be the first to greet guests. Clint Eastwood could be at our door and I wouldn't race to meet him. These days I figure I'll say hello whenever it's convenient. "I might be turning into a cat," I say with a laugh.

Sabrina's phone rings. "You'll have to wait, Reese." She silences the device. The text chime dings ten seconds later. "He knows I'm home. Says it will only take a minute."

I wag my tail once, but only because she seems to want an answer from me. "I don't really feel like moving," I say from my curled-up position beside her.

She strokes my head. "I'll text him." Her fingers move quickly over the screen. "You have two minutes. I'm about to find out if these two idiots end up together. Come on in."

His response is inches from my face but the words are fuzzy.

Sabrina growls. "He says the door is locked."

"Tell him the key is under the mat."

With a groan she slides away from me.

Reese shifts nervously on his feet. "That must be a good book."

Sabrina crosses her arms. "It is. Holly is dating this guy who is all wrong for her, but I think she's finally realized the person she loves has been next door all along."

Reese nods. "Next door? Seriously? Deacon couldn't get more creative than that?"

"It's convenient. I'll give you that. Maybe that's something he should address. Every time Holly needs something done—like changing an electrical outlet—she has Dirk come over and fix it. And he drops what he's doing to do her bidding. It would be more obvious that they belong together if he had to travel at least ten miles to do that. Thanks for pointing that out."

Reese cocks an eyebrow. "You're welcome?"

The question in his tone snaps Sabrina out of her zone. "If you came to talk about books, I'll pop open the wine." She laughs at her attempt for a joke.

Reese shoves his hands in his pockets then removes them and runs them through his hair. "Actually, I want to talk about two other idiots in love."

The muscles in my back scream as I pull myself off the couch and over to Reese. "Are you about to do what I think you're about to do?"

Sabrina zips to the kitchen for a glass of water while Reese is preoccupied with rubbing my belly. He straightens, taking the cup from her. "Thank you."

"You seem a bit nervous. Is everything okay? Is Jaycee pregnant?"

His nod quickly turns to a shake. "She said I didn't have to do this, but I want to."

I sit proudly beside Sabrina, waiting for the question to come.

He takes a long swallow. "I would like to marry your daughter."

Sabrina exhales loudly. "I don't know what I was expecting, but that wasn't it."

I crane my neck into her hand. "What else could he have asked given his nervous nelly act?"

"Of course you have my blessing." She steps forward and wraps her arms around him. "Deacon wrote this beautiful proposal scene. I'm sure he wouldn't mind if you used it. There's this gorgeous little trail...I'm sure you have your own ideas."

Reese nods sheepishly. "I've talked to the owner at the drive-in where we had our first date and they've agreed to display a screen asking the question at the intermission between the movies tomorrow night."

Sabrina clasps her hands over her heart. "Oh that's beautiful."

"I was kind of hoping we could take Huck. You know, like we did the first time."

"Of course!"

Reese shuffles his feet. "I'll see you tomorrow then." He scratches my ear and hands the cup back to Sabrina. "I'll get back to the shop now and you can get back to your other idiots in love."

Chapter 62

The proposal was a huge hit at the movies and, naturally, Jaycee said yes. They planned a spring wedding, and the next few months were filled with grueling details I was forced to listen to because the cold weather aches my bones more than it did in my youth and I can't hide outside all day with Oakley. Deacon works from our house on the days when I lack the energy to climb in the truck and go to work with Sabrina. I hate staying behind, but some days my back gives me no choice. I lie by his feet as he types, listening as he reads parts of his story out loud. His last round of edits for the book I call *Idiots in Love* is taking longer than I'd like. I've heard the same three chapters six times. Thankfully, Jaycee pops in one snowy morning to alleviate my boredom.

"I'll stick to the living room," she tells Deacon who sits at the table. "I need to finish some wedding stuff, but I promise to be quiet."

Deacon nods, his fingers moving feverishly across the keyboard.

My legs complain as I opt to spend my time curled up next to Jaycee on the couch. "I'd much rather listen to every detail of your wedding than hear another word of Deacon's story."

Jaycee opens a binder and scribbles on several pages. I wait for her to start talking to herself, too, but she only makes soft clicking sounds with her tongue as she checks things off. I yawn. Watching her work has made me tired. I close my eyes, hoping the pain in my hind quarters will subside enough for me to catch a nap.

I drag my eyelids apart when I hear a soft sob escape her lips. "What's wrong? Did I put your arm to sleep?" I move off her right arm, waiting for her to shake the tingling sensation out of it. "Deacon, I need someone in here who can speak human words. Help! She's crying," I plead, my heart wrenching for the pain my daughter is in.

The continuous tapping on the keyboard tells me he's lost in his fictional world.

I wriggle onto Jaycee's lap, hoping to knock the binder to the floor, gain Deacon's attention, and comfort Jaycee with my cold nose in her face.

She reaches around me and grabs a tissue. After blowing twice, I realize Deacon is just as clueless as any other man.

"Deacon, I swear I'll find a way to pee all over that computer if you don't get in here and talk to this girl," I bark sharply.

Jaycee sniffles but the longer she stares at the paper on her lap, the louder her sobs become.

I crane my neck to read what's written there. The words are blurry but I get the idea that she's filling in names with roles of the wedding party.

Deacon's chair scrapes the floor and a second later the ice machine drops cubes into his cup. I whimper, gaining a glance from him. His stare goes above me and focuses on Jaycee. He's at her side instantly.

"Jaycee?" He scooches between us. "What's wrong?"

She points to the list. "Every time I look at this sheet, I start crying."

He takes it from her. "The blanks...they should have your dad's name—"

Jaycee nods. "It makes me miss him even more."

I inch my body so that my head falls in her lap. "I'm not going to miss your wedding," I say, though I don't know if my body can hold out.

Deacon adjusts himself under my weight. "I know nobody can replace your dad, but you know you don't have to do the dance. You can skip that part altogether."

Jaycee wipes tears from her cheeks. "That's not what makes me cry. I don't even like to dance. Not after the recital."

"Ah. I see. Maybe your mom could walk you down the aisle."

Jaycee crinkles her nose. "She said Kelley might like to do it. He was Dad's best friend."

Deacon squeezes her shoulders. "Kelley would be a good choice."

I lick her hand. "I would be honored if Kelley stood in for me."

They sit in awkward silence for a minute.

Deacon slowly strokes my back. "I have an idea...what about Huck?"

I turn to face him at the sound of my name. My tail wags as they consider the option.

Jaycee rubs my chin. "I don't know. He doesn't get around so well these days."

My entire body shakes as I lurch upward to lick her face. "I won't let you down."

Deacon smiles, leaning backward to avoid my flailing tail. "I think he's telling us he'd be honored." He shifts to avoid me sitting directly on his lap. "If you ask me, it makes perfect sense. He's been around since your dad died, right?"

Jaycee nods. "We found him at the funeral home the day we buried Dad."

"See? He's been there for you your whole childhood; who better to walk you down the aisle?"

Jaycee covers my ears with her hands. "I know he's not going to be around much longer. I guess it would be like him passing me off to the man I'm going to spend the rest of my life with."

Deacon pats my side. "I think you got yourself the role of a lifetime."

I turn and lick Deacon square on the face. "Thank you."

He laughs—I hope from my gesture rather than my words—and stands.

"Deacon?" He stops. "If I decide I want to do the dance, would you be my partner?"

Elation seeps heavily off him. "I'd love to."

Chapter 63

Sabrina places a kiss on Jaycee's cheek, carefully checking to ensure there's no lipstick trace as she steps back. "You look beautiful."

My eyes linger on my daughter. "There have been so many times I've wished you could understand me," I say, taking in as much of the lace on her wedding dress as my eyes will allow. "But never more than I do today. You've become a woman I'm proud of and, though you don't know it, I'm honored to have the privilege of walking you to your husband."

"Mom, go," Jaycee urges.

"I need one more look," Sabrina says, tears welling in her eyes.

"There will literally be hundreds of pictures for you to remember this by." Jaycee takes her hand. "I'm not going to be late to my own wedding because you won't stop gawking at me."

Sabrina laughs. "Okay, okay."

For a few minutes Jaycee and I are alone. It had been a busy morning and I'm exhausted. I ache deep in my bones. I'd literally followed Jaycee everywhere she went, desperate to soak in every detail of the day.

The *Wedding March* plays softly in the background.

"This is it," she says, patting my head. "We're up."

We step outside and into the brightness of the sun. It's a gorgeous day, a little warm for early May. Everyone stands to stare at us. I watch my steps, careful to not touch her dress with my feet. When we reach the end of the aisle, Reese takes hold of her hands and I take my place beside Sabrina, just as we had practiced.

Finn runs his hand down my back most of the ceremony, almost lulling me to sleep. If it were any ordinary day, I'd be snoring by the time Pastor Clifford asks who gives the bride to the groom. His words trigger an impulse inside me and I proudly bark, "I do."

The crowd laughs.

Sabrina stands. "Her family and I."

I'm not sure she notices that she glanced over at Deacon, Finn, and I when she said the words, but I wouldn't have it any other way.

I don't normally like long weddings, but this one is much too short. Watching the love between my daughter and her husband in front of all these people warms my heart. I had thought I might be bitter about being a dog in this situation but, instead, I find myself feeling grateful to be allowed to attend.

The reception is held inside a renovated barn and is in full swing an hour after the ceremony ends. Even though I try my best, I find there is no way I'll make it to the good parts without a nap. The staff from Jaybird's instructed Sabrina to not lift a finger, but she's not doing a good job of listening. I laugh watching her, knowing I would've had a hard time obeying that order years ago. Today though, I realize work is not what's important in life. By the time the speeches are done and cake is cut, the music starts playing and I watch with tears in my eyes as Deacon takes my place in the Father-Daughter dance. My heart swells that she found a few more dances inside her. After the bride and groom's first dance, the floor instantly crowds with anxious partiers. I dart my way to safety beneath a table.

Lauren, the manager of Jaybird's, finally convinces Sabrina to leave them be. She takes a seat beside me to watch the dancing. A slow song starts and I leap to my feet when a woman grabs Deacon's hand.

I nudge Sabrina's leg. "Do you see that? Are you just going to sit here and let him dance with her?"

A hint of jealousy surrounds her. She taps her foot angrily against the concrete floor.

"I reckon it's time to get the white horse out, Jason," I whisper beneath the table. "I can't take that foot tapping anyway. She's way off time with the beat."

Kelley is across the room, sneaking bites from a stick of beef jerky. He slides it into the sleeve of his jacket when Amber slips by to help Lauren. I muster up what's left of my youth and dart between couples on the dance floor. Grabbing his arm in my mouth, I drag him to Sabrina's side.

"Huck, what are you doing?" The words come from both Kelley and Sabrina as they stare at my odd behavior.

I sniff his arm. At least this is distracting Sabrina, even if Kelley doesn't take the bait.

With a guilty smile, Kelley releases the jerky from his sleeve. "I guess I'm busted."

Sabrina laughs. "With all the food here, you're smuggling in jerky?"

Kelley shoots a look to his brother-in-law. "Jim just got back from a trip out west and he said I *had* to try these." He dangles the stick inches from my nose. "It's elk. Pretty darn tasty when it's not covered in dog drool." He slips the treat into my mouth.

"I'm sure it is."

"I'll see if he has any more."

The song ends. Deacon and his partner release each other. Another song starts and it's another slow one. Kelley searches for Amber but she's still busy cleaning. Deacon's lady friend takes a sip from her glass at a nearby table but reaches for Deacon's hand a second later.

Kelley extends his hand. "Care to dance?"

Sabrina slowly stands as I use my tongue to dig pieces of meat from my remaining teeth. I find a table close to the spot they choose on the dance floor and lie down, hoping my ears still work well enough to pick up the conversation.

Kelley's hand slides around Sabrina's waist. "It was a beautiful ceremony," he says.

Finn and Evie block my view, their laughter drowning out Sabrina's and Kelley's voices. But, if nothing else, I know Finn plans on slipping off to the far side of the pond with his girlfriend as soon as the next upbeat song starts. I smile to myself. The mood is certainly hitting everyone tonight, I think as Kelley and Sabrina spin a circle near me again.

"I'm just saying," Kelley whispers, "if he's too big of an idiot to make a move, maybe you should make one."

"I don't know," Sabrina responds. I can feel her nervousness from where I sit.

"Are you going to let him get away because you're too chicken to be the one to ask him out? Don't tell me you've never asked out a guy before." Amusement dances in his eyes.

"It's been too long. I'm afraid we're destined to be friends forever."

Kelley's laugh gains the attention of the couple next to them. He pulls her tighter against his chest. "That would be a mistake. Half the town is already taking bets on how long it will be until you're married." He laughs. "At the rate you're going, it will pay for the wedding."

I can't see Sabrina's face but I imagine she's rolling her eyes.

"Come on, he wrote a book about your relationship." Her face still hidden, I envision the panic her eyes hold. "You can't tell me that's not about the two of you."

Sabrina steals a glance at Deacon. "I'll admit I had my suspicions, but the couple in that story decide they're better off as friends. They don't end up together. If it *is* about us, I think that's the way he wants it."

Kelley shrugs. "Maybe he's scared to write it any other way. Like he'll be disappointed if he doesn't get his own happy ending."

The song ends and they release each other. Finn and Evie slip out the door and I decide to follow them. I need to pee anyway, but something Deacon says stops me by the drink table.

"I changed the ending to the book," he says. He's talking to Thad.

Finn and Evie slip from my sight, but I have to know how Kelley's son fits into all this.

"I'm glad you considered an alternate ending," Thad replies.

Deacon steals a bold glance at Sabrina. She smiles at him. "Something didn't feel right about the way I left things between Holly and Dirk. But Holly's son plays a major role in the new ending and I was hoping you'd have a look."

Thad nods. "As a fellow PAN, I think I'd better."

I cock my head. What's a PAN?"

"Good. I already sent you the revised copy. Thank you again for giving me so much insight into the mind of a pansexual teenager. I couldn't have done it without you."

"I expect a HEA this time."

I scratch my head. "Why are you talking in code?"

Deacon smiles. "Oh there's a happily ever after." He sighs heavily. "At least in the world of fiction."

Sabrina crosses the dance floor.

Thad taps Deacon on the shoulder. "Maybe try to find a HEA of your own." He boldly stares at Sabrina.

Sabrina matches her footsteps to arrive at the first notes of the next song. "May I have this dance?"

Deacon's earlier partner looks disappointed to find him dancing with someone new. I don't know who she is but, clearly, she isn't from around here. Everyone we know looks pleased to see the two of them finally together on the dance floor.

"Weddings make people all mushy," she says, her arms draped around his shoulders. "And wine makes people say things they normally wouldn't."

Deacon smiles down at her. "I think you're getting the stink eye." Deacon spins her to see the woman who lost out on the dance.

Sabrina smiles. "I hope she won't be too disappointed because I'd like to take you off the market permanently."

Deacon freezes, catching Sabrina when she stumbles at his abrupt stop. "How much have you had to drink?"

I move out of the way of a scooting chair. "Three glasses since Kelley told her to grow the balls you lack."

Sabrina lies her head on his shoulder. "I'll need a ride home."

"Finn is on DD duty tonight."

Sabrina lifts her head, meeting his gaze. "If I don't say this now, I fear I might never have the courage."

Deacon tilts his head and I can nearly see the gears working in his brain.

"Don't worry, pal, I'm just now figuring out that Sabrina requested this song too," I whisper against the sound of Lee Brice's song, *Rumor.*

He spins her around, cautiously dipping her. "What do you say—do we give the people what they want?"

Even upside down, I can see the confliction on her face as she whispers, "No."

Disappointment covers his face as he rights her.

I flop my head down on my paws. "You were so close. You're a couple of idiots, you know that?"

Sabrina grips his hands. "Take me home?"

Deacon nods. I slip out to warn Finn with a sharp barking sure to gain his attention.

Chapter 64

Sabrina kicks off her shoes next to the bed. "Will you unzip me?"

Deacon does as he's asked.

I watch the theatrics of her changing into something more comfortable, knowing she'll pick casual pajamas. She had insisted Finn return to the party, take Evie home, then come back to the house for the night. She doesn't have to say that's her excuse to not be alone with Deacon. We both know that's exactly what happened in the driveway ten minutes ago. Still, I wonder which of them will crack the topic open again. Deacon stays close by but turns his head as she slips from her gown and replaces it with shorts and a baggy shirt.

"Come on," I urge. "One of you has to say something. You know you want to."

Deacon pours them each a glass of water. They take them outside to the deck.

"Finn should be back in about half an hour," Deacon says casually.

Sabrina takes a large gulp from her glass. "I should explain." He waits patiently for her to keep talking.

I stare from behind the glass door where I opted to stay. Even though this is what I've wanted for a long time, I don't want a first-row seat.

"I want to kiss you," she blurts out.

I wish I could see Deacon's reaction. Instead, I wait for Sabrina to continue.

"I haven't kissed anyone in a long, long time," she whispers.

"You didn't want an audience. I get that," he says.

"I-it's complicated. All of this is complicated."

His hand slips to her lap. "Jaycee is married now and Finn is in high school. It's not as complicated as you think."

"I don't want to leap off the deep end and have it blow up in our faces. I need Finn in my life and, if I have to sacrifice my feelings for that, I'll do it."

"First of all, it would hardly be jumping off the deep end. If anything, I'd say we got in the pool then turned on the water. We can swim now."

She lies her head on his shoulder. "What if we're like Holly and Dirk?"

"You mean better off as friends?"

She nods. "I couldn't stand to lose either of you."

"That's not going to happen."

"How can you be sure?"

"Well, Finn's capable of making his own decisions. He decides who is in his life and who isn't."

"I don't want to lose you either."

He slips his arm around her waist. "Sabrina, I've been foolishly waiting around for years trying to find the right time to make a move. If you give me a chance, now or ten years from now, I'm not going to blow it. I lied when I said I didn't want to date. I was waiting on you to be ready," he admits.

Sabrina lifts her head. "But the book...you said Holly and Dirk were better off as friends. They realized—"

"Holly and Dirk are fictional characters."

"But Kelley thinks it has to be about us. Even I thought that as I was reading it."

"Maybe I found some inspiration in our relationship," he admits.

"So, that's what you think? I've waited too long?"

"I rewrote the ending."

She slowly faces him, a glimmer of hope dancing in her eyes. "Why?"

He takes her hand. "After finishing their story, I realized it would be so easy for them to continue on as friends, but that means giving up a chance to be truly happy."

Sabrina nods. "I didn't kiss you back there because I didn't want that to be what people talked about on the day of Jaycee's wedding."

"You're right. Today was about Jaycee and Reese." He runs his finger along her jawline.

"Kiss her already," I groan.

"Tomorrow we can talk about us," he says, standing.

She reaches for his hand and pulls him next to her. "I may not have the courage tomorrow," she whispers, grabbing him by the collar. Her lips find his. I know they've both been waiting for this moment for too long. They embrace for several long minutes until I wonder how far they'll take it. And

I'm afraid it may be a little farther than I want to witness when a soft moan escapes her lips.

"I think we'll have a few things to talk about," he says, quietly pulling away. "I'd just rather we do this without the presence of wine."

"I'm tired of taking the easy way out," she breathes as tires crunch the gravel in the driveway.

"Your happily ever after awaits." Deacon smiles as he opens the door.

Chapter 65

I had expected to die the next day right after Deacon and Sabrina decided to become a couple. But here I am a month later, watching Sabrina insist she had wasted enough time after my human death to spend another moment not living life to the fullest. They prance around town as a couple now and have been on several romantic dates but have yet to take things to the next level. I can't figure out why God wants me to stick around to see *that* but, clearly, there is a reason for my presence with these newfound lovebirds. Maybe it's some sort of consequence for the privilege of watching Jaycee grow up. Whatever the reason, I'm glad my days now consist of a lot of sleeping because I doubt I could handle watching the flirting more than I'm already subjected to. Thankfully, both Jaycee and Finn were happy about the new arrangement, each offering words of encouragement to their parents.

"You said Finn is staying at a friend's tonight, right?" Sabrina pulls Deacon through the front door after their third date in as many weeks. He has been reluctant to stay overnight since the wedding, not wanting Sabrina to feel pressured in any way.

I greet them with a wag of my tail from my bed in the living room. "Tonight's the night, huh?"

Deacon slowly closes the door behind them. "Yeah, but listen, Sabrina, we don't have to—"

She takes his hand, glancing toward our—her—bedroom door. "Oh, we're going to."

Even through my cataracts, I can see she dolled herself up for the night. She's wearing a flowing skirt with a top that shows a trace of cleavage, her hair has been recently colored to cover hints of gray and it still holds a hint of curl. "Would you mind letting me out? I'd rather sleep outside with Oakley tonight, if you don't mind." I clamber to my feet and take a step. Pain shoots throughout my hind quarters. "Never mind. I'm hard of hearing anyway. Just turn the TV up, would you?" I lie back down to alleviate the pain, resting my head on the corner of my bed.

"I don't want you to feel any pressure," Deacon whispers. "I thought we were taking it slow?"

Sabrina wraps her arms around his neck, quieting him with a lingering kiss. "If we take it any slower, we'll be in the nursing home before we consummate our relationship."

Deacon laughs. "Being in a nursing home might make it hard to—"

She slips a finger to his lips. "Let's not talk about what will or won't be hard at the nursing home."

He smiles. "It's been a long time since I've—"

She tilts her head. "There are matches in the kitchen, would you get them please?"

Deacon turns to do as asked. Sabrina slips into the bedroom, closing the door behind her.

I bury my head underneath the thin padding of my bed. "I thought you were supposed to feel happy after completing a mission. Why do I feel like I've lost my best friend?" I can't help but want to hold a pity party in my honor.

Deacon stands outside the bedroom door holding matches. His hand raises and lowers as if he's debating on whether he should knock or not. I laugh as he leans his head to his shoulder and inhales his armpit odor. "I get ya, buddy. I'm pretty sure I did the same thing the first time too. Although I was seventeen."

I hold my breath, realizing he's probably doing the same. "Did she dig out something I bought years ago or has she been shopping specifically for this moment?" My heart leaps into my chest as I ponder the thought and I honestly don't know which I'd rather.

The door cracks and slowly Sabrina's face emerges. Deacon tenses and I'm thankful he's too mesmerized to turn around for me to see the delight on his face. God knows it radiates off him.

Sabrina inches the door wider, revealing a new ensemble. I can't help but stare. "Thank you for keeping some things sacred," I whisper. "I don't think I could handle another man seeing you in something I bought." My heart aches, knowing Sabrina was never one for wearing lingerie except on special occasions and she probably only had a handful in the years we were married.

Sabrina takes the matches and a moment later the flicker of candlelight dances on the walls.

Deacon's chin dips as he studies her. "There's no going back from this."

Her long arm extends the length of his as she takes a step closer to him. "That's what I'm counting on."

He inhales slowly.

"That's right, get the oxygen back to your brain," I suggest.

"The last thing I want to do is lose you. Are you sure about this?"

She toys with the strap on her shoulder. "Why don't you come here and I'll show you how sure I am." She grabs him by the collar of his shirt and pulls him close.

A tear slips down my face as he enters the room without bothering to close the door.

I'm glad my hearing is mostly gone for once, but even my declining vision isn't enough to prevent me from seeing their shadows on the wall. I cringe through the painful process of standing and limp my way to the back of the house where I'll be sure to avoid the sights and sounds of their tryst.

I curl up next to Jaycee's bed, unable to hop on it like I used to. Even in the dark, away from the lovers, I'm not safe from my thoughts.

"It's been a long time," I tell myself. "She needs someone to hold her at night. After all, I won't be around much longer. I don't even know why I'm still here."

For the first time in ages, I pray.

Chapter 66

I stumble down the steps of the deck, happy to spend some time with Oakley. He's been my only escape since the two love birds moved in. Deacon and Finn finished moving their things in last weekend after Sabrina convinced them that they practically had been living together for years anyway.

Oakley greets me at the bottom of the stairs. "Never thought you'd be the old man out of the two of us," he says, watching me struggle on the last step.

"I don't know how much more I can take."

Oakley drops his head to nuzzle my neck. "That's what time does to a body."

"I'm not talking about that," I groan.

"Ah, the new roommates?"

I squat to relieve myself, embarrassed I have an audience to my weakness. "It's not that. It's seeing Sabrina so happy with someone else. Someone who isn't me."

"I'm sorry this is so hard for you. Maybe it's time to count your blessings."

I lift my head as we walk toward the shade of the old pine tree. "Sounds like you've been thinking of grandma. She used to say that when you thought the world was against you, you were picking weeds out of the garden of life when you should be picking flowers."

He laughs. "Is that the way she said it?"

I flop onto the grass. "Something like that."

"I think you have a lot to be thankful for. I know your time is running low and I'll be left by myself again, but I'm eternally grateful I've gotten this time with you."

I shift my head to put his face into my line of sight. "I'm not sure I share your enthusiasm. I mean, I know I didn't deserve the second chance I got, but how can you be so...happy about your situation? Won't you be lonely when I'm gone?"

He pulls up a mouthful of grass. "I'm going to miss you, but God has a purpose for me yet. You have nearly fulfilled yours and I can only hope that one day, before I go, I get to see my great grandchildren."

I smile at the thought of toddlers yanking on his tail and ears. "I hope you do."

"Have some faith."

I desperately want to chase the squirrel scampering up a nearby tree but I know my body won't cooperate. "I don't understand why I'm still here."

"I think we're about to find out."

I turn in the direction he stares. Faint voices from the front of the house waft toward us. "What are they saying?"

"They're backing up a trailer," Oakley replies.

I cock my head. "A trailer? Maybe it's a new car for Finn."

Oakley flicks his ears. "See? There's another flower you can pick. You may not realize it, but you got the son you always wanted."

I wince at his words. "I was happy with one daughter," I say defensively.

He takes a step toward the commotion in the driveway. "I know. But I also know Sabrina dreamt of having more children. I think she's found the son she never expected."

"I'd call that a flower."

"Do you smell cookies?"

I laugh. "I can barely smell the piles of crap in the yard. Cookies would be nice, though."

The voices grow louder as Deacon and Sabrina make their way to the backyard. Finn's voice joins theirs as they peak around the edge of the house. His hand grasps a lead. I'm not sure where Oakley got the idea of cookies; all I smell is donkey and I'm probably imagining that.

I shift my head to sniff Oakley. "Hey, I think my nose is back! You smell like donkey." Arthritis cripples my step and I fall behind him. "Well, your own special blend of donkey. Is it weird that you smell like Old Spice and wood chips? Or at least, you used to, back when I could smell. Did I ever tell you that? I don't think I did."

"You did." Oakley stops, nearly causing me to crash into his back legs. "Sniff again."

I laugh. "I'm not falling for *that* again." He steps forward as I inhale deeply. "I *do* smell cookies. Weird."

I move out of the way of his hind quarters in case he decides to pull another trick on me. My tail wags instinctively at the sight of another donkey.

I watch as Oakley cautiously greets the newcomer, but I instantly feel they've known each other longer than the few seconds we've been standing here.

"Ward," she whispers. "I knew our paths would cross again one day. I had no idea it would be like this though."

Oakley brays loudly, kicking his feet as he prances around. "Helen! I've missed you so much! Look who's here! Where have you been? Why are you here?"

I wait for Oakley to run an excited lap around the property before inspecting our new guest. I brush against her legs, making a circle around her before lifting my head to sniff her face. "Grandma, never thought I'd see you again on this side of Heaven."

She laughs. "I never thought I'd see you with four legs."

"Back at ya." I step out of Oakley's way as he returns to nuzzle her muzzle. "I think I'll give you two some time alone."

Deacon claps his hands. "I knew they'd like each other!"

Sabrina slips her arm around his waist. "I can't believe you're the second guy to randomly bring home a donkey."

Deacon leans into her. "You read the ad; how could I refuse?"

Sabrina pulls a tiny slip of paper from her pocket. "Yankee the donkey seeks luscious grassland growing wild in a spacious yard and a faithful friend. Maybe you have a chicken or goat that needs a new buddy—Yankee is your gal. From dogs to kids, she's never found a creature she didn't like. Even the fox who tried to eat Clucky the chicken became a friend to Yankee. If you're looking to protect livestock, Yankee *is not* in your best interest. Instead of chasing off predators, she'll invite them over for dinner like she did with the opossum we caught roaming around. Apparently, Yankee was leaving chunks of carrots for her new friend. I repeat, she is *not* a protector. She is an extrovert who will find lonely creatures to spend her days with. I hate to say but, Cleo, the cat, is going to be very disappointed that her napping buddy is leaving. With that being said, Cleo is NOT our cat. We don't know where she came from and you'd better check your trailer when you leave or you may end up with a stow-away. That's just Yankee for you. She also enjoys eating. I apologize for her being slightly overweight but we have ten grandkids and they love to feed her treats. She'd eat the cupboard door if she could get inside the house. And, due to the friends she's bringing home—we've added four mouths to our farm since her arrival six months ago and I fear it will continue. We must stop the madness before our farm becomes a zoo. I'm hopeful she is merely searching for the soul that matches her own and lets everyone else live their lives in peace. Since she has yet to bring in woodland creatures to clean the house, my wife says she must go."

Deacon places a kiss on Sabrina's forehead. "See? It's a cute little ad. He drafted up a second one, would you like to see it?"

She laughs. "I've heard enough. He got you with his words. How fitting."

Deacon shrugs. "I thought Oakley might need a friend when...you know."

She leans over and kisses him softly, her hand falling to stroke my head. "It's kind of cute actually."

Finn releases Yankee and Oakley proudly gives her the short tour.

Chapter 67

"It's a beautiful night," Yankee says.

I lie on the porch, too weak to make it down the stairs now. Deacon has been carrying me up and down for weeks now, three times a day.

Oakley stands beside her, his neck draped over the back of hers. "And quite the concert we're getting too."

Yankee lifts her head. "It's my favorite part of the day."

I rest my paws on my head. "He's always talking about music at night. You're telling me you hear it too?"

She slides her head beside mine. "Of course I do. You have to know how to listen."

I strain my ears, if that's even possible. "Crickets. I hear crickets." A frog croaks from the neighbor's pond. "And a frog. Sometimes an owl or something. Maybe a coyote, but that's it."

"Listen with your heart."

I stay silent a minute, listening. "Still sounds like nature to me."

Sabrina opens the door and takes a seat beside me. Something feels different about her, but I'm too exhausted to investigate. Deacon steps outside and sits on the opposite side of me. Something is definitely going on, I gather, but my eyes and ears have deteriorated so much that I'm slow to pick up on whatever it is. I wag my tail anyway. It seems appropriate.

Sabrina's hand slides over my back. "I feel guilty for being happy right now."

Deacon's hand covers hers. "We should call the kids tomorrow."

My heart sinks at the thought of leaving them, but I know my body is all used up. "I've got a place in Heaven picked out. And some special people I can't wait for you to meet," I whimper.

"He's been a good dog," Sabrina whispers.

I'm in more pain than I've ever been in, but there's no way I'm leaving without saying goodbye to Jaycee.

"I can't handle seeing him in pain," Deacon says softly.

"I'll call the vet on Monday if he makes it that long."

Deacon nods. "Probably best. He doesn't deserve to suffer."

Sabrina cups my hand, a glint of light catching something on her finger. I smile, making out a large diamond.

"Congratulations." Happy tears fall as they head inside, Deacon reminding her that I like being outside in the mild night air.

Suddenly I hear it. *Amazing Grace* sung by a choir. I listen to several hymns that take me back to my youth in church before closing my eyes.

Chapter 68

I don't know how I got back inside or even how much time has passed, but Jaycee sits beside me, tears streaming down her face. My entire body feels as if it's been run over by a car...or maybe a snowplow.

I lift my head. "Why are you crying?" More than the pain plaguing my body, the hurt in her eyes tells me this is our last meeting on Earth. "You're not going to believe the story I have for you the next time I see you."

Reese kneels beside her. "It was a pleasure knowing you, Huck." He wraps his arm around Jaycee. "That was cheesy."

Fatigue hits me hard and I slowly close my eyes. "Nobody go anywhere. I just need a quick nap."

When I wake, Reese is telling the story about the time I shoved his fish off the dock and back into the water.

"You couldn't smell the disease lurking in that fish," I argue.

"I think he was curious about it," Jaycee says defensively.

I gasp in short breaths as Finn recalls the time he used me as a floatation device to get across the creek. I smile, knowing he had no idea how deep the water was that day. Stories continue around the room until Deacon finally ends with the story about the first time I met him. He nods to Reese and Finn. Reese pats my head and leaves the room without a word.

Finn slips his arms around my neck for the final time. With his mouth next to my ear, he whispers, "I wish everyone could love like dogs do. The world would be a much better place."

I lick his cheek. "I'll put in a request when I get to Heaven."

"Enjoy *Pearly Gate Estates*." He wipes a tear, shoves his hand in his pocket, and joins Reese outside.

Deacon takes his turn at my side. "Huck, what can I say? Thank you for sharing your family with me. I promise I'll take care of your girls. You rest easy, buddy."

I thump my tail against the floor. "They're all yours now, Deacon."

Jaycee takes a tissue from him as he leaves my side. "I'm not sure I know what to do without you," she sobs. "You've been with us since the day we buried my dad and, I know it sounds weird, but it feels like saying goodbye to you makes his death more permanent. I don't know how to deal with that."

"You've got Reese now. It's time to live your own life. Go, have babies, make memories, and learn how to listen to the hymn the crickets sing. Oh, and always love like a dog."

"You were the best friend a girl could ask for."

Sabrina joins her at my side. "I never knew a dog could teach me so much. After Jason died, I didn't think I could love another living being, but there you were, refusing to give up on us. And when I refused to see what was in front of my face, you were there to guide me toward a new love. How do I ever repay you for that?"

My body aches as I curl into her. "Oh, Sabrina, you've given me more than you'll ever know."

"Will you do me a favor?" I stare into her bloodshot eyes as she speaks. "Tell Jason we're okay. Tell him I think he'd like Deacon."

My eyes droop shut and my breathing slows. "I'll drop in to check on you from time to time."

"It's time," Bobbi's voice chimes as her feline figure appears before me. "They're going to be okay. Good work, Jason."

A familiar lake looms in front of me and my form straightens as I walk to a group of children eager to show me what I've missed.

Thank You

Thanks for reading *My Life in Dog Years* by Erin Pickett. Please remember to leave a review at your favorite retailer.

To learn more about other Erin Pickett publications, please visit www.erinpickettbooks.com

About the Author

Erin grew up in a small town in Indiana and dreamed of getting away after high school, but instead she went to work in a factory and later became a waitress at a local restaurant while earning an Associate's degree in Office Administration from Indiana Business College. The thrill of exploring new places was once filled by reading until she discovered her passion for writing.

Erin is married and has three children, three bonus children, and six bonus grandchildren. She has put her days as a waitress behind her and now helps her husband with his appliance business.

Connect with Erin

Website

www.erinpickettbooks.com

Twitter (X), @erinlpickett

www.twitter.com/erinlpickett

Facebook, Erin Pickett, Writer

www.facebook.com/erinpickettbooks/

Instagram, Erin Pickett Books

www.instagram.com/erinpickettbooks

TikTok, Erin Pickett Books

www.tiktok.com/erinpickettbooks

BookBub

www.bookbub.com/authors/erin-pickett

Also by Erin Pickett

The Takeover

(2023; suspense)

The last thing they expected to encounter were terrorists. Not in rural New York. But this threat didn't come from thousands of miles away. It'd been here all along.

——————⟐——————

A Place on the Porch

(2022; Women's Fiction)

Unimaginable loss. A desperate fresh start. Will falling for a rundown house and a handsome new neighbor give her the peace she craves?

——————⟐——————

The Adventures of Logan and Scruffy

(2020; middle grade)

The kids at Logan's new school laugh at his cowboy boots. Who wears cowboy boots in New York City? No one at Van Buren Elementary, anyway. But with the help of a talking dog, Logan learns how to stand up to the bullies and even makes a few friends along the way.

Don't miss out!

Visit the website below and you can sign up to receive emails whenever Erin Pickett publishes a new book. There's no charge and no obligation.

https://books2read.com/r/B-A-UNPK-QIIYC

BOOKS 2 READ

Connecting independent readers to independent writers.